Time to Say Goodbye

Katie Flynn has lived for many years in the north-west. A compulsive writer, she started with short stories and articles and many of her early stories were broadcast on Radio Merseyside. She decided to write her Liverpool series after hearing the reminiscences of family members about life in the city in the early years of the twentieth century. For many years she has had to cope with ME, but has continued to write. She also writes as Judith Saxton.

Also available by Katie Flynn

A Liverpool Lass
The Girl from Penny Lane
Liverpool Taffy
The Mersey Girls
Strawberry Fields
Rainbow's End
Rose of Tralee
No Silver Spoon
Polly's Angel
The Girl from Seaforth Sands
The Liverpool Rose
Poor Little Rich Girl
The Bad Penny
Down Daisy Street
A Kiss and a Promise
Two Penn'orth of Sky
A Long and Lonely Road
The Cuckoo Child
Darkest Before Dawn
Orphans of the Storm
Little Girl Lost
Beyond the Blue Hills
Forgotten Dreams
Sunshine and Shadows
Such Sweet Sorrow
A Mother's Hope
In Time for Christmas
Heading Home
A Mistletoe Kiss
The Lost Days of Summer
Christmas Wishes
The Runaway
A Sixpenny Christmas
The Forget-Me-Not Summer
A Christmas to Remember

Available by Katie Flynn writing as Judith Saxton

You Are My Sunshine
First Love, Last Love
Someone Special
Still Waters

Katie Flynn

Time to Say Goodbye

arrow books

Published by Arrow Books in 2014

2 4 6 8 10 9 7 5 3

First published in Great Britain in 2014 by Century

Arrow Books
The Random House Group Limited
20 Vauxhall Bridge Road, London, SW1V 2SA

www.randomhousebooks.co.uk

Addresses for companies within The Random House Group Limited can be found at:
www.randomhouse.co.uk/offices.htm

The Random House Group Limited Reg. No. 954009

A CIP catalogue record for this book
is available from the British Library

ISBN 9780099574668

Typeset by Palimpsest Book Production Ltd, Falkirk, Stirlingshire
Printed and bound by CPI Group (UK) Ltd, Croydon, CR0 4YY

Dear Reader,

When I set out to write *Time To Say Goodbye* it was nothing like the book you see before you, which was meant to pick up the three youngsters, and then go to them as young women. As soon as Auntie and the Canary and Linnet entered the equation, however, they simply seized the story by the throat and everything changed.

I was evacuated to a farm in deepest Devonshire and had an idyllic four years there, scarcely aware of the war. The three girls, too, were happy, but their adventures and mine were very different and affected their growing up differently too. As so often happens when you are writing a book, the characters simply took over and dictated the story to me, for better or for worse etc.

Whilst I was writing the book I was carried back in time and relived those far-off days and thought perhaps one day I might write the book I meant to write, using my own experience . . . but somehow there is always another book nagging to be written, so probably the one I meant to write will be put on the back burner . . .

Hope you enjoy reading this one as much as I enjoyed writing it!

All best wishes,

Katie

Chapter One

1959

The old man sat on the bench outside his cottage door, and stared across at the village green. Presently the bus from the market town would draw up and those still remaining on board would alight. He hoped his wife would be amongst them. As soon as she got in she would begin preparations for his dinner and already he was looking forward to what, as he grew older, was becoming the main excitement of his day. His wife was a creature of habit and he knew that on this particular day, because she had been to town, the meal would be fish of some description, mashed potatoes and a slice of jam tart for pudding. If she was in a good mood – and the bus was on time – she might make a custard. At the mere thought he felt the water come to his mouth; he was fond of custard. But even as he contemplated the meal he would presently enjoy, the bus chugged to a halt and the passengers began to descend.

He acknowledged that he was a trifle deaf but knew that his sight was still quite keen; keen enough to pick out his wife's stumpy form and that of their next door neighbour, and several other familiar faces. One, however, was a stranger, and that was unusual enough for the old man to wipe his eyes and look harder. In recent years a modern estate of expensive houses had been built a bare couple of miles from the village but the inhabitants all had cars; had never, to his knowledge, caught a bus in their lives, so it was natural enough that the old man should stare at the young woman who descended on to the village street and looked about her. As he watched she took an uncertain step towards the general store, then seemed to change her mind and scanned the cottages in front of which the old man sat. He was still examining her face when his wife arrived at his side, and he greeted her with rather more excitement than usual.

'Nelly, that young woman, the one what got off the bus just after you did,' he began, but his wife, clicking with disapproval, pushed him gently through the doorway of the cottage and shut the door behind them.

'Get inside, you silly old fool,' she said affectionately. 'Ha'n't you noticed that's starting to rain? And who's to look after you if you get pneumonia? I didn't notice any girl; someone from the new estate, I suppose. Nothing to do with us, you may be sure of that.'

'I thought she looked familiar,' he said obstinately. 'I'm sure I've seen her face somewhere before, though I can't put a name to it.'

He peered at the contents of his wife's large wickerwork basket and saw a parcel of cod, his favourite. He poked it with a finger. 'Is that dinner? Are you going to do white sauce to go wi' it? And mashed taters? I'm fond of mashed taters.'

His wife laughed indulgently. 'You're fond of most food, and you can help by peeling the spuds,' she said.

The old man tottered over to the sink. 'Jam tart for afters?' he asked eagerly, all thoughts of the stranger vanishing from his mind. 'Oh, I do love a nice piece of jam tart!'

The young woman had been in a fever of impatience ever since she had got off the train and boarded the bus, bound for the village where she had spent a good deal of her childhood. But now, having reached her destination, she found herself feeling both shy and somewhat ill at ease. A while ago she had remembered that there was something special about a certain date in October, and had realised with a real shock that a twentieth anniversary was fast approaching. Twenty years ago three little girls had met for the first time on Lime Street station, waiting to be escorted to their new homes. They had been very different, those three little girls, but during the course of being traipsed about the country whilst the billeting officer tried to place them they had become friends, and without a word had decided that they meant, if possible, to remain together. They were from different small private schools and had missed the first wave of evacuees, and by the time they reached the village they had been worn out and desperate for somewhere they might lay their heads, though they were still determined to stay together. Others had been evacuated with their whole schools, so surely just three of them might find a home where they could be safe?

The young woman smiled reminiscently: three little girls with worn white faces, insisting upon visiting the lavatory at the back of Mrs Bailey's shop before they would go a step further; the billeting officer in despair; and then rescue!

But she could not stand mooning here; she had a

rendezvous to keep. The rain was increasing in severity and she hastily erected her umbrella and turned up the collar of her fawn mackintosh, chiding herself as she remembered that she had not wanted to be noticed. If there is one way of drawing eyes it is to stand outside in the pouring rain looking helplessly about, positively inviting attention. She must not loiter here.

Now, as she skulked beneath the umbrella's obscuring shelter, she took a cautious peek at her surroundings. She remembered them so well, or had thought she did. She had expected many changes, for it had been a long time since she had last set foot on this stretch of pavement. She had read stories of folk returning to a childhood home and finding that everything had grown smaller, because in the eyes of a child the thatched cottages and their patches of garden had seemed huge. Yet she was unaware of any such change, and the clump of trees which surrounded the village green had seemed enormous years ago and were enormous still. She looked about her, checking on the once familiar scene, and for a moment she wondered, for there was not a soul about. But why should there be, after all? She did not have to glance at her wristwatch to know that it was only half past ten; children would be in school and adults at work, and if she stood here much longer, gaping around her like a lost soul, someone would come out of one of the cottages and ask questions. Where did she want to go? Whom had she come to see? Or worse still, they might recognise her. It was a tiny village, the sort where everyone knows everyone else's business . . . hastily she began to walk, just as one of the women who had got off the bus glanced towards her. Ducking her head and turning it away from the bent little figure she walked straight into a puddle, a huge one, and felt it penetrate her stout brogues. She swallowed a curse and glanced quickly back, embarrassed by her own stupidity, but the old woman did not appear to have noticed. She had disappeared into her cottage, and the young woman sloshed her way out of the puddle and set off once more into the rainy morning.

In the old days the tarmac surface of the road finished within perhaps a hundred yards of the village; it used to become a lane, muddy or dusty depending on the season. But now, even allowing for the poor visibility, she could see that the tarmac stretched ahead as far as the eye could see, and as she walked the reason for this became obvious. On her left, through a discreet belt of conifers, a large housing estate had grown up. There were a great many big red brick houses with elegant driveways, double garages and gravel sweeps. Some even had forbidding wrought iron gates, though few were closed. Staring, she stepped on to the pale pink paving which divided the ordinary sidewalk from the estate. She remembered the country here as being fairly flat, but whoever had commissioned the new houses had clearly thought flatness, though useful, would not attract the right sort of buyers, and had manufactured hills and hollows around which they had landscaped the area. She peered between the branches of shielding trees, already well grown, and supposed, grudgingly, that these people – rich people – had been welcomed by the real villagers, who would have hoped that the newcomers would spend money in their small shops. And no doubt it was thanks to the housing estate that the road was both tarmacked and in good repair.

On the corner she hesitated; she could go straight ahead – now she could see that the road became the familiar lane a couple of hundred yards on – or she could take a look at the estate. Why not do just that? God knew she had plenty of time; the day stretched ahead of her, forlornly empty. Quickly, she told herself that she had always intended to explore the present village, noting changes, before the others arrived . . . if any others did arrive, that was. Suddenly, she was certain that no one would come. After all, why should they? She had noticed the date and written ahead, and receiving cautious replies had come anyway. In her heart she had hoped the others would do the same, but there was no guarantee that they would. So far as she knew, this particular October date had passed unremarked for many years.

Having decided, she made her way through the housing estate, discovering that the large and imposing houses almost hid several rows of smaller, more practical dwellings, to a point where she could see, in the distance, the opposite row of the conifers which must enclose the whole estate. Standing there in the rain, staring at the houses, she did not notice somebody coming up behind her until that someone cleared his throat, causing her to jump guiltily. She turned. He was a tall, military-looking man, with grey hair and a small bristling moustache. He was carrying a striped golfing umbrella and looked like a retired colonel, but the eyes that he turned on her were hard and cold, though his voice, when he spoke, was pleasant enough. 'Can I help you? I expect you want Doone Avenue, or possibly Totnes Heights. People often get confused because the houses on Plymouth Road hide the more . . . practical end of the estate.'

'Thank you very much, but I'm just looking,' she replied, aware of the implied suggestion that if she were visiting any of the houses on the estate, it would be one of the cheaper ones. She half turned away, but he was still staring at her, and she turned back, searching for something to say which would put this arrogant man in his place. 'It's some while since I was here last, and there have been a great many changes, not all for the good,' she said coolly. 'You wouldn't know . . . but still, it's progress I suppose.'

'The new development has been the saving of this place,' the man said haughtily, and she was glad to realise that he had recognised the implied criticism in her words. 'If it hadn't been for the estate the tarmac would have ended back in the village. And the buses would probably have stopped running. Oh yes, the local inhabitants may sneer, but if it weren't for Watersmeet Estate . . . that's why we keep an eye open for strangers, people who don't belong. A good neighbour policy, you might call it, and—'

She interrupted without ceremony. 'How often do you shop in the village?' she asked frostily. 'I dare say you pay someone to rake your gravel and clip your hedges, but I'd take a bet you pay peanuts. And how often do you catch a bus into town?'

He began to gobble and she turned away from him with a swing of her shoulders, seeing, as she had guessed, that he was unable to answer. She had seen the bus turning down the little lane which ran behind the cottages, without then registering what this meant: that despite the years between, the bus still terminated in the village, returning to the town and not coming back until it carried the workers home from their day's toil.

She turned towards her destination thinking that the conversation was over, but to her surprise the man followed her. 'Where are your manners, young woman?' he shouted angrily. 'I was still speaking; did no one ever tell you that it's rude . . .'

She laughed. 'I'm sorry, but your assumption that things were better for the villagers because of the estate rather got up my nose,' she said frankly. She looked at the newspaper in his hand; despite the umbrella, it was soggy round the edges. 'Look,' she said patiently. 'You don't even have your newspaper delivered, because you'd have to pay the boy. You walk down for it yourself in all weathers, except when the snow's too deep and then some poor blighter will have to fight his way through the drifts to earn the odd sixpence. But I shouldn't criticise you, and I wouldn't do so except that you started it.' A thought occurred to her. 'How often do you stroll up to the Canary and Linnet for the odd glass or two of beer, or even a snifter of whisky? That would help the local community.'

She thought she had got him there, for he stared at her for a baffled moment, then looked away, rubbing his chin and glancing slyly at her. 'The Canary and Linnet; no, the folk from the new estate mostly frequent the King's Head or the Bear and Billet. I take it you've friends at the – er – Linnet? Well, I'm sure I don't want to keep you so you'd best be on your way. You've not got much further to go.' Grudgingly he gave the peak of his cap a tiny jerk. 'Good day to you.'

'I'm sorry if I offended you. I'll be on my way.' She waggled her umbrella vaguely and set off, and this time he did not attempt to follow her, but simply stood staring after her with a curious expression, which she could not interpret, on his face. But what did it matter, after all? Auntie and her niece Jill had managed to make a living way back during the war when times had been really hard. Their successors would not now be reliant upon the toffee-nosed residents of the new estate, even though the majority of the airfields which had supplied most of their customers would probably have shut down after the war ended.

She walked on, trying to rid her mind of the encounter, until she realised that the tarmac had petered out and she was trudging up the lane and would soon reach her destination. She glanced to her left and then paused, frowning. The hateful man had been right when he had said that she was only a short distance from the Linnet. Yet there was no sign of it. It must be further than she had remembered. But after another hundred yards she stopped again, confused. Then she remembered the years which had passed since she had last been here. Woods grow up, hedges thicken, and now that she looked more closely she could see through the trees what must be an old building. She stepped off the lane on to the narrow path, reminding herself that there was a longer way round by which delivery lorries, and the vehicles carrying members of the forces, had reached the pub. It was only the villagers themselves who came this way. And the evacuees, of course, both those who lived at the Linnet under Auntie's gentle rule and the ones who were billeted at the Pilgrims' farm further up the lane.

She burst out of the trees into the clearing, but even as her lips began to curve into a smile, incredulity took her breath away. The old pub looked the same at first glance, but at a second . . . she put her hands to her face and felt the tears begin. The place was a ruin! A chimney stack had fallen through the roof, there was no glass in the windows and the garden, of which Auntie and Jill had been so proud, was nothing but a tangle of waist-high weeds.

She took a couple of faltering steps towards the house, then braced herself and approached it more closely, though with all the caution of someone expecting to be accused of trespass at any moment. She had seen the pub like this once before, in a dream; or a nightmare, rather. So this explained the man's strange attitude. He had known all along that the place was a ruin. He was being spiteful, paying me back for all the things I said, she told herself miserably.

A foot away from the back door, she stopped short. She knew now that they had all gone; Auntie, Jill, old Jacky – everyone. Why oh why hadn't she kept in touch? She had done so at first, and Auntie had always replied, and though her letters had been brief at least it meant she knew what was going on. Then life had caught her by the throat: a proposal of marriage, a home to run, a job in a big city, responsibilities; a new life, in fact. She remembered with shame that she had not even invited Auntie to her wedding, telling herself that it could have been seen as asking for a present, but she knew that she had been attempting to draw a line beneath the old life and begin the new with a clean sheet. Nevertheless, she had always sent a Christmas card to the Canary and Linnet and got one in return, until Auntie wrote to say that she was selling the pub and moving to a cottage in the next village. It was only this year, when deciding to organise a reunion, that she had wondered, apprehensively, how the two women were. Auntie must be very old, but she was tough; Jill was only a few years older than she herself. She would send a letter, beg to be forgiven for her neglect . . .

Then she had written to the other evacuees, only a few words, explaining how she longed to see them all again, naming this very date and saying she was trying to arrange some sort of reunion. The replies had been brief, but of course she understood: she had moved on, and so had Auntie and Jill and everyone else, presumably. But they had responded, which was a start.

By the back door of the pub stood an ancient wooden bench, green with age. She sat down and leaned back, heedless of the rain on her face, and, closing her eyes, willed herself back to that golden October afternoon when the three little girls had first come to the Canary and Linnet.

1939

When the car driven by the local billeting officer stopped outside the village post office, the three small passengers in the back seat erupted from the vehicle and glared at the fat and motherly woman who had met them at the last station and brought them on what, she had assured them, was to be the final leg of their journey. But that had been almost two hours ago and she had still not found anyone to take them in, and now rebellion was like a pot coming to the boil. When Mrs Hainstock tried to order them back into the car, three heads were firmly shaken. Imogen's shiny Dutch bob, Rita's long fair plait and Debby's untidy mop of dark brown curls were all shaken decidedly. 'You promised,' Imogen said reproachfully. 'You said it wasn't our fault that we missed the first evacuation, and you would do your best to find someone who could take all three of us . . .'

'But that was hours ago,' Debby said. 'We got to the station at eight o'clock this morning and we've been travelling ever since.' She cast a reproachful look at the billeting officer. 'We've had nothing to eat and only water to drink, and I want to be excused.'

There were murmurs of assent from Imogen and Rita, Rita adding, in an injured tone: 'And if you don't let us go to the toilet we'll just die.'

This was Mrs Hainstock's third stop since picking up the girls; the first two villages she had visited were already as full of evacuees as they could hold. She had offered to split the children up but even so no one wanted them; they simply didn't have room. But she did understand the girls' present predicament and looked hopefully towards the post office. 'I'll ask Mrs Bailey if you can use her facilities,' she began, but got no further. The girls were rushing towards the shop and she followed hastily, suspecting that the request for the use of the lavatory might be couched in less than polite terms, for desperate need pays little attention to the words it uses.

'Right,' she called after the three youngsters, 'and whilst you're in there I'll see whether there's any chance . . .'

But they had gone; were gone so long that Mrs Hainstock had visited all the possible foster homes and not found one willing to take them in by the time the girls re-joined her, still white and tired but at least relieved of their most pressing need. The three of them and Mrs Hainstock congregated on the pavement alongside the little car, and were still there when a tall woman came out of the post office, hesitated, and then approached them. 'Good afternoon, Mrs Hainstock,' she said politely. 'What's the trouble?'

Mrs Hainstock began to explain rather haltingly that she had been unable to find suitable accommodation for the three girls and would have to take them in herself, although on a temporary basis only, since her house was bulging at the seams already.

When Mrs Hainstock stopped speaking the stranger shook her head sadly, but addressed herself to the three girls. 'I'll have you, lasses,' she said briefly. 'I'm Miss Marcy, good thing you're all girls, because the only suitable space at the Canary and Linnet is the attic.'

'Oh, but . . . the Canary and Linnet? I don't think . . . that is to say . . . it's not on my list of suitable accommodation, Miss Marcy . . .'

But the three girls looked at one another, and then the tallest – Rita – spoke directly to the stranger. 'Can you really take all three of us?' she said, clasping her hands like the heroine in a Victorian melodrama. She had seized on the woman's name and spoke directly to her. 'Oh, Miss Marcy, we're so tired! I'm sure your attic would be just what we're looking for.'

'Well, it would certainly solve a few problems, but of course we could only accept your kind offer on a temporary basis, since licensed premises could scarcely be regarded as a suitable home for three ten-year-old girls . . .' Mrs Hainstock began, but she was firmly interrupted.

'My house is a respectable one, and I think the children have had enough disturbances without adding more,'

Miss Marcy said quietly, so that the girls could not hear. 'If they come to the Linnet, that's where they'll stay.' She smiled. 'I'll see that they aren't in the bar during opening times; we've a large kitchen with a back door leading directly into the garden, and the back stairs lead up to the first floor. As you know, the Linnet was a manor house until the Great War so we've plenty of room. And if you're worried, let me assure you that Jill and I stand no nonsense. The men who drink at the Linnet will respect my wishes, as they have always done. The presence of three little girls will make them even more careful to guard their tongues.' She opened the car door and gestured to the girls to get inside, directing the next remark to the three of them. 'It's only a couple of miles to my home; if Mrs Hainstock will be good enough to drive us there you'll be able to help me make up your beds – I'm afraid it may be shakedowns on the floor until I can get organised – and have a quick meal before saying good night.'

Mrs Hainstock clearly did not know whether to be delighted or horrified at the thought of her charges being taken off her hands by this strange but attractive woman, but the girls were in no doubt. Rita squeezed first Debby's hand and then Imogen's. 'I don't care where we sleep so long as we don't have to go on and on like that ghost ship . . . the *Marie Celeste*,' she whispered. 'What's wrong with the lady's house, anyway? An attic sounds nice.'

But before either girl could answer, Miss Marcy had got into the cramped little car and was telling Mrs Hainstock that she was sure the authorities would be so relieved to have found somewhere for the girls to live that they would not object to the fact that the Canary and Linnet was a pub.

In the back seat Rita raised her blonde eyebrows, Debby muffled a giggle with one plump hand and Imogen smiled and clapped her hands, but softly so that the adults in the front of the car could not possibly hear. Then the three of them leaned back and took no further notice of the discussion taking place in the front. They were sure that Miss Marcy had already won the argument; once she got them into her house they would stay there, even if it was a pub.

The car drew up in front of a pleasant building constructed out of crumbling red bricks, which were partially concealed by some sort of enormous climbing plant. Debby recognised wisteria and informed the other two that her uncle Joseph had one which clambered up the front of his house. But they had no time to do more than exchange delighted smiles before the car stopped beneath a swinging signboard, upon which were pictured a yellow canary and – presumably – a green linnet, and Miss Marcy, having watched indulgently as they tumbled, stiff, weary but exultant, out of Mrs Hainstock's small and ancient car, indicated a gravel path which led down the side of the house.

'In future you should come in and out by the back door, which you can get to via the lane which runs round the back of the pub. But today, because Mrs Hainstock has come to the front, we'll go down the side path,' she told them. 'It's a fine afternoon so the back door will be open, but in case it isn't I'll go first and introduce you to my niece, who is also my partner.' She smiled benignly at them. 'What a foolish old woman I am – I don't even know your names! But come into the kitchen and we'll get all the introductions over at once. I walk up to the post office to buy some stamps, leaving Jill baking scones, and come back with three young people and good Mrs Hainstock.' She chuckled deeply and Imogen, who noticed such things, realised that Miss Marcy had no local accent and spoke in clear, silvery tones. But Miss Marcy was ushering them into an enormous kitchen and smiling across at a flush-faced young woman who had just taken a tray of newly baked scones out of the oven, and looked round enquiringly as they entered.

'This is my niece, Jill; she and I run the Canary and Linnet between us. It goes without saying that you must treat her as though she were me, and do exactly as she tells you.'

The girl, Jill, smiled at the billeting officer. 'Good afternoon,' she said formally. 'Are these your children?' She seized four of the hot scones, split and buttered them and handed them to the unexpected guests. 'The kettle's on the boil; I'll make the tea in a minute,' she said cheerfully.

'It's awfully good of you,' Mrs Hainstock began, then heaved a sigh and gave Jill a rueful little grin. 'I'd better explain. These young ladies are evacuees and your aunt has offered to put them up, for a while at any rate.' She bit into a scone and the children realised that although the billeting officer had not had to endure the same lengthy train journey as they themselves had suffered, she had certainly had a hard and frustrating day. She had driven patiently over ill-maintained lanes, gone in and out of countless houses and cottages, and had not accepted so much as one offer of tea because she had not wanted to interrupt her ceaseless quest for accommodation. She must be at least as grateful as they were themselves that her search was over for the time being.

But Jill was looking enquiringly from face to face and Rita, swallowing hastily, spoke up. 'I'm Rita Jeffries,' she said, and jerked a thumb at the child standing next to her. 'That one, the one with brown curly hair, is Debby Viner and the one with black hair and a fringe is Imogen Clarke.'

Jill smiled and held out her hand, then retracted it hastily. 'Sorry, I can't shake hands, I'm all over flour. But I'm Jill Marcy and although Auntie is very good to call me her partner, it is actually she who owns the good old Linnet, and is the landlady.' She turned to the billeting officer. 'I'm so sorry; cooking all afternoon seems to have addled my brain. So if these lovely young ladies aren't your daughters . . .'

'I'm the local billeting officer,' Mrs Hainstock explained. 'Ever since the beginning of the war it's been my job to find places where city children will be safe from the threat of bombs and other perils. These three missed the initial evacuation for various reasons and the authorities were unable to find suitable accommodation for them in the area to which the rest of their classmates have gone. I was seconded to home them, but until your aunt offered . . .'

Jill smiled. 'I've got quite used to Auntie turning up with stray cats and dogs, an injured rabbit she released from a gin trap, and other unfortunates,' she said. 'But children are a new departure, though a very welcome one.' She turned to her aunt, who was pouring boiling water into a big brown pot. 'You'll put 'em in the attic? There are the camp beds which Mickey, Paul and I used years ago, when we went camping, and heaven knows we've bedding enough.' She smiled at the girls. 'Where have you come from? You look most awfully tired . . . anyone for another scone? But since you're going to live with us you might as well make yourselves at home. Take your coats off and sit down at the table.' She looked keenly at the three children. 'I can see what you're most in need of is something to eat, a nice hot cup of tea and then bed. I'll take you up to the attic as soon as you've finished your scones and we'll leave Auntie and Mrs Hainstock to sort out your ration books and so on whilst we do your unpacking and make your beds.'

'Thank you very much,' Rita said gratefully. It seemed as though she had elected herself as their spokeswoman, for now at any rate. She lowered her voice, glancing apprehensively towards the billeting officer. 'We all come from Liverpool, but from different parts. We met for the first time at the railway station, but we got to know one another pretty well whilst Mrs Hainstock was driving us around, so when she thought we were all big pals and would prefer to be kept together we went along with it, and now it looks as though we're in luck.'

Jill nodded her understanding. 'I'm glad you explained, because so far as I can make out children were evacuated by school, so that at least they would know someone locally. Though in my experience kids soon learn to rub along with other kids.'

By now they had finished their scones and were on their way up to the small landing at the top of the attic stairs, where Jill pushed open a door and ushered the girls into the room beyond. It was large, with a sloping ceiling and two long, low windows, more or less at knee level, overlooking the back garden and a great many trees, whose heavy foliage screened what must be the back lane Auntie had mentioned. Against the end wall was an enormous chest of drawers, closely flanked by an equally enormous dressing table, whose spotted mirror proclaimed its age. Jill, who was beginning to disentangle the camp beds, jerked a thumb at the rest of the furniture. 'Take a drawer each and start putting your things away,' she advised. 'It's not the Ritz, but it's dry and could be made comfortable, even attractive, if you want to stick posters and photographs and things like that on the walls. I'll fetch up a couple of rugs so you don't have to get out of bed on to bare linoleum, but I dare say you'll make your own arrangements once you settle in.'

Imogen, beginning to carry the clothing from her haversack to the first long drawer in the chest, smiled at Jill over her shoulder. 'It's really lovely,' she said. 'I've always wanted to go to boarding school like the girls in the Angela Brazil stories, where they had dormitories just like this one. If I'd known we were going to have so much space we could have brought more things . . .'

'Debby would have brought her teddy,' Rita whispered. She and Imogen had unpacked practical striped winceyette pyjamas, but Debby's were pink, fluffy and patterned with rosebuds. Rita had looked at Imogen just as Imogen turned to look at her, and they both grinned; already, they had realised that Debby was different from them. She kept a comb in her coat pocket and fussed with her hair when she thought no one was looking, and since the girls had been told not to wear their school uniform, but plain skirts and jumpers, they could see that Debby's clothes were of far finer quality than theirs. However, she must have interpreted the glance they had exchanged, for she blushed vividly and burst into hurried speech.

'I know my pyjamas are a bit sissy, but my grandmother bought them; she thinks girls ought to wear nightgowns, but the school said it must be pyjamas, so she chose the fanciest ones she could find.'

'Good for your gran; your pyjamas are very practical *and* very pretty,' Jill said firmly. 'And now I'll leave you to unpack the rest of your things whilst I go and get a meal organised. Would vegetable soup, ham sandwiches and a piece of gingerbread fit the bill? I made the gingerbread a couple of days ago so it's had a chance to become really sticky and delicious. It's one of the few cakes that improve with keeping.' She went to the door, opened it, and then turned back. 'Come down as soon as you're ready. I expect Auntie's laid the table, but in future that will be one of the jobs the three of you can manage. Oh, and I should have asked you if you have any questions.'

Three hands at once shot skywards, making Jill laugh, but she pointed to Rita, whose hand seemed to be waving more frantically than the others. 'Yes? What would you like to know?'

'Please, what do we call Miss Marcy and you?'

Jill laughed. 'Everyone calls me Jill, and Miss Marcy is just Auntie. Of course she has another name but she hates it and refuses to allow it to be used. Any more questions?'

Imogen looked hopefully around the room. 'Where's

the toilet?' she asked bluntly. 'I expect it's in the back yard, like at home, but what do we do if we have to go during the night?'

'Yes, it's in the back yard, and at night you'll have to use a chamber pot,' Jill said equally bluntly. 'If you're shy, no doubt you can rig up a corner so you can be private. But of course it goes without saying that you will empty your own slops. You can carry a jug of cold water up each night to wash in in the morning, or you can come down early, when Auntie and I have got the kettle on, and take some warm water back upstairs. All right? I'm afraid we don't have a bathroom as such; it'll be a tin bath in front of the kitchen fire, the same as in all the villages. You won't find many houses with bathrooms in the country.'

'It's all right, Jill, it's the same at home,' Imogen said quickly.

'Good. Then you know the score on that front,' Jill said. She pointed at Debby, whose hand was still waving in the air. 'Yes, love?'

'I just wondered how we get to school if it's in the village we passed through earlier,' Debby said shyly. 'Is there a bus that we can catch?'

Jill snorted. 'A *bus*? My dear child, a walk of two miles or so is nothing. There's a farm a couple of hundred yards along the lane where the evacuees are younger than you, and they walk to school every day. Even when Mr Pilgrim needs to go into town and gives the boys a lift, he wouldn't have room to take you as well. So I'm afraid it's Shanks's pony. If you're unhappy about it, I dare say we could try to find you another billet, but I can't guarantee we'd succeed.'

Debby looked horrified, and a ready flush rose in her cheeks. 'I didn't mean . . . you said we could ask . . . it was only a question,' she stuttered. 'I don't need a bus to take me to school, honest to God I don't. It truly was just a question, though rather a silly one. Please forget I ever opened my mouth.'

Jill smiled. 'Don't apologise; it's far better that you should know the score right from the start,' she said. 'See you presently.'

As soon as the door closed behind her, Rita flew to the attack. 'Debby Viner, who the devil do you think you are?' she asked scornfully. 'I just hope we don't get thrown out, 'cos I already like this place and want to stay here.' She glanced at Imogen. 'You're the same, ain't you?'

Imogen nodded. 'Yes, if you're asking whether I want to stay here or move on: I'm for staying. I had a good walk to my school in Liverpool and never thought twice about it. There were trams, of course, and buses, but we thought it was a waste of a penny to ride when we could walk for free.' She glanced apologetically at Debby who was staring at her, her mouth open. 'Cheer up. I wanted to know about transport too. I take it you're as keen to live here as Rita and me?'

Debby nodded so violently that her brown curls bounced. 'I do want to stay here,' she said huskily. 'It's just that I'm an only child and I suppose I'm spoilt . . .'

'Yes; well I reckon we'd guessed that,' Rita said. She had been looking severe, but apparently noticing the tears which had formed in Debby's large brown eyes she crossed the space between them and punched the other girl lightly on the shoulder. 'Don't cry, you idiot, I didn't mean to upset you. So are we all of the same mind? That we'll stay here, with Auntie and Jill, and tell our parents that we're settled?' When the others nodded enthusiastically she began to pile her belongings into the second drawer of the chest. 'Hurry up, you two. I'm starving to death, and so tired I could sleep on a clothes line. I bet that vegetable soup will be rare good, and the ham sandwiches better. I can't wait to find out.'

Downstairs in the big comfortable kitchen, Jill and Auntie looked at one another and Jill raised her eyebrows. She was slicing and buttering bread whilst Auntie was carving ham and making up the sandwiches, and now she said, 'Well? I got the impression that Mrs Hainstock wasn't too happy about leaving her charges with us; but of course she didn't stand a chance once you'd made up your mind. I wonder what she'll tell the authorities when she goes back to HQ, wherever that may be.'

Auntie sniffed. 'Poor little creatures! That Mrs Hainstock is a nice woman, but she has no imagination. I saw at a glance that those kids were lost and frightened, but making the best of it. The minute I said I'd have them I could see the relief on their little white faces.' She chuckled. 'I don't think any of them has ever been inside a public house before, but they're bright kids. They can go in and out of the back door and up and down the back staircase without setting foot on licensed premises. Then there's the small parlour which used to be the Bottle and Jug. It's nothing special, but they can go in there to do homework or play quiet games; they'll find a use for it, I'm sure. Why, the landlady of the Running Dog has *her* grandchildren living with her, has had ever since the outbreak of war, and no one objects to that, so far as I know. If you ask me Mrs Hainstock will simply give the authorities our address, and we'll hear no more about it.' She looked curiously across at her niece. 'What do you think of them? I heard you chattering and laughing whilst you made up the beds.'

'They're nice kids, from good homes, and will fit in well if only because they want to,' Jill said at once.

Auntie nodded slowly. 'I reckon you're right,' she said. 'And you'd best give them a shout, because we don't want them falling asleep now and waking up starving hungry in the middle of the night.'

When the girls made their way back up to the attic after the supper Auntie had provided, they could scarcely wait to congratulate each other on their good fortune. Rita, as usual, was the first one to put it into words. 'If we'd not made Mrs Hainstock let us go into the post office and ask the lady behind the counter if we could use her toilet, then said when we came out that we wouldn't go any further, we'd never have met Auntie,' she pointed out, wrenching her thick jumper over her head and beginning to unbutton the blouse beneath. 'I reckon it was fate.'

'Don't care what it was, so long as we can stay here,' Imogen said. 'I like that Jill. She didn't seem at all surprised when Mrs Hainstock told her we were going to live with them, did she?'

Debby was undressing with care and caution, not throwing off her clothes with wild abandon as the other two did and stepping carefully into her fancy pyjamas, yet she was still the first to be ready for bed. She'd been about to climb between the sheets but she stopped, forehead wrinkling, to reply: 'Didn't you hear her saying that Auntie was always bringing in stray animals? I suppose three girls wasn't that much of a surprise.'

Rita snorted. 'You're daft, you are,' she said derisively. 'Girls are a lot more trouble than cats and dogs.'

Debby began to disagree, but Imogen overrode her. 'You're right, of course,' she said. 'And that makes it even more important that we don't give either Jill or Auntie any reason to think we're going to be trouble. We've got to behave like three little saints, for a few weeks at least. Agreed?'

By now they were all in bed, and whilst Rita murmured agreement Debby, more practical, slipped out of bed, regarded the scattered clothing of the other two with disfavour and began to shake out each garment, fold it neatly and place it on top of the chest of drawers. Rita nodded. 'Good for you, Debby,' she said. 'Tomorrow we might ask for three chairs to put our clothes on, and a box or something so we can put a torch near our beds, just in case one of us wants to use the chamber pot.'

Debby giggled. They had been provided with an enormous floral chamber pot for use during the night, and since Auntie had said that they need not attend school for the rest of the week, she had told them to come downstairs when they awoke next day, emptying the chamber pot, if it had been used, into the bucket on the landing on the way, and wash at the big kitchen sink. 'I'll have one of the washstands carried up to the attic before you go to bed tomorrow,' Auntie had promised. 'I daresay I'm wrong to let you go to bed just as you are tonight,' she had smiled conspiratorially, 'but who's to know, eh?'

'We shan't tell,' Rita had said, beaming at her. 'It was

a lovely supper, Miss – I mean Auntie. Thanks ever so much.'

Now, Debby cast a last look around the attic before climbing back into her little bed. 'It's all very well to talk, and to say how good we are going to be, but we could start off by keeping our room nice,' she said. 'I expect at home you always kept your room tidy, didn't you?'

'Sort of,' Imogen said sleepily. 'I'll help in future, though; how about you, Rita?'

'Well, I think we ought to keep our own clothes and so on tidy, but for the actual room itself we should take it in turns,' Rita mumbled. 'Do shut up and go to sleep, you two; don't forget we've got to walk into the village tomorrow to post those dratted cards so our families know our address . . .' Her voice faded into a sleepy mumble, yet it was she who presently broke the silence in the big attic room by giving a muffled shriek, and pushing back the covers to sit upright. Even in the dark, Imogen, facing her, could see the look of shock on her face.

'Wharrisit?' she mumbled, forgetting her determination to speak correctly, for at home she was forbidden to talk with the local accent. 'You near on give me a heart attack, Rita Jeffries, screechin' out like that. I'd like to clack your lug, so I would!'

'Sorry. I forgot where I were,' Rita mumbled. 'But I just realised: who's going to plait my hair tomorrer? I can't do it meself, 'cos of them two fancy bits on each side. Oh, Gawd, what'll I do?'

Imogen chuckled. 'Cut it off,' she advised. 'Long hair's a perishin' nuisance. And if my mam heard me talkin' Scouse, I'd be gettin' a clack on the lug meself.'

'Same here,' Rita said dolefully. 'But I can't cut my hair, honest to God I can't. My mam says it's my one beauty.'

'Then I'll plait it for you, which means we'll need to get up a bit earlier once we start school,' Imogen said decidedly. 'And now for goodness' sake let's get to sleep, or it'll be morning before we know it!'

Chapter Two

Christmas came without an attack by the enemy and people began to relax. When term had ended a great many parents had reclaimed their children for the holiday, though the three girls had not been among them. No one had wanted to move them from a home where they were safe and happy, and the girls were glad of it.

'After all, Auntie and Jill took us in as a favour, and if we left they might replace us with other kids needing to be evacuated,' Rita had said wisely. The three children were roasting chestnuts, Auntie having kindled the fire in the small parlour as a special treat. 'That family of little lads who've been living with Mr and Mrs Pilgrim say they'll come back, but Jill said she reckons the Pilgrims won't have them. Apparently they'd asked the billeting officer for older boys who could help on the farm, and were pretty annoyed when they got the O'Reagans.'

'So if they can, they'll get lads of our age or older,' Imogen said thoughtfully. 'That might be rather fun.'

'Oh, you know what boys are; if they're a lot older – say thirteen or fourteen – then they'll look down on us,' Rita said. She fished the shovel out from under the coals and waved it. 'These are done; help yourselves, only remember they're really hot.'

The occupants of the Canary and Linnet had had a lovely Christmas. They had received small presents from their families and friends, and despite the threat of rationing had had a wonderful dinner. Indeed, Imogen thought, it must rank amongst the very best Christmases she had ever had. But now it was January, and the whole of the country was in the grip of what Jacky, the cellar man, a sprightly sixty-year-old, red-faced and white-haired, said was going to be the worst winter in living memory, if he was any judge. It had not stopped snowing for days and the three musketeers – Auntie's nickname for the girls – had not been able to go to school since the bad weather started. Now, with the hot chestnuts all eaten, the three of them were in the small parlour, staring disconsolately out at the whirling flakes. They were clad in every warm garment they possessed but even so, when Imogen moved back from the window she was conscious of the chill. 'Let's go into the kitchen,' she said, rubbing her hands together to restore some life to her numb fingers. 'It's not fair to make up this fire again, but there's always a fire in the kitchen and Auntie won't mind. We might be able to help her if she's cooking, or cleaning the bar.'

'Might as well,' Rita agreed with alacrity. She cast a wistful glance at the whirling flakes being blown horizontally by a spiteful east wind. 'To think how pleased we were when it first started to snow! I thought there would be snowball fights and snowman competitions, and imagined flying down Parsonage Hill on that huge old sledge of Auntie's, just as soon as the snow let up a bit. Only it never has – let up a bit, I mean – so all it's done is stop us from going to school, or doing any outdoor things.'

Debby nodded gloomily. 'I didn't like my school at

home very much, though I wasn't there long, but I love the village one,' she said. 'Miss Roxley may be old, but she's ever so nice, especially when you consider she has to teach all the kids now, from five to fifteen, which can't be easy.'

They crossed the small, dingy corridor down which customers had once trooped from the bar, presumably with their jugs and bottles, and entered the kitchen. Jacky was leaning against the sink. His cottage and that of Herbert, a retired farmhand who helped at the Canary and Linnet when needed, were a hundred yards further up the lane, and they had kept a path clear between the pub and the Pilgrims' farm, though it had not been easy.

'Mornin', girls. I just popped in to see whether Auntie wanted anything from the village shop,' Jacky said, waving the mug of tea he held in one hand. 'I reckon school won't open again until the snow stops a-fallin', but Mrs Bailey has still got some stock left.'

Auntie grinned at the girls. 'I was just telling him he'd best get me anything Mrs B can spare, because old Herbert is a famous weather prophet and Jacky here tells me that he says the snow's here to stay for a while. Which means we'll start running out of grub as well as beer, so we'd best get what we can whilst it's still possible to reach the village.'

'Aye, you're right there,' Jacky agreed. 'There's no way anyone can get down the lane now – the drifts be higher than a man's head – but if I go over the fields, pullin' the old sledge, I reckon I'll get through all right.'

The girls had been clustered round the fire, but now they turned towards Jacky, faces bright with hope. 'Can we come and give you a hand?' Imogen said, speaking for them all. 'We've been stuck in the house for days and days apart from one little half-hour, when Auntie lets us clear a path across the yard. Oh, do say we can, Mr Jacky!'

The old man laughed, but shook his head. 'Not with a blizzard blowin'. Ain't you cold enough?' he asked. 'It'll be no picnic, I'm tellin' you. Gettin' to the village will be hard, but gettin' back will be a lot worse because the sledge'll be fully laden. Just you find some other way to pass the time, young leddies. Didn't Miss Roxley give you no homework? That's what the teacher in charge usually do when the weather keep the school closed.'

'It came on too suddenly,' Auntie was beginning when the door from the bar opened and Jill, very flushed in the face and carrying a large galvanised bucket, a long-handled brush and a mop, came into the kitchen. She smiled round at everyone, then went over to the sink, tipped the dirty water out of her bucket, pumped some fresh into it and remarked that it was a miracle that the pump had not yet frozen.

'Don't you let that pump hear you say it might freeze; it's never done so in all my time here,' Auntie said reproachfully. 'But the well which serves it is very deep, so I reckon that even if we run out of everything else, we should have water.' She turned to the girls. 'And as for the suggestion that you might so much as poke your noses out of the door, you can forget it. You'd come home chilled to the bone, with icicles hanging from your ears and every garment you've got on soaked.'

'A big jigsaw would have kept us busy,' Debby said, 'or one of those board games, Ludo or Snakes and Ladders, or Monopoly; I used to play that with . . . with my grandparents.'

'I'd have bought a diary, so I could do this Mass Observation thing all the grown-ups are talking about,' Imogen chimed in. She had started to keep an account of each day's doings, but paper was difficult to come by, and anyway, what could she say except Snowing again?

Auntie, writing a list of things she would like if Jacky managed to get to the village and back, glanced across at Jill and raised her eyebrows. 'Dear me, when it comes to making your own amusements you three give up rather easily,' she said. 'I've got several packs of cards somewhere, which various customers have left in the bar. No one's likely to come in whilst the blizzard continues, so I see no reason why the three of you can't go in there and search for them. I take it you've tidied your room and so on?' She turned to Imogen. 'Suppose you write your diary in the back pages of one of my account books? Would that satisfy your urge to be an author?'

'Oh, Auntie, you are kind. But I'm beginning to think I'd better write something like "Three Go Adventuring" or "The Naughtiest Girls in the School"', Imogen said, 'because right now nothing happens to make one day different from another. It's just snow, snow, snow. But I'll help the others to find those cards.'

The three of them searched diligently and found two complete packs and several partial ones, and were glad to carry their booty back to the kitchen, for the bar was bitterly cold. They settled round the table but were soon chased off it by Jill, who wanted to set it for dinner. 'It won't be much of a meal because we're almost out of potatoes and those we have got are pretty spongy and unpleasant, having got frosted,' she said. 'Apart from that there'll be sprouts, some rather fatty bacon and the rest of the apple pie we started last night. Go and play in the parlour whilst I get things ready, there's good girls.'

The three of them gathered up the cards and Auntie's old account book and returned to the Bottle and Jug, but once there were distracted from their game by the sight, through the frosted windowpanes, of Jacky setting out across the yard with the sledge bumping along behind him. He saw the girls and waved, and Debby, giggling, said that the sledge on the end of its long rope looked like a dog on a lead and wondered why Jacky had not brought his collie, Snip, to keep him company. 'Snow's too deep and Snip isn't a young dog,' Rita said promptly. 'Brrr, it's icy in here now the fire's well and truly out. Do you know, this is the first time I've ever regretted that we didn't get a village billet? Jacky says the school's closed but I bet there are kids making snowmen and slides and things. If one of the villagers had taken us in . . .'

But the other two made derisive noises. 'Don't be so stupid,' Imogen said. 'Even your own mam wouldn't let you out on such a day. Now let's get going and have a game of pairs or snap or something, otherwise it will be dinner time before we know it. And maybe, if we pray hard, the snow will stop long enough to let us get out for a bit.'

Despite their hopes, however, the snow continued to fall all that day and the next, and they grew increasingly cold and bored with their own company. One or two customers, who had fought their way through from the nearest airfield to get a drink and a change of scene, told anyone who would listen that this bad weather might be to Britain's advantage since it gave them time to make preparations for what was to come. 'We can't get the kites off the ground whilst the snow continues, and from what we've heard the whole of Europe is suffering the same freezing weather,' a young aircraftman said. 'They're calling this the phoney war, but if you ask me it's more like a reprieve, because despite what's been happening in Nazi Germany our government has made very few efforts to re-arm. I say let the bad weather continue. Chamberlain's "peace for our time" has only proved how unsuitable he is to lead the country into war.'

But to Imogen, Rita and Debby, this meant very little. What they wanted was to get out of the house, even to go to school; in fact almost anything which would break the monotony of what they jokingly called 'house arrest'. Auntie and Jill laughed at the idea.

'Remember how you disliked the walk to and from school once the weather got cold,' Jill said. 'And anyway, whatever old Herbert says, this weather simply cannot last for ever. Any day now you'll look out of the window and see the sun shining on fields of white cotton wool and be quite cross to be herded into a classroom and made to attend to your lessons.'

And to be sure, there did come a day when the snow ceased to fall, though since the sky overhead was still dark the girls doubted that the lull would last. However, they managed to clear the yard, and the exercise brought them indoors for their dinner bright-eyed and bushy-tailed, as Jill put it. Mr Pilgrim, the farmer up the road, had sent them some eggs, Auntie had still got some of the rather fat bacon and Jill had baked bread, so it was a pleasant enough meal. As they ate the girls chatted and Imogen admitted that she had not yet tried her hand at fiction, though her diary was hardly a record of exciting events, as she had wished. 'It's nothing but snow, snow, snow,' she grumbled. 'Every night we hug our hot water bottles until they go cold and every morning we break the ice in our water jugs before we can wash. We hang around the house, play card games, help Auntie and Jill and simply wait for the weather to get better. What sort of a war diary is that? We're not far from an airfield but the planes haven't taken off since before Christmas, and when they did take off it was to drop leaflets on the Jerries, not bombs. If something doesn't happen soon, I shall get desperate.'

'Oh, you, you're always complaining about something,' Rita said untruthfully, for this was the first time that Imogen had revealed how frustrated she felt. 'It's just as bad for Debby and me, don't forget; she's been knitting herself a muffler and ran out of wool a week or more ago, and I'm trying to make myself a new dress for when summer comes from that length of gingham Auntie gave me. In fact, you're the only one who simply mooches about here moaning.'

'I am not, and it's a lie that I moan, Rita,' Imogen said angrily. 'I'm sure the school will be open tomorrow, even if it isn't today. Not that a day in school is going to make my diary exciting reading. Still, whilst we're in the village we can pop into the shop and perhaps I can buy a notebook, because writing a diary in the back of someone else's accounts isn't ideal, I can tell you.'

'Oh yes, if we can get to school then we can get to the shop,' Debby said eagerly. 'I've got my pocket money still – haven't we all? – so I could buy some Mint Imperials. They're my favourites.'

'Trust you to think of your stomach,' Rita said nastily. 'What about that jigsaw you wanted? Or since you're such a goody-goody, you'd probably like Miss Roxley to set you arithmetic questions.'

Debby's cheeks began to turn pink and her eyes filled with tears, and Imogen promptly rushed to her defence. 'Don't be so horrid, Rita,' she said. 'You're always picking on poor Debby. And it's not as though you don't care about sweets yourself, because only yesterday you were grumbling that you'd almost forgotten the taste of toffee. Now tell Debby you're sorry you were so beastly.'

At this moment the door to the small parlour opened and Jill appeared, smiling. 'It looks like we're in for a lull, since the sky has cleared,' she said. 'I'm going up to the Pilgrims' place. Old Herbert usually helps with the milking, but his rheumatism is so bad that he's set fast in his chair, so I've said I'll go up and give a hand. If you three would like to put on your wellies and mackintoshes you might do worse than come with me. I could start teaching you to milk, for a start, and it's always lovely and warm in the milking parlour. What do you say?'

'Oh, Jill, that would be lovely,' Debby said in her soft voice. 'I've often thought it must be wonderful to be able to milk. But wouldn't Mr Pilgrim mind us practising on his cows? Perhaps we should just watch at first . . . or we could clear his yard or do something else to help.'

Jill beamed, and Imogen knew she had been right when she had thought Jill was growing fond of the gentle Debby. Debby never quarrels and is always the first to make peace when Rita and I get at one another, she thought. Jill likes us all, of course, and is kind to everyone, just like Auntie, but I'll try to be more like Debby in future because Jill's the nicest person I know and I want her to like me as much as she likes Debby.

She remembered an incident which had happened a couple of nights before. Debby had nightmares, really bad ones, during the course of which she cried, shouted and even hit out, behaving quite unlike the gentle girl Imogen knew her to be. Furthermore, she sometimes talked what Imogen had thought at first was gobbledegook, although she was beginning to believe that her little friend was speaking a real language, possibly French or German. It also struck Imogen now that Debby's soft little voice never dropped into Scouse, not even when her companions were larking about, as Mrs Clarke would have put it, and imitating the broad Liverpool accent which many of their neighbours used.

But on this particular night Debby's nightmare had even managed to wake Rita, who normally slept straight through such things and, when morning dawned, denied all knowledge of any disturbance in the night. She had even accused Imogen of making it up, for as the observant Imogen was well aware – although she would not have dreamed of remarking on it – in an odd sort of way Rita was jealous of Debby. Indeed, she had several times suggested that she and Imogen should be 'bezzies'. So far Imogen had managed to wriggle out of that one by saying firmly that they were the three musketeers, as Auntie called them.

Debby's cries had grown so wild and her sobs so frantic that both Imogen and Rita had not only woken but had tried to calm her, with no success. Indeed, Imogen had been considering waking Jill when the bedroom door opened softly and the older girl appeared. She had taken in the situation at a glance, ordered Imogen and Rita back to their own beds and scooped Debby, tear-streaked and trembling, up into her arms, murmuring comforting words as she did so.

Remembering, Imogen thought gratefully that Jill had a sort of magic. Just the sound of her voice and the feel of her warm arms had been enough to bring Debby out of whatever ghastly situation her nightmare had conjured up, back to the candlelit attic; Imogen had kindled a stub as soon as Debby's cries had grown frighteningly loud.

Jill had stayed with Debby, ordering Rita to pour her friend a glass of water, and when Rita had pointed out that there was ice in the ewer Jill had spoken quite crossly. 'Then run downstairs and fetch some milk,' she had said brusquely, and as soon as Rita had disappeared and Debby was settled back into bed once more she had turned to Imogen. 'Have either of you been teasing Debby?' she had asked abruptly. And then, seeing the look on Imogen's face, had added hastily: 'No, I shouldn't have said that; I know you better. But Rita can be pretty sharp, and if she asks questions . . . but I know even Rita wouldn't have done anything to bring back memories which Debby tries so hard to forget. You'll gather that there are things in her past . . .'

But at this moment the door had opened and Auntie, clad in a long green dressing gown, had entered the room, pushing Rita ahead of her. '*What* a hullabaloo,' she had said cheerfully. 'But I can see everything's fine now.' She had crossed the room in two long strides, plonked herself down on Debby's bed, taken the mug of milk from Rita's trembling hand and beamed down at Debby, who had smiled trustingly back. 'Drink your milk, my little chickadee. Poor old lady, I gather you've had another horrid nightmare. You'll grow out of them, given time. After you've drunk up your milk, we'll all go back to bed.'

Debby drained her mug and Auntie had hesitated, looking carefully from face to face, then looked down at Debby. 'Would you like to share with Jill, just for tonight?'

Imogen had been sure that Debby would jump at the chance, but the younger girl had shaken her head firmly. 'No thank you. I'm quite all right now,' she had said. She had heaved a deep sigh and rubbed her eyes and Imogen had thought she looked, suddenly, about five years old. 'I'll try not to disturb you again, girls. Night night.'

But that had been two nights ago, and Debby had had no nightmares since. Jill had had a quiet word with Imogen and Rita, explaining that Debby lived with her grandparents because her own mother and father, and her elder brother, had disappeared into Nazi Germany and were presumed dead. 'So be especially kind to her and don't try to get her to talk about her life before you met her,' she had instructed.

Both girls had agreed to be careful, but after Jill had left them Rita had given a disdainful sniff. 'I'm very sorry her parents are dead, *if* they are,' she had said. 'If you ask me, she's just a spoilt baby.' And then, seeing the look on Imogen's face, she had come as near an apology as her nature allowed. 'Was that a nasty thing to say? Well, if so, I didn't mean it. And now let's get on with our letters home.'

Now, however, the three girls had abandoned the small parlour and were back in the kitchen, struggling into their outdoor clothing, shedding their slippers – Auntie's Christmas present to them all – and pushing their feet into the rubber boots which stood by the back door. Excitement at the thought of the walk up to the farm and even more excitement at the prospect of learning to milk made them hurry, with the result that, as they crossed the yard, Imogen was suddenly aware that her wellingtons were pinching her toes and rubbing her heels in a most unpleasant fashion. She was slightly behind the other three and hurried to catch them up, grabbing Rita's arm when she did so. 'Rita, have you got my boots by mistake? My feet are bigger than yours and these feel at least one size too small. I suppose we were in such a hurry to get out that we didn't look to see whether they were marked with our own initials.'

She expected Rita to stop and exchange footwear, but instead Rita scowled at her and shook her off. 'Don't start another fuss,' she said crossly. 'These feel okay to me; if we say anything to Jill she'll send us back to the Linnet rather than let us change in the snow. Aren't I glad the old fellers dug a path out right at the beginning of the snow though, 'cos it would be really hard work otherwise.' Imogen sighed but began to walk once more, trying to speed up, but Jill and Debby were already well ahead, and the boots were so tight that it was all she could do to hobble. The other three disappeared into the milking parlour whilst she was still only just turning into the farmyard.

Imogen said a bad word beneath her breath but slogged on, thinking rude thoughts about Rita, boots and even Jill, who no doubt was already introducing Rita and Debby to the mysteries of milking. She entered the milking parlour at last and saw her two friends watching with keen interest as Jill swished the milk into the bucket, whilst further up the long line of cows Mrs Pilgrim milked with neatness and dispatch. Rita, watching, turned as Imogen reached her side. 'Why were you such ages?' she asked, sounding indignant. 'Jill says we can watch for today and then tomorrow, if the snow holds off, we can each have a go at milking, Debby first, me second and you last.'

'It's not fair; it's all your fault because you wouldn't swap boots and let me have my own back,' Imogen said crossly. 'And if Jill asked why I wasn't with the rest of you I bet you never said you'd nicked my boots. Yours are so small I could scarcely put one foot in front of the other. Come on, let's swap now.'

Rita bent down to remove her footwear, then stopped. 'Hang on a moment! I don't believe these are your boots, nor I don't think those you've got on are mine. Just you show me the initial in them.'

'I tell you, you've got my boots,' Imogen said. She was beginning to be really angry. 'These are much too small. They couldn't possibly be . . .' Her voice faded as she bent the top of the boot back to reveal the initial I. She stared at it unbelievingly even as Rita gave a crow of triumph.

'You idiot! I know what's happened. Oh, Imogen, you really are stupid. When we came in this morning from clearing the yard, Auntie put scrumpled-up newspapers into the toes of our boots to dry them out. Don't you remember? I suppose you didn't think to take out the paper before you put them on and you've been blaming me all this time when it was your own silly fault.'

Imogen stood on her right foot and pulled the left boot off. She was tempted for a moment to pretend that there was nothing in the toe, but innate honesty prevented her. Grim-faced and without a word she pulled out the newspaper and followed the same procedure with the other boot.

Rita grinned widely. 'Told you so,' she said tauntingly. 'Wait till I tell Jill why you were hobbling along in the rear; how she'll laugh!'

Imogen scowled. 'I don't think it's particularly funny,' she said, and then, despite herself, she gave a little giggle. 'Well, I suppose it is funny, though I can't tell you how dreadfully painful it was. But let's not argue; I'm going to start making a snowman, just a little one, while I wait for Jill to finish milking. Have you ever made a snowball and then rolled it around in the loose snow until it's absolutely huge? We could do that, and clear a lot of snow at the same time.'

But it seemed that Rita was in a difficult mood. 'Make a snowman? How childish,' she said, her very tone a sneer. 'We're meant to be watching Jill, not messing around like a couple of kids.'

Imogen was about to say that they *were* a couple of kids when Jill looked over her shoulder and smiled at Rita. 'Come along, Miss Know-it-all,' she said cheerfully. Her bright gaze flickered to Imogen. 'You missed my demonstration, but I'll go over it again tomorrow . . .' she was beginning, but Rita interrupted.

'Oh, Jill, you'll never guess why she took such ages to get here . . .' she started, but Imogen had had enough.

With Jill's laughter in her ears she marched angrily out of the parlour and was crossing the yard, intending to start making a snowman regardless of Rita's remarks, when it occurred to her that if she stuck to the fields she should be able to walk to the village; had not Jacky done so, and even old Herbert, before his rheumatism claimed him? To be sure, she had no money on her, but she guessed that Mrs Bailey would be happy to sell her some aniseed balls or peppermints and accept delayed payment. She saw no reason why she should not attempt the journey. After all, if it proved too difficult she could simply turn round and come back and no harm done. Besides, Rita was in a funny mood and she, Imogen, did not fancy becoming a laughing stock. If she managed to get to the village and buy the sweets, far from being thought foolish she would be the heroine of the hour.

Of course she realised she should go back to the parlour to get Jill's permission for the expedition, but she was pretty sure that Jill would say she was not to attempt it so late in the afternoon. However, it would be an adventure, something to write about in her Mass Observation diary. At the thought she felt a little smile begin. She could buy a notebook from Mrs Bailey – the post office would keep such things – and start her diary properly at last. Jacky had been a brick and so had Jill, for both had visited the village in order to buy supplies, but when the girls had mentioned sweets Auntie had said regretfully that she had not ordered any. 'I ask for necessities, not luxuries,' she had explained, looking at the girls over the top of her little gold-rimmed spectacles. 'But I put sugar and margarine on the latest list because if she's got enough I'll teach you how to make your own toffee.'

When the order had come, however, there had been no extra sugar and only a very tiny square of margarine, so making their own toffee was just a dream which could not be realised until the snow allowed the delivery lorries to reach the village once more.

Imogen crossed the yard and hovered for a moment, unsure of what she should do. She knew both Jill and Auntie, if asked, would forbid her to go off on her own, but this was the first day they had seen the sun for what felt like a lifetime, and she thought that the very blood within her was bubbling with excitement at the promise of spring to come. She told herself that two miles when the weather was sunny would not take her more than forty minutes at the most. She could arrive back at the Linnet with pockets full of sweets and a notebook for her diary even sooner than the others, for Jill would not leave until the milking was finished and probably not even then. Like Auntie, Mrs Pilgrim was a notable housewife and would no doubt insist that her helpers be regaled with her delicious cottage cheese spread on hollow biscuits, to go with the cup of tea she would brew. Possibly there would even be a slice of cake.

The thought of the missed treat tempted Imogen to turn back and for a moment she hesitated, but then she climbed the bank and looked around her. Herbert and Jacky had come this way because it was easier with the laden sledge, and she was soon able to pick out the marks of the sledge's runners and the prints of the old men's boots. If she followed their footprints she would be in the village in no time. She cast one last look around her at the red sun turning the snowy scene to theatrical beauty, then slid down the far side of the bank and began to walk along the path the old men and their sledge had marked. For a moment she contemplated following the cleared path as far as the Canary and Linnet, then shook her head at herself. With her luck Auntie would pop out of the kitchen just as she was making her way past. No, better to take to the fields, follow where the old boys had led and arrive at the village well before closing time.

I don't suppose Jill will worry; she'll think I've gone home, Imogen told herself. And anyway, she shouldn't have laughed when Rita told her about the scrumpled newspaper in the boots. And with that thought she continued on her way.

Looking around her as she walked she realised for the first time how snow changes a landscape and decided that instead of following the old men's trail she must stick to within a few feet of the lane, for otherwise she might stray into unknown territory. The trouble was that she was a city girl, knowing only the dirty slush of snow found in a big city, and this was country snow, so beautiful that instead of watching her feet she found herself gazing to right and left, wondering at the beauty of it. The trees were heavily laden still and the wind had sculpted the drifts into the strangest shapes. Castles and palaces, huge waves which reared several feet above her head, mountains and valleys; all caught her eye as she slogged along. Every now and then she thought she saw what must be the lane, but she could not be certain.

After half an hour or so, however, she began to worry. She had not dawdled but neither had she realised that she would have to deviate from the line she planned to take in order to bypass the enormous drifts, and presently she actually found herself wishing that she had been sensible and stayed with Jill and the others. She imagined them in Mrs Pilgrim's lovely warm kitchen, sipping hot tea and crowding close to the blazing fire, and caught her breath on a little sob. She had seen no sign of any human habitation, was sure she must have bypassed the Canary and Linnet without realising it, and began to understand how very foolish she had been. She glanced behind her and was a little reassured. This way had not been trodden since the last snowfall and there were her footprints sunk deep into the soft snow. If I follow them back I'll arrive at Pilgrim Farm, she told herself. I think perhaps I'd better do that because the sun is almost out of sight and in a very few minutes it will be dusk. Yes, I'll turn back.

She did so and found herself almost immediately sliding helplessly downwards, realising as she fought to remain upright that she had been walking along the bank which flanked the ditch; she could see the top of a hawthorn hedge and gave a shriek as she crashed through snow and ice and plummeted feet first into the ice-cold water of the ditch. She grabbed at the branches of the hedge, trying to claw her way back to the bank, but she was wet to the waist and there was no feeling in the hands that tried to grasp the brittle reeds or the hedge itself. Dimly, she thought she heard shouts echoing off the snow. She tried to scream, to call for help, though she knew screaming was useless even as the water crept higher. She caught one last glimpse of a large crow peering down at her from a branch overhead, saw the dying sun slip further down the sky, and then found a boulder beneath her feet which enabled her to struggle half out of the water. Then her feet slipped, and the last thing she heard was the crow's call as her hands lost their grip and blackness enveloped her.

The Mess was crowded, every table taken when Laurie and Dave came out of the icy afternoon into the hot fug of cigarette smoke and male sweat. There wasn't a chair free, and though several of the young men greeted the newcomers, they hesitated in the doorway. Someone shouted at them to close the door as though the iced wine of the air offended them, and the shorter of the two jerked the sleeve of the taller. 'Didn't you say you knew a pub within walking distance of the station, Laurie?' he asked, raising his voice above the hubbub. 'We've been cooped up for days and days. I reckon this is the first time we've seen clear skies for ages, so why don't we take a walk and get ourselves a beer at the end of it?'

'Good idea,' Laurie said. He had been longing for an excuse to visit the Canary and Linnet again, but the opportunity had not occurred; it would have been madness to attempt the walk across the fields in the blizzards which seemed to coincide with their time off. He grinned down at Dave. 'It's not all that far off, a couple of miles maybe, and the landlady's a fantastic cook. She makes a meat and potato pie that puts my mother's to shame. Best get boots and torches, though, because we can't reach it by road. We'll have to walk over the fields.' He made no mention of the chief attraction – for him at any rate – of the pub in the woods. That girl – Jill, wasn't it? – who had smiled at him as she poured beer into a pint tankard. They had exchanged a couple of sentences and then she had moved on to serve someone else whilst he had gazed thoughtfully at her across the old-fashioned wooden bar counter. She had straight fawn-coloured hair, tied back from her face in a ponytail, large brown eyes – he thought they were brown, but they might have been dark blue – clear skin and a small, determined chin. But later, as he returned to the airfield, he realised that it was her voice which had caught his attention. It had made him want to see her again, and now Dave had handed him the opportunity on a plate. He looked narrowly at the other man. 'Are you sure you're up for it though? In all this snow it'll likely take us an hour in both directions, and it's beginning to get dark already.' As he spoke the two of them left the Mess and headed for their hut, feeling the full force of the cold now that the sun was dipping below the horizon.

Dave raised his eyebrows. 'I'm game,' he said briefly. 'I'm that fed up with being stuck indoors . . .'

The two young men disappeared into their hut and presently emerged in their bad weather gear of greatcoats, scarves and wellington boots. They headed for the gates, waved cheerfully to the guards and set off in the direction of the Canary and Linnet.

For the first half-hour or so Laurie and Dave strode out, but when he could still see no sign of human habitation ahead Dave jerked Laurie's arm. 'Hey, hang on a minute, Laurie. You said this perishing pub was only a mile or two from the station, and I'm bloody sure we've already walked a good deal further than that. Are you sure we're going in the right direction? What say we turn round and go back to the Mess?'

His companion snorted. 'Of course I'm sure! You give

up easily. Last time I came this way I was with Jigger Jones and I took his advice and made a note of landmarks. It's difficult in the snow, but if you've got eyes in your head you can spot various markers. See the top of that fencepost? That means we're well over halfway, and though there isn't a definite path you can see other people have been along here.' He pointed ahead of him, 'See that tree? I snapped a branch off when I came with Jigger. When we get to it, it means that in less than fifteen minutes we'll be in the bar of the Canary and Linnet warming ourselves at a log fire and drinking real beer, better than the stuff we get in the Mess.'

Dave sighed and jerked a thumb at the faint glow in the western sky which was all that was left of the daylight. 'Oh, all right, but even with our torches getting back is going to be no picnic,' he observed.

Laurie nodded his agreement, looking ruefully down at his blue serge uniform trousers. Although both men were wearing wellington boots and had been careful to try to steer clear of the soft snow, they had not been altogether successful. Laurie could feel snow water trickling down inside his boots, and despite gloves, scarf and his long forces issue overcoat his hands and feet were still cold. However, the thought of returning to the Mess and having to admit they had not reached their destination was a spur to continuing to fight their way onward.

Presently they reached the tree Laurie had mentioned and stopped for a moment while Laurie pointed to a branch half snapped off, dangling above the snow. 'See that? It's the marker I told you about. It means if we keep walking at our present pace we'll be in the pub in another ten minutes.' They saw another tree ahead and when they reached it Laurie grinned at the sight of a large crow perched in the branches. It seemed to be examining a pile of old clothes or meal sacks lying half in and half out of the ditch, and suddenly Laurie grabbed Dave's arm. 'What was that?' he asked. 'I heard something; was it that crow?'

'I guess so,' Dave said. He dug his companion in the ribs. 'Come on, it's not much further . . . you were right, Laurie. I can see chimneys, so we're not far off now, and since it's all downhill we can be toasting our toes in five minutes. Come *on*, will you?' He started to plough his way through the soft snow heading for a well-trodden path, but his companion did not follow.

'Hang on a minute, Dave,' Laurie said urgently. 'I did hear something, honest to God I did. It sounded like a kitten, a sort of mew. It came from over there, from the pile of stuff on the edge of the ditch, the pile the crow is staring at.'

Dave sighed, but when Laurie headed for the ditch he followed him. 'Country folk can be pretty hard-boiled,' he admitted. 'They'll drown a clutch of kittens without a second thought if they've got more cats than they need. And if it is very young kittens, the kindest thing would be to let them die quick. We can't give 'em a home.'

But Laurie was ignoring him, ploughing ahead, pointing, and presently he broke into an ungainly run. 'Something moved,' he said urgently, 'something bigger than a kitten. See those clothes, or whatever it is? I do believe someone's slipped into the ditch and can't get out.' He reached the ditch almost before the words were out of his mouth, and began to pull at the sodden heap.

'Give us a hand, old feller,' he panted. 'It's not clothing or kittens, it's a kid!'

Auntie and Jill had left Jacky in charge of the bar and were just struggling into their outdoor clothing to go in search of their missing evacuee when the back door burst open and two young men erupted into the kitchen. The taller of the two was carrying Imogen, wrapped in his greatcoat.

The women both exclaimed, and then Jill began to fill the big old tin bath with hot water whilst Auntie stripped Imogen of her soaked and freezing clothing. 'What the devil's been happening?' she asked. 'Where did you find her?' She tested the heat of the water and then dumped the child in the bath. 'Aren't you a lucky girl to have been rescued by these young men? Can you tell us what happened? My, you are in a state!'

Imogen looked up at Auntie. 'I fell . . . I fell . . .' she said, and then sighed deeply. 'I can't – I can't remember . . .'

Her rescuer interrupted. 'We think she slipped on the ice and fell into the ditch, but we didn't want to worry her with a lot of questions,' he said. He grinned at Auntie. 'I guess you're going to give her a good telling off, but she's had a horrible experience, so I doubt she'll do anything this foolish again.'

'You're right, of course; now go into the small parlour across the corridor and take off your wet things,' Auntie said briskly. 'You two will have to make do with a good wash; we'll dry your clothes out and you can borrow a dressing gown each. After that will be the time to express our heartfelt thanks, because judging by the filthy state of Imogen's clothes she's lucky to be alive.' She turned to Debby and Rita, sitting frozen with horror at the kitchen table. 'Run upstairs, dears, and fetch dressing gowns for . . .' She clapped a hand to her brow and addressed the two young men. 'My goodness, I'm so sorry, I haven't even asked you your names. I'm Auntie, this is my niece, Jill; you already know Imogen. Rita is the blonde and Debby the brunette, and you are . . . ?'

'I'm Laurie Matthews and this is Dave Crewe,' the young man said. 'We're stationed at the airfield a couple of miles away, and we were on our way here when we saw the kid struggling to get out of the ditch.'

Auntie nodded, her expression somewhat grim. As they talked she had been soaping Imogen and rinsing her off, and now she lifted her out of the tub, wrapped her in a large bath towel and set her in a chair before the fire. Meanwhile, Jill had carried jugs of hot water through to the small parlour and set a match to the fire laid in the grate, whilst the two girls thundered up the back stairs and returned with Auntie's green dressing gown and Jill's fawn one. Laurie and Dave thanked them, closed the door on them and stripped off their soaked clothing. Huddling as close to the fire as they could, they shared a rather unsatisfactory wash, for they had taken it in turns to carry Imogen and had managed to transfer a good deal of the muddy ditch from her person to their own.

As the two young men returned to the kitchen Jill placed a bowl of bread and milk in Imogen's hands, but the child could not grasp the spoon so Jill fed her whilst Auntie, looking stern, began to tell her that she had let them all down by her behaviour. 'You've done wrong and we all know it. But for the quick thinking of these two young fellows, you'd be dead and I'd be in deep trouble. You were in my charge and you knew very well that you were supposed to come straight home from Pilgrim Farm. I've not heard the full story yet, but from the state of you I'd guess you've come nearer death today than any of us would have thought possible. I won't ask you how you came to leave the path Jacky and Herbert had made to the village, because I realise you probably don't know yourself, but I'm telling you that for two pins I'd send you home to your mam and let her try to keep you out of mischief. I dare say, after this little adventure, you realise the country around the Canary and Linnet is just as dangerous as the slums off the Scotland Road in Liverpool.'

'I'm s-s-sorry,' Imogen muttered.

'Fine words butter no parsnips,' Auntie said severely, but Jill shook her head.

'She isn't taking anything in, Auntie,' she said quietly. 'I think she should go straight to bed and tell us her story in the morning.' As she spoke she lifted Imogen in her arms and headed for the stairs, but was intercepted by Laurie who took her burden from her.

'Show me where to go,' he instructed.

Jill went ahead of him and opened the attic door, indicating Imogen's bed. 'I do believe she's asleep already,' she said in a low voice. 'Don't bother to take the towel off, just roll her into the bed with it wrapped round her. It's my belief she'll sleep till morning, so you'll have to make do with our thanks – mine and Auntie's – until Immy is well enough to thank you herself.'

'I'm just glad we got her out in time,' Laurie muttered. 'Poor little bugger, she's had a lesson she'll never forget.'

As though the words had somehow reached her sleeping mind, Imogen's long lashes lifted and her eyes focused on Laurie for one moment before the lids were lowered again. 'Thank you,' she said drowsily.

'Glad to have been of service,' Laurie said, grinning, but Imogen's eyes didn't open again, so he and Jill turned and left the room. They descended the stairs and re-entered the kitchen.

'Now Imogen's settled, how do you fancy bacon and eggs and some of Jill's home-made bread?' Auntie said. 'You'd be all the better for something hot inside you, and though it's small thanks for saving our foolish child's life it's the best we can do for now.'

'That'll be grand,' Laurie said quickly. 'Are you really going to punish her? Don't you think she's been punished enough?'

Auntie smiled. 'I won't send her away, if that's what you mean,' she said, 'but fair's fair, young man. Jill and I are what you might call *in loco parentis* to these children; I imagine you've gathered they're evacuees. You must think I don't take very good care of them . . .'

'She does, honest to God she does; take care of us, I mean,' Debby said. 'And Imogen is very good as a rule. I suppose she never thought she was being naughty because she's doing this Mass Observation thing and has been desperate for something exciting to happen.'

Jill, who had been slicing the loaf, pulled a face. 'I don't imagine she wanted anything as exciting as being nearly killed. And I don't suppose we'll get an explanation out of her for a day or two. All I can tell you is that so far as I can recall, Debby was watching me milk the cows and Rita was cleaning the channel—'

Rita interrupted. 'If you're going to punish Imogen, Auntie, then you really ought to punish me as well,' she said miserably. 'I was in a bad mood, and I – I think I took it out on Imogen.' She turned to Jill. 'If you remember, there was a bit of a row over who was wearing the wrong wellington boots. In fact, none of us were. Imogen hadn't remembered that Auntie dried out our boots with scrumpled-up newspaper after we cleared the yard. In her hurry to go up to the farm, she put her own boots on with the paper still in and thought she was wearing mine. When we discovered the truth I – I jeered at her, made it sound as though she had been a real twerp, and I suppose she hated being laughed at and decided to show us all that she wasn't the idiot I'd called her. She must have decided to come home, or perhaps go into the village. But of course I don't know how she came to fall into the ditch except that she's always been a bit of a dreamer. If she was wandering along, thinking about what she would write in her diary, I suppose she could easily have slipped down the bank.'

'Well, no point in apportioning blame,' Auntie said briskly. 'I just want all of you to give me your word of honour that you'll never go off by yourselves. There are other dangers in being alone in a strange place, too, which I won't name . . .'

Debby nodded wisely. 'Mad axemen who hate little girls,' she said. 'There was an old man who lived a few doors away from my grandmother in Liverpool. He bred pigeons, for racing you know, and was always inviting children to visit his pigeon loft, but we were told not to go with him, so we never did.' She turned to Jill. 'That's what Auntie meant, wasn't it?'

Jill, breaking eggs into the big black frying pan, smiled, but nodded too. 'That's right; never forget there is safety in numbers,' she said cheerfully. Then she turned to address the two young men in their borrowed raiment. 'Sit yourselves down; I want to dish the eggs up before they go hard.'

By the time Laurie and Dave left the pub they had little need of their torches, for the moon was up and they could see their way clearly. They had eaten well but had refused Auntie's offer of a beer or even something stronger, thinking it best to stick to hot strong coffee. 'It'll keep us awake; not that there's much fear of either of us falling asleep on the walk home,' Laurie had told the two women after they had redressed in their dry clothing. 'Thanks very much, Miss – er – Auntie, I mean. As you can imagine, whilst this weather lasts there won't be any flying, so we'll pop in again in a day or two to check how young Imogen is getting on.'

Warm and well fed, they found the path they had made with ease, and when Dave started singing 'Good King Wenceslas' as they trod in the footsteps they had made when heading for the Canary and Linnet it seemed very appropriate. The moon shone down on the cheerful scene, throwing blue shadows on the silvered snow. Presently, they passed the spot where they had rescued Imogen and pointed out to each other how easy it must have been for the child not to see the ditch, hidden as it was by the depth of the snowfall and the drifts.

'She was lucky we came by,' Dave said presently. 'They're nice, aren't they, Laurie? Jill and Auntie, I mean.'

'Very nice,' Laurie said. He cast a look at his companion. 'That girl; there's something about her face. A sort of calmness . . . I don't know how else to describe it . . .'

His voice faded away and Dave said brightly: 'Imogen, do you mean? I didn't really notice.'

Laurie gave a snort of laughter. 'Not the kid, you fool,' he said derisively. 'I meant Jill, the one who cooked our supper. There was something about her – I'm not sure what – but I'd like to see her again.'

He looked across at Dave, a slow grin curling his mouth. He and Dave had both joined the Royal Air Force back in '38, passing out as fighter pilots after eighteen months' intensive training, and by now they knew each other pretty well. Laurie knew that Dave liked his girlfriends to be what he would have described as 'hot stuff'. He realised of course that Jill could not be so described, for she wore no makeup, her hair was not permed or curled but fell, rain straight, to her shoulders, and her open friendliness did not indicate that she was looking for romance.

Laurie, immediately attracted, had watched her whenever she was unaware of his scrutiny and thought she had a quality of peacefulness, rare in someone so young; he knew her to be not yet seventeen. But Dave, nodding slowly, seemed to understand. 'I've often wondered what sort of girl you'd go for, and now I know,' he said triumphantly. 'You like plain Janes, nice little homebodies who fuss around a feller; a stay-at-home girl, in fact. Well, you certainly found one there.' He shrugged, then punched Laurie lightly on the shoulder. 'You'll have no competition for that one; not from me at any rate. I like my women to have sex appeal.'

'And you want them to be willing; in fact that's all you care about really,' Laurie said with a grimace. 'I'm a bit choosier than you, old fellow. I want someone I can talk to.'

'If you want someone to talk to, what's wrong with me?' Dave said plaintively. He turned to grin up at the taller man and spoke in a squeaky voice: 'Gee, honey, let's discuss the theory of relativity . . .'

But before he could go further Laurie had bent down and made a snowball, and Dave's sentence ended in a splutter as the missile got him right in the teeth. 'Better the theory of relativity – which I'm bloody sure you don't understand – than assessing every woman you meet on a "will she won't she" basis,' Laurie said reprovingly. 'But that's what you get if you simply grab for any girl you find bedworthy. I like to get to know a girl . . .'

'. . . before you even ask her to dance,' Dave said, grinning. 'Well, you're a relic from the past, Laurie Matthews, but if you ask me, life's too short—'

'Shurrup,' Laurie said at once. 'Tell you what, how about making up a foursome? Auntie and Jill, you and me . . .'

This time it was Laurie who found himself spluttering through a mouthful of snow, but when the conversation looked like deteriorating into a snowball fight he backed off at once. 'Pax, pax, you idiot!' he said, spitting snow. 'I admit Auntie's a trifle long in the tooth to accede to your rampant demands, so I'll have to revisit the Canary and Linnet with no masculine support. And now stop fooling around and let's get a move on. The Met boys say we're all set for a thaw, so I mean to make the most of the snow and visit the pub whenever the opportunity offers. And don't you go offering to come with me, because you'll only queer my pitch.'

Jill was a light sleeper and was the first to hear the little whimpering cries coming from the girls' attic bedroom. Her first thought was that Debby's nightmares had started again, but when she hurried up the stairs and opened the door she saw, in the dim snowlight coming through the window, Imogen sitting up in bed. She was very flushed, and when Jill lit the candle which stood on the dressing table she saw that the child's pupils were very enlarged and she looked terrified. Jill sat down on the bed and put her arms round her, giving her a gentle hug. 'It's all right, my love, you're safe in your own bed,' she said soothingly. 'Can't you get to sleep? Did you have a bad dream? Jill's here, and won't leave you.'

Imogen gave a low moan. 'Falling, falling . . . the ice won't hold,' she muttered, in a hoarse wavering voice which Jill scarcely recognised. 'I'm in the water . . . get me out of the water. Tell the men I'm sorry I was bad, I'll never be bad again if they'll only get me out!'

Jill smoothed the hair off Imogen's forehead and realised that the child must be running a temperature, for the hair was damp and the forehead almost frighteningly hot. But probably it was no wonder, considering what had happened to her. Jill, who had had very little experience of illness, tried to lie Imogen down again, but the child flung her arms round Jill's neck and refused to let go.

'If I let go I'll drown,' she said, then withdrew from

Jill a little. 'Who are you?' Her big frightened eyes scanned the room. 'Where am I?' Jill began to reply but was interrupted. '*Who* am I?' Imogen demanded, her voice breaking on a sob. 'Am I the lady in the brown dress? Am I going to die?'

Poor Jill, realising that she needed to fetch Auntie, tried once again to detach Imogen's arms from round her neck, but before she could loosen the child's grip another voice spoke. 'Jill, it's me, Debby. Shall I fetch Auntie? She did say to call her if Imogen got worse.'

'Oh, Debby, I wish you would,' Jill said breathlessly. 'I think Imogen is running a fever, and I don't know what to do. But Auntie will.'

Debby took her dressing gown off the hook on the back of the door, slid her feet into her slippers and in a moment could be heard softly thumping down the first flight, presently returning with Auntie close behind. Jill greeted her aunt with great relief, for although she had managed to detach herself from Imogen's grasp the child had begun to moan and to complain that she ached all over and could not move without pain. It was clear that she still imagined herself half in and half out of the ditch.

'Rheumatic fever,' Auntie said in an undertone, as soon as she had examined Imogen, 'or something very like it at any rate. We'll have Dr Vaughan from the village up here as soon as it's light, but in the meantime I think she'd benefit from a couple of aspirin and a long cool drink.' She turned to Debby, for Rita was still slumbering peacefully. 'Go down to the bar, dear, and bring me up a bottle of cordial and a glass of water. I'd best mix it myself.'

This sounded infinitely sensible to Jill, but although

Imogen was burning hot she rejected the very idea of a cool drink. 'I'm cold enough already,' she said fretfully. 'I'm freezing, and my hot water bottle's gone cold . . . oh, how I do ache!'

This made Auntie look grave, but she still maintained that they should wait until day dawned before getting a message to the doctor. 'In the meantime I think the three of us had better get dressed so that there's someone with Immy all the time. I just hope the doctor can give her something to ease the pain and reduce the fever. Aspirin tablets will help because aspirin lowers the temperature.' She smiled across at Debby. 'Do you think you could put the kettle on, dear, whilst Jill and I take it in turns to dress? We'll be a good deal more able to cope with the situation when we have a hot cup of tea inside us.'

Jill agreed that this was so, and had just succeeded in lowering Imogen on to her pillows when she spoke. 'I'd like a hot cup of tea,' she said feebly. 'One with lots of milk so's I can drink it straight down . . . oh, I would like that!'

Jill and Auntie exchanged relieved smiles. 'If she wants a cup of tea she can't be all that bad,' Jill said bracingly. 'I've heard folk often get feverish in the small hours; maybe it's just that.'

But the doctor, when Jacky fetched him the next day, put an end to such hopes. 'If I could get her to hospital then she could have the treatment she needs, but since that's impossible you and your aunt will simply have to follow my instructions,' he told Jill. 'The child's suffering from exposure, of course, and when I sounded her chest I could hear bubbling. But keep her in bed, keep her warm, make her take the medicine I will give you three times a day and get her to take a great many hot drinks. She won't be hungry whilst she's so feverish – her temperature is almost 105 degrees – but broth will help her to keep up her strength. I'm sure Mrs Pilgrim will sell you a chicken, or even a couple of pounds of bones if that's all that's available . . .'

'Bones?' Jill said. 'What use would bones be?'

'Boil them to make stock, you silly girl,' the doctor said. 'If you add a carrot, an onion and half a swede to make it more palatable it will give her strength, and she needs strength to fight the infection. At the moment the main danger is that she may contract pneumonia, but she's young and strong, so we'll hope for the best.'

Auntie and Jill took the doctor's advice, obtaining a chicken from the sympathetic Mrs Pilgrim, as well as a couple of pig's trotters which, she told them, when boiled for long enough would make pork jelly. 'My mother thought it a cure-all for just about every disease you can mention,' she assured Jill who, accompanied by Rita, had slogged her way up the lane to the farm. 'Let me know if there's anything more I can do for the poor little dear.'

Jill thanked her from the heart and promised not to hesitate if she needed anything more, but in fact now that they were organised she thought she and Auntie were managing pretty well. They had abandoned their own rooms to Debby and Rita and now slept in the attic, one on either side of Imogen's bed, so that there was always someone handy. She was very weak and could not reach the chamber pot without help, and once she began to sweat, which the doctor assured them was a good sign, they changed her sheets whenever they became too damp for comfort.

For the first couple of weeks Imogen was not herself, frequently talking as though she were still struggling out of the ditch, but gradually she began to improve and the last time the doctor visited her he was sufficiently pleased with her progress to say that she might come downstairs for an hour if she felt so inclined.

Imogen thanked him, but her voice was lacklustre, and despite her efforts to be cheerful she was still apt either to fall asleep or to begin to weep bitterly, though when asked the reason for her tears she just muttered that she had bad dreams and that shame over her behaviour still haunted her.

'You've had pneumonia,' Rita told her, as she sat on the end of her friend's bed, reading her a letter from her mother. Auntie and Jill had decided not to tell Mrs Clarke how very ill her daughter had been, so she thought Imogen had had a nasty cold and nothing more.

'If my mam ever found out that I'd gone off by myself and got into trouble she'd be terribly cross,' Imogen had admitted to Jill and Auntie as she gradually began to improve. 'She's very strict, my mam. I don't think she'd take me back to the city because of the danger, but she would be very angry.' She had looked from Jill to Auntie. 'So if you wouldn't mind . . .'

Jill and Auntie had agreed to her request and Auntie thought they had done the right thing. Mrs Clarke, though no doubt an excellent official doing important war work, corresponded with her daughter rarely, and when she did write the letters were always short and mainly concerned with her work.

Rita finished reading the letter and handed it over to her friend. 'There you are! You know she's well and busy;

and now are you going to get out of that bed, you lazy little beast?' She grinned at Imogen. 'You've timed your recovery nicely; the snow's all gone and the fellers from the airfield come over whenever they're free. The couple who hauled you out of the ditch always ask after you; they'll be right glad to see you up and about. I know Auntie and Jill keep them informed, but the blokes would like to see you for themselves.'

Imogen heaved a sigh. 'Since I'm only allowed to get up for an hour, I'll come down for the midday meal, save one of you having to carry up a tray,' she said wearily. 'Oh, Rita, I'm still weak as a kitten! But I'll come down if Auntie thinks I ought.'

'Right,' Rita said decisively, standing up and heading for the door. 'And you'd better write to your mother, because if Auntie or Jill write again Mrs Clarke may get suspicious.' She reached the doorway, then turned back. 'Is there anything you want?' she asked rather impatiently. 'I hope not, lazybones, because I'm on duty to give an eye to you today, and I'm sick and tired of toiling up all these stairs.'

Imogen gave a very small spurt of laughter. 'I'm not the lazy one; I've been ill,' she pointed out. 'And now you and Debby are back in school it's Auntie and Jill who have to keep toiling up and down with trays. Don't go for a moment, Rita; just tell me what the weather's like. I'd really like a breath of fresh air, but not if it's still cold.'

Rita sighed. Imogen reflected that the other girl had always been short of patience, so it was no surprise when she answered rather brusquely. 'One minute you say you're weak as a kitten, and the next that you want to go outside for a bit,' she said. 'If you ask me, it's far too cold, but it's for Auntie to decide.' And with that she shot out of the doorway and Imogen could hear her feet clattering down the stairs.

Imogen huddled under the covers again. She knew really that it would take all her strength just to get down the stairs, and heaven knew how she would manage to get up them again. She was still languid, having to be coaxed to eat more than a few mouthfuls, crying if she was left alone for long yet finding conversation tiring. The doctor no longer visited, a sure sign that she was better, yet she had twice put off the chance of going downstairs. Today, however, she knew she really must make the effort. Auntie would not let her have a pen and a bottle of ink in the attic, and fair was fair; Auntie and Jill had a lot to do and she knew in her heart that she should write personally to her mother. Also, Auntie kept telling her that her appetite would return once she did something other than lie in her bed, and she supposed that the older woman was right.

What I ought to do is practise when I'm here with no one watching, she decided. Yes, that's a really good idea, because I know very well that if I'm all weak and wobbly when I do go downstairs Rita will have a go at me, and that will upset Jill and Auntie.

Having decided, she swung her legs out of bed and stood up, reflecting that since she had been using the chamber pot whenever she needed it for some time now, she really should be able to walk across to the door, take down her dressing gown and put it on, push her feet into her slippers, descend the two long flights of stairs and go into the kitchen.

She was wrapping her dressing gown round her and tying the cord when it occurred to her that perhaps Auntie would expect her to dress; certainly there was a small pile of her clothes on top of the chest of drawers. If I can dress myself and get down the stairs then Auntie will be really pleased, she told herself. I ought to do something to please her for a change; I've been awfully selfish when I think about it.

Rather reluctantly, for it was cold in the attic, she took her dressing gown off again and pulled on her woolly vest and knickers, her thick blue jumper, a grey pleated skirt and grey knee socks. She had dressed sitting on the bed, but now she stood up and for a moment the room swung giddily around her. She closed her eyes briefly and opened them again to find the room stationary once more, and not giving herself time to think she headed for the door. Clutching the banister, she tiptoed down the stairs and went quietly into the kitchen.

Jill was rolling out pastry and Auntie was stirring something in a pan over the heat. They both looked up and exclaimed with pleasure at the sight of her, downstairs after so long. Jill rushed to make her sit down in a chair close to the fire and Auntie pulled her saucepan off the flame and came over to give the newcomer a hug. 'Well done, you good girl!' she said approvingly. 'Rita said you were going to come down for lunch and I meant to ask Jill to go up and give you a hand. We thought you'd come down in your dressing gown, didn't we, Jill, but this is a great deal better.'

Jill was beaming. She broke off a piece of pastry to hand to the invalid, which made Imogen laugh. It was so typical of Jill to want to express her pleasure by giving food, even though all she had was the raw topping for the pie she was making.

'And how do you feel, my love, after your excursion?' Auntie said anxiously as Imogen nibbled the uncooked pastry. 'Do you realise this is the first time you've come downstairs for a whole month? Bronchial pneumonia is no joke; in fact it's very serious. I don't think you'll be going back to school this term.'

'Oh, Auntie, I must,' Imogen said, dismayed. 'I've missed no end of lessons; if I miss any more they'll keep me down a year and I'd hate that.' She looked appealingly at Jill. 'Surely, if I get up and dress all next week, I'll be able to go back to school after that?'

Jill laughed. 'I think Auntie was teasing you,' she said. 'After all, Rita and Debby have only been back in school themselves for a week because of the snow. Now it's cleared I see no reason why you shouldn't return to your classes. Give yourself next week to grow accustomed and then start off slowly. As it is, Miss Roxley's running three days for evacuees and two days for village children one week, and the following week two days for the evacuees and three days for the village. There simply isn't room in the school to have everyone there at the same time, especially now that the Pilgrims have some new evacuees.'

Imogen pricked up her ears. 'Young ones? Like those little boys they had before?' she asked curiously.

Auntie shook her head. 'No. I met Mrs Pilgrim in the post office a couple of days ago and she told me she'd got two twelve-year-old boys from a private school that's been evacuated to Hemblington Hall, only there wasn't enough room for everyone so some of them have had to go elsewhere; I reckon you'll be having some new pals.'

'Then all the more reason for me to go back to school as soon as I can,' Imogen said. Jill bent and opened the oven door and a glorious smell tickled Imogen's nostrils. 'Gosh, that smells good,' she said appreciatively. 'I do declare I'm hungry!'

Auntie and Jill exchanged satisfied glances. 'Those are the words I've waited to hear,' Auntie said. She turned to Jill. 'I'd suggest we give the young lady one of those little buns you've just made, except that I don't want to spoil her lunch.'

Jill laughed, but went over to the windowsill and picked up the cooling tray. 'I don't think it will hurt her to have a bun for her elevenses,' she said. 'And since we've plenty of milk I'll heat some up in a pan to go with it.'

Chapter Three

Having got herself downstairs without any ill effects, Imogen decided to remain with her friends in the cosy kitchen so that she might catch up with what had been happening whilst she had been bed-bound. However, as soon as the meal was over Jill ordered her back to the attic. 'You may not be tired now, but if you overdo it today you'll spend the next two days in bed feeling worn to the bone,' she said, and turned to Debby. 'Why don't you give Imogen a hand with getting back to bed whilst Rita dries the crocks?' She smiled at Imogen. 'And don't think you're cured, because convalescence isn't just a word, it's what everyone needs after a long illness. So far as you're concerned it means taking things easy and getting yourself right. Learning to walk before you can run, in fact.'

Once in the attic and beginning to undress, Imogen realised the truth of Jill's warning. She was very tired and anxious to climb back into her bed, and glad that Jill had chosen Debby to assist her rather than Rita, who could be so sharp. It wasn't that Rita thought she was malingering, it was just that the other girl was quite incapable of putting herself in another's shoes. Imogen had once heard someone described as having 'tunnel vision'. She had not understood at the time, but Jill had explained it. 'When someone has tunnel vision it means they can only see straight ahead and can't spare a glance for what is happening left or right,' she had said, looking thoughtful. 'Rita's a bit like that, but she'll change as she gets older. People do.'

Now Imogen, cuddling down in her bed and watching as Debby carefully folded every garment and placed it in its exact position on the chest of drawers, was grateful for the younger girl's uncomplaining help. Rita would have helped too, of course, but such assistance would have been accompanied by remarks about being forced to give a hand, and she would never have dreamed of picking up cast-off clothing and replacing it on the chest of drawers.

Having finished tidying the clothes away, Debby turned to smile at her. 'Is there anything else I can do, Immy?' she asked softly. 'Would you like a drink? Only Jill seems to think that you need to sleep, so if you'd rather I'll come back at teatime and see whether you want to come downstairs for supper or whether I should bring it up here.'

Imogen laughed. 'It's Rita's turn to take care of me today, really,' she reminded the other girl. 'I don't want a drink or anything yet, but if you truly don't mind, Debby, I'd really appreciate you popping in again just before supper. I'm sure I'll be fine to come downstairs, but I wouldn't mind a bit of help.'

Debby nodded and left the room. 'Sweet dreams, Immy,' she whispered. Imogen settled down and was asleep almost before the door had closed; asleep and dreaming.

The dream started as her dreams had had a way of doing since her accident. She was walking along a narrow path through the snow, admiring the beauty of the drifts and the branches of the trees which arched overhead. She was lazily content to walk slowly, and every now and then she reached up and shook a branch so that its burden of snow fell all around and on top of her. However, since it was dream snow it was neither wet nor unpleasant, but simply pretty. She walked further, and the snow which had been piled up on either side of the tiny path gradually lessened until, at the base of a mighty beech, she saw clumps of snowdrops and knew that spring was on its way. Further along, the gold and purple of crocuses could be seen breaking the monotonous whiteness. Imogen walked on dreamily, seeing the snow underfoot gradually giving way to green grass, brown earth and here and there bright yellow celandines. She knew she was dreaming, though in an unreal sort of way, and presently she found herself entering a lane which wound its way through the trees. She continued to walk along it, wondering whether it would lead her to the Canary and Linnet or whether it would take her elsewhere, because dreams, she knew, had an uncanny habit of switching from one scene to another without warning.

But this dream, it seemed, was somewhat different, and presently she found herself turning off the lane and following a path which led to the Linnet. She went towards the back door and then stopped abruptly. This was not the happy place she knew. The back door, that heavy oak door which Auntie bolted every night to shut out the world, was swinging on its hinges. The windows gaped glassless, like empty eye sockets, and when she looked up she saw that the great branch of a tree lay across the slated roof, no doubt letting in both wind and weather.

Without her realising it her hands had flown to her face, and she felt tears gather in her eyes. She sank down on the old bench by the back door, and even as she did so she heard a voice calling her name.

'Imogen, Imogen, where are you? We've come, like you said, but where are *you*?' Imogen stared wildly round her but could see no one. She grabbed at the back door, meaning to pull it open, but with the realisation that her hands could not feel the wood came the reminder. 'It's a dream!' she shouted. 'It's only a dream; the Canary and Linnet is safe and well and the voice is in my head . . .' But even as she spoke she glanced to her right and saw a woman in a brown dress, her hair whipped into a wild tangle by rain and wind, coming towards her.

For some reason the intrusion of another human being into the dream was frightening. 'Go away. I've been ill. How dare you come into my dream,' Imogen shouted, her voice thin. With a tremendous effort of will she turned from the abandoned house, and as she ran and dodged between the trees, gasping with fright and effort, she awoke.

For a moment she simply lay there, almost unable to believe that she was safe in the attic room at the Canary and Linnet, that the dream had been just that. But she could not continue to lie there whilst the dream had possession of her thoughts. She sat up in bed, aware that she was trembling in every limb, and pulled her mother's letter from under the pillow. She had let Rita read it to her, but she was quite capable of doing so for herself, and now, as she read, she took comfort from Mrs Clarke's prosaic words. She had been to visit Elspeth, Imogen's eldest sister, who had joined the ATS; she described her duties with both the Women's Institute and the ARP. It was such a practical letter that it reduced the dream to just that: a dream which had undoubtedly come about because Imogen herself had done too much and was overwrought as well as overtired.

Imogen cuddled down the bed again. In all her time as an invalid she had had many dreams – many nightmares, in fact – but none quite as real and frightening as the one from which she had just awoken. It was poor Debby, wishing me sweet dreams just before she left, Imogen told herself. You can't start taking any notice of dreams, otherwise you'd be afraid to go to sleep. Why, when I was ill I remember dreaming that I'd got into that ditch to rescue a kitten I'd heard mewing, and when the two men came on the scene they pushed me back in the water and walked off with the kitten, saying they would take it back to Mrs Pilgrim, because farmers need lots of cats. But the dream hasn't made me hate kittens, or those two fellers either. So I'll soon forget the Canary and Linnet being a ruin.

But despite her brave words Imogen could not get her dream out of her mind. Who had been calling her? It was a voice she thought she ought to have recognised, yet she had not done so.

Imogen sighed and turned her pillow over so that her hot cheek rested on cool linen. It was nothing but a dream, so the voice could have no existence in reality. She glanced at the two other beds to check that their occupants were not there – this was a habit – before sticking her thumb in her mouth. Debby might have smiled, Rita would undoubtedly have scoffed, but it was the only sure and certain way that Imogen knew to court dreamless sleep, and within five minutes of feeling the comforting thumb in her mouth, she slept.

Jill was sitting at the kitchen table writing a list of requirements which Auntie was dictating. They took it for granted that they would have all the goods to which rationing entitled them but there were extras, what you might call under the counter provisions, which Mrs Bailey would sell them if they were available. Dried fruit was impossible to obtain, as were many other things which came from abroad, but, along with every other housewife in Britain, they were growing used to substitutes. All their customers at the Linnet were very fond of Woolton pie, for which Jill had her own secret recipe. She made a delicious stock by boiling bones which the butcher saved for her, and sold the vegetable pie in slices to the young aircraftmen who came to the pub when they could get away from their station, always eager for a beer, a sandwich and either a sausage roll or a slice of Woolton pie. They were fed on the station, of course, but complained that, though filling, cookhouse grub was nowhere near as tasty as that which the Linnet could supply.

Now, Jill counted up the items which Auntie had mentioned and stood up. 'The kids can come with me, then they can give a hand,' she said cheerfully. 'In fact, if that poultry meal you ordered has arrived, they can help me carry it home.'

Auntie nodded. She had decided that since they had a huge garden as well as the old outbuildings, it would make good sense to get some poultry so that they might collect their own eggs. Accordingly, the three girls had decided to present Auntie with chickens on her birthday, and, encouraged by the way the young hens had thrived, she thought that they might try keeping a pig. Mrs Pilgrim had promised her one from the next litter her sows produced and the children were looking forward to becoming farmers, as Rita had put it.

Now, Jill glanced at Auntie from under lowered lids. 'I wondered about getting a dog,' she said rather hesitantly. 'Not a puppy, that would be too much work, but a fully grown dog. I think it might be good for the girls, and especially for Imogen, because she finds it irksome never to be able to go out alone, only with her pals. I know a great many dogs were put down when the war started, but I'm sure there are others the RSPCA must know about . . .'

Auntie nodded thoughtfully. The two women could hear vague sounds from the attic, where the girls were giving their bedroom a spring clean. Spring and the Easter holidays had arrived simultaneously and outside a gentle sun shone down on bursting buds, the tender green of new leaves, and nesting birds flying in and out of the trees and hedges around the Canary and Linnet.

Across the table Auntie's greenish-hazel eyes met Jill's innocent blue ones. 'Come clean, young woman,' she said severely. 'You know of a dog needing a home and you can't wait to get it aboard. Out with it, young Jill!'

Jill giggled. 'Well, I was wondering about old Mrs Monroe's Rufus,' she admitted. 'The old lady can't cope by herself any longer so she's going to live with her daughter. But the daughter doesn't like dogs and anyway, she says her home is unsuitable for an animal; she lives in a flat in the heart of Liverpool and says most people have already got rid of their pets. I'm sure Mrs Monroe would be delighted if we offered to take Rufus. He's about two or three, I think; not old at all but very quiet and reliable. The girls don't talk about their homes and families much but I don't believe any of them has owned a dog, and I've seen the fuss they make of the ones in the village and the sheepdogs at the farm, so I know he would be very welcome.' She stood up, list in hand. 'There are old rabbit hutches, chicken runs and a kennel in the end outbuilding, so if you wanted him to sleep outside . . .'

'Ha very ha,' Auntie said sarcastically. 'I can see how long that would last! The damned critter would be sleeping on the foot of my bed before you could say knife. No, if we're to have a dog he's not going to live chained to a kennel. What good would he be as a companion to the kids or a guard against burglars? He can have a mat on the kitchen floor.' She sniffed disparagingly. 'If he was outside and heard an unusual noise, he'd stuff his paws in his ears, curl up in the straw and go back to sleep. Besides, straw is full of fleas and I don't mean our girls to face life covered in flea bites. What sort of dog is he, anyway? I dare say I've met him, but none of the dogs I've seen hanging around outside the butcher's has been intelligent enough to say: "I'm Rufus; give me a home!" Is he one of these here collies, black and white with a pointed nose, which looks as if it's been rolling in cowpats? If so . . . don't you laugh at me, young woman!'

'No, he's not a collie, and I don't think I can describe him other than saying he's black and shaggy,' Jill said, on the edge of laughter. 'Tell you what, Auntie, I'll bring him back with me when I've done the shopping, and you can decide for yourself whether you want to add him to our family.'

Auntie subjected Jill to a hard stare. 'You're relying on the fact that once I've seen him I'll be putty in your hands,' she remarked. 'But you're right: we could do with a dog. The children will promise to look after him, to take him on regular walks and to teach him not to interfere with our poultry; not that they will, of course. Promises are like pie-crusts: made to be broken. And now you can save my old legs by trotting upstairs to see if the girls have finished their spring cleaning.'

'Right you are,' Jill said cheerfully. 'But you're wrong when you say the girls won't look after the dog, because I'm sure they will. In fact, I'm sure they'll look after the pig, if you get one. Children love animals and birds – you've seen how they talk to the hens, and of course hunting for the eggs keeps them occupied for hours. The only snag will be if they're allowed to get too friendly with the pig, because when it's old enough . . .'

There was a moment's silence whilst both Jill and Auntie envisaged the outrage the girls would show when they realised the fate the pig was going to suffer. Then Jill pointed out rather sharply that the girls would have to come to terms with life and death. 'We'll have to explain that pigs are bacon and are needed for the war effort,' she said rather uncertainly. She brightened. 'Or we could keep a piglet as a pet as well as the baconer. They're very intelligent animals; the girls would love it.'

Auntie sighed with relief. 'You're a good girl, Jill,' she said approvingly. 'Yes, when we get round to repairing the old pigsty, we'll definitely do that. And now you'd best check on the girls, because there's an ominous silence from the attic.'

'Right,' Jill said. She was heading for the back stairs when Auntie called her back.

'Hang on a minute,' she said. 'How do you think Imogen is getting along? She's doing well at school and spends ages writing up her Mass Observation diary, even though no one's allowed to read it. She's eating well, and she's always eager to help us in the house, but she's – oh, she's different. Before the accident she was just like the others, chattering away, giving her opinion on every possible subject, always asking for help if she was stuck with her homework, and the first to volunteer when we needed something doing. And arguing! She and Rita were always at odds, or bosom friends. But she doesn't chatter any more.'

'She never did talk about her family,' Jill pointed out. 'I know she's got a couple of brothers and several older sisters, but she never mentions them by name. I think the strangest thing is the way she thanked Laurie and Dave very prettily for saving her life, but when they come in for a drink she slips out of the bar and misses all their stories about life on the station. It's not like her, Auntie. Debby has always been quiet, but Imogen and Rita hardly ever stopped talking. And they did argue, though it was usually amicable enough. Now, if there's a disagreement, Imogen retreats like a snail into its shell.' She laughed. 'It drives Rita mad because she can't get a reaction! What do you think, Auntie? I've talked about it to Laurie, but of course he never knew her before the accident . . .'

Auntie had been staring at the fire in the grate, but

now she transferred her gaze to her niece's face. 'It's a puzzle; I'll have to give it some thought,' she said slowly, then smiled. 'And you've been discussing Imogen with Laurie, have you? Well, why not? I know he likes you, and I'm pretty sure you like him, so naturally you share worries. But tell me, why wouldn't you go to the flicks with him when he asked you?'

Jill, halfway across the kitchen pulled a face. 'Nosy, nosy,' she chanted. 'Curiosity killed the cat! As it happens it was your whist night, but I promised him I'd be happy to accompany him another time.'

Auntie began to say that she would have given up her whist night with pleasure, but Jill was already mounting the stairs. Auntie sighed. With Jill and the children about to go into the village there was only one person left to clean down, and that was herself. Not that she minded; she was proud of the bar, which was always spotlessly clean. In each of the windows was a large vase which she tried to keep full of flowers, pussy willow catkins, or simply young budding branches which unfurled their leaves faster in the warmth of the bar than they would have done out in the garden.

She began to fill a bucket with hot water, puzzling again over the changes which had come over Imogen since the accident. When the child had first taken to her bed she had complained of nightmares, which was scarcely surprising. But that had been many weeks ago, and she had said nothing about it since, so Auntie had assumed that the nightmares had left her. She had expected Imogen to chatter away to Laurie and Dave, possibly even let them read a page or two of her diary, but this had not happened. She had never thought of her as a secretive child, but now she wondered whether her unnatural quietness had something to do with the diary. She remembered that when she had handed a fat exercise book and a pencil to Imogen a couple of days after she had first come down to the kitchen, the child had said ruefully that she might as well try her hand at fiction since real life, for one under house arrest, meant she had virtually nothing to write about. Auntie wondered rather uneasily just exactly what Imogen was recording in that notebook. She could ask – had done so – but Imogen's replies were always evasive.

Further speculation was ended as the three girls, shepherded by Jill, burst into the kitchen. They charged across it, grabbed coats, hats and scarves from the hooks on the back of the door, scuffed their feet into their wellingtons and turned to grin at Auntie. 'Our bedroom is clean as a new pin,' Rita said triumphantly. 'Even my clothes have been folded and put away . . .'

'Thanks to Debby,' Imogen interposed. She smiled at Auntie. 'She's the only really tidy one; she seems to like being tidy, whereas Rita and me would just bundle the stuff into the chest of drawers and hope no one notices.'

Auntie looked across at Jill, who was also getting down her outdoor things. 'Are you satisfied that the attic is as clean as a new pin?'

'It'll pass,' Jill said cheerfully. 'See you later.'

Auntie waved them off and began to clean down the bar. She noticed that the catkins were shedding yellow pollen all over the wide windowsills, and tutted, picking up both vases and carrying them out to the compost heap. As she returned to the house she decided she would go for a walk with the children after lunch to collect wild flowers for the bar. She knew where tiny daffodils grew wild amongst a particular patch of shallow-rooted beeches, and decided that she would enjoy an outing now that the mild spring weather had arrived.

Back in the bar, Auntie remembered Imogen's diary. It wasn't a proper diary – the village shop did not stock such things – but it was a nice fat notebook and the last time she had seen Imogen writing in it she had realised that despite the child's complaint that nothing ever happened she had somehow managed to fill quite half the pages. Auntie fetched a cloth and cleaned the windowsills, then began on the little round tables and the long benches and chairs. There were one or two ring marks, but very little mess despite the fact that, with the finer weather, she had more customers than ever. She had brushed the floor before she began to clean the surfaces and now she gave the long wooden bar a treat: she beeswaxed the counter top, rubbing it as hard as she could until it shone like polished glass. Then, having checked that all was prepared for the meal which the children and Jill would expect when they returned, she set off for the attic. It was sneaky, not the sort of thing she would ever have dreamed of doing once, but she intended to take a look at Imogen's exercise book. As I told that young air force feller, I am *in loco parentis* to those children, she told herself. I've every right to know just what she's recording in that diary of hers. In fact, it's my duty to snoop a little.

But once in the attic she realised that it was not to be so simple. There was no sign of the notebook. She searched the beds, looked under the rag rugs, opened the chest of drawers and went carefully through the neatly piled clothes, and would have abandoned her search had she not suddenly noticed that near the head of Imogen's bed a board creaked when stood upon. She gazed at it thoughtfully, then saw that it did not fit tightly against its neighbours. A tentative pull and the fat red notebook was revealed. Feeling half ashamed, she lifted it out and turned the pages, telling herself that since it was supposed to be either a children's story or part of the Mass Observation project, it might, one day, be read by anyone. Nevertheless she felt guilty, and doubly so when she read the words which Imogen had printed on the cover. *Mass Observation*, it said. *Imogen's War. Private, keep out.*

Guiltily, and it has to be admitted with trembling hands, Auntie opened the book and flicked through the closely written pages, stopping at random. The entry was dated a couple of weeks earlier.

Had an omelette for lunch, and baked apple for afters. Got bad marks in arithmetic, came fifteenth out of twenty, but top in English. We're writing a diary, ha ha, so of course all I have to do is crib a few pages from this book. Found Debby crying over something she'd read in the newspaper. Gave her a hug. Rita came in – we were in our bedroom – and said we were soppy. Didn't argue.

Auntie flipped over a couple more pages and what she read brought a puzzled frown to her brow.

Had that dream again last night. It was just the same as before, but when I get the dream it's as though it were the first time. I go into the trees, heading for the Linnet, only when I find it, it's a ruin. It's strange, because I'm wearing a brown dress, rather long, and very smart brown shoes. Brown is a colour I really don't like at all, I've never had a brown dress, and we always wear wellingtons, though I suppose when summer comes it will be sandals and plimsolls again. Then someone calls me by my name, not just a shout, and I search amongst the trees and round the side of the Linnet but can't find anyone. I start to shout back, to tell the person to get out of my dream, and then I wake up. I used to be very frightened and I still am, a little. I don't know why I should dream the same dream, but I expect it's all a part of falling in the ditch and nearly dying. So I've made up my mind that I won't dream it any more. I'm sure I can control a dream!

Auntie turned the page, then realised that the dream Imogen had written of must have happened only the previous night, for the rest of the book was blank. She gave a little shudder; how very, very odd. But hopefully, as Imogen had seemed to indicate, the dream had come for the last time and would not be repeated. Was it the reason for the change in the child's attitude? Even before reading the diary, Auntie had wondered why Imogen, after the most subdued greeting, always made herself scarce if Laurie and Dave were in the bar. Other young men did not have the same effect, though even with them Imogen listened more than she spoke. But I am no psychiatrist, Auntie told herself, replacing the diary in its cramped little hiding place. Thank God for Jill! The two of them would talk it over, and since a trouble shared is a trouble halved would no doubt find a reason for the changes in Imogen, who was a great favourite with them both.

Auntie was back downstairs in the kitchen when she heard Jill and the children coming up the lane, and realised that she felt a good deal better about her activities having decided to share them with Jill. As the children trooped across the front yard, she pulled the kettle over the fire and set out mugs, so that all was in readiness for elevenses when the back door opened. 'Did you get the poultry meal?' she asked. 'Oh, I see that you did . . . my God, is that a dog or a hearthrug?'

'Oh, Auntie, you know very well it's Rufus,' Jill protested. 'Isn't he lovely? And he's been so good. Imogen has walked all the way from the village with her hand in his collar and he hasn't pulled away from her once, has he, Immy?'

'Not once,' Imogen agreed, and Auntie saw that her cheeks were flushed and her eyes bright. 'He's handsome too, isn't he, Auntie? A real beauty. We bought some dog biscuits and the butcher gave us a bone; he knows it's in Jill's basket but he's too polite to try to grab it. At last I've got something to put in my diary – something nice and exciting, I mean.'

Auntie looked rather doubtfully at what appeared to be a black doormat with a pair of shining brown eyes at one end and a wagging tail at the other. 'Well, he's not the most handsome dog I've known, but if he's got a nice nature that's far more important,' she said. 'We'll have to see how he settles. And don't forget, Jill and I are much too busy with the pub to look after him . . .'

As expected there was a chorus of promises that they would do everything necessary, even offering a share of their pocket money for their new pal. Rita, on her knees, said she had an old hairbrush he could have, for fond though they were the girls admitted that Rufus could do with grooming. In fact they would have taken him up to the attic for that purpose had Auntie not firmly intervened. 'Once you start brushing there'll be a great deal of loose hair about, so take him out to the yard right now,' she ordered them.

'I'll get the brush; I know the one Rita means,' Imogen said eagerly, and whilst Rita was saying indignantly that she might fetch the brush but they must take turns in wielding it, Imogen was already at the foot of the stairs. She was away rather longer than seemed necessary, but came down eventually with the brush and handed it to Rita.

'I bags first go, because Imogen had him all the way from the village,' Rita said firmly. She turned to her friend. 'You can help Jill unload the shopping and Debby can carry the poultry meal over to the outhouse.' And having given her orders she grasped Rufus's collar and towed him out through the back door and into the yard.

Jill began to unload the shopping, telling Imogen to put the flour in the big crock and to stand margarine, lard and butter on the slate windowsill in the pantry, but though Imogen picked up the nominated items she hesitated, and then put them back on the table and swung round to face Auntie. 'When I went up to the attic just now I saw that someone had pulled up the floorboard near the top of my bed. Was it you, Auntie?'

Auntie felt her cheeks grow hot, but she met Imogen's enquiring eyes unflinchingly. 'Yes,' she said.

There was a short silence. Auntie wondered whether she should pretend that she had not read the diary, but before she could do so Imogen spoke. 'Oh,' she said, and without another word began to help Jill to put away the shopping. As soon as the task was finished and Jill had disappeared into the pantry to check that nothing had been forgotten she turned towards the back door but Auntie, feeling terribly guilty, caught her hand when she would have passed.

'I shouldn't have done it,' she said in a low voice. 'I only looked to see if you'd decided to write for the Mass Observation project or whether you were doing a story for children, as you said you might. I – I didn't read much, perhaps a page and a half . . .'

Her voice trailed off but Imogen turned, gave her a brilliant smile and squeezed her hand. 'It doesn't matter, Auntie. If you'd been my real mother you'd have read every line, and nagged me about poor handwriting and bad grammar. I honestly don't mind you or Jill reading it – or Debby for that matter – but Rita would only scoff. You know what she's like.'

Auntie beamed at her, feeling as though a heavy weight had been lifted from her shoulders. 'I'm glad you're not cross with me,' she said. 'You see, Jill and I have been worried about you, because although you're back in school and very much better, you aren't yet your old self. You're very quiet, Imogen. You and Rita used to squabble a lot, but you laughed and talked a lot, too. That doesn't happen any more. I thought your diary might give me a clue to what's causing the change in you.'

Imogen laughed. 'I didn't know I was different,' she said. 'And I don't think my diary would be any help. Did you – did you read about that odd dream I've had?'

Auntie nodded, shamefaced, but said nothing.

Imogen frowned. 'A dream is just a dream,' she said in a low voice. 'And it's a dream I don't mean to have any more. The next time I find myself walking along that lane I won't go into the trees; do you think I could do that, Auntie?'

'You could try,' Auntie said doubtfully. 'But in time, you know, the dream will fade and fade until it quite disappears. And since I don't mean to let the old Canary and Linnet become a ruin whilst I'm alive, comfort yourself that the dream is meaningless.'

Imogen squeezed Auntie's hand and then stood on tiptoe and kissed her cheek. 'I love you, Auntie,' she said raptly. 'I wish I'd told you about it before because I'm positive, now, that I'll never dream it again.' She laughed. 'And as for squabbling with Rita, she'll get a shock when I start contradicting her again, instead of letting her get away with bossing me and Debby about.' She turned towards the back door. 'And now I'll go and have my turn at brushing Rufus,' she said gaily.

As she disappeared Jill came out of the pantry, and Auntie raised her brows. 'Did you hear all that?' she asked. 'Oh, Jill, I know it was sneaky of me, but I've been truly worried about Imogen. She's been so quiet. Well, we've both noticed it, haven't we? Do you think I did very wrong to read her diary?'

Jill's cheeks gradually flushed and she looked self-conscious. 'Well, I've been thinking and I believe I've got the answer,' she said. 'I believe poor Immy's got what we used to call a crush on Laurie and she doesn't know how to handle it. So she goes all quiet and instead of wanting to be near Laurie she avoids him like the plague.' She saw Auntie's expression and laughed. 'Don't worry, it will pass! She's young for her age and her mother, I gather, isn't the cuddly sort – her father died years ago. So poor Immy doesn't know quite how to behave. But you are in charge of the children and have every right to know what they're up to. And judging from Immy's reaction, she doesn't resent what you did, which is all that matters.' She smiled and Auntie realised, not for the first time, that her niece was turning into a remarkably pretty young woman. Her thick, bright brown hair was pulled back from a heart-shaped face, but when it was loose it curled to her shoulders and the eyes which met Auntie's were a deep and brilliant brown. No wonder Laurie wanted to take her to the cinema, Auntie thought.

But Jill was staring at her, waiting for a reply. Auntie cleared her throat. 'I'm glad you think I've done no harm,' she said. 'And by now those children must have brushed the dog until he's all but bald, so you'd best give them a shout whilst I warm the milk and lay out the biscuits.'

Chapter Four

May came, and with it the war ceased to be phoney and became real. By the end of the month the evacuation of Dunkirk, as it became known, had begun. From every British port the little ships plied across the calm blue sea, collecting the BEF and carrying the soldiers back to Britain. Horrific stories filtered through even to the children at the Canary and Linnet. Jill had a cousin who had been nursing in France and received a letter in which the older girl described how the Luftwaffe had bombed hospitals and dressing stations, had flown low and strafed nurses helping patients to board ambulances, had fired on the long lines of troops in the water, wading chest deep, because it was too shallow for the big ships to come any closer. *I know very little about the rules of war, if there are any such things, but the Nazis don't play by rules,* she had written bitterly. *My fiancé was taken prisoner; we know nothing more than that. I'm just glad that thanks to the government's foresight in evacuating them early on, children are safe.*

At first, Auntie had wanted to keep all news of the war from the children, but Jill had told her that that was not fair. 'They must listen to the wireless every evening before they go to bed, because it's their war as much as ours,' she had said. 'God knows, we all hope it will be over and won before the girls are old enough to join one of the services or help in some other way, but we owe it to them to tell them the truth. Believe me, Auntie, they would hate to be kept in the dark, and if you imagine that other children won't be well aware of what's going on you're being wilfully blind! Everyone talks in front of their kids – we do it ourselves – and I'd much rather they listened to the news and heard the truth than listened to gossip, or ignorant conjecture.'

Having thought it over, Auntie was able to tell Jill that she agreed with her completely, so every evening the family at the Canary and Linnet settled down to hear the news. As the men streamed back to their homes from the ports they were welcomed like heroes, though within a few days it was realised that though Churchill had called Dunkirk 'a miracle of deliverance' he was right when he had also admitted that it was 'a colossal military disaster', for though nearly four hundred thousand men had been saved, they had left behind all their weapons and military equipment. If the Nazis decided to invade, Britain was in a poor state to drive them back.

Nevertheless, Churchill's speech, as old Jacky put it, gave them back their pride. 'We shall fight on the beaches . . . we shall never surrender . . .'

Even Imogen, Rita and Debby knew that the war was coming nearer. But then so was summer, and as if to make up for the dreadful winter, the summer promised to be a glorious one. Everyone was expecting that Hitler would take advantage of the weakened state of the country by beginning to invade, and on their way to and from school the girls were perpetually casting their eyes skyward in the expectation of seeing nuns floating down from every aircraft which passed overhead, nuns whose secret identity would be given away only by their heavy army boots.

But the girls treated such stories with the contempt they deserved. 'As if any soldiers, even the stupidest, would expect us to believe in nuns floating down from the sky,' Rita said scornfully. 'And where would they put their guns and bayonets and things?' She had asked the question of Jill, who laughed and rumpled her hair.

'I think the floating nuns would be what you might call pathfinders, who would somehow get news back to the rest of the German army where it would be safe for them to come ashore,' she said. 'Personally, I think it's what they call propaganda; remember the leaflets that the chaps told us both sides dropped when war was first declared? It's just talk, and you should take no notice of it. You don't hear Alvar Lidell mentioning nuns on the wireless, do you? So let's wait and see what really happens before we start to panic.'

The truth was, however, Jill thought with some amusement, that far from panicking the girls simply behaved as they always had. Except that now, everywhere they went, Rufus accompanied them. At weekends they would take a packed lunch of anything Auntie or Jill could provide and go off into the woods, where they had built a shelter out of the bendy branches of the willow trees which overhung the river. They would have liked to spend a night there, but this was going a step too far, or so Auntie thought. Jill, who had spent a good deal of her childhood living in the country, thought that it would do the girls no harm to rough it for a change, but was wise enough to realise that Auntie would worry herself sick if the children were not under her roof by nightfall. However, the rule about never going off alone was relaxed, and provided she took

Rufus with her Imogen was allowed to roam much more freely.

As time passed, Jill began to realise that the children were far more different from one another than she had at first supposed. Debby, though she did her share of searching for eggs, feeding the poultry and cleaning out the pigsty, did not really enjoy these chores, but much preferred to help in the house, and Rita, though she also did her share, enjoyed playing organised sports. She was happy to stay after school in order to play netball and rounders, and always took part in the trips which the school organised so that the children might learn to swim in a nearby pool.

Imogen, however, was not particularly keen on such things, and much preferred to wander off with Rufus. She was becoming a real country girl and soon got to know the best hedges and trees for nests, knew that if she and Rufus sat quietly in some hidden corner of the woods they would presently see the wild things which lived there emerging from holes and thickets to go about their business.

Her Mass Observation diary, which she now encouraged Auntie and Jill to read, soon became more like a nature notebook, though she always included a short piece on whatever war news the wireless provided. Indeed, the beautiful willow shelter had been her idea, she had done most of the work on it, and now that the other two were no longer particularly interested it had become her favourite hideout. It was near the banks of the river, and sitting quietly in her willow tree cabin, with an arm round Rufus's shaggy neck, she could watch the comings and goings of frogs, water voles and water birds as well as rabbits, hares, and the odd fox, returning to his cubs with a dead bird dangling from his jaws.

So when, on a beautifully sunny Saturday morning, she took her packed lunch and told Auntie and Jill that she meant to spend the day out of doors, they reminded her that she must be in for high tea no later than half past five and waved her off without trying to persuade her to go with the other two, who had announced their intention of accompanying Auntie when she cadged a lift into the nearest market town with Mrs Pilgrim. The farmer's wife was going shopping, and since she intended to pick up some sacks of poultry meal she meant to take the wagon, so there would be plenty of room for the girls. Rita had already tried to persuade Imogen to go with them, saying it would be far more fun in town than simply mooching about in woods and meadows, but Imogen, though she was rather tempted, for she loved the hustle and bustle of the town, was firm. Rita was inclined to be indignant, for the three of them usually set off on any adventure together, whether fishing for tiddlers in the river, digging out a pool where the water might one day be deep enough to swim in, or simply improving the swing which Jill and Laurie had helped them to make, but she could not deny that they almost always split up at some stage.

So now Imogen waved the other two off, with a half-promise that she might join them later, for the whole sunny day stretched before her and the willow cabin, though a delightful retreat, might not have much to offer on a day so hot and still. She knew from experience that dawn and dusk were the times when there was maximum activity in the woods and copses. Added to this was a fact which she had forgotten until she and Rufus arrived at the willow cabin. All the girls had promised Auntie that they would never paddle, fish, or even play around the margins of the river when they were alone. At this time of year the water was low and nothing could have seemed less dangerous than the gentle swaying of the waterweed and the occasional plop as a fish surfaced. But a promise was a promise and Imogen had no intention of going back on this one, so she settled down with her notebook and, though she knew very well that she should not start to eat her lunch for at least a couple of hours, she detached the apple from the neatly packed sandwiches, the hardboiled egg and the small bottle of lemonade. She was burying the apple core, dreamily considering how nice it would be to come back here in a few years' time to find a flourishing apple tree ripe with fruit and, so to speak, all her own work, when Rufus gave her a nudge.

It was clear the dog had expected to be given the core – he was fond of apples – and he gave a disappointed whine. He went over to the grave, giving it an experimental poke with one paw. Imogen laughed but shook her head and tore a crust off one of the sandwiches, which Rufus accepted, though with rather less enthusiasm than he would have shown towards the apple core, for his tongue was lolling out and it was pretty clear that what he really wanted was a drink.

Imogen looked at him doubtfully. He was an intelligent and obedient animal but he was a real water-dog and loved bathing in the river. If they went down to the bank at this particular spot, Imogen was pretty sure that he would leap joyfully into the water, get himself a drink, and then, knowing nothing of prohibitions, set out to swim strongly for the opposite shore, because this was what the children usually did on such a hot day.

Imogen had been sitting on a substantial log which they had brought to the cabin when it was first completed, but now she stood up and, leaving her satchel, walked down to within a couple of feet of the water. As she had expected, Rufus did not wait for her to suggest that he might like a drink but sprang straight in, lapped for a moment and then, when she called him, made for the opposite bank. He scrambled out and looked expectantly at her, no doubt wondering why she had not followed his excellent example, for though there was plenty of shade under the trees the sun beat down strongly on the calm water and even more strongly on the meadow beyond, where Mr Pilgrim's milking herd grazed. This morning they were beset by flies, however, and Imogen knew from experience that once the flies had discovered her they would accompany her wherever she went, in a huge buzzing column above her head, so any thought of crossing the river, even if she had been allowed, died from her mind. But if she and Rufus walked a good deal further she remembered Jill telling her that there was an ancient wooden bridge across the river, which was the way Laurie and Dave came when they visited the pub in the evenings. So she whistled to Rufus, who came reluctantly out of the water and shook himself violently, so that for a moment Imogen was well speckled. And I've not been within a yard of the bank, she told herself with an inward grin. Thank you, Rufus, for cooling me down.

The pair of them returned to the willow cabin and Imogen hitched the satchel on to her back. Then she and Rufus set off for what would be pastures new, since she had never gone so far along the bank, and had not even set eyes on the wooden bridge. Telling herself that with every yard she covered she was enlarging her knowledge of the area, she ambled contentedly along, occasionally stopping to pick wild flowers or make a mental note of trees which, later in the year, would bring rich pickings in the shape of nuts, cherries and even wild apples. After half a mile or so she began to wonder whether she had let her attention stray at some point and had already bypassed the bridge without noticing it.

But just as she was considering turning back, she saw the wooden bridge ahead of her. It looked pretty sturdy, and was obviously quite strong enough for a herd of cattle to cross it, since there were ample signs that several cows had done so probably less than an hour ago. 'Found it!' Imogen said aloud. She looked reproachfully down at Rufus. 'You thought it was just my imagination, didn't you?' she enquired, giving him a severe look. 'You should have more faith; after all, it was Jill who told me there was a bridge and Jill knows everything, doesn't she, old fellow?'

Rufus was a most satisfactory companion; his ears had drooped when Imogen had accused him of lacking belief, but now he grinned up at her, his eyes shining and the expression on his face saying more loudly than words that he knew himself forgiven. Imogen laughed and rumpled his already rumpled head. 'I love you, Rufus,' she told him. 'You're the best friend a girl ever had. Only for the Lord's sake avoid the cowpats as we cross the bridge, because if either of us treads in one we'll be forced to put up with the pong all day, since we're not allowed to wash our feet in the river.' They crossed the bridge and were well into the trees, for this was heavily wooded country, before Imogen stopped and struck a pose. 'We are explorers, entering an unknown region,' she told the dog. 'No one has ever been this way. When I eat my packed lunch I'll write up my diary and tell the world all the wonderful things we've discovered in this new country.'

And new country it certainly was, for presently, walking away from the river, she came upon a most majestic beech wood. The trees were on a gentle slope and were larger and more beautiful than any Imogen had yet encountered. There was beech mast and moss underfoot and to Imogen's delight she saw that there had once been bluebells, though at this time of year they were long over. 'Next year we'll come in May,' she told Rufus, slinging her arm round his shaggy neck. 'This is a wonderful place, the sort of place where fairies live. Of course I don't believe in fairies, because people old enough and sensible enough to write diaries for the Mass Observation could not possibly do so, which means that if, presently, I see a tiny boat emerging from under the roots of this huge beech with little men no bigger than pins at the oars I shan't write it down in my diary, but even though I know it's not real it will have a special place in my heart.'

She stopped by the mighty beech, the roots of which spread out to form exciting black pools, and looked upward. The branches did not even begin until ten or twelve feet above the ground, but each one was as thick as a man's thigh and so well leafed that when she sat with her back against the trunk and tilted her face right up she could not see the brilliant blue of the sky. With a sigh of satisfaction she settled herself comfortably and began to open her satchel, whereupon Rufus, edging close, gave the little purr of satisfaction with which he greeted the hope of a snack for himself. Indeed, past experience told him that whatever food there was would be shared, though the water which had gathered in the roots of the beech would be his alone, since he had no taste for lemonade.

Leaning comfortably against the bole of the tree, Imogen undid the greaseproof paper in which the sandwiches were wrapped and examined the contents: lettuce and tomato and cheese and pickle, her favourites. She had just begun to divide the first sandwich – a cheese and pickle one – between herself and Rufus when a voice interrupted her. 'Imogen, Imogen,' it called softly. 'I know you're there, Imogen. I can see you; can you see me?'

Imogen was so frightened that the whole sandwich, only partly severed, fell from her hand on to the mossy ground, and Rufus, misunderstanding, ate it before she could move a muscle. But the voice had scared her so much that she could not have eaten the sandwich even had Rufus not already done so. She looked round wildly, but could see no one. Could it be Rita, playing a trick on her? The gentle Debby never played tricks on anyone, but in any case the voice belonged to neither of them. She knew it wasn't Jill or Auntie, but supposed it could be someone from the village school, for who else would know her name? But the voice was speaking again, and this time in a sort of chuckling half-whisper.

'Imogen, do you believe in fairies? I'm sure you do. I expect you'd like to come and see fairyland with me, but there's a price you have to pay to the Lordly Ones. You must put your sandwiches and your lemonade on the other side of my tree and then walk away, out of the wood. You must count to ten and return to this very tree – no other will do – and as you get nearer you will find yourself shrinking and shrinking until you're small enough to come into fairyland with me.'

Imogen looked very carefully all around her and then, with considerable caution, looked up. It was a hot and windless day, yet the leaves of the biggest branch above her head were vibrating ever so slightly. Imogen frowned. What sort of person could climb up that ice-smooth trunk to gain the first mighty branch? But then she thought she saw a tiny, tiny movement as though someone lying on the branch shifted to get her into focus, so when she spoke at last her voice was firm. 'I dunno who you are or how the devil you gorrup that tree, 'cos the trunk is smooth as glass,' she said, with only the slightest tremble in her voice. 'But I *don't* believe in fairies, or in fairyland. I reckon you're just some kid from the village what fancies lettuce and tomato sandwiches and fizzy lemonade. Well, you can forget stuffin' yourself wi' my grub, you cunnin' little weasel, and bugger off!' She had deliberately used the tone and words which she had often heard in the courts of Liverpool, though she could not have said why.

And the voice which answered her immediately took up the same accent. 'If you ain't a-goin' to obey me fairy command then I'll bleedin' well strike you deaf and dumb,' it said indignantly. 'Aw, c'mon, gairl, I'm fair clemmed; gi's a sangwidge.'

All fear banished by the well-remembered Scouse accent, Imogan giggled and looked up. A narrow, weaselly face looked down at her through the delicate green of the beech leaves. It had eyebrows which slanted up at the corners and gleaming hazel eyes, and its dark hair grew in a widow's peak on its forehead, increasing the devilish look. As she watched, the boy – for it was definitely a boy – gave a reluctant grin, revealing very white pointed teeth. 'If I come down will you set your dog on me?' he asked, then added with a chuckle, 'But he don't look much like a ravening wolf from up here, so I guess I might as well come down.' The grin widened. 'Course, if you'll close your eyes I'll fly down, provin' I really am one of the fairy folk.'

Imogen snorted. 'Fairy folk?' she asked incredulously. 'You're pretty bloody substantial for one of them. And anyhow, I want to see how you got up there and I shan't see that with me eyes shut!'

The boy sighed. 'Well don't go telling anyone else, 'cos I've not let on to a soul,' he said. And Imogen was not much surprised when a good length of knotted rope came whistling past her ear and landed with a thump on the ground. It was easy, now, to see how the boy had got up there. He must have thrown the rope over the lowest branch, pulled it until the ends hung evenly and then shinned up it. He had then pulled the rope up and stowed it amongst the leafy foliage whilst presumably climbing even higher up the tree in a more conventional fashion, and indeed, when he presently came down the rope with all the ease of long practice, he admitted that she had got it right.

'Most of these beeches are the same: no hand- or foothold for ten or fifteen feet, but then you can go up almost like ascending a staircase,' he assured her. 'And the view from the top . . .' He whistled softly beneath his breath. 'I'm telling you, it's bleeding fantastic. Apart from the woods and copses and that – and this beech wood in particular – the ground's pretty flat. Well, it would have to be, else they wouldn't have put an airfield here, would they? So once you're right at the top of this tree you can even see the planes and that: runways, huts, everything. It looks like one of those models you see in the Boy's Own annual. I've made a sort of lookout 'cos I thought if everyone's right and the Germans do plan an invasion, then I'll get me a gun and some ammo and lay on the platform picking off the Nazis one by one.'

Imogen gave him a long, hard look. He was taller than she by several inches and thin but wiry. He was wearing a patched grey shirt and grey shorts, grey knee socks both of which had descended to his ankles, and the scruffiest pair of plimsolls she had ever seen. From below she had registered that his hair was dark and curly but now she realised that it was also cropped exceedingly short; a convict cut, her mother would have called it. He had a narrow face in which those peculiar eyebrows were the most striking feature, but now she saw that, far from being weaselly, his face lit with humour when he grinned and his slanting eyes smiled at her with a good deal of understanding.

'Know me again?' he asked. 'Remember me from . . . oh, earlier times?' His hand, which was extremely dirty, hovered over the sandwiches. 'Going to give me one?' he asked, though his fingers had already closed on the next cheese and pickle. 'Oh go on, give us one!'

'What would you say if I said no? Or rather, what would you do?' Imogen said. 'Yes, all right, we'll share, only I'll do the sharing 'cos your hands are filthy.'

'Filthy? That they ain't,' the boy said indignantly. 'Well, if they're a bit black it's 'cos I've been tree climbing, but they were dead clean when I left home this morning.'

Imogen chuckled. 'Fair enough. And we'll have to drink out of the same bottle 'cos I've only got the one.' She put a protective hand across the neck of it. 'And not one swig of this will you get until you tell me who you are, and why I don't know you. I'm Imogen Clarke and I live at the Canary and Linnet – so c'mon, who are you and how do you know my name?'

'I'm Winston Churchill,' the boy began, then laughed and dodged as Imogen aimed a punch at him. 'All right, all right, I'm an evacuee like you and commonly known as Woody. Your name's unusual; I heard someone calling out to you in the village when I was last there. Most of my school live at Hemblington Hall, but Josh and meself were two of the lucky ones. There wasn't room for everybody at the Hall, so Josh and myself were sent to Pilgrim Farm. It's grand up there: no teachers, no one nagging us. How about you? What's this Canary and Linnet you mentioned? Are there lots of you there, or are you the only one?'

'Oh, there are three of us, all girls,' Imogen said. She passed him the lemonade bottle and a sandwich. 'I remember Auntie telling me that Hemblington Hall had been taken over by a school, and that Mrs Pilgrim had taken two of the boys. And they were talking about it in the post office once when I was queuing for a stamp so that I could send a letter home. Young Mrs Bonner was saying that the Hall was now a prep school – what's a prep school? – and she had a job there helping Mrs Catchpole in the kitchen. Apparently Mrs Catchpole used to cook for the squire when he lived at the hall.' She stared at him thoughtfully. 'So why didn't Mrs Pilgrim give you a packed lunch? It's Saturday, so I reckon you'll have the day off, same as me.'

The boy swallowed a mouthful of sandwich before he replied. 'A prep school means they only take boys up to the age of thirteen; after that you go on to the big school, which is for boys from thirteen to eighteen. As for a packed lunch, I could have asked Mrs P for some food but there was a big bustle on at the farm when I left. The men were driving the cattle down to the market – my pal Josh has gone with them – and I knew if I asked for grub they'd expect me to give a hand, so I kept shtum and slipped out when no one was looking.' He cocked one of his strange slanted eyebrows. 'Satisfied?'

'Ye-es,' Imogen said after a thoughtful pause. 'So the reason I don't know you is because you aren't at the village school. But surely you must leave Pilgrim Farm at around the same time as we leave the Canary and Linnet – it's a pub, by the way – so why haven't we met before?'

'Because we only came to Hemblington Hall a couple of weeks ago,' Woody explained patiently, 'and we've been helping to bring the hay in. Did you say you were living in a pub?'

'That's right. But I don't really understand why there wasn't room for all of you at the Hall. I mean, I could understand if ten or a dozen of you had to go somewhere else, but surely they could squeeze in two?'

The boy grinned his odd, saturnine grin, and reached for another sandwich. 'The Hall isn't that huge, you know. By the time they had turned the ground floor into classrooms, offices and so on, and the bedrooms into dormitories, it was pretty cramped. They asked for volunteers to live out and I can tell you my hand shot up at once. There are six of us – four above the feed merchant's in town, and Josh and I at the Pilgrims'. They've promised to get us bicycles so we can cycle to and fro, but I bet they don't succeed; bikes are already like gold dust, and anyway we enjoy the walk.'

Imogen snorted. 'It's plain you weren't here in the winter,' she said. 'We were cut off from the village for weeks, and most of the time we couldn't even get out of doors because of the blizzards. If we have another winter like the last one you wouldn't be able to cycle even if they did provide you with bikes.'

Woody's eyes lit up. 'No school for weeks,' he said reverently. 'I shall pray for snow.'

'Oh, will you?' Imogen said mockingly. 'But suppose the snow starts when you're in school, and you can't get back to Pilgrim's, bike or no bike? How would you like that? And snow in the country isn't like snow in the cities . . .'

But the boy interrupted. 'Don't you worry your head about me and Josh,' he said. 'At the first sign of a flake we'd tell whichever master was in charge that we mustn't be late for tea at Pilgrim Farm. They're so keen to keep on the right side of the folk who've taken us in that they'd probably let us go hours before it was necessary. Still, it probably won't happen. It would be just my luck for next winter to be as mild as summer.'

Imogen giggled. 'Well, time will tell,' she said. 'You don't have a wristwatch, do you? Only I'm supposed to be home by half past five, and it took me the best part of an hour to get this far, so I suppose I ought get moving.'

She stood up, brushed crumbs from her skirt and slipped a hand through Rufus's collar. 'Come on, old feller, we can't sit here chatting all day.'

Woody scrambled to his feet as Imogen began to put the sandwich wrappings and the empty bottle back into her satchel. 'Hang on a minute,' he protested. 'Aren't you going to climb up to my lookout? I told you the view was tremendous, but you don't have to take my word for it; you can see it for yourself.'

Imogen looked up and up and up to the very top of the tree, where the sun glinted on the topmost branches. Just looking up at it made her feel dizzy, and she hastily lowered her gaze to the dangling rope. 'No thanks,' she said firmly. 'Rufus needs a longer walk, and if I get a move on we might actually reach the airfield – and don't worry, I know better than to get near the perimeter fence. You might think I don't look much like a spy, but if the guards are the sort of men who believe in nuns floating down from the sky they might believe that wandering schoolgirls are spies as well.'

'It's a fair way; you'll be late for your tea,' Woody said warningly. 'I know what it is, you're scared I'll see your knickers when you start to climb. Suppose I promise to keep my eyes averted; would you go up then? Or are you a real little ninny, scared of heights and no good at climbing anyhow?'

Imogen realised that Woody's invitation amounted to a dare, so she sighed and stood up. If she refused to climb the tree her reputation would rapidly sink to a low from which it might never recover. But she had one last card to play. 'I don't mind the climb, because it will prove that I'm as good as you any day of the week,' she said, 'but it's Rufus. He'll get terribly upset if I go somewhere he can't follow. Auntie only allows me to go out alone if I'm with him, you see.'

Woody gave her a thoroughly evil grin and put an arm round Rufus's shaggy neck. 'I'll stay with your diddums dog and reassure him if he gets scared,' he said mockingly. 'I had meant to climb with you, show you the best footholds, but we wouldn't want Rufus to try to follow you up the rope, would we? So I'll stay down here while you go up that tree as fast as a monkey on a stick.'

Imogen grasped the rope, cast a malevolent glance at Woody and began to climb. She reached the first wide branch and grabbed the one above. By concentrating fiercely on her hands and feet and trying to ignore the increasingly enormous drop below her, she got halfway up the tree, then wedged herself into a fork to consider her next move, for she knew that when it came to descending she would be unable to ignore her dizzying distance from the ground. She considered staying where she was for a further five or ten minutes and then going down and saying how she admired the view, but this plan was foiled when Woody's head suddenly appeared below her, a taunting grin on his face.

'Rufus is just fine; in fact he's curled up by your satchel,' he said breezily. He looked hard at Imogen and the taunting grin softened into doubt. 'Are you all right? If you've had enough we'll go down together; me first so you don't have to look at the drop. It wasn't nice of me to tease you. Not many girls would have even got past the rope, let alone reached this far up.'

Imogen longed to take him up on his offer, for she

had felt dizzy a couple of times, but having got so far she realised that she did want to see the view, so she shook her head. 'Thanks for the offer, Woody, but I reckon having got this far I might as well go the rest of the way. Only if you wouldn't mind coming up behind me . . .'

'Sure thing,' Woody said, and together they finished the climb and reached a sunny spot from where gaps in the foliage enabled them to see for miles, and for a moment Imogen simply sat on the branch, catching her breath, marvelling how Woody had managed to discover such a perfect lookout. But then she saw the view, and it was every bit as good as Woody had promised. Below them, tiny aeroplanes were scattered over the green grass; tiny men moved back and forth; there were huts with corrugated iron roofs, office buildings and no doubt air raid shelters, though these would be underground. It was a world in miniature, Imogen thought with wonder. Neither said anything for a few minutes, but then Woody heaved a sigh and pointed up into the blinding blue of the sky above. 'I know I told you the lookout was at the top of the tree, but the upper branches are too whippy for comfort,' he admitted with a wry grin. 'Still, it's pretty impressive, wouldn't you say?'

'I would. I can't imagine how you came to find it because you don't realise it's the tallest tree around until you're up here, but if I had a hat I'd take it off to you,' Imogen said, and meant every word.

Woody grinned. 'Luck,' he admitted. 'And I read an old diary, written by one of Mrs Pilgrim's sons – she has two – when he was twelve or so, which mentioned a great view from the tallest beech. Only there was no airfield in those days, of course. If you can help me to nail some planks across the branches to form a solid wooden floor then it'll be as good as any tree house, only a whole lot higher.'

Imogen stared at the model airfield until her eyes watered and she had to look away into the shadow cast by the uppermost branches. 'I'm game,' she said. 'Who climbed up first, you or Josh?' she asked idly after a few moments. 'You don't seem to have any fear of heights at all; I suppose Josh must be the same.'

She was looking at Woody as she spoke and noticed the appreciable pause before he answered, and when he did so he was grinning. 'Oh, well, I can see I'll have to tell you the truth because if I don't you'll find it out anyway. Josh hates heights. He doesn't think much of tree climbing, either. He's a great guy, as the Yanks say, but he's never been up to the lookout . . . never even seen the airfield. So if the Huns do invade he'll have to do his sniping from the ground.' He looked at her, a grin hovering. 'There's a nice little hut down by the river which some kids made out of willow wands; I reckon he can hide in there and pick the enemy off as they cross the river.'

'Hey! It wasn't kids who made the willow cabin, it was us girls, and if anyone's going to hide in it to snipe at the Jerries it'll be us,' Imogen said. 'Well, it'll be Rita and me, because Debby wouldn't hurt a fly, not even a German one.'

'She would if she became a member of the resistance group I'm thinking of forming,' Woody said. 'As for your den by the river, it's really good. You must tell me how you wove the wands to form the walls and roof sometime.

And now we'd better be getting down, because I reckon it takes longer than going up.'

'Right,' Imogen said. 'You go first as far as the rope.'

It was several minutes later before her hands closed on the rope once more, and she saw Rufus's face, not tiny as a wild pansy but its normal size, staring up at her with what looked very like anxiety in his golden-brown eyes. He was certainly delighted to see her, prancing around and uttering little yips of excitement, and Imogen was glad to collapse on the soft moss and clasp the dog in her arms, for it hid the fact – she hoped – that she was shaking all over and could not have stood up to save her life.

Seconds after she had landed on terra firma Woody joined her. He patted her shoulder, and sank down beside her. 'Phew!' he said. 'Tell you what, you should have been a boy. Any of that lemonade left?'

'No, it's all gone. But Auntie put a couple of barley sugars in the front flap thing, so we'll have one each whilst we recover,' Imogen said. She giggled. 'Isn't it odd? You tell me I should have been a boy and I know it's meant as a compliment, but if I said you should have been a girl you'd be mad as fire!'

Woody, accepting the barley sugar, laughed with her. 'Yeah, it's a funny old world,' he agreed. He peered upward through the branches. 'Look, the sun's beginning to sink, and I reckon it really is time we were heading home. We might as well walk together as far as this Linnet place. Aren't you lucky to have an auntie willing to take you in? I reckon that's why they allowed you to be evacuated to a pub, because it's the first time I've ever heard of kids going to licensed premises.'

They had made their way out of the beech wood and were skirting a pasture where a couple of horses grazed. Imogen chuckled. 'It's plain you're a newcomer to the district,' she commented. 'Auntie isn't any relation to me or Debby and Rita; she's really Miss Marcy, but everyone calls her Auntie. I *think* it's because she and her niece Jill run the pub together, and since Jill is her real niece she's probably always called her Auntie, and everyone else follows suit. Tell you what, if you don't mind going a tiny bit out of your way you can come into the Canary and Linnet and meet Auntie and Jill for yourself. You'll like them; they're two of the nicest people I know. But tell me about yourself. Do you have brothers and sisters? And though you do a pretty good Scouse accent, I don't believe you're from Liverpool. Where do you come from when there isn't a war?'

'Southampton; and I'm an only child,' Woody said briefly. 'But ports are dangerous places in wartime, which is why the whole school was evacuated, even the masters. Me and Josh have been best friends ever since we started at St Hilliers, and of course it's a boarding school, so I didn't see that much of my parents except during the hols. Dad's in the Navy and my mother's wrapped up in local affairs, so I don't see much of them even then, but by a great piece of good luck Josh lives next door so the pair of us do just about everything together.' He looked enquiringly across at her. 'You?'

'I *am* from Liverpool, the youngest of five, two brothers and three sisters; they're all much older than me and living away from home.' She pointed to the horses, who were coming over to see if the children had carrots or sugar lumps. 'Wish I had a pony,' she said. 'The Pilgrims have several horses; perhaps one day they'll teach us to ride them.' She sighed deeply and hitched her satchel higher up her shoulders. 'Wonder what Rita and Debby are doing now. They were going to the market too; wouldn't it be odd if they'd met your Josh?'

When the high-sided cart, pulled by Magnum the great shire horse, drew up outside the Canary and Linnet, Debby and Rita were ready and waiting. Debby had never ridden in the farm cart, but Rita assured her that it would be a delightful experience. Jill had decided to come along with them as well, leaving Jacky and Herbert to look after the pub. Auntie had announced her intention of buying some soft drinks for the bar, if she could find any, and Jill had a list of groceries – mainly cooking ingredients – which she hoped she might be able to purchase in the larger town.

Debby and Rita had come along for various reasons, mostly to buy anything they could find in the way of sweets, since they seldom had a chance to spend their pocket money in the sparsely stocked village shop. Clambering into the cart behind Jill and Auntie, and greeting Mrs Pilgrim, they took their seats on the wooden ledge which ran along the inside of the cart and prepared to enjoy the ride. Mrs Pilgrim was an essential user, so had a petrol allowance, but the old Morris Minor was so small that when Mrs Pilgrim shopped she was unable to take casual passengers, which made the trip into town a rare treat.

Rita settled herself comfortably, patting the blue gingham skirt of her best dress and adjusting the angle of her panama hat, and Debby noticed Auntie and Jill watching her friend with amused smiles. Rita looked up and caught the amusement on Auntie's face and guessed the cause. 'You never know who we might meet in town,' she said gaily. 'Oh, I do like an outing! And I like looking neat and wearing my best dress, 'cos we don't often get the chance at the Linnet, do we?'

Auntie smiled rather grimly. 'All you're likely to meet is a family of pigs with a net over them so's they can't escape, or a couple of rabbits, their noses wiffling at you through chicken wire,' she observed. A sudden thought seemed to strike her. 'Oh, I've just remembered; I suppose you're fishing for one of the lads at Hemblington Hall.' She made a tutting sound. 'You're starting young, my girl.'

The cart swung into motion and Rita, who had been straightening up indignantly at such a suggestion, squeaked and clutched her hat. 'I don't care about boys; boys are stupid,' she said scornfully. 'All they think about is playing football or whacking cattle with sticks. I don't like boys and nor does Debby, do you Debby?'

Debby had been writing a shopping list before the cart had picked them up and now she bent her head and examined it. 'I don't know any boys,' she mumbled. 'But I expect they're all right, really.' She too was wearing her best cotton frock and Jill had marked the occasion by tying back the soft, dark brown curls with a piece of satin ribbon, so she felt her appearance would not let the side down.

As the cart swung into the road, Mrs Pilgrim shook the reins and adjured Magnum to increase his pace. 'Better get a move on,' she remarked to her passengers, ''cos we've a deal of shopping to do before lunch.'

Auntie turned to smile at the children. 'I hope you're bringing good appetites to market as well as those fancy dresses, because I mean to take you both to the King's Head for meat and potato pie and chips. You too, Mrs Pilgrim. If it wasn't wartime someone would be selling ices, but I doubt they'll do so today, hot though it is.'

'I say, thanks, Auntie,' Rita said in an awed voice. 'I wondered why you only made a packed lunch for Imogen.' She grinned delightedly at Debby. 'Wait till we tell poor Immy that we've had a proper grown-up lunch at the King's Head! She'll be mad as fire.'

Auntie and Jill both chuckled, but Debby looked up and shook her head. 'She won't be mad at all, she'll just say "Lucky old you" and start telling us what a wonderful day she's had,' she said. 'Not everyone is like you, Rita. You shouldn't always criticise, it's not nice.'

Auntie's eyebrows shot up at this remark from the gentle Debby, but Jill gave a subdued cheer. 'Well done, you,' she said, pointing at Debby, and then, turning to Rita: 'Never judge others by yourself, Rita. Debby is quite right: there isn't a mean bone in Imogen's body; she'll not grudge you your day out, I promise you. And there are nice boys and nasty ones, just as there are nice and nasty girls.'

Debby, watching, noticed Rita's cheeks flush at the reproof and burst into speech before Rita had a chance to reply. 'Jill's right. My brother was nice – he was ever so kind . . .'

'Oh, you!' Rita interrupted scornfully. 'Brothers are different; they're family, and you have to like family whether you want to or not. Look at poor Immy with two older brothers and three older sisters. I suppose she likes them . . . not that she mentions them often.'

Jill interrupted. 'I think we've had enough talk about relatives,' she said gaily, and Debby, who had ducked her head, looked up quickly, then reached out and squeezed Jill's hand.

'Where will we go when we reach the town?' she asked, and was glad to hear her voice was steady. 'I'd like to go round the market; if I've got enough money I might even buy a pet. Could I, Auntie?'

'Ooh, I'd like that,' Rita said at once. 'Not a chick, but perhaps a duck – a duckling rather – to swim on the pond which the RAF men are going to dig for us. I'd love a duckling of my own.' She turned to Jill. 'Laurie and Dave did offer to dig a pond out for us, didn't they? I'm sure they won't have forgotten.'

'Or a rabbit,' Debby said softly, following her own train of thought. 'I do love Pandora the piglet, but she isn't cuddly. A rabbit or a guinea pig would be nice.'

Chapter Five

When they reached the market Mrs Pilgrim unloaded three of her passengers, Auntie reminded the girls that they were to meet at noon outside the King's Head, and then she and Mrs Pilgrim drove off to the feed merchant's. Jill was just suggesting that Debby and Rita might like to go round the indoor market where poultry, rabbits, guinea pigs and various other small creatures were being sold when a familiar voice hailed them, and Debby looked up and smiled as Laurie came towards them.

'Well, fancy seeing you,' Jill said, and Debby realised that there was no surprise in Jill's voice, or in the glowing face she turned towards Laurie. 'I know you said you'd try to come into town today, but I thought you couldn't possibly arrive until after lunch.'

'Special dispensation,' Laurie said breezily. 'The Hurricane needs some work on her before we can take off tonight, and I've been flying pretty continually lately, so I had a word with my squadron leader, and provided I'm back on the station by seven o'clock I should be okay.' He tucked Jill's hand into his arm as he spoke and Debby smiled to herself.

Rita had commented only the previous evening, as the girls got ready for bed, that she rather thought Jill had her eye on the handsome young pilot officer. But Imogen had disagreed. 'You're wrong,' she had said loftily. 'He's too old for her. Why, Jill's only seventeen, and Laurie's really old, twenty-two or three at least, I should think.'

'Oh, you. Just because you think the sun shines out of Jill, no one else is good enough for her,' Rita had said scoffingly. 'Besides, she's not even pretty. Oh, I don't deny she's ever so nice . . .'

But Debby and Imogen had fallen upon her, knocking her on to her bed and threatening to pour cold water over her if she did not eat her words. Rita had promptly retracted, vowing that Jill was as beautiful as the day and saying that the man she married would be 'jolly lucky'.

Now, Debby caught hold of Jill's free hand and spoke quickly. 'Rita and I will go to the indoor market and see if there's anything for sale that we can afford. And we'll come to the King's Head at twelve. That will give us two hours; plenty of time to look at absolutely everything.'

Jill and Laurie agreed that that would be fine, but as soon as they had disappeared into the crowd Rita jabbed a sharp elbow into Debby's ribs. 'I'm not going round the bleedin' animal market,' she said defiantly. 'I'm goin' to the shops. So you can choose, baby Debby; it's either the animal market by yourself or the shops with me. Only don't you go hangin' about wasting time, 'cos I mean to enjoy my freedom.'

But Debby felt she had had enough of being bossed about. She did not argue – arguing with Rita was useless – she simply turned on her heel and began to wriggle through the crowd, heading for the enormous barn which housed the indoor market. She heard Rita's yelp of surprise but ignored it, and soon the two were separated by the crowd and she was staring into the contents of the first wire-fronted cage. It held a large grey rabbit with four little ones, and the description on the card on top of the cage, read *Doe and four kittens, Miss Letitia Brown.*

Debby smiled to herself. She was sufficiently knowledgeable now to guess that kittens must be the official term for baby rabbits. Once, she would have puzzled over it, but now she simply accepted it. Beside her, however, a thin brown boy wearing heavy horn-rimmed spectacles stood staring at the rabbits with a puzzled frown. He was wearing a patched grey shirt and shorts with plimsolls on his feet, and when he saw Debby staring at him he grinned. The grin lit his rather serious face, and when he turned his head slightly to read the card again it seemed enlightenment dawned, for he turned to Debby. 'Am I right in supposing that baby rabbits are called kittens?' he asked, and Debby nodded.

'I'm pretty sure you're right,' she said, returning his grin. 'Though why they don't just call them baby rabbits I can't imagine.'

'Me neither,' the boy said. He took off his spectacles, polished them absently on his shirt sleeve and replaced them on his rather aquiline nose. Then he moved a little further along the line of cages. 'Are you just looking, or do you mean to buy?'

'Bit of both,' Debby replied. 'I'd like a rabbit, but I've only got three and sixpence. And I've not got a cage or a run or anything, so I suppose I'll end up just looking.'

'I'm just looking,' the boy said. 'I live on a farm so there are animals everywhere, and this morning I helped to drive the cattle all the way from the farm into the pens. Mrs Pilgrim – she and her husband own the farm – gave me half a crown to buy myself some dinner, but

I did wonder whether to go hungry and blow it on a hamster or a rabbit or something. Are you an evacuee like me? Or do you live here properly, so to speak?'

'I'm an evacuee; my name's Debby. I came in with your Mrs Pilgrim in the cart.' Debby went on to tell him all about Auntie, Jill and the Canary and Linnet as the two of them moved slowly along the line of cages.

The boy listened, and then told her that his name was Josh and he and his friend Woody were the only evacuees living at Pilgrim Farm. 'Of course we go to Hemblington Hall for lessons,' he explained. 'The Pilgrims expect us to help around the house and farm for an hour or so when we get home, but after tea we can do as we like. What about you? From what I've heard, those two ladies who run the pub are as easy-going as Mrs P.'

When the line of rabbits came to an end, by common consent they went outside and toured the entire market together, talking as they went. Debby was surprised by her ease with this boy, for she was normally shy with strangers. They saw pens packed with bleating sheep and others with fat sows and their little ones, and watched cattle being auctioned by a fat man whose sonorous voice rose above the market din. They were about to move on to where Mr Pilgrim's cattle awaited their turn in the auction ring when Debby suddenly clutched Josh's arm. 'Oh Lor', I've just remembered! I'm supposed to be meeting Auntie and the others outside the King's Head at noon, and judging from the position of the sun it must be noon now. Why don't you come with me and have your meal at the same time as us? Then I could meet your pal Woody. Didn't you say you were going to meet him?'

This was definitely a bow at a venture, and Debby was not particularly surprised when Josh shook his head. 'I said nothing of the sort and well you know it,' he said reprovingly. 'Woody's got a den down by the river where he watches birds and that. And lately he's got what he calls a lookout. It's up a tree, a really tall one. He wanted me to go with him, but I'm not keen on heights and anyway I didn't want to miss the market.' He grinned at her. 'Even though it meant helping to drive the cattle in. When you wear specs you get half blinded by the dust the cattle's hooves make on a hot day, and the mud they throw up on a wet day is even worse.'

'I don't wear specs, but I can imagine how it must be,' Debby agreed. 'Only you haven't said you'll come to the King's Head for your dinner. Oh, be a sport! Even if I can't meet Woody, you could meet Rita. She's not my particular friend – when there are three of you you can't really have a particular friend – but she's not bad. Bossy and rather rude sometimes, but not bad. So will you come with me?'

Josh patted her shoulder, but shook his head. 'Thanks but no thanks,' he said breezily. 'The men get cheese baps and beer from the Drovers' Arms; they'd wonder what was up if I went off to the King's Head, which is where the farmers' wives go. We'll have to meet up again sometime, though. I don't suppose you want to help to drive Mr Pilgrim's new stock back to the farm?'

Debby was pleased to note that his voice sounded hopeful; it made her feel that she really had made a friend. Nevertheless, though regretfully, she shook her head. 'Can't do that, I'm afraid. Auntie means us to go back in the wagon with Mrs Pilgrim. When we reach the Linnet we'll have to help unload the sacks of poultry meal and so on, and they're jolly heavy, I can tell you.' A thought struck her. 'You know that den you said you use, down by the river? If it's made of willow wands, sort of twisted to form walls and a roof, with just a little gap so's we can get in and out, Imogen, Rita and me made it long before you came to Pilgrim Farm, and I think it was mean of your pal to pretend it was him.'

Josh's dark eyebrows shot up. 'I never said he built it, I just said he goes there,' he protested. 'Tell you what, tomorrow's Sunday. All us Hemblington Hall boys go to Sunday service at the church in the next village, but afterwards me and Woody have our dinners at the hall and then walk back to the farm. We finish dinner by about half past two, so we could meet at the den at about three o'clock.'

Reluctantly, Debby shook her head. 'Sundays are special, because Auntie and Jill have the day off,' she explained. 'We go to morning service in the village, and after lunch Jill darns her stockings while Auntie writes letters to friends in the forces. She told us once that before the war she and Jill used to catch a bus to the seaside and have a day on the beach. They can't do that now, of course, because the beaches are mined and you aren't allowed on them, but even so . . .'

'Oh, well, it was just an idea,' Josh said peaceably. 'We're bound to meet again soon, living so close.' They had wandered into the main street and now he looked up at the clock above the chemist's shop and whistled under his breath. 'I say, it's past twelve; you'd better get a move on.'

Debby squeaked. 'Oh dear, I'm going to be late! 'Bye, Josh. See you sometime.'

'Bound to,' Josh called after her. 'If it doesn't happen by chance I can always pop into the pub for a whisky and ginger!'

Jill and Laurie wandered around the market, hands linked, talking. Jill thought him the nicest man she had ever known, but was aware that he was only offering friendship. He had already told her that in his opinion wartime relationships tended to be overdramatised, and she had read this as a kindly warning. Don't go taking me seriously, he seemed to imply. I've other things on my mind right now; relationships can wait.

Laurie told her that the general belief in an invasion by the Jerries was pretty widely held in the Mess, and when it came he and his crew, who had discussed it endlessly, believed that the enemy would attack the airfields first in order to put them out of commission. Once the British planes were destroyed it would be a far simpler matter to send an invasion fleet across the Channel, knowing that there would be no retaliation by an air force already battered into submission. But when Jill gave a little shudder Laurie smiled at her reassuringly. 'My old dad had a saying: "a dog fights best with its back to the wall when defending its own",' he quoted. 'And that's the position we are in at the moment. We're defending everything we hold dear, so if they come they come at their peril because, as dear old Winnie says, "we shall never surrender".' He spoke in his best imitation of the Prime Minister's well-known tones and Jill gave a small breathless laugh.

'That's it,' she said approvingly. 'And now since this is a day off let's not talk any more about the war. What would you like to do next?' She glanced at the small watch on her wrist. 'Are you interested in pictures? Auntie says that if we go round behind the corn hall there's an exhibition of paintings by local artists in the hut and some of them are quite good. Want to have a dekko?'

'Good idea; I'd like that,' Laurie said. 'In fact if I can buy a picture which isn't too expensive I might get it for my mother's birthday. And then we'll go on to that little tea room close by the church and have some elevenses.'

'Lovely,' Jill said contentedly. 'I told Auntie not to worry if I didn't meet them at the King's Head for lunch, so we can spend the day together, if you like.'

Auntie watched Jill and Laurie wander away as the cart swung into the feed merchant's yard. She liked Laurie very much, was pretty sure he was fond of her niece, but told herself that it was early days. Jill was her dear girl, but Auntie knew that she had never had a boyfriend, and was very sensibly taking things slowly. Laurie, on the other hand, was an extremely personable young man who must, she felt sure, have the experience which Jill lacked. When Jill was putting her jacket on that morning Auntie had been tempted to suggest that her niece might wear something a little smarter, since she guessed that Jill and Laurie meant to meet up. But she knew this would be blatant interference and might be resented. After all, Jill was only seventeen and would probably have a good many boyfriends – casual boyfriends – before settling down with any particular one.

At this point Mrs Pilgrim pulled on the reins and jumped down to go to Magnum's head. She tied him up, then returned to the cart and addressed her passenger. 'Best get our buying over before we go into the market,' she said briskly. She cocked an eye at Auntie. 'I see your niece have got herself a feller . . . nice-looking one, too. Ah well, that's life.' She chuckled. 'Before you know it we'll be hearin' wedding bells, and you'll be advertisin' for a new barmaid.'

Auntie opened her mouth to say indignantly that Jill was not a barmaid but a partner in the business, then changed her mind. 'I think she's a bit young for marriage yet awhile,' she said cautiously. 'But if she did marry Laurie she wouldn't want to move away. Still an' all, never meet trouble halfway. I dare say the lad's got no more idea of marriage than my Jill. Now how much pig meal do you reckon I'll want?'

Debby arrived at the King's Head breathless and panting, to find the others just about to go into the pub without her. She apologised for her tardiness and explained that she had forgotten to keep her eye on the clock, but whilst Auntie smiled and said it wasn't important Debby received an angry glare from Rita. 'A fine friend you are,' Rita said contemptuously as they entered the dining room. 'You never even tried to find me, did you? Oh no, why should you bother? You'd found yourself a boyfriend, and had no further use for me.'

Debby giggled. She thought of Josh with his enormous spectacles, his skinny body, and what she thought of as his hooky nose. They had got along well, but she had never considered him as a boyfriend for one moment.

Still, once again she told herself that it was no good arguing with Rita, so instead she tried the apologetic approach. 'Oh, Rita, I'm sorry. I didn't realise you were looking for me,' she said. 'Why didn't you come over? I was only with that boy – his name's Josh, he's one of the Pilgrims' evacuees – because we were both looking at the rabbits in the big barn. I thought you only wanted to see the shops, and you know I'm not much interested in clothes.'

Rita sniffed. 'What's the use of being interested in clothes when you're stuck out in the country, with no one to care if you look pretty or ugly as sin?' she asked sulkily. 'My mother taught me to take care of my appearance; your mother – and Imogen's for that matter – don't seem to give a tuppenny damn what you look like.'

Debby felt a hot blush rise up her neck and into her face. She said stiffly: 'You know very well I don't have parents any more. Sometimes I think you're really horrid, Rita Jeffries.'

She was pleased to see that her friend looked a little ashamed, but being Rita she did not intend to admit it. Instead she shrugged and turned away. 'Oh well, it doesn't matter. It's just that you and that boy, Josh or whatever his name is, were laughing and chatting, and I knew if I went over and joined you I'd have felt left out.'

Debby felt a stab of guilt. In a way, Rita had hit the nail on the head. Had she joined them, Debby knew very well that her own pleasure in the day's outing would have been, if not spoiled, at least lessened. The truth was, Rita was not easy. She wanted to be in charge of everything, tell everyone how they should behave, make all the decisions. Debby had once heard her telling Auntie that because she was an only child she had always mixed with grown-ups and regarded other children as being in some way inferior to herself; a remark which had made Auntie laugh. 'Go on with you!' she had said affectionately. 'How can you say such a thing, let alone think it?

Rita had opened her mouth to reply and had suddenly noticed Debby, quietly slicing a loaf for sandwiches, and shrugged. 'Oh well, it's what my mother says,' she muttered. She had turned from Auntie to Debby. 'Do you want a hand with buttering those slices?'

But now they were taking their places round a large table and Auntie was ordering pie and chips for everyone, whilst Debby pointed out that Jill had still not arrived.

'I think she and Laurie are making their own arrangements,' Auntie said. She peered at the handwritten menu which the elderly waitress had given her. 'I see there are puddings, despite wartime shortages. It seems you can choose between apple pie and custard or rhubarb crumble; which is it to be, girls?'

Despite Imogen's invitation to visit the pub, Woody decided that this would have to wait for another day. Mrs Pilgrim, the least fussy of hostesses, laid down few rules, but one of the ones she took most seriously was mealtimes. What she described as high tea was served at half past five and anyone not putting in an appearance at the kitchen table, hands scrubbed and clothing neat, would have received a severe lecture, if nothing else. Mr Pilgrim, many years older than his wife, always backed her up, but he was, on the whole, easier on the boys than she was. So far as he was concerned five minutes either way was forgivable in boys who did not own wristwatches, but his wife thought this no excuse. 'They got tongues in their heads, ha'n't they?' she had asked, the first time Josh and Woody turned up for high tea at twenty to six. She had turned to the boys. 'Just this once I'll let you off, so wash up, get them boots off and your slippers on and sit yourselves down . . . no, I don't want to hear what you've been a-doin' of; it's stew and dumplings, so no talking till your plates are wiped clean.'

Woody explained this to Imogen as they hurried along the dusty summer lane, and she was in full agreement that he must most certainly not waste time popping into the Linnet, but should go straight to the farm. 'Auntie's not like that about mealtimes; we eat whenever the food's ready, because of licensing hours and the pub,' she explained. 'The Linnet's a free house, which means it's not tied to a brewery, but even so Auntie isn't supposed to let us into the bar when the pub's open. We do go through it collecting empty glasses and sandwich plates, but we don't serve the customers or anything like that. But you'd better get a move on, because it's after five already.'

'Oh, cripes! I'd better hurry,' Woody said. 'Cheerio, Imogen; been nice meeting you.' He paused. 'Any chance of getting together again?'

Imogen laughed. 'We're bound to bump into each other,' she said, and turned eagerly towards the pub. As she crossed the lane and went into the yard she wondered about Woody. He was older than her and came from Southampton – a port, like Liverpool, her own home town – but she was not sure whether she was particularly keen to meet him again. He was no beauty, that was for sure, but then you didn't judge friends on their looks. She thought him bossy, and wondered, with an inward smile, how he would get on with Rita. They both wanted to rule the roost, that was the trouble, and she found that she disliked the thought of two boys turning up at the willow hut and trying to take over. But then she supposed there were ploys which might be more fun with five than with three. For instance, there was the pond which the air force men had promised to dig out when they had time to spare, but as more and more aircraft appeared in the skies above the pub she had realised that it would be a good deal quicker if they dug the pond themselves. After all, we're the ones who want to keep ducklings and encourage water birds to come to the Linnet, she told herself.

She actually had her hand on the back door knob when the cart rumbled into the yard behind her and Rita and Debby bounced down and began to lug out the sacks of meal and grain. Auntie got down rather more cautiously and grinned at her. 'Have a good day, poppet?' she enquired genially. 'You missed a jolly good lunch, but Jill said she'd put you up all your favourite sandwiches . . .' she delved in her large cracked leather handbag, 'and I managed to find a sweetshop selling those fat striped humbugs you like.' She produced a rustling paper bag which she thrust into Imogen's hands. 'There you are, a little treat; mind you don't eat them all at once. And now we'll allow these great strong girls to drag the sacks across to the barn whilst you and I start getting the tea.'

'Where's Jill?' Imogen asked presently, as Auntie began to empty the contents of her shopping bag on to the scrubbed wooden table. 'I thought she would be coming back with you.'

'Oh, she met that young air force officer,' Auntie said absently. 'I did say she mustn't forget that the cart would be leaving town at around five o'clock, but she said she and what's-his-name – Laurie – would most likely make their own way back.' She smiled at Imogen. 'You know what people are; they'll probably go to a flick, as you call the cinema, and come back on the last bus, or if he's feeling generous I suppose he might get a taxi.'

Imogen filled the kettle at the sink, glad to keep her back to Auntie for a few moments. Of course she knew that Jill and Laurie liked each other, but it still hurt whenever she saw them together. If only I'd been born ten years earlier, she thought mournfully, carrying the heavy kettle across to the Primus stove, for Auntie did not light the Aga in hot weather. Or even five years earlier . . . but then he never notices me; why should he? Jill's the nicest person in the world, and just because he saved my life . . . well, no use to even think about it. I won't even be eleven for a few more weeks, and by the time I'm old enough to have a boyfriend not only will Laurie be as old as old, but he'll probably be married to Jill and have several babies of their own.

At the thought, two large tears welled up in her eyes and she had to hook out the hanky she kept up the leg of her knickers and pretend to blow her nose whilst dabbing crossly at the unwanted tears. You, Imogen Clarke, are a fool, she told herself. He'll never look at you, not just because you're too young but because Jill is the prettiest girl in the world, as well as the nicest. So stop mooning over him and get on with your life.

As she turned from the Primus stove she became aware that Auntie was talking to her and hastily returned her attention to the matters in hand. '. . . we've all had a good cooked lunch, but I bought a couple of Cornish pasties – they're probably more potato than meat but they always go down well – and one each of those little fancy cakes, the ones the baker sells off at the end of each day's trading. Do you think that'll do?'

'I know the ones you mean; they used to be called French fancies before the war, because they were topped with icing sugar, but now they're just plain,' Imogen said. 'You're quite right, everyone likes them. I'll lay the table, shall I?'

As she spoke the back door burst open and Debby and Rita erupted into the room. 'Hiya, Immy,' Rita said, her voice rather higher than usual. 'We had a great day, didn't we, Deb? We went all round the market and looked in the windows of all the shops and had a wizard lunch.' She gave a small crow of laughter. 'Bet you wish you'd come with us when I tell you Auntie bought us pie and chips and rhubarb crumble. And we met a boy from Hemblington Hall . . .'

Imogen's eyebrows shot up. 'Did you,' she said. 'Well, what a coincidence! I met a boy from Hemblington Hall as well. His name is Woody and his pal is called—'

'Josh,' Debby and Rita shouted in chorus, whilst Imogen exclaimed: 'Well I never did,' and Debby said in a voice too low for Rita to catch: 'Trust Rita to make it look as though she was in on everything.' She raised her voice. 'Not that it matters, of course, because I don't suppose we'll meet the boys again. That Josh is very nice – you'd like him, Immy – but no matter what he may pretend he won't want to go about with girls, particularly girls younger than he is.'

'You're probably right,' Imogen said rather regretfully. She had not been particularly keen to get to know Woody, but she had been fascinated by his lookout and knew she would never dare to climb that mighty beech if he were not present. But she had already decided that she would persuade Debby and Rita to go to the airfield the next time they set out on one of their expeditions, though she knew, really, that if the Germans did invade she would be far too afraid to carry on the sort of guerrilla warfare against them that Woody had in mind, even if he truly could acquire guns and ammunition.

But nevertheless, she was disappointed when Sunday came and went without her seeing hide or hair of the boys from Hemblington Hall. As the girls walked back from church, neat in their best dresses, their panama hats set very straight upon their shining, newly washed hair, she voiced the thought aloud to Debby, being careful to do so when Rita and Jill, talking earnestly, had got some way ahead of them. Debby's eyebrows shot up. 'Didn't I tell you?' she enquired. 'I thought I said; they go to the church in the next village.'

Imogen thought this over. 'But the boys you and I met are living at the farm, not at the Hall,' she pointed out. 'Surely they'd go to our church, even if the other boys didn't.'

'Well, they don't,' Debby said rather impatiently, and it occurred to Imogen that her little friend had begun to come out of her shell. But she did not comment, merely waiting for Debby to continue. 'Josh said they go to church and have their midday dinner with the rest of the school, and are only free from around half past two. But we're busy then, writing letters, helping Auntie and so on.'

'Oh, now I understand,' Imogen said. 'Poor things! Well, in that case, I imagine we're not likely to see much of them.' She looked curiously at Debby. 'You liked that boy Josh, didn't you?'

She was watching her friend's face as she spoke and saw she had coloured slightly. Debby made no reply for a moment but then she heaved a sigh. 'Yes, in a way I did,' she admitted. 'He's not like the boys I met when I was living with my grandparents in Liverpool, or the village boys. They don't think much of girls, but Josh . . . well, if I say he was like another girl you'll think he's a pansy, which he's not. Oh, dear, I can't explain . . .'

'Did Rita like him?' Imogen said, when the silence stretched and it seemed as though Debby was not going to expand on her last remark. 'Come to think of it, she's not said much about him, so perhaps they didn't get on.'

Debby gave a muffled giggle and lowered her voice, though there was no possibility of their being overheard by the couple ahead. 'She didn't meet him. In fact, from what she said, she must have caught a glimpse of Josh and me looking at the animals and then lost sight of us. She pretended she chose not to join us – two's company three's a crowd you know – but I can't imagine our Rita letting that put her off, can you?'

Imogen laughed. 'Rita holding back from being an unwanted third? Pigs might fly!' she said gaily. 'Oh well, from what you say we're unlikely to come across either of those two chaps by chance. Unless we meet in our willow hut.'

'Don't you think we might see them if we go to the lookout in the beech tree?' Debby said tentatively, confirming Imogen's feeling that her shy little friend really was coming out of her shell if she was prepared to actually look for the boy Josh.

However, she had to shake her head, though she did so reluctantly. 'I found it by chance, and I don't know whether I could find it again,' she admitted. 'All I can really say is that Rufus and I crossed the wooden bridge and then turned right and wandered along by the river until we turned off into the wood. And coming home it never occurred to me that I might be lost because Rufus and I were with Woody and he led us straight to the rickety bridge.'

Debby gave a delighted chuckle. '*Hippity hop, clippity clop, over the rickety bridge*,' she quoted. 'Was there a troll guarding the way? Or was he only after the three billy goats gruff?'

Imogen was about to reply that the bridge wasn't *that* rickety when Rita, no doubt attracted by their laughter, joined them. 'No sign of your boyfriends,' she said jeeringly. 'The only boys in church were from the village, so I suppose your new pals don't believe in God. I'm surprised Mrs Pilgrim didn't drag them out by their ears.'

'Oh, Rita, of course she didn't,' Debby said impatiently. 'The Hemblington Hall boys go to a different church, that's all.'

'That's stupid,' Rita snapped. 'The fellers you met live with Mrs Pilgrim.'

'You're the stupid one,' Debby said, highly daring, and Imogen, watching with amusement, saw Rita's cheeks begin to glow; how the other girl hated to be in the wrong! But Debby continued to speak quite calmly. 'Josh told us – oh, but I forgot, you weren't there – that the school goes to the next village for Sunday worship.'

'Oh,' Rita said. 'Oh yes, that makes sense. There must be an awful lot of them. They ought to open up the plague church, the one Auntie told us about. Then they could have the place all to themselves.'

By this time they had reached the Canary and Linnet and were looking forward to Sunday lunch, which was always delicious. Before anyone could speak again, Auntie was unlocking the door and ushering them into the kitchen.

As soon as lunch was finished and the washing up done the girls knew that they would gather round the table to write letters home. And today, Imogen thought gleefully, she really would have something interesting to tell her mother. She had made a new friend and seen with her own eyes, albeit from a distance, the airfield from which so many of the Canary and Linnet customers came.

For two whole weeks there was no sign of the boys from Hemblington Hall, and Imogen decided somewhat regretfully that their chance meeting was probably going to be the only one. She felt sorry, but thought that for the sake of peace it was probably a good thing. She and Debby could scarcely mention Josh and Woody in Rita's presence without the other girl beginning to bridle and make pointed, often spiteful, remarks.

At the end of the second week Imogen, Debby and Rita set off for the willow hut, with three packed lunches and three bottles of Auntie's homemade ginger beer to keep the wolf from the door until teatime, when Auntie had promised to serve a meat and potato pie along with the peas whose pods were full to bursting in the kitchen garden. They had just settled into the hut and were discussing what they should do next when they heard voices. Imogen frowned. 'No one ever comes this way but us,' she said. 'I wonder if . . .'

But she had no chance to complete the sentence before a tanned face appeared in the aperture through which one gained admittance to the hut, a tanned face crowned with tight curls and enlivened by a wicked grin. 'Hello, girls!' said Woody. He turned to someone behind him. 'I told you we'd find them here! Come along in, Josh, and let's introduce ourselves.'

Imogen woke early because she had not pulled their bedroom curtains properly the night before and sunshine was pouring in through the gap. Cautiously, she sat up on one elbow so that she could see the alarm clock, which squatted on the small table between her bed and Debby's. Today, she and the others had planned an expedition to a stretch of water which the boys told her was known locally as the Broad. Here, the boys knew from past experience, the water was deep enough for swimming, and Woody had assured Imogen that she would find it a lot easier to do a breast stroke or even a crawl rather than the dog paddle which was all their rather shallow river allowed.

The expedition to the Broad would be the furthest they had ever gone into strange country and Imogen hugged herself at the thought. They had not mentioned it to either Auntie or Jill. 'I just know they'll forbid it because they're old, and old people don't believe young ones have any sense,' Rita had said crossly. 'Must we mention the Broad, Imogen? After all, it's a long way off so we may never actually reach it.'

Imogen glanced at the alarm clock, which in term time was set to go off at seven o'clock. They did not use it in the holidays; it simply wasn't necessary. Mostly, the three of them got up at seven o'clock anyway because after they had done their chores, such as weeding the vegetable garden and looking after the poultry and Pandora the pig, they were free to please themselves. Of course there were other calls on their time: occasional shopping trips to the town and visits to the village for their rations and anything else they might find, but by and large Auntie and Jill were happy for them to take Rufus and a packed lunch, and stay out all day.

Naturally, both adults had insisted upon meeting the boys and had thoroughly approved of them both, had invited them to pop in whenever they were passing and had asked them to remember that the three girls were young and foolish.

'We shall rely upon you lads to keep our girls safe,' Auntie had said impressively. 'Remember, they will follow your lead just to prove that girls are as good as boys, so make sure you lead them into good ways, and not into mischief.'

Lying in her bed now, for the clock read half past six, Imogen reminded herself guiltily that one of their ploys Auntie and Jill would never have countenanced had they known about it was the lookout. Debby had refused categorically to even ascend to the first branch, saying that she and Josh would remain on the ground, but thinking it over now Imogen realised that this had its advantages. For a start, she knew that at first Rita had felt excluded; five is an awkward number and because she and Woody had met for the first time on market day, as had Debby and Josh, it was only natural that when they paired up it would be Rita who would be left out. This was a new experience for the other girl, and not a pleasant one. But when Debby and Josh made no secret of the fact that they hated heights and had no intention of climbing the tree, Rita came into her own. She scrambled up like a monkey, swinging from branch to branch and causing even the fearless Woody to tell her sharply to stop showing off, and be a bit more careful. 'You're so keen to prove you're tougher than the rest of us that you don't think of anyone else,' he had said severely. 'It didn't occur to you that I was coming up a couple of branches beneath you and you were kicking bits of bark and leaves into my face. If I hadn't been such an experienced climber I might have let go of the branch to brush away the muck, and fallen to my death.'

Imogen had expected Rita to give a sharp retort, but it seemed that Debby was not the only one who was beginning to change, for when Rita did speak it was quite humbly. 'I'm sorry, Woody,' she said. 'You're quite right. I'll be more careful next time.'

'Good; see you don't forget it,' Woody had said sternly. 'Remember what your auntie said? We're older than you, me and Josh, so we're the ones in charge.'

Imogen, watching, had seen a flash of rebellion in Rita's eyes and had waited once more to see her friend try to take Woody down a peg or two. But to her relief, this did not happen. In fact the five of them very soon took it for granted that whatever they did, they would do together.

Having ascertained that there was no need for her to get up yet, Imogen lay down again, but the sun was now directly on her face so she slid out of the sheets – she had kicked the blankets off long ago – and went over to the window. She began to draw the curtain properly across, then hesitated; wouldn't it be rather a waste to spend the lovely morning lying in bed? If she got up right away she could go down to the kitchen, light the Primus under the kettle and make a pot of tea. She could take a cup to Auntie and another to Jill, and then she could start the preparations for breakfast.

To think was to act. Imogen went over to the washstand and began to pour water from the ewer into the round basin with its pattern of poppies. Having washed, she put on the faded shirt and shorts which Jill always referred to as their working clothes, though really, Imogen thought, buttoning the shirt, it would have been more accurate, perhaps, to call them everyday clothes; now that the summer holidays had arrived they were what she and the others wore every day except Sunday, or when they were taken into town to help carry Auntie's shopping.

Imogen tiptoed across the wooden boards, avoiding the one that creaked, and was opening the door with all possible stealth when a sleepy voice addressed her. 'Whazzup?' Rita's voice demanded. 'Izzit time to gerrup?'

Conscious of a decided feeling of disappointment, Imogen realised that she had been looking forward to surprising Auntie and Jill on her own, both by taking them a cup of tea and by starting the breakfast, thus easing the day's work for the two of them. But as she paused, a hand on the doorknob, she looked back and realised that Rita had spoken more or less in her sleep, so instead of answering she went quietly out of the room, leaving the door slightly ajar.

Downstairs, she lit the Primus, made the tea and carried two cups up the stairs. She had to stand them down to knock on Auntie's door, then pushed it open and beamed as Auntie sat up with every evidence of surprise and pleasure and took one of the cups. 'How lovely,' Auntie said, sipping. 'And you've brought one for Jill as well. Goodness, you are getting off to an early start this morning! Have you anything in particular planned?' She glanced towards the bedroom window. 'It's going to be another lovely day by the look of it. Well, after the winter we suffered I should think we jolly well deserve a good summer.' She glanced at the old-fashioned brass alarm clock on her chest of drawers. 'I'll just drink this, then I'll get up and come downstairs,' she said. 'I know the fine weather's lovely for us but it's just what Herr Hitler wants if he's to knock out the Royal Air Force and send his troops over the Channel. They're calling it "the Battle of Britain". . . but I missed the news last night so must catch it this morning. And I hope it won't interfere with your plans, Immy dear, but the accumulator needs recharging, so if you and the others don't mind you might take it down to the blacksmith's – the garage, I mean – and get it done. I take it you're meeting your pals? Are they calling for you, or are you calling for them?'

'I don't know that it matters,' Imogen said. 'If we're early, we'll walk up towards Pilgrim's and meet them. But either way, we'll take the accumulator down to Mr Tidnam's and pick it up on our way home.'

Auntie nodded. 'Right, but make certain you've got it

home in time for the news,' she said. 'Going anywhere in particular?'

Behind her back and feeling thoroughly guilty, Imogen crossed the fingers of the hand not holding Jill's cup of tea. 'I s'pose we might go to the Pilgrims' tree house if we have time, but we won't know until we meet the boys,' she said untruthfully, and salved her conscience by the recollection of Rita's suggestion that they might never actually reach the Broad. 'Is there anything else you want from the village? Apart from having the accumulator recharged, I mean?'

'Torch batteries, if they've got any,' Auntie said. She smiled at Imogen. 'Hope springs eternal, they say. Oh, and if you see any toothpaste . . .'

Imogen laughed. 'You'd better make a list,' she said, thinking that the expedition to the Broad was fast disappearing. 'And now I'd best take this cup of tea to Jill before it goes cold.'

By the time the girls set off they were already uneasily aware that their day out was unlikely to include a trip to the Broad. The boys, too, had been held up and explained with much detail what had happened.

'That darned young bull that Mr Pilgrim is so proud of got out of the bull pen,' Woody said. 'Someone made a mistake somewhere, we aren't sure who, but when old Herbert opened the bull pen the Minotaur – that's what they call him – instead of charging into the enclosure where the cow was, ignored that gate and broke through the one which leads to Parson's Piece. There was lots of shouting and hullabaloo, but he took not a blind bit of notice. He went charging straight across the meadow and crashed through the gate on the opposite side. Apparently, old Herbert says there was a heifer down at the river . . . well, anyway, the Minotaur stopped when he reached his lady love and after they'd said hello he was quite easy to catch and bring back to where he belonged. But it's made us late, so I'm afraid we probably shan't reach the Broad until mid-afternoon. Want to change our plans? We can just muck about down by the river, or walk as far as we can in the time, because we've got to get back as usual for five thirty tea.' He fell into step with the girls and Josh followed suit. 'Come on, shall we save the Broad for another day? And by the way, what made you three late?'

'Oh, Auntie wanted some messages run,' Imogen said. 'Stuff she couldn't wait for, and Jill was busy dealing with the delivery from the brewery so it was up to us to go down and get our rations and so on.' She looked enquiringly up at Woody. 'I s'pose what you're saying is that we might as well muck around here and perhaps go to the Broad another time.'

The five of them had met just about halfway between the farm and the pub, and now stood in a small group, discussing what best to do. 'We've left the accumulator in the village,' Imogen went on. 'That means we've simply got to get back to Mr Tidnam before he closes. Auntie was fed up last night because the newscaster's voice was too faint for her to hear, though she turned the volume up as high as it would go.'

Woody's eyebrows shot up. 'Don't you have two?' he asked. 'I thought everyone had two so whilst one was being recharged you could still get the news with the second one.'

'That's right; we've got two as well,' Imogen assured

him. 'But Auntie forgot to pick the recharged one up. That's why we've got to be back in good time, otherwise she won't know what's going on, and you know how old people fuss about the news.'

'I see,' Woody said rather gloomily. 'Still, I suppose we can go to the Broad another day when we can get away soon after brekker.'

'We could go to the lookout,' Rita said brightly. 'The river will seem tame after we've talked about nothing but the Broad for ages.'

Debby began to speak, but was immediately interrupted by Josh. 'Trust you to think of your own fun and nobody else's, Rita Jeffries,' he said scornfully. 'You know very well Debby and I don't like heights.'

'We're not even thinking about going to the lookout today – well, nobody but Rita is,' Woody said quickly. 'Shall we go down to the river? I know it isn't deep enough to swim in, but mucking about in the water will be cooler than just tramping to nowhere in particular.'

'If we don't set out somewhere soon we might as well not go anywhere,' Debby remarked. 'Come on, fellow adventurers, let's hear some sensible suggestions.'

Imogen smiled at the younger girl. 'Good for you, Debs,' she said approvingly, and turned to the others. 'Come along, ladies and gentlemen; suggestions for today's expedition, if you please?'

'Tell you what,' Woody said after some thought, 'why don't we go along to the airfield? Me and Josh went to the end of the main runway a couple of weeks ago – we were taking a message to an old bloke who used to work for the Pilgrims – and we stayed for ages, watching the planes take off and come back. It's nowhere near as far as the Broad and it was dead interesting . . . it's only a small airfield by most standards, and there are no heavy bombers or anything like that, it's just Spitfires and Hurricanes, but you'd be surprised at the row they make on take-off, and there's a spot where you can lie in long grass and see everything.'

'Shall we have a vote on it?' Imogen suggested. 'Hands up who wants to go and watch the planes take off?'

Four hands shot skywards, including Imogen's own; it was only Rita who did not seem interested.

'Right, that's settled by a majority of four to one,' Woody said briskly. 'Let's set out at once, then we can have our dinner in the wood. Josh and me know where there's a stream where we can eat our sandwiches sitting on the bank with our feet in the water.'

The small group followed this plan to the letter, though it was tempting to stay beneath the shade of the trees; Woody actually suggested they might have a little snooze before going further, but this was shouted down by the rest of the company. 'Come on, Grandpa Woody; if we stop for a snooze we shan't see any planes at all,' Josh said. 'And from here on we've got to keep our heads down because we're getting near the perimeter fence. There are guards patrolling it, of course, but the grassy hollow Woody and I picked last time was pretty good. We reckoned we could see everything without being seen . . . but you'll see for yourselves in a minute.'

And presently they found the dip in the ground and tumbled into it just in time to avoid being spotted by two guards, rifles slung on their shoulders, solemnly marching along the perimeter track on the inner side of the fence. Once they'd gone by Woody began to tell the others what they would see. 'I told Laurie, last time he came up to the farm to see if we had any eggs to spare, that I wanted to join the RAF as soon as I was old enough, and learn to pilot a Spitfire,' he said. 'Only when Laurie told me how wizard the Hurricanes are I changed my mind. It seems they're not as fast as the Spits, but they're a good deal sturdier. And he says that Flotsham has been lucky so far and not been raided because of its position. Lots of trees with the huts built under the cover of the foliage, and grass runways, camouflaged so that they don't stand out. I can tell you, seen from the air, it only looks like an airfield when the planes are getting ready for take-off. Once they're gone . . . well, it could be anywhere.'

Josh had described their hideout as a grassy hollow, but in fact it had once been in a cornfield and now the stiff stems of the remnants of the crop surrounded them. It was difficult to see out, and to make matters worse the hollow felt extremely hot after the cool shade of the trees, with the sun beating down on their heads and the breeze unable to penetrate the surrounding stalks. Rita began to grumble first, as Imogen had known she would. She said it was a bad spot; their view of the runway was very restricted, but if it occurred to the guards to look in their direction she was sure they would be easily spotted. Woody was beginning to tell her that if she wanted to go she could do so when they heard a loud-speaker boom out and saw, in the distance, the figures of men in what Imogen guessed must be their flying kit running as hard as they could towards the planes which were lined up in readiness.

'They're being scrambled,' Woody hissed in Imogen's ear. 'That means the enemy have been picked up crossing the Channel or the North Sea either on the radar or by the Royal Observer Corps. They telegraph the news to the airfields, who have to get into the air as soon as they can. I don't understand everything Laurie told me but it seems that height is terribly important, and that's where we lose most men and machines. The Luftwaffe have time on their side, time to gain height I mean, so they can bounce on the aircraft below them rather like a cat bounces on a mouse, from above, d'you see?'

'And the Huns attack out of the sun,' Josh put in, having to raise his voice above the roar of the engines as the planes began first to trundle and then to race across the grass. 'You can imagine how hard it is to spot somebody hundreds of feet above you when in addition to everything else he's coming at you out of the sun and you have to fight bedazzled. If the warning comes early enough our chaps can climb and then they can pick off the enemy, because by and large the Spits are faster and nippier than the Messerschmitts and the Junkers. And of course both Spitfires and Hurricanes are a great deal more manoeuvrable than the Stukas.'

After his conversation with Laurie, Woody, who had been keen on aircraft, according to him, ever since he could toddle, had immediately rushed home and consulted his books on flying. He had learned that the Stuka was a dive bomber which, when it descended towards a target, let out a hellish scream, no doubt adding to the terror of a normal bombing raid. Woody explained all this to his companions, and as the last plane left the ground he said cheerfully, 'Well, that's all the show for now. From what I remember it's a matter of fuel almost as much as firepower. Our aircraft can stay in the air for two or three hours but then they have to get down. The Luftwaffe must have bigger fuel tanks, I suppose, because they have much further to travel.'

'But not so far now they've got French, Belgian, Dutch . . . oh, all sorts of airfields on the continent, so they don't have to come all the way from Germany,' Josh said, and Imogen noticed that both he and Debby were very pale, and that Debby was clutching Josh's hand convulsively; so convulsively that her knuckles were white.

'So they won't be back for two or three hours then?' Imogen said presently when the roar of the engines had faded to a faint murmur. 'No point in hanging around here to be spotted the next time the guards go past . . . only I expect they'll be looking up, don't you? They'll want to make sure that any planes going over are ours.'

Woody's head popped up so that he could look across at the airfield, for like everyone else he had gazed skywards until there was nothing in sight. Now he stretched and yawned, then grinned at his companions. 'Well, that's it. Shall we go back through the wood and begin to make our way homewards? No point in—'

'Shut up a moment,' Rita said in a peremptory fashion. 'They're coming back; they must have been recalled. Laurie said they were in radio contact with base, so presumably it was a false alarm.'

Woody cupped one hand behind his ear. 'Yes, I can hear the engines . . .' he began, then frowned. 'Hang on a minute. I've got to know the sound of our engines and I don't think . . .'

Now they were all on their feet and staring up into the blue sky even as Woody shrieked at them to get down. 'They aren't ours,' he shouted. 'Where's the bloody ack-ack?' He stopped speaking and dived for the ground, pulling Imogen with him. The roar of the engines was right overhead and it seemed to Imogen that all hell had broken loose. The planes came in fast and low, out of the sun, as Josh had predicted, raining down bullets as they came, attacking everything indiscriminately. Imogen, peering between the cornstalks, saw one of the guards bowled over as though he weighed no more than a husk of wheat, saw the other run to him, and then heard the hellish scream which Woody had just been describing. She looked up. A huge plane, which seemed to be two or three times the size of the Spitfire and Hurricane attacking it, was almost upon them. She saw the bomb doors open, saw the monstrous fish hurtle downwards and put both hands over her ears as it hit the ground and exploded, throwing up great sprays of soil and choking smoke before the pilot pulled out of his dive and headed back the way he had come. Imogen watched as the Stuka gathered its defensive fighters around it like a man pulling on a cloak, and then the whole lot climbed into the blue and disappeared. The guards did not appear to have seen the children; the one on the ground was clutching his shoulder, and his companion was bending over him, assisting him to rise. Relieved, Imogen watched as the pair disappeared in the direction of the huts.

She looked around at her four friends and wondered for a moment how they had managed to get so dirty, then realised that the bomb which had exploded so near their hideout had thrown earth and grass some considerable distance. She examined their expressions: Woody looked excited, almost as though what they had watched had been on the cinema screen, whilst Josh, though pale, was bright-eyed; now that the action was over she saw he was both frightened and furious and was swearing beneath his breath, had probably been doing so from the moment the planes attacked. That was not like Josh, who never swore. Debby was wiping dirt from her face and Imogen saw that she was crying; there were two white tear tracks running down her filthy cheeks. Rita was flushed and excited, hopping up and down and saying that she hoped Laurie would meet them on his way home, and blast the whole lot of them out of the sky.

It took a good five minutes before Imogen herself had stopped shaking and realised that it was the same with the others. In fact it was not until she said sharply 'Where's Rufus?' that they all came back down to earth.

Chapter Six

Everyone stopped what they were doing and stared about them. There was no sign of their faithful friend, not so much as a tuft of fur, and certainly no indication that he had been hurt, but belatedly Imogen remembered that when it was clear no more sandwiches were forthcoming he had become bored with their uncomfortable hideout and wandered off. She had a distinct and horrible impression of having seen him sniffing along the perimeter fence and she could still see the little puffs of dust where the fighter plane had strafed the perimeter track. They had been standing in an untidy little group but now Woody said briskly: 'Well, the raid's over. They won't come back; there'd be no point. And it does rather prove that Flotsham is well camouflaged because the huts are still standing. Now let's concentrate on finding Rufus.'

They did not have to look far. Close against the perimeter fence, about ten yards from their hollow, they saw a pathetic heap of black fur. Imogen was the first to reach him; she flung herself down on her knees and clasped the dog round his neck. 'And he never even had the Spam sandwich I saved for him, and they're his favourite,' she mourned. 'Oh, darling Rufus, you should have stayed with us.' She rummaged in her satchel and produced the Spam sandwich she had been saving for later, waving it under the dog's black nose, and letting her teardrops fall on to his much loved face.

Debby and Rita joined her whilst the boys stood a respectful distance away, letting the girls get over the worst of their grief. Rita was the first to recover. She rubbed her eyes briskly and stood up. 'We ought to bury him here, because if we take him home Auntie will know that we must have been at the airfield during the raid and it'll spoil everything.'

Woody sighed, then absently leaned over and stroked Rufus's silky ears. 'Poor old beggar, you have landed us in the soup,' he murmured. He turned to Imogen. 'Have you realised how much weight he's lost since coming everywhere with you girls? He used to be quite tubby but now he's very slim, which is a good job, because carrying him back to the Linnet is going to be pretty tough work.' He cast a reproachful look at Rita. 'Just how do you imagine we can dig a grave for a large dog like Rufus without so much as a spade between us, Rita? We'll have to say he ran off and must have overstrained his heart or something, because so far as I can see there's no blood anywhere.'

'I suppose it's blast,' Josh said as the two boys lifted Rufus, not without difficulty, and began to make for the path through the trees by which they had come. 'I've heard stories about blast . . . gosh, he's pretty heavy. The girls are going to have to take a turn at carrying him.' They had not gone more than half a dozen yards, however, when he stopped short. 'Hang on a minute,' he exclaimed. 'Who did that?' He was carrying Rufus's front end and even as he spoke Imogen, who was walking along beside him, squeaked and gasped.

'He licked your ear; I saw his tongue come out!' she said. 'I don't think he's dead at all, I think he was just knocked out when the bomb fell.' She flung her arms round the dog, rubbing her face against his as Rufus began to struggle. 'Oh, thank God! I do love Rufus so much, and if he had been killed it would have been our fault because we didn't make him stay in the hollow with us.' She dug in her bag and produced the rather battered sandwich once more, waving it enticingly in front of Rufus's dazed eyes. 'How about a mouthful, sweetheart?' she said in her most wheedling tones. 'It's your favourite, it's Spam.' The dog sniffed at the food, then accepted it, and as he gulped it down she turned and gave Rita a hug. 'Oh, Rita, I bet you're as glad as I am – and the others too, of course.' She looked towards Debby, who was grinning from ear to ear and rubbing her eyes with both grimy fists.

'Put him down and see if he's all right to walk,' she said huskily. The boys gently lowered the dog to the ground, whereupon Rufus's knees buckled and he looked appealingly up at his one-time carriers. Woody, who had had the lighter end, giggled. 'The lazy old beggar obviously enjoyed having a lift,' he said cheerfully. 'But the sooner he learns to walk properly the better.'

The return of Rufus from the dead was so dramatic, so welcome, that their recent terror over the raid became almost insignificant. At first the dog walked along dreamily, as though only half awake, but after ten or fifteen minutes it was as though his brain had cleared and he began to examine every tree, lifting his leg against favoured ones and behaving, in short, in a perfectly normal manner. Woody dug in his pocket and produced a boiled sweet which he had been saving for the journey home, and the speed at which Rufus both accepted it and gulped it down made them all laugh.

'Well, whatever was the matter, he's over it now,' Josh remarked. 'Good old indestructible Rufus, you've saved our bacon. If you really had snuffed it there'd have been all sorts of fuss, but as it is we can tell Mrs Pilgrim and Auntie that we heard the planes and saw the Stuka diving without them getting wound up. And that means our expedition to the Broad is still on even though we missed out today.'

They were tramping along, happily discussing the raid and boasting about how clever they had been to get so close without actually risking life and limb, when Debby suddenly jerked at Imogen's arm. 'Immy, the accumulator!' she said. 'You know how keen Auntie was for us to fetch it before Mr Tidnam closes. Well, I reckon even if we run all the way he'll have shut up shop by the time we get to the village. Oh dear, we'll be in awful trouble.'

Josh gave her a reassuring smile. 'No you won't. Old Tidnam lives in the cottage next door to the garage. All you have to do is knock and he'll be happy to oblige.'

'You can do the knocking then,' Imogen said. 'I don't mind Mr Tidnam – well, I like him – but his wife's a different kettle of fish. She doesn't like kids and she gets ever so cross if you go round after hours, as she calls it. If I knock and she answers she'll give me a right earful and tell me to come back at half past eight tomorrow morning. It's all very well for you to laugh – I think she quite likes boys – but this wouldn't be the first time I've put her out by arriving just when she's serving Mr Tidnam's tea. Oh, be a sport, Josh!'

They were emerging on to the village street and Josh was beginning to say that he didn't mind bearding the Tidnams in their den when Debby grabbed his arm. 'You won't have to; here comes Jill!' she said excitedly. 'She's pushing her bike and look, she's got the accumulator dangling from one handlebar and a shopping basket from the other. Oh, what day of the week is it?' She beamed round at her companions. 'Is it the day the fish and chip van comes? I'm sure I can smell the fat hotting up.'

Everyone's pace immediately quickened. Mr and Mrs Ryder owned and ran a mobile fish and chip van, visiting those villages which had no such shop of their own. It came round once a week, and Mr Ryder dispensed his delicious product to anyone who could afford a threepenny bag of chips or a ninepenny piece of fish. His van stood on the village green for a full hour whilst customers queued and, as Woody was apt to say, got the delicious smell for free.

Of course, had he and Josh lived with the rest of the school at Hemblington Hall, he would never have got so much as a whiff of the Ryders' offerings, for the teachers thought the boys at their school were sufficiently well fed without adding anything else. 'They think fish and chips are common,' Woody had told the girls. He had scowled. 'But the masters nip down and get a paper of chips at the van, and a pint of beer or Guinness or something, whenever they think no one's watching.'

As they waved enthusiastically at Jill they saw that their noses had not deceived them: the queue was already a long one and Mr and Mrs Ryder were working like demons, he dipping the fish in batter and frying it whilst Mrs Ryder dug into the pile of golden chips with her stainless steel scoop and tipped the contents on to squares of newspaper, added salt and vinegar as required and handed the packets to the customers at the head of the queue.

Jill was waving back and pushing her bicycle towards them at a dangerous speed considering the weight of the goods on the handlebars. Rita hurried towards her and gripped the handles, straddling the front wheel. 'Is that the accumulator we were supposed to pick up from Mr Tidnam? And do you need any help carrying fish and chips?'

Jill laughed, but she was looking strained and worried, Imogen saw, her normally fresh complexion pale. 'Yes, I'm going to buy chips to go with the meat and potato pie that Auntie made earlier. But I'm going to make a telephone call first. You lot can join the queue . . .' she delved into her pocket and produced a handful of change, 'and get five portions of chips. You lads won't need any because it's after five now and you're supposed to be back at the Pilgrims' by half past, aren't you? Their place is in an uproar because of the raid, so I don't suppose it will matter if you are a bit late. Did you know that Flotsham airfield has been bombed? From what I can gather, Laurie and Dave should have been airborne and halfway to the coast before the attack happened, but I'm just going to ring the Mess to – to see how they got on. It would be awful if the Luftwaffe caught them on the ground.'

'Oh, they didn't,' Debby said, clearly anxious to relieve Jill's mind of at least one of its worries. Josh kicked her ankle, but having started Debby obviously felt it would look strange to stop. 'We saw the Hurricanes take off and it was ages before we heard enemy engines.'

Jill had been heading towards the red telephone box, but at Debby's words she stopped short and turned round. 'Are you sure of that?' she asked eagerly. 'Where were you, exactly?'

Debby looked baffled and Woody struck in. 'Dunno; there are so many woods and streams and meadows, and we don't know the names of any of 'em,' he said vaguely. 'Just you telephone, Jill. Laurie was telling me a couple of weeks ago that they only have fuel for a couple of hours and can't chase the Nazis right across the North Sea or the Channel or whatever, so they have to return home quite soon.'

'What time would you say they were scrambled? Oh – that means—'

'That means they reached the planes and got into the air,' the children said in a laughing chorus, Rita adding: 'We may not be supposed to go into the bar but we hear everything that's going on because Auntie leaves the door ajar.'

Jill laughed with them. 'Kids are the same the whole world over; ears on legs,' she said, causing her audience to giggle helplessly. 'Tell you what, join the queue and ask for chips for five but keep your eye on the telephone box and if I come out and give you the thumbs up sign make it seven instead.'

Just before they reached the head of the queue they saw Jill give the thumbs up sign. On the walk home, however, her relief at knowing Laurie and Dave were fine – Laurie had added a Ju88 to his tally of 'kills' and Dave and another Hurricane pilot had both claimed responsibility for downing the Stuka – didn't prevent her from enquiring more closely into her charges' afternoon activities, and in the end they had to reveal that they had been near enough to the airfield to see the action. Jill's broad smile faltered for a moment and a frown creased her brow, but then it cleared. 'I suppose if you were exploring in that direction you had little choice, because aircraft cover large areas so very quickly,' she said. 'But I think we won't mention to Auntie that you were near enough to see anything. I don't want to worry her, and anyway, there's nothing anyone can do about it. If you were in a town or a city you'd be in a much worse position. As for being near a port . . . well, you understand what I mean, I hope. I know Flotsham is only a couple of miles from the Linnet, but it's a small airfield with only fighter planes and unlikely to be targeted a second time, especially if two of the attackers were downed as they made their way home.'

Woody and Josh agreed fervently with this. 'Our school was bombed weeks ago – not Hemblington Hall, of course, the one outside Southampton,' Josh said. 'Besides, we none of us want to be moved, do we?'

Four heads were shaken in a very determined fashion. 'If they move us, we'll wait a couple of weeks and then come back here,' Imogen said at once. But at this point they reached the pub and Woody and Josh made their farewells and headed for the farm, whilst the girls and Jill joined Auntie around the kitchen table, and watched eagerly as she cut generous portions of meat and potato pie and surrounded each wedge with chips.

There was a knock on the door and Jill jumped to her feet as Laurie and Dave entered. Imogen saw how her cheeks flushed and her eyes glowed with pleasure and relief, and guessed that the same expression must have appeared on her own face. She cast a cautious glance around through her lashes but saw that no one was looking at her; attention was fixed on the two pilots. They were sliding out of their jackets and hanging them on the hook behind the door, talking animatedly as they did so, and Auntie was extracting the rest of the meat and potato pie from the depths of the Aga. Jill took the opportunity, whilst urging the two young men to sit down, to squeeze Laurie's hand tightly, and although he swung his broad shoulders between the children and Jill for a moment Imogen saw him lift Jill's hand, uncurl her fingers and drop a kiss into the palm. Then he led her back to her place at the table and sat down in the vacant chair next to her. 'There you are, sweetie,' he said cheerfully. 'Back home with scarcely a scratch. And that includes the good old Hurricane.'

Dave, pulling out the chair next to Rita's, grinned up at Auntie as she handed him a laden plate. 'I reckon the attacks are getting weaker and weaker,' he said triumphantly. 'I tell you, looking back on the early days of the Nazi offensive, there were times when the air was so full of Messerschmitts that you could scarcely fail to down two or three. It was good for morale as well as for the war effort, and even though the Luftwaffe have finally got their act together I reckon we could have finished them off by now if only our radar – and the Royal Observer Corps – could pick them up more quickly so we could attack from a height.'

'Well, it seems to me you put up a pretty good show today,' Auntie observed, placing full plates before the young men. 'There are several chaps in the bar talking about the raid, and it seems not one hut was touched, and the only casualty was a guard with a bullet through his shoulder.'

'There was nearly another . . .' Debby began, and was immediately nudged into silence by Rita's elbow.

'Yes, one of the cows had a narrow escape, someone said,' Rita broke in. 'The poor thing had an ear shot off. Bloody Nazis. As if the cow could know anything about the war!'

Auntie pulled a rueful face. 'Do you suppose that all the children – some of them little more than babies – who were killed when the Nazis entered Poland knew, or cared, anything about the war?' she asked quietly. 'War doesn't discriminate, my love, which is why we have to stop it. And now let's forget all about it until we turn on the news.'

When they had finished their meal the children began to wash up and clear away whilst Auntie turned up the volume of the wireless so that those in the bar could hear.

Imogen herself paid more attention to the news, she realised, than she had ever done before. The raid had brought the war into their lives and it had become real. As the announcer's voice, calm and authoritative, began to relay the war news she saw again the fighter plane spitting bullets and the huge size of the dive bomber. She remembered the chaos the bomb had wrought and she knew that it had changed her view of the war in a way no mere announcements could. She saw again in her mind's eye the way the guard had been bowled over like a ninepin and realised how, if the bomb had been nearer, she might not be standing in Auntie's kitchen calmly washing up the supper things and listening to Alvar Lidell, in his calm unhurried voice, telling of raids in other parts of the country.

Every now and then she stole a look at Laurie, noticing for the first time that there were dark circles under his eyes and he seemed thinner than when he had rescued her from that ice-bound ditch. Astonished, she found herself understanding something Auntie had said: that a boy had brought her home that night, but the boy had become a man. And she knew, now, that it was the war which had done it to him. She had never tried to imagine what it was like to fly a Hurricane into battle; now she realised that it must be a lonely thing. She opened her mouth to voice the thought when the news had ended, but quietly closed it again. A day or two ago she might have questioned him; now she knew better. What Laurie wanted was to rest, relax, and forget, for the time being at least. So she smiled at him as he came back into the kitchen from the bar, holding a foaming pint pot in one hand. 'We're going to ring our mums tomorrow to let them know we're all right, thanks to you fellows,' she told him. 'Do you phone your mum and dad regularly, Laurie? I know Dave does.'

Laurie grinned at her and Imogen thought all over again that he was not only the nicest man in the world but also the best-looking. However, he was shaking his head. 'My dad is in Rhodesia, pilot training,' he informed her. 'And my mum rings the Mess two or three times a week. Now, when I've finished this beer Dave and I are going to trot home to our little beds so we're fresh and fit if the call to scramble comes as soon as it's light. Isn't it time you were off to bed as well? Oh, and I never asked you about your boyfriends. They okay?'

'They're very well indeed, thank you,' Debby cut in before Imogen could answer. 'We've been with them all day.' She cast a rather apprehensive look at Auntie and Jill. 'We meant to go the Broad – can't remember the name of it, the one nearest us – but we caught up with shopping and things so we never got there. Still, we can go another day.'

Laurie's eyebrows lifted. 'Good thing you weren't there. That was where we had a dogfight with the Messerschmitts and a couple of Junkers,' he told her, and Imogen, listening eagerly, thought his voice trembled a little. 'There were bullets flying everywhere. There was an old fellow in a rowboat . . . everyone else seems to have kept well clear. I'm glad you'd not got that far.'

Dave broke in, wiping a moustache of froth off his upper lip before he spoke. 'You've never seen anything like the way that old chap worked at the oars, though, once he realised what was happening,' he said. 'He fairly skimmed across the water, like one of those water boatmen you see on the Broad – the insects, not the people – so let's hope he got clear away.'

The children agreed fervently with this wish and then at Jill's insistence made their way up to bed. Imogen, slipping between the sheets, knew that the war had truly come home to her at last. She realised that in her heart of hearts she had believed that those one loved would in some miraculous way be kept safe. As a small girl on holiday in the country she had grazed on the hedgerows in a similar manner to that adopted by sheep and cows, telling herself that God would not let a little girl eat anything poisonous. Her mother had remonstrated, pointing out that the prettiest berries were likely to be the most poisonous, but she had simply not believed her. God loved little children, therefore he would not let harm come to the young Imogen. But now, having actually seen the fighter planes strafing the airfield and the bomb bursting dangerously close, having believed for several terrible moments that her darling Rufus was dead, she no longer considered herself safe, because why should God let one sparrow fall and save another? It didn't make sense.

Next morning when she woke she would telephone her mother and get her to check on other friends and relatives. She closed her eyes and slept, only to be haunted by a vision of the Stuka as it dived to deliver its bomb and the picture of Rufus as he lay against the perimeter fence, to all appearances as dead as mutton.

She was not the only one to suffer from nightmares. Rita slept soundly, as usual, but Debby wept in her sleep and cried out a couple of times, and when at last it grew light Imogen got into the other girl's bed and they talked softly of various plans for the future, including a trip back to Liverpool before the school holidays ended.

'I know our mums and grans and so on don't want us to go back into danger,' Imogen admitted. 'But after yesterday . . . well, I'd just like to see the city for myself.'

Debby agreed and Rita, when she awoke, agreed too, though somewhat reluctantly. They went down to breakfast feeling that, for the time being, they had done all they could, but later that day, going into the village to fetch the second accumulator, they heard some news which hardened their resolve to return to Liverpool, if only for a couple of days.

Queuing in the post office, they heard an old man discussing the raid with a friend. 'A cow got a bullet which took a lump out of its lug,' he told his friend. 'But that in't the wust, not by a long chalk that in't. You know old Ebenezer what sets his eel traps on Flotsham Broad? He were out there when the planes were overhead and them bloody bullets flyin'. They say he fair flew across the water and into the reeds, probably hopin' to keep his hid down and stay clear. But his old woman got worried when he din't come in for his tea, and went a-searchin'. Found him lyin' in the bottom of his old boat, wi' bullet holes right across his back. Dead as a herrin', so they say. Bled to death, poor old bugger.'

Afterwards, Rita said that her companions had actually turned green, but since Imogen immediately said that they were not the only ones Rita had to admit that the news had shaken her too. 'It's because Laurie and Dave were talking about it last night,' she said. 'Poor old man. And the worst part is . . .'

'Shut up!' Imogen and Debby said in chorus. They all knew what the worst part was: it was impossible to tell whose bullets had killed the old man. Apparently a Spitfire had been only yards behind the Ju88 and the bullets could have come from either aircraft.

There might have been an argument, or at least more discussion, but at that moment they reached the head of the queue and Debby, always the peacemaker, gave a little squeak. 'Fruit gums!' she said. 'I wonder if Mrs Bailey will let us have a tube each?'

This incident strengthened the girls' resolve to go home, though when Auntie telephoned Mrs Clarke, Mrs Jeffries and the elderly Viners, it soon became clear that the girls' relatives were not enamoured of the idea. Old Mr and Mrs Viner had moved out of the city centre and now lived on the Wirral as paying guests of an elderly couple who had a couple of rooms to spare. They had offered to take evacuees, but the plan had fallen through when it was realised that the old couple just could not cope. They volunteered immediately to take the Viners in and charge a very reasonable rent. 'Very welcome my granddaughter would be, but there's nowhere in a village so tiny – and already bursting at the seams – who could put her up overnight,' Mrs Viner had explained to Auntie, in response to the suggested visit.

Mrs Jeffries had said uncompromisingly that her boarding house was full of sailors. 'Not suitable company at all for a young girl like Rita,' she said primly.

And Mrs Clarke, though anxious to see her daughter and to reassure Imogen that so far Elizabeth Court had escaped damage, thought it would be more suitable if she came to them. 'If you could put me up just for the one night, that would be fine,' she said. 'Of course it would mean taking a couple of days off – I'm sure Immy has told you that I'm an ARP warden as well as organising the canteen vans for the WI. I know the girls want to come home for a visit but between you and me, Miss Marcy, to have them in Liverpool just as the raids are hotting up is unlikely to lessen anyone's worries. How would it be if I got in touch with the other parents and we all came down together? A taxi from the town to the Canary and Linnet, shared three ways, wouldn't break the bank.'

Auntie thought this a very good idea, and when she returned from the village telephone box and told the children what she and Mrs Clarke had arranged everyone seemed to think it a good solution to their worries. Partly, this was because the children's immediate anxiety had lessened by the time the final arrangements for parents to come a-visiting were made. Overhead the battles still raged, but the Luftwaffe's attacks on airfields decreased as the British pilots in their turn became stronger and more confident. When Laurie and Dave visited the pub they were pale and hollow-eyed, but always smiling. They kept a tally of the aircraft they downed and it grew steadily, and even when they were posted to a much larger airfield in Lincolnshire they kept in touch with Jill and Auntie by telephone. Their confidence continued to grow, as did the confidence of the general public. Everyone now felt they had a personal hand in the war. Schoolchildren spent their pocket money on the 'Buy a Spitfire' fund, housewives handed in enamel saucepans – though Auntie was heard to remark that she did not see what use could be made of such domestic utensils – and the authorities came along and took away gates and garden fences.

The Linnet, deep in its grove of trees, had no fences to be taken, but there was a big fuss at the Pilgrims' farm when the salvage men, as they were called, tried to commandeer the bull pen. Mrs Pilgrim advised them in a honeyed voice that they were welcome to it so long as they didn't mind disputing ownership with the Minotaur. The salvage men, after one horrified look at the bull's massive body and glittering eyes, decided that he might be best behind bars, and went on their way leaving the bull pen intact.

Rita awoke on the morning of the parental visit not sure whether excitement or apprehension was uppermost in her mind. She supposed she loved her mother, because it was her duty, but she had never liked the boarding house or the constant turnover of different guests, mainly seamen whose ships had come into port for maintenance work. And she had been away from home now for the best part of a year, as indeed had Imogen and Debby. She knew she had changed and supposed that her mother would have changed, too. The dreadful thought that they might not recognise each other began to haunt her. They would walk into the village after breakfast to meet the ten o'clock bus, for Mrs Clarke and Mrs Jeffries had chosen to spend the night at a guest house in town rather than arrive at the Canary and Linnet after their children were in bed. Debby's grandparents, in the end, had been unable to come after all. Mr Viner had written to Auntie explaining that his wife's rheumatoid arthritis was now so bad that she could only walk very short distances with the aid of two sticks. He felt he could not leave her, but promised that as soon as she had a good spell they would undertake the journey.

Debby had not seemed unduly disappointed, and when Imogen had commiserated with her she had reminded her friends that she scarcely knew the old couple, having been evacuated a matter of weeks after they had arrived from the Continent. 'I should have known they wouldn't be able to come, but as soon as Auntie will let me I'll go and visit them,' she had said cheerfully. 'I shan't come to meet the bus, though, if you don't mind. I'll walk up to the farm and spend some time with Mrs Pilgrim after I've finished my chores.'

Now Rita stared very hard at her two friends, assured herself that they both slept still, and swung her legs out of bed. She padded over to the window and drew back the curtains a little, then gasped. The view was entirely obscured by thick mist, and even as she rubbed at the windowpane, thinking that perhaps it was merely condensation, she heard a squeak from behind her and turned to jerk her thumb at the window. 'It's fog, one of those pea-soupers that we used to get when we lived at home. It would come rolling up the Mersey and envelop all the streets down by the docks, and your mum would walk to school with you 'cos of the traffic not being able to see too clearly. I didn't know they happened in the country, though.'

Imogen joined her at the window and gave her a playful push. 'It just shows how often you get up early,' she said mockingly. 'At this time of year you get what they call autumn mists which disappear as the sun rises. Don't worry, by the time we've had our brekker and walked into the village it'll be another lovely sunny day.'

And so it proved. Before they had even gone downstairs the fog had become a mere mist through which the sun shone brightly. Despite their intention not to wake Debby the other girl got up as soon as they had done washing and dressing and the three of them clattered down the stairs together. In the kitchen, Auntie and Jill were busy, Auntie dealing with breakfast whilst Jill ironed the neat white blouses, grey cardigans and pleated skirts which Imogen and Rita wore for best.

Jill looked up from her work and smiled at them. 'You're going to look smart as paint whether you like it or not,' she said, then turned the smile on Debby. 'Not you, chick; you can wear your scruffy old togs, but Imogen and Rita must have their breakfast and then change.' She laid the last garment she had been ironing over the back of a chair, dusted her hands briskly and picked up the ivory-backed hairbrush which they all shared. 'Sit down and eat up. Who wants plaits or a ponytail? I've already ironed the ribbons – blue for Rita, red for you, Imogen – so once you've eaten your porridge you'll be free to leave.'

It was tempting, Rita thought, to linger over breakfast, to put off the moment when they would see Mrs Jeffries and Mrs Clarke descending from the bus. But Imogen was eating fast, her eyes sparkling with excitement, so Rita had, of course, to follow suit, and presently, carefully avoiding dusty patches, they found themselves emerging from the lane and walking rather awkwardly across the village green, to sit down on the rustic bench near which the ancient bus would presently draw up.

Sitting there in the sunshine, Rita began to feel a little better, and wondered whether she would sound silly if she shared her worries with Imogen. She was pretty certain the other girl would understand her apprehension; surely she must be feeling it herself. Rita was glad Debby had decided not to accompany them; she would have scorned to admit to the younger girl that she was afraid of not recognising her own mother. Rita was the oldest of the three, though only by a few months, and Debby the youngest, but as she sat on the sun-warmed bench and watched as the villagers came and went it occurred to Rita that Debby had changed a lot. When they had first arrived at the Canary and Linnet Debby had been prone to nightmares, was painfully shy and most definitely a follower rather than a leader. Perhaps the latter still applied, but she was no longer shy and the nightmares had ceased long since.

I wonder whether it was us or the boys who changed her, Rita thought. But whichever it was, she's just like the rest of us now. She takes things in her stride and if a row erupts she doesn't cry or run away but joins in. Goodness, I'd quite forgotten how even the smallest disagreement used to upset her. Now she can hold her own even when things get nasty, not that they do, or not often at any rate.

She was still pondering this fact when Imogen, who had been gazing thoughtfully into the middle distance, her thoughts obviously miles away, spoke. 'I say, Rita, wouldn't it be strange if our mums walked straight past us! I'm several inches taller than I was when we left home, and I believe you're the same. And we've grown our hair, so I bet we look quite a lot different.' She hesitated, then looked shyly at her companion. 'My mum was rather strict, not a bit like Auntie and Jill . . . but of course she's my mum, so I love her.' She peered into Rita's face. 'That's right, isn't it? You have to love your mum and dad; it's one of the rules. You see, since Dad died Mum's always worked, so probably you know your mum better than I know mine.'

Rita felt an enormous wave of relief break over her and the sun, which had appeared to go behind a cloud at the thought of the imminent meeting, came out again and fell warm on her neatly plaited hair and long bare legs. 'Oh, Imogen, you've made me feel a whole lot better,' she breathed. 'And as for not knowing your mum very well, I sometimes feel I hardly know mine at all. The hotel is one of the best, you see; it's extremely popular and there's always a queue for beds, so Mum has to work awfully hard and when I lived at home I worked awfully hard too. I'm afraid there were times when we had fearful rows and I stormed out of the house because I never seemed to have any time to myself.' She giggled. 'But of course she's had to manage without me now, so when the war's over and I go home I think things will be better between us.'

'Here comes the bus,' Imogen said, jumping to her feet. 'Tell you what, let's have a bet: I bet my mum is first off the bus. Sixpence if I'm right.'

'Sure. And I've got sixpence that says my mum will be first,' Rita said firmly. 'Oh, I see her! She's got a new coat, and a new hat. She and Mrs Clarke must have sat next to each other, and now they're neck and neck!'

'Oh, oh, and my mum's done her hair different,' Imogen squeaked, and then, as the two women descended from the bus, all doubts and fears disappeared. Imogen flew into Mrs Clarke's arms, hugging her tightly whilst tears filled her eyes, though all she could say was: 'Oh, Mum, oh, Mum, it's so good to see you. Oh, I've missed you so much; I hadn't realised how much until I saw you coming off the bus.'

Imogen would have said her mother was down-to-earth and undemonstrative, but as the older woman held her back and smiled reassuringly Imogen saw that tears had filled her eyes too. But Mrs Clarke was not one to give way to emotion. 'My goodness, how you've grown, love,' she said. 'And you've not only grown tall, you've grown pretty. My, I wish your dad could see you now.'

She turned to where Mrs Jeffries was giving Rita a long surprised look. She was an angular woman with bleached blonde hair pulled back from her sharp face. She had light blue eyes, white eyelashes and brows and a peevish expression. However, she greeted her daughter pleasantly, saying briskly, in a strong Liverpool accent: 'Well, Rita, it's plain you've landed on your bleedin' feet! It's nothin' but the best if you live in the country, by the look of you. Oh aye, whiles your poor old mam struggles to put bread on the table, you've been livin' off the fat of the land. But we'd best get to this Canary and Linnet and them ladies what have been lookin' after you, 'cos we've only got till six this evening and then we'll have to be off.'

Imogen and her mother exchanged startled looks. So this was the elegant hotel owner they had heard about! Somehow, Rita had managed to give a very different impression of Mrs Jeffries. But just because she spoke with a local accent, that did not mean Rita need be ashamed of her mother, Imogen thought, and saw the thought reflected in her mother's face. Resolutely, Mrs Clarke tucked her hand into Mrs Jeffries's elbow. 'Off we go,' she said cheerfully, 'I can't wait to see the Canary and Linnet, can you?'

Later, after supper had been enjoyed and farewells said, Rita and Imogen climbed wearily up the stairs, closely followed by Debby, and began to undress. They had been chattering all day, talking about life at the Canary and Linnet, about the village school and about their companions, who had disappeared on some ploy of their own. The girls had listened too, of course, sometimes with amusement and sometimes with dismay, for it appeared that during their journey the mothers had agreed that it would be foolish to keep the truth from their children.

Imogen's little cousin Ruth, who had been evacuated

to North Wales, had been injured when a plane had crashed quite near her school as the children made their way home after classes. 'London's getting the worst of it so far, and the Channel ports,' Mrs Clarke told her daughter. 'Our chaps do their best to intercept the Luftwaffe and stop them getting to the ports in the west – Barrow-in-Furness and Liverpool are the main ones, with both food and armaments going through – but I suppose eventually, when the Nazis have done their worst down south, it'll be our turn.' She had smiled affectionately at her daughter, with the warmth and tenderness which showed her love more clearly than words could do. 'And I don't want you listening to the wireless and deciding you'd better come home,' she added firmly. 'It's not as though there's anything you could do. In fact the truly useful thing is what you are doing, you and your pals: you're keeping hope alive for the next generation. So no heroics, young lady. I can see Auntie and Jill take very good care of you and that's how it should be. We all have our war work, you as much as Mrs Jeffries and I, and yours is to keep safe until it's all over.'

So now, as they got ready for bed, they told Debby all about their day and Imogen admitted that she had been afraid her affection for her mother might have dwindled both because of their time apart and because she loved Auntie, Jill, and the life they were leading so much. 'But it's all right,' she said contentedly. 'I've got enough love for them all.'

Debby looked enquiringly at Rita. The two girls had never got on particularly well because they were totally different, but now Rita smiled and nodded. 'I agree with every word Imogen has said,' she told the younger girl. 'And I'm real sorry that your folk couldn't come to the Linnet, Debby. Tell us how you spent your day!'

Ever since school had started once more the girls had formed the habit of waiting for the boys on the lane which led to the village. Sometimes, of course, none of them went to school, but helped with the harvesting of whatever crop was ripe for market, but on this particular morning both parties were heading for school. As soon as she caught sight of Josh and Woody, their heads together over something, Imogen hailed them. 'What's up, you two?' she said, her voice sharpened with interest. 'Don't say it's the post! I reckon I'm owed at least two letters; if they've come today perhaps my mother will tell me how my cousin Lizzie's birthday went off. They had a party despite the war . . .'

Woody, grinning, shook his head. 'No, it's not the post,' he assured her. 'It's a book Josh's mum sent him; it's really good. We've been taking it in turns to read a page aloud.'

Josh looked up and grinned too, pulling his spectacles down on his nose so that he could look at the girls over the top of them. 'You can borrow it if you like, when we finish . . .' he began, then stopped short. 'Here comes someone; a boy on a bike. But he's going in the wrong direction for school.'

'It's the telegraph boy from town,' Imogen squeaked. 'Oh, God, even the sight of him makes my stomach turn over. Is he heading for the Linnet, do you suppose? Only if so we'll have to go back because it might be from one of our relatives. Was there a raid last night, do you know?'

'Dunno; we left the house before Mrs P turned the wireless on,' Woody said. He brightened. 'But you're right, of course. If the boy's heading for the farm, me and Josh will have to go back and you girls might as well come with us. We can always say the Pilgrims needed help with the early plum crop.'

The three girls laughed. 'Trust you to find an excuse not to go to school,' Imogen said jeeringly. 'Of course, it might be for the cottages further up the lane . . .' She stopped speaking abruptly as the telegraph boy swerved towards the pub, cycled briskly across the car park, leaned his machine against the venerable oak and knocked loudly on the front door.

'Go round the back!' Imogen screamed. 'They're in the kitchen; they probably won't even hear you knock.' The five of them had run across the car park as she spoke and now they galloped round the corner of the house and up to the back door, well ahead of the telegraph boy. Imogen, dispensing with good manners, flung the door open without so much as a knock. 'Auntie, there's a telegram,' she said breathlessly. 'We saw the boy coming up the lane and thought we'd best come home.'

Auntie was washing up the breakfast things whilst Jill dried and put away, and as the five children piled into the kitchen they both stopped what they were doing to stare. 'What on earth . . .' Jill began, and even as Imogen watched the colour seemed to drain from her face and her eyes grew large and dark. Her voice sunk to a whisper. 'My God, suppose it's Laurie!'

As the telegraph boy tumbled into the room clutching the little yellow envelope, Jill would have snatched it from him, but he shook his head chidingly. 'Are you

Miss Marcy?' he asked suspiciously. 'Miss Lavinia Marcy?'

Woody gave a crow of triumph, quite forgetting himself. 'So that's why you wouldn't tell us your Christian name, 'cos you knew folk would call you Lavvy,' he said on a choke of laughter, pointing at Auntie. He turned to his companions. 'Well, kids, now we know who the telegram's for, I suppose we might as well head for school.'

He turned and would have gone out of the kitchen but Imogen, who had gone as pale as Jill, grabbed his arm. 'Wait!' she said urgently. 'Let Auntie open it. Grown-ups don't send telegrams to kids.'

But Auntie had already opened the telegram and was looking rather helplessly at Debby. After a moment she moistened her lips and spoke. 'Debby, dear, this won't come as a complete surprise to you, but I'm afraid it's very bad news.'

Before she could say anything further, Jill had abandoned the drying up and had put her arms tightly round Debby, who turned her head to hide her face against Jill's bosom. 'I s'pose it's Gran,' she said in a muffled voice. 'Is she . . . is she . . .'

'She's very ill,' Auntie said gently. 'She's asked your grandfather to see if you might return to the city so that she can say goodbye. Oh, my dear child, I'm so *very* sorry.'

Debby sighed and gently disengaged herself from Jill's embrace, though she kept hold of her hand. 'Grandma's very old, and in her last letter she said the Red Cross had lent her a wheelchair because she couldn't walk any longer.' She turned to Auntie. 'I'll have to go to her. She must be – very ill,' she said quietly. 'It must be important for Grandpa to send a telegram.'

Auntie laid the telegram down on the table and crossed the room to give Debby a kiss. 'Of course you must go,' she said. 'Jill will go with you, won't you, Jill?'

'Of course I will,' Jill said warmly, and Imogen could tell that the sheer relief of the telegram's not containing bad news about Laurie meant that Jill would have agreed to almost anything. 'We'll go at once.' She turned to Auntie. 'How long can you spare us for?'

Auntie smiled. 'As long as it takes,' she said. 'Now bustle about, everyone . . .' She crossed over to where her coat hung on its peg beside the back door, fished in its pockets and produced a sixpence which she handed to the telegraph boy. 'Off with you, lad,' she said briskly. 'You have work to do just as we have.' She began to push him towards the back door, but he resisted.

'The sender paid a bob for a reply; that's six words and your signature,' he said reproachfully, producing a small pad of paper and a pencil from his jacket pocket.

Auntie glanced helplessly at Jill, then pulled herself together. 'Will be in Liverpool asap Debby,' she said after a moment's thought.

The telegraph boy scribbled and then eyed her reproachfully. 'You've got another word,' he said, but Auntie, chuckling, hustled him out of the door. 'Get back to the post office and send that,' she said. Then she turned to Jill. 'Pack everything you're likely to need in your old blue haversack so that it's easy to carry, and you do the same, Debby dear,' she commanded, 'and you others get off to school. There's nothing more you can do here.'

For the first leg of the journey Jill and Debby scarcely talked at all, for the carriage into which they crammed themselves was filled to capacity, mainly with men and women in uniform. But when they left that train at a small station and found that their connection had been delayed, Debby felt able to talk freely and realised it would be a relief to tell Jill a little more about herself and her grandparents.

'I was born in Leipzig, but when I was five we came to Liverpool and my parents opened a small shop,' she said. 'My father was a tailor, and my mother worked with him. They made what they called bespoke garments, which meant that the customer would go to the shop, tell Mother or Father what they wanted, and have it made to measure. My father often said that they would never grow rich but would, he hoped, always be comfortably off. He planned to buy a place in the country for his retirement, and my brother Aaron contributed his savings when he got a really good job in an import-export business.'

'I see,' Jill said slowly. 'But I thought your parents were killed in Germany, before the war started. I assumed a traffic accident . . .'

'No, not a traffic accident,' Debby interrupted. 'Naturally we had heard of the terrible things which were happening in Germany because it was in all the papers. We still had other relatives in Germany and Austria, and after what happened on "Crystal Night" my parents dispatched my brother to see what he could do to help.'

Jill stared at her companion with mounting horror. 'I hadn't realised you were Jewish, Debby. It's perfectly frightful how your people have suffered,' she said. 'So how did your parents become involved?'

'They had a letter from an uncle telling them that my brother had been taken away to a concentration camp, but he also said that one could buy freedom for one's relatives, if one had the means. My parents would have done anything to save Aaron. They sold up the business, sent me to live with my grandparents and went off to try to rescue Aaron. None of them ever came back. My grandparents told me I must never tell anyone I did not know well that I was Jewish. And now you know as much as I do,' she added with a wry smile. 'We think my parents and my brother are dead, but we don't actually know for certain. They might still be in a Nazi camp. But they've not been in touch . . .'

Jill looked at her, and Debby read in her eyes the compassion which filled her friend. 'I didn't mean to upset you, but I had to tell you because when we see Gran and Grandpa they'll assume that you know,' Debby said gently. As she spoke, the train for which they waited drew up alongside and they both rose to their feet.

'I'm glad you told me,' Jill said softly beneath the rattle and roar of the train. 'Dear Debby, what a load you've had to carry all these months! But I'm sure if you told Immy and Rita they'd understand and support you. There'd be no need to go into details.'

'I wouldn't mind telling Immy; in fact it would be a relief. Sometimes I think she already knows,' Debby said as they climbed aboard the train. 'Josh does; I didn't have to tell him, he guessed from something I said, but he won't tell a soul. He's very quiet, isn't he, Jill? Very – very discreet.'

'He is,' Jill said. 'Look, Debby dear, would you rather I didn't come to the hospital? It could be easier for you to talk without a stranger listening.'

They were sitting side by side, and at Jill's words Debby reached out and gripped her hand tightly. '*Please* come,' she said urgently. 'I – I can't face seeing Gran and Grandpa alone.'

'Then of course I'll come with you,' Jill said, and presently, as the compartment began to fill up, they talked of other things until Liverpool Lime Street was reached.

Jill and Debby were shocked by the bomb damage, but hurried to the hospital just in time for old Mrs Viner to take her granddaughter's hand and murmur some words in a language which Jill guessed was German, though its import was clear enough, for the tired eyes which fixed on Debby's face were full of affection. Then, within moments, her old head with the thin strands of grey hair brushed across the scalp had fallen sideways, and the nurse who had accompanied them to the bedside sighed and indicated that the visitors should leave. 'She's gone, my dear,' she said, turning to Mr Viner. 'In such pain she has been; you would not want her to linger longer. A good woman she was, and had a good, quick end. Now I think you should take these two young women to Sister's office. I will arrange for a tray of tea to be brought, and the rabbi will be along later so that you may make funeral arrangements. You'll see the almoner, no doubt. She will deal with any queries you may have.'

Despite his grief, Mr Viner proved to be both intelligent and resourceful. He explained to Jill that Jewish funerals always follow a death as rapidly as possible, and he had already made all the arrangements. Jill suspected that Debby's grandfather was a good deal younger than his wife, or perhaps it was pain rather than years which had aged her, but at any rate she thought him perfectly capable of managing on his own. He agreed with alacrity that he should come and visit them the following summer. 'Though I shall now move back into the city, where I can be of some use,' he told them. 'I could be a firewatcher, an air raid warden, a home guard . . . anything the authorities need.' He smiled engagingly at Jill. 'An old man I may be – well, an old man I am – but I can still do my bit.'

Three days later, Debby and Jill got off the train and headed for the bus which would take them the rest of the way home. They were just in time to climb aboard before the conductor tinged the bell, and they reached the village as dusk was deepening, delighted and surprised to find Auntie and Imogen waiting for them. Auntie seized their shoulder bags and heartily kissed their cheeks. Jill flung her arms around Imogen, who was hugging Debby. 'How wonderful to see you; we never expected to be met,' she said. 'We couldn't let you know which train we'd be catching because of all the changes – we could have arrived here at any time. Yet you still managed to meet the bus; I do think you're clever!'

Auntie nodded. 'Yes, but if you were going to catch a bus at all, it would have to be this one,' she observed. 'I do hope Rita's remembered to take the macaroni cheese out of the oven, otherwise it'll be hard as nails. But of course we'll brew fresh tea and I can always make up some egg sandwiches; the hens have been doing us proud whilst you've been away. Come on, let's hurry!'

Chapter Seven

Laurie had been on duty for five days, and when the call to scramble had gone out that morning he was so befuddled that he had pulled on his uniform over his pyjamas. In fact he had not woken up properly until he was sliding back the Perspex hood of his Hurricane and climbing into the pilot's seat. It was early, and though the sun was up, just edging over the flat Lincolnshire horizon, Laurie was still quite cold and knew he would be colder once he was airborne. Before him, Dave's Hurricane roared into life, tore across the runway and lifted until it was well clear of the trees which surrounded the airfield; and then, as Laurie always put it to himself, the plane headed for the stars. Not that there were stars out now; what they were heading for was their ceiling of 34,000 feet.

As he pulled the stick back the nose lifted like a hound on the scent and he retracted the undercarriage, glancing around him as he flew. He was intent upon gaining as much height as possible so as to have the advantage over the enemy. If the Spitfires and Hurricanes could manoeuvre themselves into the right position they could pounce on the Luftwaffe without being dazzled by the rising sun, always a problem when a dawn raid came from the east. No doubt by now they would have overflown the coastal defences and the bomber pilots would doubtless think that they could attack their targets with impunity. The big clumsy Dorniers, the Me110s, and the Ju87s, no doubt with their bomb bays loaded, would be relying on their fighter escort to keep them safely in the air. Well, they could bloody well forget that; he was so high now that he guessed the German pilots would be scanning the air around and below them and would scarcely bother to look up, believing that their early start would give them a degree of immunity from the British fighters.

It was still cold in the tiny cockpit but Laurie knew from experience that heat would come when the action started. And here they came at last, black against the rising sun, perhaps heading for Liverpool or Barrow-in-Furness. Well, they would not get there, not if he and his fellow fighter pilots could help it. Quickly he rubbed both hands across his uniformed knees, to dry his sweaty palms, then grabbed the joystick and began to tilt it. He checked that there was no one in his path and dropped towards the nearest Dornier like a hawk to its prey. Beside him, perhaps no more than thirty yards away, he saw Dave in the same position but with a Heinkel in his sights. Laurie steadied his aircraft, which seemed very small and light compared with the heavy bombers, and raked the enemy with bullets from the eight Browning machine guns mounted in the wings. He saw the big plane stagger, then burst into flames as he attacked the fuselage, saw the port wing come up and the starboard one point to earth. He repeated the mantra he had taught himself for just such an occasion and had used now many times. 'It's just an aircraft violating our air space; I'm killing a plane not a person; if there are men aboard they'll bale out . . . here comes another!'

He had a Messerschmitt correctly placed for an attack.

He could even see the pilot crouching over his instruments, unaware of what was about to happen. Laurie's finger was on the firing button and he was pouring a stream of lead into the Messerschmitt, then jigging violently to the right to evade retaliation, when he remembered what a friend had said to him. 'My CO told us that the Huns are yellow, so when we confronted one in battle we should just drive straight at him, as though intending to ram, and he'd fall away and return to base.' His pal thought it a foolish trick and was not surprised, upon returning to his airfield, to find that his CO had bought it. In fact, he said, all they found of him was his shirt buttons.

Laurie was grinning at the recollection of the story, which had doubtless circulated in every Mess in the country, when he saw that he must have hit a vital spot: the Messerschmitt was losing height rapidly, with smoke streaming out of its tail. Laurie killed the thought that there were men in there, men desperate to get out; men just like him, longing to live. Useless to dwell on it. He slid away from another encounter and began, once more, to gain height.

By this time dog fights were taking place wherever you looked; the German escort had arrived, though a little late, to protect their bombers. Laurie glanced at the fuel gauge, then nodded to himself. The big Heinkel had had enough and was returning the way it had come. He must go to Dave's assistance, follow the bomber, down it if possible . . . He saw out of the corner of his eye another machine in a steep nosedive, flames roaring out of it. Sickly, he remembered stories he had heard in the Mess, stories which spoke of pilots who never flew without a pistol shoved in their waistband or flying boot, so that they could use it on themselves if the plane took fire, anything rather than the agony of burning to death. They had all seen the wrecks of men . . . he dragged his mind away from scenes which were too ghastly to consider; he had no pistol. If only one could slide back the Perspex hood . . . simply jump, pray your chute opened . . . but even if it did not it would be a quick, clean death, better than . . .

As though the thought had given birth to the fact, something bounced off the nose of his aircraft. It was a chunk of someone's wing and the next moment he realised, with horror, that it had gone clean through the propeller. He would have to bale out, but first of all he must put the plane into a glide, try to get clear of the carnage which surrounded him. He knew pilots who had baled out too soon in the middle of a scrimmage only to find the sky full of obstacles, and had suffered for it. He would keep the plane on an even keel for as long as possible, and would not jump until the sky was relatively clear. It demanded an iron will and a degree of self-control which he was not at all sure he possessed, but he had infinite faith in his aircraft and told himself he would come off all right, provided he kept his head and didn't jump too soon out of sheer funk.

At that very moment his sweaty hands slipped on the joystick, as though the Hurricane was trying to tell him that the moment had come. She was pulling towards earth now, but a quick glance all around him showed that the sky was relatively clear. He had slid back the hood as soon as he had seen the propeller go and now he looked earthwards. Where was he? He realised he had not the faintest idea, could not see anything but fields and woods . . . ah, there was a river below. At least he knew he had not crossed the sea; the ground beneath him was his native land. Laurie began to pull himself out of his seat and gave the Hurricane, whose nose had begun to point downwards as soon as his hand left the stick, a grateful pat. She had been a good little plane and he was sad to part from her, but part they must. His weight tipped her to one side, he saw the wing go down, poised himself, then jumped.

The rush of air should not have been a surprise, but somehow it was; somehow he was not prepared to be seized by the slipstream and forced to do a double somersault. Beneath him the fields, the river and the woods whirled and suddenly, for no apparent reason, he thought of Jill: sweet, generous, and beautiful in a calm and steadying way.

As though seeing a picture of her was an omen, he seemed to hear her voice at the same moment, cool, comforting, yet urgent. 'Pull the ripcord!' Jill's voice said. 'Pull the bloody ripcord!'

Before she had finished giving the command Laurie had obeyed. To his relief the canopy unfolded, though the jerk it gave him was frighteningly hard and abrupt. Then it took him a moment or two to gather his senses and look around him. The sky was almost clear except for one other parachute drifting down towards earth, probably several miles off, and a plane on fire hurtling downwards and clearly out of control. Laurie stared, but could not tell whether it was British or German. He was low enough now to see that he would come to earth on farmland, and he thought, thankfully, that once he had got rid of the chute he should be able to walk to the farmhouse and telephone to the airfield to give his position.

But the ground was coming up awfully fast; he remembered lectures on how to steer a parachute but could not remember any helpful details. At least he would not be descending into enemy country . . . and suddenly he realised that there were people below him: a couple of kids, a man with a pitchfork, a fat woman in an apron and a girl in the practical clothing of the Women's Land Army. He waved to them and the Land Girl waved back, but the old man with the pitchfork made jabbing motions and Laurie grinned to himself. Britain was dangerously short of armaments, but this was the first time he had considered a pitchfork as a weapon of war.

Now he could see the river Waveney and the outline of Oulton Broad, which meant that the town on the horizon would be Lowestoft. He landed with a crash amidst the reeds on the edge of the river and took a hasty step, trying to avoid being enfolded in the falling canopy, but as he put his right foot to the ground his boot turned sideways and he heard a crack and felt a sudden sharp stab of pain. Unable to stop himself, he gave a gasp and a yelp and fell heavily sideways, giggling helplessly despite the pain as the silken folds of the canopy enveloped him. He was crawling out of the muddy reeds on to the bank, still wrapped in the canopy, when he felt a thump followed by a sharp pain in his shoulder, felt blood begin to trickle down. He realised he had not buttoned up his flying jacket and that whatever had hit him had inflicted quite a lot of damage, though he heard a voice – he presumed it was the Land Girl's – expostulating. 'Have you a care, Mr

Grundy. You can't see nothin' through that there silk; he might be as English as you or I.'

This advice was ignored as a voice cried triumphantly: 'Come you here, my fine feller! I'm a Home Guard I am, and we's a force to be reckoned with. See how you like life in Britain behind bars.' There followed a wheezy chuckle. 'I've heared tell you Nazis allus say "For you the war is over." Well in't that the truth?'

The pitchfork jabbed again and Laurie gave an indignant shout. 'Stop that!' he commanded. 'I'm as English as you are. Get me out of this perishing parachute, but go carefully; I think I've broken my ankle.'

They disentangled him from the parachute and the Land Girl and the old man helped him to the farmhouse, for he could not put any weight on his right leg, and his shoulder needed to be cleaned and dressed. Mr Grundy, told he must apologise for his attack, was unrepentant. 'Us can't take no risks; for all I know you could ha' been Herr Hitler hisself,' the old man said. 'I were only doin' me duty; you should ha' hollered out the moment you reached land. I only did what were right and proper.'

The Land Girl, slim and blonde, shook a chiding finger at the old man. 'You never give him a chance to say so much as one word before you jabbed him with that there pitchfork,' she said reproachfully. 'I dare say it's the first time in your life that you've ever apologised to anyone for anything, but that'll larn you! Come along, own up that you were mistaken.'

As they helped him towards the farmhouse Mr Grundy stuck out his lower lip and mumbled something which Laurie could not catch, but the Land Girl must have heard, because she gave a stifled giggle and as they helped him into the farmhouse kitchen and into a chair she rounded on the old man once more.

'Everyone make mistakes, Mr Grundy; you in't the only one,' she said reproachfully. 'Now you can just eat humble pie. That's a dish you've never tasted before, so make the most of it.'

By now Laurie felt so ill and weak that he had little interest in the old man's humiliation, but he was forced to intervene because he could see that getting an apology out of Mr Grundy would be like extracting teeth. 'It's all right, Mr Grundy; only don't go being so free with your pitchfork again,' he said wearily. 'Do you realise you could have got me in the face? You might have blinded me; killed me even.'

Mr Grundy snorted, had begun to say what a fuss to make over a little scratch, when the fat woman in the apron, who was Mrs Threadgold, the farmer's wife, interrupted. 'Yes, that's typical of you, my man,' she said briskly. 'Off you go and get on with your work.' She turned to Laurie. 'Ginny will telephone to your CO if you'll give her the number, and you can drink the cup of tea I'm making whilst I find some dry clothes for you to change into. My son Bob's in the air force . . .' she cast a quick glance at him, 'and he's about the same size as you, so you can borrow his togs.' She smiled and shook her head as Laurie began feebly to say he was quite all right. 'That you in't,' she said firmly. 'You can't see yourself, but where you in't covered with blood, you're covered with mud. So we'll clean up that wound in your shoulder and I'll lend you Bob's stuff so long as you promise to return it as soon as you can. Don't worry, we won't take off your trousers, 'cos of that there ankle. I reckon they'll send an ambulance from the nearest airfield, which may take an hour or two. No point in you sitting around waiting in them wet clothes.'

Laurie accepted the tea eagerly and drained the cup, but found he could not fancy the shortbread biscuits which were offered. He was suddenly terribly tired, and when the Land Girl, Ginny, had made the telephone call and told him he would be picked up in a couple of hours, he was grateful for his hostess's suggestion that she should take some bedding through to the front parlour and let him sleep on the sofa until the RAF team arrived.

'Where did the old chap go?' Laurie asked as Ginny and the farmer's wife helped him through into the parlour. He gave a feeble chuckle. 'Home Guard, is he? Well, if another flier arrives on your land, tell him to keep his pitchfork to himself. So far as I can recall we are supposed to treat the enemy who fall into our hands as prisoners of war, not lumps of manure!'

Mrs Threadgold laughed, but nodded. 'He's a proud man, our Mr Grundy. He won't risk having to apologise twice in one lifetime.' She turned back the blankets she had spread on an old-fashioned plush sofa. 'In you get. I put in a hot water bottle wrapped in a couple of meal sacks, so you won't soak the sofa or get that all muddy. Now you just go off to sleep and I'll give you a call when your transport arrives.'

Laurie was glad to obey, but for some time sleep refused to come. Over and over he slid back the Perspex hood, steadied the Hurricane on an even course and waited for the right moment to jump. Once, in a dream, he landed on the spire of St Nicholas's church in

Lowestoft, and Mr Grundy came along and hooked him down with his pitchfork. Several times he avoided the town but landed in the middle of Oulton Broad, and when he would have swum to shore a man in Home Guard uniform prevented him, saying he would have to swim back to his airfield because no Germans were allowed here.

When at last the transport arrived the young MO grinned at the neat dressing on Laurie's shoulder. But when he tried to take off his right flying boot Laurie's left leg kicked out so suddenly and unexpectedly that the MO could not dodge. 'You've got me right in the courting tackle,' he said reproachfully. 'Bang go my chances of fathering a large family.'

Laurie apologised, but warned the MO that his foot and his boot seemed to have become inextricably attached. 'Oh well, the boot's as good as any temporary cast for holding the bone in position,' the MO said as two hefty airmen began to load Laurie on to a stretcher, despite his protests. 'Best keep it as still as possible until we can get you hospitalised. Have you thanked these good people for taking care of you? By the way, what's under the shoulder dressing? The blood's seeped through, so I suppose you got tangled up in the canopy and jabbed yourself with your knife when trying to cut yourself free.'

Laurie, who had completely forgotten the penknife everyone carried in order to cut themselves free of the parachute should they land in enemy territory, or become entangled and be unable to use the release, muttered something appropriate; he did not intend to admit that he had been apprehended and mistaken for a Nazi by an extremely elderly member of the Home Guard.

At the hospital in Norwich he had to endure a great deal of discomfort as he and his boot parted company, but after the ankle had been realigned, dressed and plastered he was happy to get into the bed allotted to him, to have some hot soup, and go to sleep.

It proved to be a dream-haunted sleep, however, and, waking in the small hours in a sweat of fear, imagining himself pulling the ripcord and finding that the canopy remained obstinately closed, he caught the eye of a passing nurse and asked her if she could rustle up a cup of tea.

The nurse, saying that she was about to have one herself, agreed to bring him a cup and, when she did so, sat down on the end of his bed – a strictly forbidden proceeding – and asked gently: 'Nightmares? We've had a great many chaps who've had to bale out, some who've got pretty badly injured doing so. They find it difficult to sleep for nightmares at first, but don't worry, they'll grow less and less terrible as time passes. Most of the night staff understand and will stop for a chat and a cuppa whenever possible. Do you have a girlfriend? What's her name? Is she near enough to visit you?'

'Yes. She's called Jill, and she's not too far away,' Laurie said wearily. 'In my dreams she keeps telling me to pull the ripcord . . .' he grinned tiredly at the nurse, 'only either it won't work or I can't find it. She shouts and shouts, but the wind carries her voice away . . .' He turned his face into the pillow and said nothing for several moments as he fought with his emotions. Finally he turned back to the girl perched on the end of his bed. 'It'll come right, won't it?' he said huskily. 'I've never suffered from bad dreams before; well, not since I was a little boy. Then it was crocodiles in the bath or lobsters in the lavatory pan.'

The nurse giggled. 'My boyfriend's on an armed trawler patrolling the North Sea. It's very dangerous – just like your job – so I have my share of nightmares. What with U-boats and Nazi craft sneaking out of ports on the Continent, and the weather . . . well, I expect you can guess how it is; nightmares come easy. But I'll tell you something which should stop your bad dreams as nothing else could.' She jerked a thumb at the cage they had put around his foot to keep the blankets off it. 'That'll mean you'll be on leave for at least a few months. Oh, they'll maybe find you work to do, but it won't be flying, not until you're A1 and that foot is completely mended.'

Laurie felt a wave of relief rush over him. Weeks and weeks when he would not have to race for his Hurricane, leap into the seat and defend his country! Heaps of time to visit Jill at the Canary and Linnet whenever the air force had not found him anything else to do! He grinned at the nurse. 'Thanks,' he said fervently. A doubt shook him. 'Are you sure, though? Douglas Bader lost both his legs – I'm not sure when – and he still carried out sorties.'

'That was different. With you, we're talking about a break which hasn't even begun to heal. Douglas Bader lost his legs well before the war even started.'

'Oh. Right. Understood,' Laurie said, and smiled gratefully as the girl stood up. 'Thanks very much, nurse. I do believe I'll be able to sleep now.'

Laurie remained in Norfolk for the three months it took his ankle to heal, and during that time the relationship between him and Jill warmed and deepened. In fact, by the time Christmas had come and gone it was clear to everyone that the young people were in love and would marry when circumstances allowed. Clear to everyone except Imogen, that was. She was still shy in Laurie's presence but watched him with glowing eyes whenever he came to the Linnet, laughed at his jokes, and always saw that he got his share of any treats going; generally showing, as Rita disgustedly put it, that she still had a crush on Pilot Officer Laurence Matthews.

As soon as Laurie was fit to fly Jill began to fear that he would be posted once more to some other part of England, for by now the Battle of Britain was over and won so far as fighter planes were concerned. Now the Luftwaffe were concentrating on night raids and heavy bombers. Liverpool had been targeted around Christmas and the air had fairly buzzed with telephone calls, but though the bombs had caused considerable damage none of the girls' friends or relatives had been hurt.

When Laurie next turned up at the Linnet, he had significant news. 'I'm being posted, but not to another fighter station,' he told the assembled company. He caught hold of Rufus's front paws, for the dog was welcoming him ecstatically. 'Down, boy; I don't want paw marks all over my number ones.' He had arrived at supper time and Auntie was aware that all the girls were listening eagerly, spoons poised over the plums which she had bottled the previous summer.

Jill spoke first. 'Oh, Laurie, does that mean you won't be flying?' she asked eagerly. 'I know your ankle is fine now, but perhaps the MO put in a report to say that it needed more time . . . that would be wonderful.' She was smiling hopefully, but her face fell as Laurie shook his head. 'No, you've got the wrong end of the stick. To be honest, old girl, the last thing I would want is to be grounded. As the air force is always telling us, it costs a great deal of money to train a bloke to fly successfully, and now what they're wanting are pilots for the heavy bombers which will teach Germany, eventually, what it's like to be a target. I'm to go to Church Broughton where I'll be trained to fly Wellingtons – Wimpeys, the fellers call them. I've no definite date yet, won't have one till our rail passes come through – Dave's coming to Church Broughton as well – so I've put in for a spot of leave.'

Jill's face, which had fallen almost comically, brightened. 'Oh, Laurie, remember we've talked about Eve, who was my best friend throughout our schooldays?' she said eagerly. 'She's in the Land Army now but she still lives at home. She's engaged to an armourer in the air force so she spends all her spare time with him, which means we've not met for ages, but of course I've told her all about you in my letters. Dear Laurie, if Auntie can manage without me for two or three days I'd love to take you to visit Eve and her mother. Her brother's in the army and her father works for the Min of Ag in London, so they've plenty of spare bedrooms. They'd make us welcome, I know it.' She turned to Auntie. 'Could you manage without me for two or three days? Oh, please say you can!'

Auntie pretended to consider, head on one side, then nodded slowly. 'Of course the girls can't help in the pub, but I'm sure Jacky will be pleased to earn a few bob extra,' she said. She smiled benignly at her niece. 'You'd best go into the village as soon as you finish your supper and give young Eve a ring.'

Jill ran round the table and gave Auntie an impulsive hug. 'Oh, Auntie, you're the kindest woman in the world,' she said. 'And I'll work twice as hard when I get back to make up for being away. But I'll go and ring Eve and okay it with her mother.' She ran over to the back door and began to put on her outdoor clothing, kicking off her slippers and thrusting her feet into rubber boots. 'What's Church Broughton like?' she asked as Laurie opened the door and began to usher her into the yard. 'Is it far—'

The slamming of the back door cut the sentence in half. Auntie pulled the jug of custard towards her and raised her eyebrows. 'Any more custard, anyone?' she asked.

Imogen watched enviously as the days passed and Jill prepared for her holiday. She just wished that Laurie had shown an interest in her own family, but the sensible part of her mind knew that this was very unlikely to happen. After all, he had shown no interest in Jill's best friend – it had been she who had made the suggestion that they should spend his leave with someone called Eve, a name which Imogen had never heard Jill utter before. But it was no use wishing, so when Jill left, in a flutter of excitement and wearing her very best dress, she had waved her off as though Laurie meant nothing to her, and had promised Jill that she would help Auntie in every way she could.

The three days of Laurie's leave were icy cold, and passed, for Imogen at any rate, on leaden feet, and of course when Jill came back and Laurie went off to Church Broughton Imogen had to face the fact that she might not see him again, perhaps until the war was over. She knew he wrote to Jill, but visits over such a distance were impossible, and as spring arrived life at the Canary and Linnet became so interesting that she only thought of Laurie a couple of times a week instead of many times a day.

May dawned brilliantly and with it came the worst raids on Liverpool so far. For eight days the Luftwaffe concentrated on smashing the city, the docks and the rest of Merseyside. During this time Imogen thought of Laurie not at all but spent sleepless nights worrying over what was happening to her mother and other relatives still living in the port. She begged Auntie to let her return to the city, promising faithfully to arrive in daylight and leave before the nightly raid began, but both Auntie and Jill were adamant. Rita and Debby had joined Imogen in her pleas for a return to the city, but though Auntie and Jill were sympathetic Auntie was adamant that whilst the girls might invite their relatives to visit the Canary and Linnet – she would put them up for as many days as they cared to stay – she would not allow a return to a city under fire.

'What good would it do the war effort if you three were killed?' Jill had asked. 'Well, it would be four, because naturally I would go with you. So I'm afraid for the time being you'll have to make do with telephone calls and letters. Comfort yourselves with the thought that when I spoke to Laurie the other night he said one of his pals speaks good German and listens in to their radio transmissions. The Nazis call an all-out attack on one city a blitzkreig – blitz for short – and he says the attack, though ferocious, never seems to last above a week.'

By the time it was safe to return to Liverpool both Mrs Clarke and old Mr Viner had telephoned to say that there was little point in Debby and Imogen's returning to the city because though the damage was almost unbelievable they had been lucky. Mr Viner, though he came into the city every night to fulfil his duties as a firewatcher, was still living on the Wirral in a neat and undamaged little house, whilst Mrs Clarke had moved in with Imogen's eldest sister and said cheerfully that they had been fortunate; bombs had fallen close, windows were glassless and boarded up, but otherwise all was much as Imogen remembered it.

Rita's mother, however, told a different story and had peremptorily ordered that her daughter should return to her for at least a week if not more. *The worst of the raids are over, but my boarding house is my living, and I need all the help I can get to bring it back to what it were before them bleeding Huns attacked*, she said in her letter to Auntie requesting Rita's return.

> *She won't be much good I don't suppose, being only a kid, but she's better than nothing. Two of me boarders was killed when their factory was flattened and others have moved out – too near the docks – so I'm short-handed. There isn't no glass in any of the windows and you wouldn't believe the dust what's got into everything. I'd have young Rita back for good, only folk would say I were bringing her into danger and I won't be having that. What gets me most is the unfairness. Lavender Lodge, what's only a few yards up the road, is owned by a Jewish couple, the Sterns, and they get all the help they need. I telled the ARP warden it weren't fair – they're foreigners after all – but he said as how it were their friends and relatives rallying round and nothing to do*

with the authorities. He said as how I ought to put the word about, but so far not one of me relatives have so much as put a nose around the door, which is why I'll have our Reet back to help clear up.

Auntie had been reading the letter to herself, for Rita had handed it to her silently. She waited a moment, until Imogen and Debby had thundered upstairs to do their room, before she spoke. 'Your mother needs you, poppet. But it's only for a week or so after all, and everyone's going to be missing school because getting the hay in is more important than two times two makes four. Do you want Jill to go with you, or one of the girls? Only I don't know that I ought to offer their services just in case something bad was to happen . . .'

Rita broke in before Auntie could finish the sentence. The letter was bad enough since Mrs Jeffries referred to the boarding house whereas Rita had always called it the hotel, but actually to have anyone from here see the place would be unbearable. She shook her head decisively. 'No thanks, Auntie; Mam wouldn't like it. Strangers seeing our home, you know, when it's not at its best.' She had looked anxiously at the older woman. 'She – she won't try to keep me, will she? Of course if the war was over it would be different, but . . .'

'Of course she won't. My dear child, she actually says she only wants you for a week or so,' Auntie said quickly. 'But we'd best not linger; run upstairs and pack a few essentials – pyjamas, toothbrush, that sort of thing – and then I'll come with you to the station and buy your ticket. A return, naturally.'

Considerably cheered by Auntie's conviction that Mrs Jeffries would not try to keep her longer than a week, Rita did as she was told, said a rather subdued goodbye to her friends – they were already working in the hayfield – and when they reached the station clung to Auntie's neck for a few moments in a very untypical way. 'Just a week, Auntie; I'll be back in just a week,' she muttered. 'Only it will seem like a year.'

It was the first time Rita had returned to the city since she had left it in 1939, and she was appalled by the extent of the damage the Luftwaffe had inflicted. She was also shocked at the state of the boarding house, which seemed to have shrunk in her absence, and far from being the smart hotel which she had described so often to Imogen and Debby was clearly a cheap lodging house used mainly by seamen waiting to join their ships. Mrs Jeffries was living in what had once been the kitchen, and when she had got over the shock she had felt upon seeing Bide-a-Wee Rita decided that her best hope of escaping back to the Canary and Linnet would be to take over the task of cleaning up. Mrs Jeffries seemed to have abandoned all thought of doing any work herself and agreed with everything her daughter suggested, provided it meant that she herself could spend all day gossiping and drinking tea with others in a similar position. By the end of the week Rita and her mother had organised everything and the place was looking as respectable as it was ever going to be. They had employed a young boy to do the actual clearing, found a builder who agreed to replace at least some of the glass, and Rita had reinstated the girl who had been helping her mother, telling that lady brusquely that it was no use whining; if she wanted her living back then she must delve into her Post Office savings and pay at least a small wage to anyone willing to work for her.

Furthermore, the weather was kind and very soon their rooms were full, her mother had been persuaded to start cooking breakfasts and Rita had informed her that she now intended to return to the Canary and Linnet. 'You, Lizzie and Matt can manage very well without me now,' she said. 'Lizzie is quite happy to have a shakedown in the box room, since her own home was bombed. Don't pull such a face, Mam. You know very well that if I came home for good I'd insist on having my own room and that would be one less for you to let.' Rita grinned to herself at the look on her mother's face. Mrs Jeffries was fat and lazy and did not like being forced to work. Once I'm gone poor little Lizzie will find herself doing Mam's work as well as her own, Rita thought, but I'm damned if I'll stay here to become Mam's slave. I'll be off on the first train tomorrow, so I'd best drop Auntie a line; maybe someone will meet me, you never know!

Back at the Canary and Linnet, Rita reflected that the experience had taught her a lesson: she knew that when the war ended she would not want to become a house slave to her mother. Before then I'll have a talk with Auntie – or maybe with Jill – to see whether I might be able to get a job somewhere locally, she planned. It's not that I don't love my mother, I think it's more her way of life that I don't like. Now if I ran Bide-a-Wee, I'd charge a bit more, but I'd give a bit more as well. Look at Lavender Lodge. Mam hates Mrs Stern because they're successful and I know they take a lot of people who would otherwise come to us, but Mam doesn't seem to notice how beautifully clean the Lodge is and how businesslike, yet friendly, the Sterns are. They're foreigners of course, taking the bread from our mouths you could say, but Mam just lets it happen and never fights back. If I were in charge I'd put it about that Lavender Lodge is owned by a Jew-boy, and say the food was poor and the accommodation none too clean. All's fair in business, they say, and I bet Mrs Stern tells her boarders that our place is a real rat-run. It would be quite fun to run a successful hotel, but no fun at all to run a scruffy boarding house. Still, no point in worrying; I'm back where I want to be, and Mam won't winkle me out again without a fight.

It was mid-May and Laurie and his fellow pilots from the Lincolnshire airfield to which he and Dave had been posted when they finished their training had been attacking targets on the Continent when Laurie's plane was heavily damaged by flak whilst overflying Paris. The next time he and Jill spoke on the telephone he told her that his aircraft was in for repairs, which meant he might get a forty-eight at the weekend; was there any chance of her coming over to Lincolnshire so they could spend some time together?

Auntie, smiling at her niece's eagerness, agreed only a little ruefully, the girls promised to be extra helpful and Woody said he would come over if needed to undertake tasks such as chopping wood, carting coal and helping the cellar man, jobs he considered too much for the girls' feeble strength. 'It's odd, when you think we're only a few years younger than Jill, yet it still takes two of us to carry in the log basket, or a big sack of spuds, whereas Jill can do it with one hand tied behind her,'

Rita said after school on Friday as she and Imogen tottered across the yard with a sack of swedes to put into the woodshed. 'Of course I want Jill to be able to see her boyfriend, but—'

'He's not . . .' Imogen began, and then seeing the look in her friend's eyes changed what she had been about to say, 'he's not able to get away often,' she substituted. 'And it's nice to know Jill will be enjoying herself, and not just working like a slave to keep us all fed and watered. And a forty-eight isn't very long.'

'True,' Rita said absently. 'It's a pity Laurie can't come all the way to the Linnet . . . then you'd get a chance to see lover-boy in person, and—'

'Shut up!' Imogen screamed. 'If you start, Rita Jeffries, I'll . . . I'll . . .'

But Rita, laughing, said she was sorry and diplomatically changed the subject.

And then when they retraced their steps a surprise awaited them. They burst into the kitchen, already asking Auntie who owned the rather natty sports car which was parked only feet from the back door, to find Jill and two men in RAF uniform sitting at the big kitchen table and drinking tea whilst Auntie placidly buttered scones.

'Laurie!' Imogen squeaked, then put her hands over her hot cheeks. 'Jill! How ever . . .'

'I got a lift from a friend,' Laurie explained. 'So you won't have to lose Jill after all. Auntie says she can put me up for a couple of nights.'

'And the car?' Rita said, voicing Imogen's thoughts. 'Is it yours, Laurie? Will you take me for a spin?'

'I wish it were mine, but actually I've only got an eighth share in it,' Laurie explained, and Imogen, who had not seen him for many months, saw that he was pale and strained, not at all like the Laurie who had fought to keep Britain safe in his little Hurricane, and had never seemed conscious of danger. 'Oh, I should introduce you.' Laurie struck his forehead with the back of his hand. 'Ricky, the fair one's Rita and the dark one is Imogen. Girls, Ricky's my tail gunner and it was his idea to car-share. So when the CO said we could have a forty-eight we worked out a route across country, and when Jill telephoned me this morning I told her not to set off because I was coming to the Linnet instead of her coming to me. We arrived half an hour ago.'

'And now you know as much as the rest of us,' Auntie said, glancing fondly at her pink-cheeked niece. 'Debby is upstairs, making up the bed in the spare room, and you two can make yourselves useful. Ricky here – I'm sorry, Ricky, I don't know your surname – has just popped in for a mug of tea and a scone, and then he'll be on his way and you can have Laurie all to yourselves.'

Rita was beginning to say that no doubt he and Jill would catch the bus into town and see a flick, or go dancing, when Debby came clattering down the stairs and burst into the kitchen. She beamed at the assembled company, dusted her hands rather ostentatiously, and slid into a vacant chair.

'Bed made up, floor brushed and furniture dusted,' she announced. She turned to the two young men. 'It was my turn, you see. We do everything by turns: housework, a bit of cooking – Jill taught us to make bread and butter pudding, with chopped up carrots instead of sultanas – and yard work, like feeding the pigs and the poultry . . .'

'And shopping,' Imogen broke in eagerly. She shot a sideways look at Laurie under her lashes. He was grinning, and looked, she thought, more handsome than ever.

'Very praiseworthy; the sharing, I mean,' Laurie said. He took a scone off the plate Auntie was offering. 'Thanks very much, Auntie.' He turned to Ricky. 'You're in for a treat; these ladies make the best scones I've ever tasted. God knows how they do it with rationing and restrictions and all; I suppose they have some secret recipe.'

Auntie put the plate of scones down in the middle of the table and grinned. 'That's right; the hens have been laying well,' she said, not bothering to explain further that scones made with eggs were extra rich. She smiled across the table at Ricky. 'I understand from the lad here that you weren't able to get in touch with your mother to tell her you were coming, so I'll give you half a dozen scones which she may be glad of. And Imogen here can make you a couple of sandwiches to eat on the way.'

Imogen jumped eagerly to her feet and went across to the pantry, returning with a newly baked loaf, a pat of butter and a jar of strawberry jam. 'We all went in the cart to the Ellises' farm and picked the strawberries, so Mr Ellis gave Auntie a big basketful to make into jam, because we'd all worked so hard,' Imogen said, addressing herself to Ricky, though she was well aware of Laurie's laughing eyes on her and felt the heat rise in her cheeks once more. 'At the village school they call us the strawberry dodgers, because we don't have to attend classes when we're helping on the land.' Out of the corner of her eye she saw Laurie grinning.

'From what I've heard you lasses don't just help with the strawberry harvest at Ellis's, you throw yourself into any farm work that's needed,' he told her, 'because of course it's more fun than lessons. Jill said . . .'

Jill interrupted hurriedly. 'Don't tease them, Laurie; they work like slaves, and so do the boys up at Pilgrim Farm. Any time now they'll be cutting the hay and the girls will be first at the field to turn the crop as soon as it's ready.' She watched approvingly as Imogen sliced and buttered bread and spread strawberry jam with a prodigal hand. 'Don't know where we'd be without our excuses,' she finished.

'Wish we could take time off for harvesting,' Laurie said wistfully.

Imogen lowered her eyes to her task. She was terrified that Laurie might realise how she felt about him, and brought up another topic of conversation. 'Oh, that reminds me: how's Dave?'

She was looking at Laurie as she spoke, and saw his lips quiver before he turned his gaze away from her and across to Jill. There was a moment's uncomfortable silence, and then it was Jill who replied. 'Hopefully, in a German POW camp. I didn't tell you before, girls, but Dave was shot down somewhere over France. But Laurie saw his parachute open, didn't you, Laurie? And he saw British Spitfires follow him down. Only it takes time for news about POWs to get through.'

There was a shocked silence in the kitchen. Imogen could hear the clock on the wall ticking and a blackbird, the one that nested in the lilac tree which grew against the outhouses, giving his strident alarm. She could hear her own breathing and the thump of her heart. She longed for someone to break the silence, yet could not do so herself, and it was Debby who finally spoke.

'What do you mean, the fighters followed him down?' she asked, and Imogen could tell that she was keeping her voice level with an effort. 'Why should they do such a thing? It seems very strange.'

Again, there was a silence before Laurie answered. 'In the heat of battle . . .' he began, then hesitated, and Ricky swallowed his mouthful of scone and answered for him.

'Some of the Huns see a parachute open, know it's from a British plane and chase it down, guns blazing,' Ricky said cheerfully. 'It's not always the easy option, baling out,' he added.

There was a shocked silence before Imogen, forgetting that she did not want to draw attention to herself, spoke. 'You mean they'd deliberately kill one of our chaps who had jumped because his plane was on fire or something?' she asked in an incredulous voice. 'I shouldn't have thought even a German could be that wicked.'

'Oh, mostly they're too busy trying to down the big bombers,' Ricky assured her. 'I'm sure Dave reached the ground safely.' He turned to Laurie. 'He went down over occupied France didn't he?'

Laurie nodded. 'Yes, and as soon as we have definite news we'll let you know,' he assured the company. 'And now you'd best be on your way, Ricky.'

Ricky grinned, getting to his feet and taking the neat packet of sandwiches and the bag of scones which Imogen was holding out. 'Thanks very much,' he said. 'My mum will be glad of the scones. Laurie, don't forget I'll pick you up at ten o'clock on Sunday.' He opened the back door and everyone accompanied him outside to watch him get behind the wheel of the little sports car and drive out of the back yard with a cheery wave.

Jill and Laurie decided that they would catch the bus into the town, see a film or simply have a wander round the shops, and stay out for supper. Imogen, who had been told to feed Pandora and clean out the pen, ably assisted by Rita, began work at once. She waited for Rita to make some remark about Laurie and when it came, as it inevitably did, she parried it by saying smartly: 'I saw your face when Laurie said Dave was probably a POW. I didn't know you'd got a crush on him!'

Rita began to deny that she had any interest in Dave other than friendship, ending reproachfully, 'You shouldn't joke about someone who might be dead or injured. We all like Dave . . .'

'. . . and we all like Laurie,' Imogen said defiantly. 'And now let's get on with the work.'

By the time Jill and Laurie returned the girls felt well pleased with how they had coped. When the pub opened they collected empty glasses and took orders from the drinkers which they passed immediately to Auntie behind the bar, and at ten o'clock, when they would normally have been in bed for at least an hour, they were glad to greet Jill and Laurie and tell of their helpful work.

Imogen said very little whilst Rita and Debby filled Jill and Laurie in on the evening's happenings, though she had worked as hard as anyone. She was still shy of saying too much in case Laurie guessed how she felt about him.

Auntie smiled complacently round the shiny kitchen and caressed Rufus's soft ears. 'Everyone pulled their weight, even Rufus here,' she reported. 'Old Mr

Weatherspoon came up from the village with a message for one of the customers and was paid for his trouble in cider, which is strong stuff. I wouldn't have liked to see him trying to make his way back to the village alone, so I lent him Rufus. I told him to keep the dog by him until he reached his own cottage and then to tell Rufus to go home, which he did.' She beamed at the company. 'How about that for intelligence, eh?'

Everyone agreed that Rufus was bright as a button and worth his weight in gold. Very soon after that Auntie sent the girls off to bed, for it had been a long and tiring day – a day which Imogen hoped to relive, particularly the bits with Laurie in them, before she went to sleep.

Imogen was awoken from the middle of a pleasant dream in which she was swimming in beautiful calm blue water, surrounded by fish, with seagulls floating above her head. Sighing regretfully, she buried her head in her pillow and tried to go back to sleep. Woody had taught her to swim, more or less, but they still had not managed to find a sufficiently private stretch of water where she could be taught proper strokes instead of the rather desperate doggy paddle which was all shallow water allowed. But as everyone knows, sleep does not always follow the rules so, although disappointed, she was not particularly surprised when she remained wide awake. She glanced across at the alarm clock; gosh, it was midnight. She had gone to bed soon after ten and must have plunged straight into not only sleep, but also the dream sea. What a nuisance! Previous experience told her that she would probably lie awake for at least an hour now, since her mind would assume it to be morning. She glanced at the two other sleepers, thinking that if one of them were awake she might tell her about the swimming dream, but it was pretty obvious that the day's hard work had affected her friends quite differently from the way it had affected her, for they were fast asleep. Debby was even snoring gently, and Rita suddenly gave a snort and turned her head restlessly on the pillow.

Imogen was wondering why when she saw that a broad band of moonlight lay right across Rita's face. She had been half hoping that one of the girls might wake, but even as she saw Rita's eyelids flutter she realised that this was the last thing she really wanted. Rita would start on again about Imogen's feelings for Laurie, and she could do without that. Sliding out of bed she crossed to the window. Below her, the yard and the garden beyond looked magical in the silver light, and Imogen was suddenly struck by a desire to go out. She could get dressed and make her way to the great beech tree which they called the Lookout and watch for the moment when the fighters would be scrambled. But of course, though it was fun to imagine, she knew very well that she would not even start to get dressed, far less set off on a moonlight walk. Only an idiot would do such a thing

Imogen closed the curtains and returned to her bed, and was about to pull the covers back over her when her tummy gave an indignant rumble and she became suddenly aware that she was hungry. Every night, Auntie made what she called a bedtime snack, which was a cup of cocoa and some of her home-made ginger biscuits. But tonight Imogen had been too involved with not appearing to notice Laurie that she had scarcely touched her cocoa and had not eaten so much as one ginger biscuit. *That* was why she had awoken! She really was an idiot, because going to bed hungry was never a good idea. But this, she knew, could be easily remedied. She would sneak downstairs, fetch the tin of biscuits from the pantry, help herself to a handful and return to bed. She could of course confess to her theft in the morning, but doubted whether she would bother to do so. If she wanted to be really devious she could knock on Auntie's door and peep around it, secure in the knowledge of Auntie's frequent boast that she (a) could fall asleep on a clothes line and (b) would not wake if a brigade of Scottish pipers, all playing at full blast, were to march round her bed. Then she could say that she had tried to ask permission for taking the biscuits, but not having a Scottish piper, let alone a brigade of 'em . . .

Giggling at the thought, Imogen got out of bed and padded across to the door. She took her dressing gown off the hook and slipped it on, then she opened the door very, very softly, crossed the small landing, and began to descend the stairs. Halfway down she thought she heard something and stopped short, but the kitchen was all in darkness save for the glow of the fire in the range.

Odd! It must be just her imagination; it really was hunger which had sent her on the prowl. There had been no sound which might have woken her, no clink of glass, no stealthy footfall, so it seemed unlikely they had been visited by burglars, and what was there to steal? Nothing . . . oh, hang on a moment! Beer might be difficult to stick in one's pocket, but there were those upside down bottles containing spirits, which she supposed, vaguely, men might want to steal, and if so, it was her duty to go quietly across the kitchen and peep round the edge of the half-open door into the bar.

She crossed the kitchen and went to the door which opened directly into the bar. It was in complete darkness, and she realised that the silence was also complete, but nevertheless, having got this far, she felt she should check everything. There was the Jug and Bottle, their private sitting room, rarely used now summer had come; she had best take a look in there.

She did so, stealing soft-footed over the polished lino-leum. Nothing. Deciding with a good deal of relief that there were no burglars to be apprehended, Imogen returned to the kitchen, visited the pantry for long enough to grab a couple of biscuits and pop them into her pocket, and then, having a good look round in the gloom to make sure that she had left no tell-tale signs of her midnight visit, returned to the stairs. She was halfway up the first flight when, ahead of her, she heard a door open softly, followed by the creak of a board. She stopped abruptly; she had thought it might be fun to startle another night-time wanderer by saying 'Boo', but now she knew she would do no such thing. Instead, she shrank against the wall and stared upwards . . . and saw Laurie slipping into the room which she knew was Jill's, shutting the door gently behind him.

Shock affects everyone differently. For what felt like a long time but might only have been a few minutes, Imogen sagged against the staircase wall and waited for her heart to stop beating so loudly that she half expected Laurie to open the door again to see what was making the noise. Cold was spreading up from her toes as though she were standing in a tub of icy water, and it was this which finally got her moving. Shivering and mouse-quiet, she completed her climb of the staircase, slipped into the attic room, hung her dressing gown on its hook and climbed back into bed. She tried to tell herself that what she had seen had been perfectly natural. Probably Laurie was lonely on his own in the spare room, for she knew he shared his life with his crew, perhaps even slept in the same hut or the same quarters, whatever the expression was. Yes, that must be the answer: he was lonely and he loved Jill, so what was more natural than that, seeking company, he had gone to her room. She tried to imagine him sitting on the edge of Jill's bed, waking her up, starting to chat . . . only another picture kept intruding, that of Laurie pulling back the covers and getting into bed beside Jill.

But it's only a single bed, Imogen reminded herself desperately. Auntie said there wasn't really room in it for one, so what on earth would be the point of cramming two people in such a bed?

Imogen sighed and, for the first time for many months, began to suck her thumb. Anger was beginning to build. How dared Laurie and Jill do whatever it was men and girls did in bed? Once, she reminded herself, she had known so little about what went on between males and females that she would have simply accepted the first picture: that of Laurie and Jill wanting companionship and being content to simply chat. But now she had spent over a year watching the various antics of the farm animals, the strutting cockerel and his harem of hens – Auntie had bought a cockerel so that they might rear their own chicks – and even the fat wood pigeons who came to steal the corn thrown out for the poultry and stayed to mate with complete abandon whenever they felt so inclined.

Sadly, Imogen realised that so far as the facts of life were concerned she had cast the innocence of city children behind her and now knew far more than she wished to. Almost in the same instant, however, she realised that whilst she had been conjecturing, the deathly cold which had gripped her had gone. She felt warm and comfortable; perhaps it might even be possible to go back to sleep. She glanced across at the alarm clock, which now read half past one, and pulled the sheet up over her shoulder, snuggling her head into the pillow but removing her thumb from her mouth because, she told herself, she no longer needed its comfort. She was almost asleep when a thought occurred to her which had her sitting bolt upright. What would she do in the morning when she had to face Laurie and Jill across the breakfast table? She knew that what she had seen should make no difference to how she felt about them, but she also knew that things would never be quite the same again. How she wished she had never given way to her urge for food . . . and with the thought she remembered the ginger biscuits, still in the pocket of her dressing gown. She jumped out of bed and fumbled in the pocket, and was returning with the ginger biscuits in her hand when a sleepy voice said: 'Immy? Why are you out of bed? It's not morning, is it?'

Imogen had jumped quite six inches at the sound of the voice and now she turned reproachful eyes on Debby, who was sitting up and staring at her. Annoyed at being caught out she scowled at the other girl, though she doubted whether Debby could see her expression in the gloom. Thank God for the ginger biscuits, she thought devoutly; no need to say anything about Jill and Laurie. But Debby was still sitting up, still staring, so Imogen broke into reluctant speech.

'I got hungry, I don't know why. Well, perhaps I do; I didn't have my bedtime snack because I was listening to what Jill and Laurie were telling us. Anyway, I sneaked downstairs and helped myself to a couple of bickies; I've only just got back.' She flourished the biscuits. 'I'm not as hungry as I thought, though; do you want to take one off my hands?'

'No thanks,' Debby said promptly. She snuggled down the bed again. 'What I really want is to go back to sleep. You are a wretch, Immy. It took me ages to drop off with you snoring like Pandora, and now you go and wake me!'

'Sorry,' Imogen mumbled through a mouthful of biscuit. 'Did you know it's well past one o'clock? I say, Debby, it's a grand night! If neither of us can sleep why don't we get dressed and go for a little wander?'

Debby shook her head decisively. 'If it's fine tomorrow they'll be working with the hay and we'll be busy from dawn to dusk,' she said reproachfully. 'So let's get to sleep again as quickly as we can.'

Imogen sighed. 'I don't know why I suggested it,' she mumbled. 'Night night, Debby; see you in the morning.' But though she realised that Jill and Laurie had every right to be together, she made up her mind that if she could put a spoke in their wheel, she would do so. They aren't married, so they shouldn't sleep in the same room, she told herself righteously. She doubted she would get so much as a wink of sleep, yet within seconds of the thought, she slumbered.

Next morning Imogen was down early, helping Auntie with the breakfast since Jill was lying in for a change. Imogen, toasting bread, laying the table and making a large pot of tea, asked what plans Jill and Laurie had made for the day.

'They're going over to Oulton Broad; I've got a cousin who owns a boat which he's agreed to lend them, so since the weather seems set fair they should have a good day,' Auntie told her. 'What are your plans, poppet?'

'Haymaking, I think. The boys are coming round to help out as soon as their chores at the farm are over, and we'll all go off to the hayfields together,' Imogen said. 'I wish we could borrow a boat on the Broad some time.' She looked hopefully at Auntie. 'People fish on the Broads, don't they? It'd be fun if we could catch a few fish and bring them home for you to cook.'

Auntie laughed. 'It's not impossible, and your summer holidays start soon,' she said. 'I'm sure Matthew – that's my cousin – will lend you a boat then, provided one of you can row.'

'I bet Woody can; he can do everything,' Imogen said. She cocked her head at the sound of footsteps thundering down the stairs. 'Here they come, all eager for brekker.' The kitchen door opened and Laurie came into the room. He was smiling, and Imogen realised that the pallor and strain which she had noticed on his face the day before had disappeared. Suddenly, she was no longer embarrassed by the memory of the night. She was not embarrassed at all, in fact. 'Grab a chair, Laurie,' she told him. 'Auntie will dole out your porridge and pour you a cuppa whilst I butter your toast.'

When Jill appeared, looking flushed and pretty, Imogen did suffer a momentary pang, but then she remembered it was Jill's kindness which had taken the strain from Laurie's face, and smiled at the older girl. 'Aren't you lucky to be going for a boat trip? But Auntie says when the school holidays come, she'll get her cousin to lend us his boat,' she said. 'How many slices of toast can you eat, Jill?'

Chapter Eight

Things had changed considerably since Laurie's visit, Imogen thought as she got into bed one April night, almost a year later. Jill and Auntie had had a number of discussions and finally it had been agreed that it was Jill's duty – and wish – to join one of the services. She had become a Waaf and then a plotter, working in a big underground control room outside the city of Norwich, just ten miles from the Linnet, which meant she was able to visit them whenever she had leave.

Naturally enough she wanted to be with Laurie whenever possible, and once or twice they had come to the Linnet together. Imogen noticed that Jill was thinner and looked worn out, though a couple of days' rest did wonders. The girls had grown used to what were described as 'hit and run raids', the heavy bombers roaring overhead on their way to attack ports or factory complexes, and no longer bothered to get up and go down to the Anderson shelter Auntie had insisted on installing the previous year. Sometimes the noise kept them awake, particularly the whine of the air raid siren, which, if the wind was in the right direction, came to them clearly from the village, but the shelter itself would have grown disgustingly damp and smelly had Auntie not decreed that they should give it a thorough spring clean once a month.

Once, there had been no question of aircraft flying at night, but now it was done as a matter of course. America had entered the war at the end of 1941 when the Japanese had bombed their fleet in Pearl Harbor, and their air force had taken over daytime raids, leaving night flying to the British. Auntie had said the Japs should get a medal, because having the Americans on the Allies' side must, she thought, shorten the war by many months, perhaps even by years.

But now it was 1942 and Imogen awoke to the familiar sound of planes overhead and Rufus's howling. Auntie often remarked that he was better than any alarm, since he seemed to hear the raiders as soon as they crossed the coast and began to howl at the top of his voice, showing the whites of his eyes and not ceasing his lament until the skies were clear once more. Imogen sighed and burrowed her head into her pillow. It would be another hit and run raid on the airfields, she supposed; no need to get out of bed.

She was just beginning to snooze once more when there was a sound like all the devils in hell screaming at once, followed by a deep boom. Debby, who had actually been snoring, gave a squawk and sat bolt upright, eyes rounding. 'What was that?' she quavered. 'Immy, what was that huge bang?'

Imogen was beginning to answer that it must be a bomb, jettisoned by an enemy plane on its way home to Germany, when it was succeeded by another tremendous, earth-shaking boom, and others began to follow in quick succession.

Imogen jumped out of bed and saw that Rita was doing the same, whilst Debby, still foggy with sleep, seemed unaware of the danger. Pulling on her thickest woolly, she said urgently, though in a rather muffled voice, 'Get up, Debby. It's a raid; what they call a blitz, I think, like the one in Liverpool last year. You'd better get dressed. Put on warm things and we'll get down to the Anderson shelter.'

Another enormous crash was accompanied by a flash of light so brilliant that it lit up the room like daylight despite the blackout curtains, and Debby, pushing her feet into her slippers, went over to the window, meaning to peer out. 'Don't!' Rita said sharply. 'Blast can push that window in straight on to your face. Look what happened to my mum's hotel when next door was hit. It cost a deal of money to get the windows put back in and the chimney rebuilt. Bloody Luftwaffe! So hurry up and come downstairs. I expect Auntie's trying to do all the things we were told to do in a bad raid: she'll be making flasks of tea, cutting sandwiches and getting out the biscuits . . .'

Debby obediently retreated from the window and finished dressing at record speed, heading for the stairs just ahead of the other two. They burst into the kitchen to find Auntie busy as Rita had said and Rufus, mouth open and eyes turned skywards, adding his own particular warning to the one which was doubtless still sounding, though they could hear nothing above the heavy drone of the engines and the crash of the bombs.

Auntie looked up as they entered the room and jerked a thumb at the line of coats and boots beside the back door. 'Get 'em on,' she said brusquely. As Rita had surmised she had packed a basket with food and flasks and now she began to don her own outer clothing. 'I told you the Anderson shelter would come in useful one day, and now we're going to prove it. But don't go out until there's a lull; then run like hell, get down into the shelter, pull the curtain across, and stay there.'

'What about you?' Imogen said. She felt cold with fright. 'Oh, Auntie, what about Jill?' She pointed to the bright orange glow lighting the sky. 'They're bombing Norwich. It's on fire, and Jill's there!'

'She's in the control centre, and that's underground; she should be safe enough,' Auntie said briefly. 'I'll bring the basket; you girls grab Rufus in case he tries to run off – dogs do, I've been told – and then get into that shelter.'

Rita and Debby rushed over to the back door and thrust it open. Imogen saw that the sky overhead was black with aircraft, cutting out the stars, though the moon still shone down on the Canary and Linnet as though it cared nothing for those below.

They had to wait a moment before a lull came, by which time Auntie and her basket had joined them, and they all charged for the Anderson shelter. They were too frightened to giggle when Auntie, coming last, slipped on the top step and entered the shelter on her bottom, smiling ruefully as the girls helped her to her feet. 'More haste less speed,' she quoted. She sat on one of the wooden benches and thumped her basket down beside her, whilst the girls tried to comfort Rufus by pulling him on to their laps – he took up all three laps, for he was a big dog – and assuring him that they were safe and he could stop howling. Rufus, rolling his eyes pathetically, did not appear to believe them and was only persuaded to shut up by a sandwich placed between his paws, which he immediately gobbled. Then he slid off the girls' knees and went over to the doorway, though he made no attempt to push aside the heavy curtain, clearly believing that he really was safer here than in the kitchen of the Canary and Linnet.

'I say, Imogen, what were those things that looked like huge candelabras?' Debby said presently. Her voice trembled a little, but Imogen realised that the question took her mind off their more immediate troubles.

'I think they're called flares, and the bombers drop them so that they can see their targets,' she replied. 'Haven't you heard people talking about them?'

'I think perhaps I have, I've just not seen them before,' Debby said cautiously. 'I've heard them talking about incendiaries as well; they light up the scene too, don't they?'

'Oh, Debby, you're such a baby,' Rita said, but without the usual edge to her voice. 'I remember reading that incendiaries are just smaller bombs which are supposed to set fire to buildings. Last year, when Liverpool was attacked, incendiaries landed on a warehouse full of margarine and stuff which went up with a whoosh, and another one might have landed on the *Malakand*, the ship which was full of ammunition. Or that may have been a bomb – they're not really sure. It was in all the papers, anyway.'

'Oh yes, I remember,' Debby said meekly. She turned to Auntie. 'How long is this going to last?' she asked. 'Is it a blitz, like the May blitz in Liverpool last year? That went on for over a week, didn't it?'

Auntie waited for a lull in the crashes, booms and explosions before she answered. 'I imagine it's one of what they're calling the Baedeker Raids,' she said, and smiled at her companions. 'Apparently the word has gone round that Herr Hitler sits in his office with a Baedeker guide – that's a well-known travel book – spread out before him and simply sends the Luftwaffe to the principal cities it mentions.'

The girls nodded their understanding, and as soon as the thunder of the heavy bombers returning began to pass overhead they would have left the shelter to see how much damage had been done – if any – in the village and surrounding countryside, but Auntie would not allow it. 'It's still not daylight, though it won't be long before the sky starts to lighten and the stars disappear,' she said. 'You've been patient for six hours, so being patient for another couple shouldn't strain you unduly. And as soon as it's light enough – and the all clear has sounded – we'll go and cook a sustaining breakfast and then check up on the damage.'

'I hope Pandora's all right,' Imogen said when the two hours were up, the all clear had sounded, and they were crossing the yard towards the kitchen. 'I expect the telephone wires might be down so we shan't be able to get in touch with Jill. I wonder if Laurie's station was raided last night – he's quite near Lincoln, isn't he?'

'I shouldn't think so; I believe the Luftwaffe attack one city at a time,' Auntie said as she pushed open the back door and ushered the girls inside. 'But there's no knowing how long the blitz on Norwich will last. I imagine it depends both on the weather and on the amount of damage they think they have inflicted. But I'm pretty sure the air force will have kept up communications between stations; even if the phones are out they'll be the first ones to be reinstated, and until then they'll use messengers. I don't think you need to go to school today – no one will be able to concentrate after having so little sleep – so when you've had your breakfast and checked the animals and hens you can hold the fort for me here whilst I go into the village and try to telephone. If I can't I'll take a bus into the city, get in touch with Jill somehow and make sure she's all right. Either way I'll be back well before dark. Can you manage by yourselves? One of you must run down to Jacky's cottage and ask him to open the bar at lunch time, though I don't know whether we'll have any customers. Still, licensing laws aren't meant to be flouted, so we'll have to be open at noon, blitz or no blitz.'

The girls assured her that they could manage easily and began to make porridge, tea and toast, and as soon as the meal was finished Debby started to wash up, whilst Imogen wiped and put away. Rita pulled on her coat and boots and set off for Jacky's cottage, and Auntie left for the village.

'I wonder whether the ack-ack batteries round the city downed any of the German aircraft,' Imogen said idly as she and Debby began to lay the table for lunch. 'I didn't hear a plane crash, but then how could we possibly have done so? And I dare say one gun sounds very like another in all that noise blazing away.'

'We'll find out when Auntie gets back,' Debby said. She peered into the pantry. 'There's not a lot of food in here, so I reckon we're in for a cold lunch. There's a bit of bacon, but I don't think we ought to use that, so I fear it'll be jam sandwiches and an apple or two for afters. Are there still some left?

Rita, having returned from her errand with the information that Jacky would be along well before noon, nodded. 'Bound to be,' she said with easy optimism. She was fond of apples and had, with her companions, harvested a great many from the Pilgrims' orchards, carried them up to the loft above the stable and laid them with tender care on beds of new-mown hay. Mrs Pilgrim had impressed upon them the importance of leaving at least an inch around each fruit. 'You've heared the saying one bad apple spoils the barrel,' she said. 'Well, that applies just the same to fruit kept in the apple loft, so be good kids and treat them with kid gloves, because a bruise can ruin an apple in a matter of minutes.'

Mrs Pilgrim had, of course, been referring to her own produce, for the Pilgrims had three acres of fruit, but the girls realised that her advice would hold good for Auntie's apples as well. Her five trees were old but productive, and the children had gathered pounds and pounds of fruit and stowed them away in the small room next to their bedroom as though they were, in truth, as delicate as the strawberries they had picked the previous year.

Now, they went up to the attic and brought down a dozen fine Bramleys which, Imogen said, she would make into a pie. 'And we'll make some custard, so it will be better than only jam sandwiches,' she added. She smiled at Debby. 'Won't Auntie be delighted to find we've used our initiative? She's always telling us we ought.'

The three girls, proud of the trust that had been placed in them, worked hard all morning, and when the boys appeared, having also been kept home from school, told them flatly that they did not intend to leave the Canary and Linnet that day.

Woody pulled a face. 'We thought we'd go up to the Lookout and see what we could see from there,' he said discontentedly. 'I wanted to go into the city but as it happens we're a bit short of cash for the bus fare, so that's a non-starter. Are you serious when you say you won't leave the pub? I don't see why you shouldn't come with us once your chores are done.' His voice, which had started to break some months before, suddenly soared on the last few words into falsetto, in the unreliable way the voice of a boy in his teens often does. Imogen smiled to herself as he looked hopefully at Rita, knowing, Imogen thought, that she was the one likeliest to say she would go to the Lookout with them. Imogen herself had never altogether conquered her dislike of heights, though she tried to hide it from Woody, fearing he might despise her.

But to her relief Rita also shook her head. 'Not today, Woody,' she said firmly. 'Auntie's gone to find out how Jill got on last night so we all want to be here when she returns. And then there's Laurie. If he's been flying he rings Jill at her Mess to reassure her that he's okay. So you go off to the Lookout and come back later. I expect Auntie will be back by about five or six.'

'And you know what Mrs P is like about high tea; we'll miss out if we wait for Auntie to come back,' Josh said. He turned to Woody. 'I'm pretty sure you don't want to go up to the Lookout by yourself, so why not stay here with me and give the girls a hand? I dare say they'll feed us.'

This was agreed, and when Auntie had still not

returned by five o'clock the boys left and the three girls, having done all that they could towards an evening meal, decided to walk into the village and meet the six o'clock bus. 'I'll be glad to get out of the house for once,' Debby admitted, making the other two smile, for as a rule she was the most domesticated of the three, always eager to help Auntie and Jill indoors. She saw the smiles and giggled. 'Bet you never thought you'd hear me say that,' she admitted. 'But it's a glorious day and we've finished all the housework, so a walk to the village would be fun.' She looked from Rita's face to Imogen's, began to speak, hesitated, and then looked rather anxiously at her companions. 'Has it occurred to you that if there was nothing the matter, Auntie would probably have caught the next bus home?'

Imogen felt the blood drain from her face, and clapped a hand to her mouth, speaking between her fingers. 'Of course!' She turned to Rita. 'Why didn't *we* think of that? And we can't contact her because we don't really know where she's gone. Let's hope she found Jill okay and the two of them are doing what they can to help. But we'll go into the village anyway, because if Auntie isn't on the six o'clock bus there's only one more, the one that brings people back from the city when they've been over there to see a flick or go to a dance or something.'

The three girls duly met the six o'clock bus, but Auntie was not on it, though others were; old Mrs Jackson who helped out at the general shop when they were busy, two girls who worked in one of the munitions factories in the city whom they remembered from the village school, though they were a couple of years older, and the bus driver himself. He remembered taking Auntie into the city that morning but said she had not been amongst the queues of people eager to get out of the city as evening deepened.

He was an elderly man with kindly blue eyes and now he sensed the girls' anxiety and jerked a thumb at old Mrs Jackson. 'I saw Miss Marcy go off with the old 'un; why not ask her if she knows where your auntie's gone,' he said, and Imogen thanked him and was about to approach the old lady just climbing down from the bus when a car drew up with a screech of brakes, the passenger door shot open and Auntie clambered out.

'Oh, girls, I knew you'd worry so I set out to thumb a lift,' she said breathlessly. She indicated the driver of the car, an elderly farmer whom the girls knew slightly, since the previous year they had helped him to harvest a field of peas and another of carrots. 'Mr Carter there saw me before I'd gone more than a hundred yards, realised I'd missed the bus and made room for me . . .' she chuckled, 'though I had to share the seat with a bag of pig meal. But at least it got me home, or would have done if I'd not seen you lot hovering by the bus stop and got him to drop me off.' She rapped smartly on the driver's window and raised her voice to a shout. 'Mr Carter, you're a prince! Thanks ever so much; next time you come into the Linnet you can have a pint of the best on me.'

The old man mouthed something through the glass, presumably an acknowledgement, and drove off, starting with a series of kangaroo-like bounds before the old car settled into its stride and carried him out of sight. Only then did Auntie turn to the girls. 'Jill's in hospital,' she said quietly. 'She was making her way from her billet to the control centre right at the beginning of the raid, and she said the dive bombers – those awful Stukas which scream as they descend – must have seen her and her fellow workers racing across the airfield and tumbling down the steps. They were strafing anything that moved and poor Jill got three bullets across her shoulder and upper arm. Others weren't so lucky. But no use to be angry, because war is war . . . only one of the girls, Lucy, had her eighteenth birthday today and they'd planned a party for her.' She was silent for a moment. 'So young – not even quite eighteen.'

By now they had begun to walk towards the pub, Auntie in the middle with Imogen on one side, Rita on the other and Debby carrying her basket, though it contained little beside her handbag and the greaseproof paper which had held her sandwich lunch. 'Will Jill be all right?' Debby asked anxiously. 'I'm so sorry about the other girls; were many of them injured?'

Auntie began to speak in a reassuring voice, but then seemed to change her mind. 'Yes. Jill was one of the lucky ones,' she said grimly. 'A great many people died, and many more were injured. The hospitals are packed, but the doctors and nurses say they can cope.'

'Can we go and see her?' Imogen asked eagerly. 'Oh, poor Jill. Does she feel very dreadful, Auntie?'

Rita cut in before Auntie could speak. 'Of course she does,' she said crossly. 'When you say she was hit in the shoulder, Auntie, was anything broken?'

Auntie nodded. 'Yes, her collarbone. And when it's safe of course you can visit her, but only one at a time, I'm afraid. Visiting is usually between seven and eight, but I'm sure the hospital will make an exception in your case. And now let's talk about something a little more cheerful. What are we going to have for supper?'

The blitz on Norwich continued for the rest of the week, though with varying severity, but Auntie refused to let the girls go into the city until the raids had been over for a week, and then she would not let the boys accompany them.

'Patients at the hospital are only allowed one visitor per bed; the girls will have fifteen minutes each and that will be plenty long enough, for Jill is still very weak.' She saw the disappointment on the boys' faces and relented a little. 'Why not meet the bus and come back to the Linnet for supper? Then the girls can tell you just how Jill is.'

'We could go next week . . .' Josh began, only to be put firmly in his place.

'Laurie is coming all the way down from Lincolnshire whenever he can manage it,' Auntie said. 'I spoke to the sister in charge of the ward and she says Jill is a grand girl and determined to be back at the control centre just as soon as she's able. She'll get some leave – bound to – so you'll be able to see her then.'

The girls were given permission to take an afternoon off school and set off for their first visit, and were shocked and appalled by the state of the city. When they got off the bus Rita lifted her chin and sniffed, reminding Imogen sharply of the Bisto Kids. 'What's that glorious smell?' Rita asked curiously. 'I've smelt it before, but I can't put a name to it . . .'

A passer-by, overhearing, grinned broadly. 'That's clear you aren't local,' he said. 'Them bloody Nazis hit the Caley's factory; that's chocolate you can smell.' He looked at them curiously. 'Know where you're headin'?' He pointed. 'This here's Surrey Street, and up there's Ipswich Road. Any help to you?'

Rita was inclined to say that they could find their way very well, thank you, but Imogen was not so proud. She gave him the name of the hospital and listened gratefully to his instructions, and presently the girls found themselves pushing through the revolving doors and being directed to the ward by a harassed but friendly nurse.

After explaining who they were to the sister in charge, the girls went on to the ward, a long room with a dozen beds on either side. They had just begun to walk along between the rows when Debby gave a squeak. 'There she is!' she said joyfully. 'Look, she's trying to wave.' She began to run towards a figure at the far end of the ward, then remembered where she was and slowed to a walk. Imogen, following close behind, was shocked: Jill was white as a ghost and seemed to have lost weight simply by lying in bed. Her hair hung limply on either side of her face, her eyes were blue-shadowed, and there were hollows beneath her cheeks, but when they got closer her eyes lit up and her beautiful, gentle smile illumined her pale face.

'Girls! How lovely to see you! Auntie said you were going to come and visit, but she wasn't sure when. Laurie came two days ago, and now that I'm able to leave my bed I telephone his station each morning to make sure he's come back safe from whatever sortie he's on. How are you all? And how are the boys?'

'We're fine, and so are they,' Imogen said at once. 'But oh, we do miss you, Jill! It's daft really because you've been in the WAAF, and away from us, for nearly a year now. But you always came back to the pub whenever you had the chance.'

'Did you know the bombs hit the Calcy factory?' Rita put in. 'When we got off the bus all we could smell was chocolate; we wish we could have brought you some, only I expect it's all ruined. But we did bring you some mint humbugs.' She handed over the sweets and gradually the shyness which had gripped the three girls when they saw how pale and pulled Jill looked dissipated, and by the time a nurse came along, saying rather reproachfully that two of them should have waited outside and gone in separately, so as not to tire the patient, they were chattering freely.

On the bus going home, however, Rita gave vent to her feelings. 'Bloody, bloody Nazis,' she muttered. 'I'm sure our chaps would never target people on the ground.'

Imogen raised her eyebrows. 'I'm sure it was dreadful, but as Auntie says, it's war,' she told her friend. 'And even if our chaps don't deliberately fire on people, they bomb them. You mustn't try to pretend that the RAF don't hurt women and children – babies, even – because what choice do they have?'

'And remember, Jill and her friends are all Waafs,' Debby reminded Rita when she remained obstinately silent. 'And from what I've read in the papers the Nazis do much worse things than shoot at girls in uniform. In fact I know they do; my family didn't leave Germany without a very good reason. I wonder how long Jill will be able to stay with us when she comes out of hospital? She won't be able to plot aircraft across the control board until her collarbone knits, or whatever it is they're supposed to do.'

Rita took the opportunity to tease Debby, though not as cruelly as she sometimes did, saying she now had a mental picture of Jill's collarbone, needles in hand, quietly knitting away at an air force sock.

When the bus reached the village they found Woody and Josh waiting for them. 'How was Jill?' Woody asked eagerly, and before any of the girls could answer he added: 'But you needn't tell us now. Auntie's invited us to supper because she knew we'd want to hear how Jill's doing, so let's save it till then. Auntie says she might be out of hospital next week.'

'Yes and the sister on the ward told us they'll release her to Auntie's care, which is great,' Imogen said joyfully. 'Jill says she'll lie on the couch in the small parlour and as soon as she's able she'll start doing the books again.'

Rita giggled. 'Auntie does do them – the books I mean – but because of coupons and restrictions it's awfully hard work. As soon as the bar closes you can see her scribbling away. We try to help – counting coupons and checking the stock – but sometimes I think we only confuse her, so she'll be tickled pink to get Jill back, even if it's only for a week or two.'

When they entered the Linnet, they found Auntie sitting at the table carving what looked like a joint of pork. The smell was delicious, and when Auntie bade them to take their places around the table they obeyed with alacrity.

'I smell stuffing, the sort you make yourself,' Debby said ecstatically. 'Gosh, and roast potatoes; what have we done to deserve such a feast, Auntie?'

Auntie continued to carve the meat and divide it between the plates she had set ready. Then she began to dish up the potatoes and spoon some delicious stuffing on to each plate. 'Mr Huggit killed a pig,' she explained. 'This is our share, so make the most of it. Now tell me, did you have a good visit? And how was my poor little niece?'

'Sister says she'll be home before next weekend,' Rita informed her, helping herself to carrots and cabbage as the tureen was passed around the table. 'The MO says she won't be fit for work for a long time, so you'll have help with the books again, Auntie.'

'Well, isn't that the best news anyone could hear?' Auntie said at once, beaming around the table. 'I knew Jill did the right thing when she joined the WAAF, but my goodness, don't we miss her! What with coupons, rationing and all the masses of paperwork I have to fill in and send off just to get a barrel or two of beer, I seem to work from dawn till dusk, and then from dusk till dawn. But having my Jillywinks back, even for a short while, will be a great relief.' Her tone suddenly sharpened. 'Have you eaten all your meat already, Debby? Or did I give you a very tiny helping?'

'It's all right, Auntie; I'm almost a vegetarian so I passed most of it to Woody. Can I have a bit more stuffing, though? And is that apple sauce? I love apple sauce.'

Imogen, in front of whose plate was a round dish of apple sauce, pushed it along the table without comment, but Rita remarked that Debby had not been backward in coming forward when Auntie had made toad in the hole the previous week. Imogen was about to jump to Debby's defence when Josh forestalled her. 'Sausages are mostly sawdust,' he said briskly. 'I say, Auntie, I feel really mean eating your share of Mr Huggit's pig, because Mrs P will get her share as well. But knowing her, she'll send us down tomorrow with liver or kidneys or a couple of pork chops, to make up.'

'That's true,' Auntie nodded. 'Now let's eat up, because I've an apple pudding steaming on the back of the stove and some custard made up in the jug. Goodness, how I'm looking forward to having my niece home once more!'

For one reason and another the youngsters had not visited the Lookout since the previous summer, and when the raids on Norwich started and they saw with their own eyes the terrible results of the Luftwaffe's attacks, visited Jill in hospital and heard sad stories on every side it had seemed a childish pastime. But now it was June, and Jill had returned to an airfield not far from Laurie's, though she was now training as an R/T operator. Laurie had visited her a couple of times while she was at the Linnet, and on those nights Imogen took care to stay in her room, even when for some reason she might otherwise have padded down the stairs to the kitchen. She had no wish to repeat her previous experience.

Now that the weather was set fair, however, Woody suggested one Saturday that they really should visit the Lookout. Last autumn's leaves would have piled up and the debris of the winter might make climbing the great beech both difficult and dangerous unless they first went prepared to test and clear every branch. Auntie and Jill had never been told much about the Lookout, though they knew it existed; they had no idea how high one had to climb to reach the position from which they could see the airfield, so Auntie agreed to lend brushes, rakes and other implements needed to clear the platform the boys had built. As they wended their way through the familiar countryside Woody turned to Imogen. 'We're getting too old for mucking about with the Lookout and pretending we'd carry on a guerrilla war from there if the Nazis ever landed,' he said rather discontentedly. 'I've joined the air force cadets; did I tell you? And as soon as I'm old enough I'll join the regulars. I'd like to fly, of course, but I believe they're getting pretty damned fussy; you have to pass all sorts of exams before they'll even let you put a foot on the runway.'

Rita, overhearing, snorted. 'Oh, rubbish; you're talking through your hat,' she said scornfully. 'My cousin Albert—'

'Sod your cousin Albert; we've heard all we want to hear about him,' Woody said at once. 'And anyway he's not a pilot . . .'

'He's air crew; he might be a pilot for all I know,' Rita said defensively. 'You're just using it as an excuse because you don't want to leave school. But if you do decide to join up – before your age group gets conscripted, I mean – then you'll probably end up as an armourer or a plain old motor mechanic.'

'I don't see that it matters if he is, because he'll still be helping with the war effort,' Debby the peacemaker said. 'You can't pick and choose in wartime, Rita. You have to do whatever job the air force needs most.'

Rita went pink. 'I wouldn't be content to muck around with engines if I were a man; I'd want to do something really useful, like piloting a heavy bomber the way Laurie does. But of course it's different for you, Woody; you're only a boy.'

Woody's normally easy-going freckled face turned scarlet and his eyes blazed. 'At least I'll be a man one day, even if I'm not yet sixteen,' he said angrily. 'But you, Rita Jeffries, will never be a man, because you're just a silly little girl who thinks she's oh so marvellous . . .'

Rita, who was carrying a long-handled brush, suddenly whirled round and round, shouting she was glad she would never be a horrible boy, and let go of the brush, which flew across the clearing and hit Woody's head with such force that he was knocked over. There was a general outcry and Rita rushed to apologise and pick him up, but Woody scrambled to his feet, the light of battle in his eyes. Imogen saw that he had a bruise the size of an egg on the side of his forehead, a bruise which was dripping blood, and noticed how he swayed and clutched the nearest tree for support. She turned on Rita, too angry to guard her tongue as she usually did with the other girl.

'You wicked girl, Rita Jeffries!' she shouted, her voice trembling. 'You could've killed him, and all he did was say you weren't a boy, which is pretty damned self-evident. You're wicked . . . and if you had killed him, it would have been murder, so tell him you're sorry!'

'I'm not sorry; he started it,' Rita yelled, but her voice was trembling. She turned to Imogen. 'Oh, come off it, Immy. It was an accident, and anyway I said I was sorry . . .'

Debby tried to break in again, still apparently wanting to make peace, but now Imogen was yelling at Rita and neither of them paid any attention until Josh's voice rose over the hubbub.

'We've got to get him back to the Linnet, or at least

to the village,' he said urgently. 'That whack on the temple ought to be seen to.' He turned to Rita. 'You can do what you like, but I reckon it will take the rest of us to get him back to civilisation, so you can help if you want or go your own way.'

'I'm not coming back with you. He'll be all right, and someone's got to clear the Lookout,' she said sulkily.

'No, I think not,' Imogen said firmly. 'I think we should all go back to the village. Then if he's okay we can do the clean-up of the Lookout later.'

Rita had begun to say that she needed no advice from Imogen, thank you very much, when Woody swayed and dropped to the earth, frightening all of them, Imogen was sure, though Rita tried to pretend indifference.

Josh immediately took charge. 'I'm not at all sure whether we should move him, with a head wound I mean,' he said uneasily. 'But I think we have to; we can't leave him here. Come on, troops!'

In fact even as they heaved Woody to his feet he came round, and though glad of their support he managed to walk all the way to the village, where the doctor took a look at his head, patted him on the cheek and said in rallying tones: 'You'll live, my lad. Tripped and fell, did you? Well, take more water with it next time!'

Woody laughed dutifully, but when they left the surgery and found Rita hanging about outside he vetoed any idea of returning to their original plan to clean up the Lookout. 'If you don't mind I'll just walk very slowly back to the farm and have a lie down,' he said. And then, with a return of his usual spirit: 'And don't you glare at me, young Rita, because if it wasn't for you my head wouldn't be banging like a trip hammer, and I'd be first up that perishing tree.'

Imogen looked warningly at Rita. She had noticed how sharp-tongued her friend had become, and wondered whether it had something to do with the damage to Rita's mother's house. She had consulted Auntie on a day when Rita was not around, and Auntie had told her that she did not think that was the cause. 'She's the oldest of you; if you were back in the city she'd probably be leaving school at Christmas,' she explained. 'She's neither fish, flesh nor good red herring; not a child any longer but not a woman yet either.' She glanced almost shyly at Imogen. 'I can remember when I was her age how it felt to be neither one thing nor t'other; part woman, capable of having a child, and part child . . . dear me, I'm not explaining very well. Perhaps you can't understand until it happens to you . . . can you understand, love?'

Imogen had wrinkled her nose. 'It sounds perfectly horrible,' she said after a moment's thought. 'And I'm not that much younger than Rita. But I do understand what you mean, because I think I may be young for my age. For instance, Rita spends her pocket money now on ladies' magazines and reads every word, whereas Debby and I still get the *Beano* and *Dandy*, and laugh like drains at all the funny bits.'

'Well, there you are then,' Auntie had said comfortably. 'And I'm glad you and Debby are still children, though very sensible ones.'

But now, standing on the pavement outside the doctor's small surgery, it seemed that Imogen's warning glance had not been necessary. With one of the abrupt changes of mood which had become almost commonplace, Rita smiled at Woody and held out her hand. 'I'm really sorry I whacked you with the broom,' she said penitently. 'I didn't mean to, honest to God I didn't. And you're right, you can't possibly climb up to the platform whilst your head is still swimming. I'll go and see that all's well there, then join you at the farm.' She turned to Imogen. 'You go with him. I can manage alone.'

'Tell you what, Woody and I will go back to the farm whilst you lot go to the Lookout,' Josh suggested. 'With you and Imogen on the job you'll have it shipshape in no time. And you can take Rufus, because I know Auntie doesn't like you going off alone.'

This was agreed, and as soon as they reached the Lookout Debby settled herself comfortably at the foot of the tree, an arm round Rufus's shaggy neck, whilst the other two began the climb.

They reached the platform which, in truth, was only a couple of planks nailed between two stout branches, and found, as Woody had predicted, that the leaves had piled up in the autumn gales along with a great many broken twigs, and even small branches. Imogen leaned over the side and shouted to Debby to get away from the bole, and then she and Rita began to clear the debris. Naturally enough a good deal of this fell on the branches below, and in order to make the climb safe the girls had to clear such things as ancient birds' nests and even an empty meal sack on the way down. They had almost finished their task and were thinking hopefully of their satchels at the foot of the tree and the sandwiches and lemonade therein when Rita grabbed Imogen's arm and pointed away to their right, where the forest became even deeper and more tangled. 'See that huge old yew, or whatever it is?' she asked. 'What's that thing hanging in the upper branches?' She giggled. 'It looks like an enormous chrysalis . . . gosh, I hope it isn't a bomb, because if so it's an unexploded one, and I suppose we ought to inform the authorities. What do you think?'

Imogen peered in the direction Rita had indicated, but at first could see nothing, for the trees were in luxuriant leaf. But after a moment she thought she could see a sort of thickening and nodded her head when Rita said: 'Well? I don't believe it is a bomb – they're pretty dark, aren't they? This thing is quite light-coloured. I wonder if it's visible from the ground?'

'Dunno,' Imogen said vaguely. 'But I'm awfully hungry, so let's get down and eat our sandwiches. Then we can take a closer look at the bundle, or bomb, or whatever it is.'

Rita agreed, but when the two girls reached the ground they realised they could no longer see the yew tree and would have to fight their way towards it through the tangled undergrowth. 'And we probably won't be able to see the bundle even then,' Rita said ruefully. 'How the undergrowth has grown up since we were here last!' She glanced at the sun, high overhead. 'Anyway let's have our lunch before we do anything else. If we can't spot whatever it is, I suppose I'll have to go up to the platform and shout directions to you, but you'll have to be jolly careful because if it is a bomb it might go off if a bird landed on it. Agreed?'

'I don't know what you're talking about,' Debby said aggrievedly, having listened to the conversation without understanding a word. 'If you can see a bomb from the platform we ought to go away from the horrible thing, not towards it. But I don't understand . . . bombs hit the ground. How can you see something on the ground better when you're high up in the air?'

'It's something hanging in one of the trees, Debby,' Rita said in a tone of exaggerated patience. 'We don't really think it's a bomb. It looks more like a bundle of canvas, or something like that. You remember the storm a few weeks back? If someone was camping out in the woods I suppose their tent might easily be blown into a tree. Perhaps it's just that.'

As they talked the girls had been getting out their food, and now they settled down to the serious business of eating. Only when they were folding up the paper which had contained their picnic did the talk revert to the bundle in the tree. Then the three of them got to their feet, settled their satchels on their backs and began to make their way in what they hoped was the right direction. It was a difficult and unpleasant walk, for they had to more or less hack their way through young saplings, waist-high grass, and a great swag of ivy which must have been torn off a tree and now dangled across what had once been a path. It was made even more difficult by the fact that they could not look both up and down at the same time, and when at last Rita gave a triumphant shout Imogen was too tired to feel anything but relief. She peered up, at first unable to see anything against the dazzling blue of the sky, then realised that what she was looking at must be the object for which they searched. And now, seeing what she had taken for a mere thickening of the branches clearly for the first time, Imogen was in no doubt as to what it was. 'It's a parachute, and it looks as though it's wrapped round something,' she said uncertainly. 'Could it be a man? Only I don't remember a plane crashing or coming down on fire last night, do you?' Both the other girls shook their heads, but Rufus, who had been staring up into the tree, gave a short sharp bark and, rearing up on his hind legs, began to paw at the trunk, glancing at the girls as though to say that if they didn't try to climb it, he would.

The girls looked at one another, then Imogen seized a branch which grew conveniently a couple of feet above her head. 'Good job it's a yew; they're always the easiest to climb because their branches grow out sideways and make a sort of step ladder,' she said. She heaved herself up, then turned to look down at the girls below. 'Suppose – suppose it's wrapped round a corpse?' she said, her voice trembling. 'If it's the body of some poor pilot I'll probably faint and fall out of the tree.'

Rita laughed. 'And then there'll be two corpses,' she said drily. 'If you're that scared you'd better let me go up.'

She made as if to hoist herself up into the branches, but Debby squeaked and grabbed her arm. 'Don't leave me here with only Rufus for company,' she said. 'Oh, oh, oh!'

'Oh, Debby, what's up *now*?' Rita said crossly. 'I wasn't going to climb up whilst Imogen is still climbing, because she'll kick bits of bark and rubbish into my face. But why did you yelp?'

'It moved – I saw it move – it's got a sort of boot thing and it moved, I tell you,' Debby said hysterically. 'Oh, I don't like it; I wish we'd never come. Suppose – suppose . . .'

But high up in the old yew tree Imogen was looking into the scarred and terrible face of a young man – she assumed he was young – wearing a flying helmet and a leather jacket. She thought he must be dead, trussed up like a hen for market, but when some movement of hers caused him to swing towards her he gave a groan, proving, at least, that he was not yet a corpse.

Imogen summoned up all her courage and spoke to the inert figure. 'It's all right, we've found you, you'll soon be safe,' she said. She leaned over, looking down at the three faces looking up at her. 'It's all right. It's a man and he's alive, though he's quite badly hurt,' she shouted. 'Rita, if you can come up and give me a hand perhaps we could untangle him from his chute. He seems to have got wrapped up in it somehow. It's no use simply cutting away his harness because that's all that's holding him up, and he'd just crash through the branches and . . . oh . . .' She breathed a sigh of relief as Rita joined her on the branch. 'I think we ought to fetch help and not touch him in case we do more damage.' She jerked a thumb at the booted leg dangling close against the trunk of the tree at a very odd angle. 'I should think that leg is broken, probably more than once. He's unconscious, but I think he's been here for quite a while; we're probably only just in time.'

'Mm-hm,' Rita said. She turned and began to climb down the tree, and when she and Imogen were both on terra firma once more she looked hard at the other girl. 'He's a Nazi; I s'pose you realise that,' she said. 'By the look of him he's nearly dead anyway. I think the best thing to do would be to say nothing and do nothing either. He's our enemy, don't forget. It's what a German girl would do if she found Laurie or Dave in deep woodland, completely helpless. Why, don't you remember what Ricky told us? That their pilots are ordered to shoot any RAF chaps floating to earth on a parachute? And even if you're stupid enough to want to save the life of an enemy, how are you going to find him again? No one comes through this part of the wood.'

Debby had been watching, mouth open, as Rita spoke, but now she broke in. 'Do I gather that the man up there is a member of the Luftwaffe? But what's that got to do with anything? He's a man, fighting for his country . . . oh, Rita, how could you possibly leave anyone, anyone at all, to die such a dreadful death?'

Imogen noticed Rita's cheeks flush. 'But if we tell Auntie – or anyone else for that matter – they'll guess about the Lookout, and that will be the end of that. We shan't be allowed near the beech wood ever again.

'And remember, if it hadn't been for me spotting him he'd have been dead long before anyone happened to find him,' Rita said. 'Why, for all we know he might have dropped the bombs which destroyed the city. You two are soft. We've all got reason to hate the Nazis – look what they did to Jill . . .'

Debby spoke up once more. 'I think you're just being silly, trying to get a rise out of us,' she said quietly. 'My family have suffered more than most at the hands of the Nazis but that doesn't mean that all Germans are bad, any more than all English are good. So let's stop being stupid and get this fellow help. You two go back to the village and explain what you've found and Rufus and I will stay at the foot of the tree to mark the spot, because it really is awfully difficult to find in this thick undergrowth. The moment we hear you approaching I'll start shouting to guide you to the yew tree, and I dare say Rufus will join in. I don't need to ask you to hurry, because I'm sure you will. Tell them to bring a ladder, because grown-ups don't climb trees. And as for losing the Lookout, we'll meet that threat when we come to it.'

'Thanks, Debby,' Imogen said gratefully. She knew how the other girl hated being alone. 'We'll be back as soon as we can.'

Chapter Nine

Debby watched Imogen and Rita disappear, keeping her arm round Rufus just in case he decided to go with them, but instead he reached up and licked her cheek as if to say 'Don't worry, I'm staying with you.' Debby was so touched that she kissed him back, and then settled down. She calculated that it would be at least half an hour before rescue could arrive, probably considerably longer, and began to wait with what patience she could muster. To pass the time she imagined Woody in the farm kitchen regaling Mrs Pilgrim with stories of how he came by the enormous bump on his head. Debby smiled to herself. If there was any justice, Rita should be worrying over what Mrs Pilgrim would say, for that lady had a tongue as sharp as Rita's own at times. However, Debby knew that Woody would not dream of telling tales. He had invented a fall to explain away the bruise to the doctor and would doubtless stick to the same story for the Pilgrims.

Sitting with her back to the old yew and glancing to where her companions had disappeared, she saw a fallen log, and was just admiring the crop of tiny scarlet-capped toadstools which grew mossy and bright in its shelter when Rufus yipped and glanced upwards. Debby followed his gaze and saw a tiny movement again from the figure so tightly swaddled in his parachute. She stood up, feeling her heart begin to hammer in her breast. Suppose he was dying, wanting to know that he was not alone? Debby looked doubtfully at the tree. She had watched Imogen scaling the branches as easily as though it had been a staircase and she knew that Rita had done the same. But I am afraid of heights, Debby reminded herself. I can't, I really can't, climb that tree. And if I did, if I managed somehow to get all the way up to where that man is dangling, what could I possibly do for him?

She had been staring up at the bundle which she now knew to be a man, her eyes watering against the brilliance of the sunshine, and now she looked at Rufus, who was whining and staring upwards. As she watched he reared up on to his hind legs, his front paws on the craggy trunk of the yew, and then he turned his head and there was something in his expression which brought the blood rushing to Debby's cheeks. It was as though he was saying 'You've got to do something! If I wasn't a dog I'd be up that tree before you could say knife!'

Debby took a deep, steadying breath and began, very cautiously at first, to climb the tree. And the climb proved not to be so bad after all, so long as she did not look down.

She reached her objective and looked for the first time into that strange damaged face. His flying helmet hid his hair completely, but she saw that he had a high-bridged nose and square cheekbones with hollows beneath. His mouth gaped, but his chin was deeply cleft and the stubble on his jaw was dirt-streaked. She imagined that the burns which she could see on his face and neck had happened before he had baled out and the livid cuts and bruises would have been inflicted as he had plunged through the upper branches of the great trees, to come to rest in the fork of the yew. At the sight of his ruined face she felt both fear and revulsion and wished with all her heart that Imogen had been with her; not Rita, who would scoff at her fears, but Immy who would understand. Leaning close, she saw that the man's eyes were closed and forced herself to put out a tentative hand, meaning to touch him, but before she could do so his heavy lids lifted and he spoke. His voice was hoarse and cracked, and when she snatched her hand back he spoke again. '*Wasser* . . . water,' he croaked, and with the word she noticed his dry, split lips and realised his desperate need.

Water! Of course, he had been caught up there for hours, possibly days, with the sun beating down on him, unable to move so much as a finger; his thirst must be almost unbelievable, and at the thought of what he must have suffered both fear and revulsion left her. It might have been Laurie or Dave, or even Josh. She stiffened her back; they were a long way from the river or a stream, but even as she began to tell him rather shakily that she would try to fetch water she remembered the bottle of cold tea in her satchel.

'Right. I'll fetch you a drink,' she said, speaking slowly and clearly. When he had asked for water he had spoken in German; she supposed Rita was right that he was an enemy, but suddenly to Deb he was just a young man in need. 'I won't be gone long. Stay there!' It was not until she was halfway down the tree that she realised the foolishness of her last remark. Stay there, indeed! The poor devil had no choice but to stay there, but then he was in no state to quibble over her choice of words.

At the bottom of the tree Rufus greeted her wildly, leaping up and licking her chin, giving little whines of pleasure as though he knew how frightened she had been and was congratulating her on her courage. He stood close to her, pressed against her knees, whilst she extracted the bottle of cold tea from her satchel. It was only about a quarter full and she wished she had not drunk so greedily earlier in the day, but then she remembered how they had been told on a first aid course in the Guides that only small drinks should be given to sick or wounded people. Satisfied, she slid her arms through the straps of the satchel, gave Rufus's head a valedictory pat and began to climb once more. She reached the man, but he seemed to have lost consciousness again and when she tried to trickle some tea into his half open, smashed mouth he did not swallow and it occurred to her that he might choke if she continued. How she longed for someone to join her, to tell her what she should do! Then she remembered how Mrs Pilgrim had once fed a tiny motherless lamb by dipping the corner of a soft cloth into a pan of warm milk and giving it to the little creature to suck. Hastily, Debby produced the handkerchief she kept in her knicker leg – luckily it was quite clean – splashed a little tea on to it, and wetted the man's lips and dry, almost stick-like tongue. At first there was no response, so she squeezed the handkerchief in order that a few drops might fall into the man's mouth, and presently had the satisfaction of realising from the convulsive movement of his throat that he was swallowing, though his eyes remained closed. She was still slowly feeding him the liquid, drop by drop, when she heard a commotion from below, and realised that rescue had arrived. She turned to the young man. 'Can you hear that?' she whispered. 'That means Imogen and Rita and the men from the village are coming to get you down. I wonder how they found us, though? Because I said I'd wait at the foot of the tree and keep calling out once I heard them approaching.'

Understandably, the young man made no reply, and Debby was about to explain that she would have to stop feeding him the tea and return to earth when she heard a voice echoing up from the ground below.

'Well, how typical of Debby to wander off without a thought for the rest of us!' Rita said. 'Good thing it's the only yew tree in this part of the wood; good thing I spotted the bundle when Mr Huggit and Mr Pilgrim would have gone straight on past. If it hadn't been for me . . .'

'Well, I like your bleedin' cheek!' That was Josh, who must have got wind of what was happening and joined the rescue party. 'If it hadn't been for Rufus we'd still be wandering around in quite the wrong direction, calling Debby's name and trying to spot the parachute.'

Debby peered down through the branches. 'I heard you, Rita Jeffries,' she said furiously. 'Just remember who it was who wanted to leave the poor chap to die, because he was a German and not one of our boys. Just remember . . .'

But, perhaps fortunately, Imogen's voice cut across Debby's furious denunciation. And looking down, Debby could see that there were now several more faces upturned towards her and regretted her words. 'Debby! How on earth did you get up there?'

Despite her anger, Debby could not help giggling. 'How do you think?' she asked. 'I didn't fly, and I didn't fall from the sky like this poor fellow did. I climbed up because he was desperate for something to drink and now I shall climb down.' She hoped that no one, particularly Rita, could hear the tremble in her voice. She had climbed down the tree to fetch the bottle of tea without any qualms, but then she had been so intent on relieving the unfortunate airman's thirst that she had barely given a thought to the perils of the climb. Gritting her teeth, she started to descend, whilst below her Mr Pilgrim and one of the farmhands began to erect a ladder and the other men who had joined the rescue party manhandled an ancient door, to which Debby guessed they would presently strap the injured flier.

The moment Debby was on the ground Imogen gave her a hug. 'You're braver than the lot of us, isn't she, Rita?' she said. 'We all know you're afraid of heights, so climbing the tree would have been harder for you than for anybody else. Dr Vaughan doesn't like heights either so he isn't going up the ladder; he'll examine the airman once the other men have got him safely to the ground.'

Debby began to reply but then sank down on the ground beside Rufus, because her knees were trembling so much that she was afraid of falling. She looked up at Rita and saw the other girl's reddened cheeks and trembling mouth, and was sorry for drawing attention to her outburst earlier. 'I'm awful sorry I said what I did, Rita,' she apologised in a subdued tone. 'I know you didn't mean a word of it.'

Josh, who had been watching the men erecting the ladder, came over to them and ruffled Debby's already ruffled hair. 'Now you've given me the lead I suppose I'll have to start climbing trees too,' he said cheerfully. He turned to Rita. 'Care to give me lessons? I've heard Woody say you're as good as any monkey when it comes to climbing.' He lowered his voice. 'And as for leaving the fellow in the tree, of course you didn't mean a word of it, you were just reacting. I mean, we all hate the Nazis, but I've heard Laurie say that it's not a personal thing; when our fellows bomb a German city they try not to think that there are people down there as well as factories and so on.'

It was clear to Debby that Josh was trying to show he did not believe Rita had meant the horrid things she had said, and all might have been well had Rita not decided to justify herself just as the door, with the young man strapped upon it, came gently to earth. All three of them got up and went over to look at the injured man, and Josh was just wondering whether the bloody furrow which slashed his badly burned face was, as Imogen had thought, a rope burn and not the path of a bullet, when Rita spoke once more. 'Look at that bullet mark. It was probably fired by one of our gunners trying to down a German bomber,' she commented. 'If so, this bloke deserves to be in prison for a hundred years.'

Debby had had enough. 'For God's sake shut up; save your breath to cool your porridge, as Auntie says,' she snapped. 'If you're trying to prove how horrid you can be, you're doing a good job of it.' She glanced around, at the doctor kneeling beside the injured airman, at the men reassembling the ladder and at the others limbering up to lift the door. 'There's nothing more we can do here,' she said briskly. 'Let's go home.'

Auntie was making a Woolton pie when the back door burst open and the three girls and Josh came into the room. Auntie had already heard, on a trip into the village, that an airman and his parachute had somehow managed to get tangled up in one of the forestry trees, and guessed at once that the children she regarded as her own responsibility must have been involved. So when they came into the kitchen and all began talking at once she had to disappoint them. 'Hush,' she said reprovingly. 'You don't have to tell me that one of our brave boys ended up caught in a tree, because I heard the news when I went into the village to see if anyone could sell me some onions. And I was lucky, so I'm making a Woolton pie for our supper tonight. I take it that you four were in on the act? Where's Woody?'

'Oh, he had a bang on the head and felt dizzy, so he went back to the farm,' Josh said quickly. 'Don't worry, he saw Dr Vaughan and he said Woody was fine.'

'Yes, Woody's okay, but it was us – us girls – who found the man wrapped up in his parachute right at the top of an old yew tree,' Imogen said excitedly. 'And he wasn't one of our chaps, Auntie, he was a German, probably a Luftwaffe pilot. On the way home the men were talking and someone said he must have been dangling from that tree for at least two days, unable to help himself. The doctor said he had a lot of broken bones and was badly de . . . dehydrated, so he'll be in hospital in the city for a good while until he's well enough to go to a POW camp. And guess what, Auntie? Old Debby climbed the yew tree whilst Rita and I went for help, and you know how frightened Debby is of heights.'

'I've heard tell,' Auntie said cautiously, 'but of course I've only seen you climbing trees in the orchard. So he was a German flier, was he? Well, that's one less to shoot down our brave boys.'

'That's what I said,' Rita put in. 'But these ninnies seem to think we ought to be pleased that he got down alive. *I'm* not pleased. I don't want him turning his guns on our air force as soon as he's well enough . . .'

'Oh Lor', she's off again,' Josh said wearily. He turned to Rita. 'At first I understood why you were so against the idea of helping the chap in the tree – he was a German after all – but when I heard how badly he was injured . . . for goodness' sake, Rita, he'll be no threat to anyone.' He turned to Auntie. 'We took him to the village and Dr Vaughan telephoned for an ambulance. The poor fellow was unconscious all the time, but the doc says he's broken both legs, one arm, and several ribs . . . and he's horribly burned. Honest to God, Auntie, he's a mess.' He glanced across at Rita. 'I suppose you could say he was fighting for his country the same as we're fighting for ours. And now let's forget it.' He turned to Auntie. 'I told Mr P I was coming here with the girls and wouldn't be home in time for tea – would you mind if I invited myself to supper? I love your Woolton pie. But perhaps you'd rather I didn't stay?'

Whilst he had been talking Auntie had placed the pie in the oven, and now she smiled reassuringly at him. 'Ridiculous boy, of course you must,' she said. 'Why should you not? Everyone's a trifle overwrought after so much excitement and I'm sure Rita never means half the things she says. Now run upstairs, girls, and tidy yourselves. By the time you've done that it will be almost time to eat. Off with you; Josh shall pay for his supper by laying the table whilst you're gone.'

Upstairs in their room there was an uncomfortable silence whilst the girls washed and changed into clean cotton frocks, but when they were ready, and still had not said a word, Imogen spoke. 'Pax,' she said, smiling at Rita. 'The subject of the airman is now closed. Will you shake on it?'

She half expected Rita to refuse, but after a moment Rita took the offered hand. 'I suppose since he's now a prisoner of war there's nothing more to be said,' she remarked. 'And now let's get at the Woolton pie before Josh eats the lot.'

On Monday Auntie announced that she was going into the city since she had to see an official about acquiring another pig. 'If I've time I'll pop into the hospital, see how your young German airman is getting on,' she told them at breakfast. 'No school today – Mr P needs your help with the haymaking. You'll have the harvest lunch and tea which Mrs P provides, so no need to even think about cooking, and I'll be home in time for supper.' She glanced across the table to where Rita was pushing her porridge spoon moodily round the dish and addressed her. 'Rita, love, no quarrels today please. When I get back you and I must have a talk.'

Imogen saw Rita flush and said quickly: 'It's all right, Auntie, we'll all be good as gold, and we won't even mention the Jerry.' All the girls agreed and they had an excellent day, without so much as one cross word. The boys walked them home, and when Auntie returned a surprise awaited them. She came into the kitchen lugging two obviously heavy baskets, a wide smile on her face. Imogen, toasting bread on a fork extended to the small flame under the Primus, had begun to ask whether she had managed to get some baked beans – they had just opened the last can – when she dumped her baskets and clapped her hands for attention. Josh emerged from the pantry giving a military salute and Woody, pouring tea into mugs, stopped short. 'What's up, Auntie?' he enquired.

'Your airman's not a Jerry,' Auntie said triumphantly. 'He's a foreigner all right, though. He's Polish, his name is Stan Mielczarek and he's stationed at RAF Crumpton, up in Lincolnshire, quite near dear Laurie.'

For several weeks after Stan's rescue there was a certain degree of harmony at the Canary and Linnet. The weather was fine and the girls spent more time helping at the farm than they did either at school or at the pub. But as Imogen told Jill when the older girl came home for a forty-eight, Rita was still difficult, apt to take offence over almost nothing and frequently abandoning them as they worked in the hay, or rode the great wagons – wains as Mr Pilgrim called them – back to the farm. Sometimes when they returned to the Linnet it was to find that Rita had made herself a sandwich and gone off to bed, and if they climbed the stairs and tried to persuade her to join them for supper she just hunched an offended shoulder and told them to bugger off. So when Auntie visited Stan in hospital and got permission for the youngsters, including the boys, to visit as well, Imogen and Debby doubted whether Rita would go. 'After all the things she said about him, even after she knew he was one of us, she can't possibly want to see him, even in a hospital bed,' Debby said. 'But you never know; she's really unpredictable, isn't she, Immy?'

Imogen agreed that this was so and was both pleased and surprised when Rita said stiffly that she had been the first to see the bundle in the tree and therefore had every right to visit the hospital.

'Of course you have; if it hadn't been for you spotting him the three of us would have finished cleaning the Lookout and gone home,' Imogen said at once. She looked anxiously at Rita. 'Only – only you won't say anything nasty to him, will you, Rita? Auntie says he's in a poor way . . .'

'I can say anything at all, because even if I said I hoped he ached all over he wouldn't understand a word,' Rita snapped. 'Anyway, I don't mean to talk to him. I shall just stand in the background and stare whilst you jabber on. Bloody foreigners! For all we know he might be a spy.'

Debby and Imogen exchanged anxious glances; what was the matter with Rita this time? She had always been sharp-tongued but now she either did not speak to them at all or said something so horrid that it killed any conversation stone dead. When questioned, Auntie shrugged rather helplessly but said that they must not mind. She thought that Rita must have worries unconnected with the Canary and Linnet. 'She never reads bits of her letters aloud, or tells us what's been happening to her mother,' she reminded them. 'She's at an awkward age. But I'll have a word with her, tell her that I am trusting her not to make trouble.'

Later, Auntie expanded on her visit, saying he was a nice young man with rather limited English. 'But by the time he's able to leave the hospital and go back to his flight at RAF Crumpton he'll be chattering away like the rest of us,' she said. 'He's intelligent; he was studying at university to get a medical degree, so he's hoping to be a doctor one of these days. But at the moment he's just a lonely young man, unable to leave his bed, and, the sister on his ward told me, pathetically grateful for any small kindness.' Here she handed Imogen a small jar of homemade toffee. 'Just a little present,' she murmured, and Imogen saw that she was avoiding Rita's eyes. 'I know Mrs Pilgrim is sending him one of her carrot cakes, and the hospital staff will see he gets your gift as well.'

So the five of them, for Woody insisted that he was entitled to accompany them even though – and here he shot a fulminating glance at Rita – he had not been present at the rescue, set out and boarded a bus which would drop them outside the hospital gates. Rita always behaved better when Woody was with them, Imogen remembered, and thought there was a good chance that the visit might be quite pleasant after all.

They reached the hospital and reported themselves to a neat little nurse on the reception desk in the front hall. She entered their names in a sort of visitors' book and then summoned another nurse to lead them to ward H, where their guide gestured vaguely at the patients. 'He don't speak much English and you're only allowed thirty minutes,' she said briefly. 'I'll come and fetch you when your time's up.'

'Hang on a minute,' Woody said, since the others seemed struck dumb. 'Which one is he?'

But the nurse had whisked round and was already halfway back to reception, leaving Woody staring at the girls and Josh whilst they scanned the young men in the beds on either side of the ward.

Imogen stared hopefully but it seemed to her that she had never seen so many legs and arms encased in plaster, or young men wearing identical striped pyjamas, or faces and heads swathed in bandages. 'They all look alike,' she whimpered, but Rita gave an exasperated snort and pointed.

'He's that one; don't you remember the burns and the bullet mark on his cheek and brow? Goodness, I never even thought he might be a blond.' She turned to Woody. 'He might have been handsome once, but he's hideous now.' She looked at Imogen, and for the first time for ages gave her a small, tight smile. 'Good thing he's sleeping, and can't hear me,' she said.

Before they left the hospital, however, Stan awoke. Auntie must have explained that his rescuers had been youngsters for he smiled round at them before muttering a few words which they took to be thanks. However, it was not a very satisfactory visit, for Stan could not remember how he came to land in the tree, nor why he had been swaddled so securely in his parachute. He remembered nothing about the rescue, not even Debby feeding him with cold tea; in fact it seemed he remembered nothing from the moment he had abandoned his burning aircraft until he woke in a hospital bed.

Their visit had been limited to half an hour and Debby, looking round at the others, could see relief on every face when the bell for the end of visiting sounded. It was difficult conversing with someone who had so little English and she knew they were all glad that it was time to say goodbye and leave him. As they crossed the foyer, heading thankfully for the outside world, however, Woody saw a doctor and stopped him to enquire how long the patient in the third bed from the end – the Pole with the unpronounceable name – was likely to be incarcerated here.

The young doctor blew out his cheeks and frowned. 'He's a strong young man but a good deal damaged. My personal opinion is that he'll be here for months rather than weeks.' He grinned as he saw their obviously downcast expressions. 'I expect he was hard work this evening, but as his health improves so will his grasp of English and his interest in what is going on about him. If you visit say once a week for the next month I'm sure you'll notice changes for the better every time you come to the hospital.'

For the first month the girls trailed dutifully to the hospital once a week, though the boys said they were far too busy. But after that first month both Imogen and Rita felt they were wasting their time sitting beside the bed whilst Debby regaled Stan with stories of any happening she thought might interest him.

Once, when Imogen and Rita had gone further up the ward to talk to another airman, hospitalised after breaking both legs, Stan had lowered his voice to a hissing whisper. 'I have not said how my memory has begun to return, but you, little Debby, were my good angel. You gave me tea out of a bottle and spoke to me kindly. It must be boring for you spending so much time telling me about your life, but it is what makes *my* life worth continuing. Your friends won't come to see me so often now they're really needed on the farm; before I came to England and joined the RAF I worked with my father on his farm in the university holidays so I know that everyone gives a hand at harvest time. But please, little angel Debby, don't you desert me.'

Debby had taken his hand and pressed it to her cheek. 'I *like* coming,' she said truthfully. 'But you're right, of course: Imogen and Rita truly are needed on the farm . . .' As she spoke the bell for the end of visiting rang out and she jumped to her feet and beckoned to her friends.

'Come along, you two,' she said briskly. 'If you run we can catch the early bus.'

The three girls were harvesting the wheat along with their schoolfellows and most of the boys from Hemblington Hall. The day was hot and sunny, an ideal day for the work in hand, and it seemed impossible to Imogen that anyone could be cross or bad-tempered on such a day and doing such a task, but Rita was quite clearly in one of her fractious moods.

Debby, realising this, burst into speech. 'I wrote to Stan last night. He sent me a card with his new address on it – he's at RAF Sandwich, still up in Lincolnshire, with all his old flight or whatever they call it.'

The binder passed them, spitting out the neatly tied sheaves, and the girls pounced on them and carried them to where the men were expertly stacking them into stooks. They handed their burdens over and went back to catch the next lot, and it was not until then that Rita voiced her thoughts. 'I don't think you ought to bother about him – that Stan – when they're beginning to appeal for people to send letters and parcels to our chaps in POW camps,' she said. 'From what we've read in the newspapers our POWs, particularly the ones in the Japanese camps, are having a terrible time. We put the German prisoners to work on the farms, but they say that the Japs and the Germans make our men do all sorts: huge construction works like building bridges and railways and tunnels and canals . . .'

Imogen took a deep breath. Long experience had told her that arguing with Rita was a lost cause. Rita was only interested in her own point of view, so, as Auntie was fond of saying, Imogen might as well save her breath to cool her porridge. So she waited without saying a word whilst Rita went on and on, and, when she ran out of steam, said calmly, 'Yes, Rita, I'm sure you're right and we ought to be corresponding with some poor chap in one of the enemy's POW camps. I mean to do so; I've sent away for an address. Have you?'

Rita mumbled something to the effect that she'd been too busy, but would get round to it sometime, and Imogen did not challenge this blatant lie, knowing that it would only lead to another argument. All she said was: 'All right, all right, I think you've made your point, but there's nothing to stop Debby writing to Stan as well, is there? And anyway, I like Stan.' She looked defiantly at Rita. 'If it wasn't for his burns he'd be rather good-looking, don't you think? His hair's the same colour as this corn, and his eyes are lovely.'

Rita gave a contemptuous snort just as the two mighty carthorses who pulled the binder came level with them once more. 'Trust you to judge somebody by his looks,' she said scornfully. 'I like a man to look like a man, not like a pretty little girl. And you'd better get on with the work before somebody notices you slacking.'

Imogen bit her lip but Debby, who had run forward

to pick up a couple of sheaves, grinned and winked, and somehow the gesture turned Rita's nastiness into a joke. As the binding continued the girls parted company, Imogen going off to help build the stooks whilst the other two continued to carry the sheaves to where the men needed them. Once or twice Imogen glanced towards her friends, but could hear nothing of any conversation between them. And presently Woody came charging up with Josh in tow to say that they had been sent back to the farmhouse to help Mrs Pilgrim carry up the harvest grub. 'She's got lemonade for us and beer for the rest,' he said breathlessly. 'Can you be spared to give us a hand?' By this time the girls were separated by the whole width of the field, but Imogen made wild gestures and though Rita remained obstinately where she was Debby came and joined them at a quick trot. She was looking flushed but agreed eagerly to accompany them to the farm.

'What about Rita?' Woody asked. 'Didn't she understand what we meant when we beckoned to her? It's awful hot and everyone's been working all out since breakfast; I should have thought she would be keen to take a bit of a break.'

Debby looked conscience-stricken. 'Oh dear, I've been so careful to stay calm when Rita flies off the handle, but this time I lost my temper, really lost it, I mean. I – I told her things I always promised myself never to tell a soul. Oh, Woody, she just went on and on, you know how she does, and I'm afraid I let rip.'

Woody, Josh and Imogen stared at Debby as though they could not believe their ears, but then Woody laughed and the other two followed suit. 'I don't believe it! Little

Debby Viner actually losing her temper?' Woody said. 'I never thought to see the day! Has it put Rita in such a bate that she won't speak to any of us for a few hours? If so, it's a jolly good job. And what exactly did you say, anyhow? Come to that, what did she say to make you answer back?'

Debby shrugged. 'Oh, just the usual: my cousin Albert in the air force, my uncle George who's on an ack-ack battery near Portsmouth, my poor mother who can't run her hotel properly until she can get someone to replace all the windows and re-tile part of the roof.' Debby sighed. 'Honest to God, I wouldn't have lost my temper if I hadn't heard it all before about a hundred times, I should think.'

By this time the four of them were heading for the gate which led on to the lane, but Imogen was still puzzled. All of them, including the boys and Auntie, often referred to Debby as 'our little peacemaker', so not unnaturally Imogen wanted to find out just what Debby had said. But when she pressed her for an answer, Debby went very red and shook her head. 'I had no right to say what I did, and I don't intend to repeat it,' she said obstinately. 'What's more, I'm jolly certain that Rita won't repeat it either. In fact I'm quite hopeful that when I tell her to forget it and apologise for – for speaking out of turn, she'll forgive me and we can continue to be friends.'

'If you ever were friends,' Woody muttered, but he said it so quietly that Imogen thought she was the only one who heard. He raised his voice. 'Oh, these little tiffs blow over, and it'll be a change for Rita not to be the one who started it. And now let's get a move on, because we shan't be very popular if the workers have to wait for their midday break.'

As they emerged on to the lane, Imogen glanced back and saw that Rita, with a sheaf of wheat in her arms, was walking purposefully over to the men building the stooks. As she watched, Rita turned to look at her and it occurred to Imogen that the other girl looked rather pale. She beckoned, but with a typical gesture Rita tossed her head and turned to face forward once more. Imogen sighed and wondered again what on earth Debby had said, then decided that it really didn't matter. She knew the younger girl too well to think she would ever deliberately hurt anyone. No doubt in the heat of the moment she had reminded Rita of some peccadillo which the other would sooner forget. So what? Rita was far too fond of pointing out the faults of others; it was about time she had a taste of her own medicine. Imogen hurried to catch the others up.

When the four of them returned to the harvest field, accompanied by Mrs Pilgrim and a good deal of food and drink, Rita was nowhere to be seen, but when the meal was spread out she appeared and went to sit as far away as she could get from Debby, Imogen and the boys. Once more, Imogen beckoned to her to join them, but Rita merely tightened her lips and shook her head with such vigour that her long blonde plait bounced on her back. At one point Debby, very red in the face, went over to Rita and whispered something in her ear, then pointed to where the other three sat, but all Rita did was cram a sandwich into her mouth so that speech must have been impossible and shake her head vehemently. After another try, Debby shrugged and Imogen heard what she said quite clearly. 'All right, I know it was wrong to say what I did, but all I can do is apologise and I've done that twice already. Can't you pretend I never opened my mouth? I know I never should have done, but something you said flicked me on the raw. Oh, Rita, please forgive me.'

For a moment Imogen, listening and watching, thought that Rita was about to give in, but then Rita shook her head again, saying nothing, and after waiting for a couple of minutes Debby, who had sat down on the grassy verge next to Rita, sighed and got to her feet. 'All right. See you later,' she said, and re-joined Imogen and the boys.

The rest of the day was spent in the harvest field. Everyone was well aware that the fine weather might not last, so they worked until it was too dark to see. The boys offered to accompany the girls back to the Linnet but Imogen assured them that she and Debby – and Rita when she turned up – could see themselves home perfectly safely, so the boys went off to the farm whilst Imogen and Debby loitered, waiting for Rita to put in an appearance. When she had failed to do so after ten minutes, Imogen tucked her arm into Debby's, giving it a little shake. 'Don't worry. You know what she's been like lately, keeping herself to herself, spending hours reading her silly magazines, going to bed to get out of the washing up and then grumbling that the rest of us leave her all the nasty jobs. What *we* have to do now is pray that it won't rain before it's Mr Pilgrim's turn for the threshing machine, what they call the drum. When the fellows are sure that the stooks are dry, they'll make them into stacks; I still don't understand how they construct them so that they're pretty well weatherproof even without that sort of canvas hood they sometimes put over them. And I don't know how the drum separates the corn from the ears; I might ask Woody tomorrow.

He means to join the RAF as soon as he's old enough, but he thinks when the war is over he's going to be a farmer because he thinks we'll always need food whatever else we manage to do without.'

'I wonder what I'll do, when the war's over I mean,' Debby said. 'I used to think I'd like to go to university and get a degree in languages, but now I'm not so sure. You've got to be awfully clever to go to university. The thing is, all my family find learning languages easy. My parents spoke French, German, Polish and even some Russian as well as English. I remember my father saying that if you had languages you could take your choice so far as work was concerned. How about you, Immy? What do you want to do?'

Imogen considered as they walked along the country lane in the deepening dusk. 'I don't know,' she said dreamily. 'I'd like life to go on like this, for ever and ever. Do you know, I can hardly remember what it was like before the war? Living at the Canary and Linnet is the best thing that's ever happened to me, though of course it would be even better if Mum was here. I do love her, but when I think of our life in Liverpool . . . well, I don't think I could ever be happy there again.'

'I know what you mean,' Debby said after a thoughtful pause. She chuckled. 'Fancy having to go back to school every day, with no breaks for farm work or strawberry picking, no following the digger and picking the lovely new potatoes out of the loose earth . . .'

'No sitting round the fire on winter evenings passing round a bottle of milk and shaking it vigorously when your turn comes to make it into butter; no searching for the hen who lays astray and finding a whole clutch of beautiful brown eggs cunningly hidden away at the very bottom of the hedge,' Imogen said, joining in the game. 'No sneaking into the bar for empty glasses and listening to the jokes and chaff of the drinkers, no Auntie handing you the mixing bowl when she's been making her famous carrot cake and telling you to scrape it out and to share it with the others . . .'

'Oh, Immy, I just wish . . .' Debby began, then straightened her shoulders as they crossed the back yard of the pub. Only of course it wasn't a back yard any more, because they had turned it into a vegetable garden, and a very good one, too. 'No point in wishing, and anyway, I'm sure we'll have good times when we return to city life. There are cinemas, theatres, proper tennis courts, clubs you can join, oh, all sorts.' She looked hopefully at her companion as Imogen began to open the back door. 'We'll like it all right once we get home. Don't you think so, Immy?'

'Oh, sure,' Imogen said, hearing her own lack of enthusiasm with some dismay. Then she cheered up. 'Only I expect the war will last for ages yet, don't you?'

'Oh, Immy!' Debby said reproachfully, and they were both laughing as they entered the kitchen, to find Auntie snoozing over her knitting. She was making socks for soldiers, and very odd they looked, for Auntie was by no means an expert at the turning of the heel and, now that Jill was no longer around to do it for her, produced some surprising results. However, the opening of the back door roused her and she adjusted her spectacles and tried to sit up straight, saying as she did so: 'What's so funny? If you're laughing because I closed my eyes for a moment . . . I wasn't asleep, if that was what you were thinking.'

'It was; and you must have closed the pub early,' Imogen observed, seeing that the door between the kitchen and the bar was open, showing the bar to be empty of its usual customers. 'Is Rita back yet? There was a bit of a row – would you call it a row, Debs? – and she didn't walk back with us, but we want to make our peace.'

Auntie removed her specs, rubbed her eyes, then yawned. 'It's possible that she might have come in very quietly, not wanting to disturb me,' she said. 'But remember she's sleeping in Jill's room until the harvest is over because she says you two keep her awake by talking . . . not that I believe you do, for one moment, or if you do, young Rita chatters away as merrily as either of you two. But she does like to grumble occasionally.'

'Oh, damn!' Imogen said. 'I'd forgotten that. I'll go up and tell her she should never let the sun go down upon her wrath – that sort of thing – and she'll probably be quite chirpy and good-tempered by morning.'

Debby looked doubtful. 'Suppose I come and say sorry all over again?' she suggested as the two of them bade Auntie goodnight and began to ascend the stairs. 'It's me she's cross with, remember. And I don't mind apologising, honest I don't.'

But when they reached Jill's room and tapped gently on the door there was no response, and though neither Imogen nor Debby would have admitted to being afraid of Rita's tongue when roused from sleep they decided, by unspoken but mutual consent, not to disturb her until morning.

They prepared for bed in unusual silence, Debby

replying in monosyllables to everything Imogen said, and Imogen being far too tired to say much. But as she rolled between the sheets she said sleepily: 'Oh, Debs, just what *did* you say to offend Rita?' She remembered something suddenly and sat up, a hand flying to her mouth. 'You didn't tease her about the geranium petals?'

For a moment she thought that Debby was asleep, but then she heard a sleepy chuckle. 'No, I'd forgotten all about the geranium petals. And it was Woody who put her back up when he asked if she'd thought of using soot to darken her eyelashes. I thought she was going to hit him, but then he went on and told the story about someone who went to see a sad flick in the old days before the war, and her mascara, if that's what it's called, ran all down her face and made her look like a panda.'

'So what was it?' Imogen persisted.

But Debby, sleepy though she undoubtedly was, sat up on one elbow and spoke firmly. 'For goodness' sake, Immy, I told Rita I'd forget all about it and forget I shall. You won't learn anything, not if you nag all night, so will you kindly shut up and let me get some sleep!'

Imogen lay down with a defeated sigh. She knew when that note entered Debby's voice that she was serious. No use nagging; so far as the other girl was concerned the subject was closed. She cuddled her head into her pillow and smiled to herself. Apparently it had occurred to Rita – or perhaps she had read it in a magazine – that if she rubbed scarlet geranium petals on her lips it would look just as though she were using a real cosmetic, now that such things as lipsticks and rouge were simply not available. So Rita had disappeared into Jill's bedroom the previous day armed with a handful of geranium flowers and had come down with scarlet lips and a round scarlet patch on each cheek. If she had applied the petals with discretion it might have looked quite nice, but she had overdone it, not keeping to the natural outline of her mouth but trying to enhance it, and when the boys saw her they had been quite rude. Rita had pretended to take their teasing in good part and had rubbed off the offending colour on her hanky, but once the boys had gone home Rita had snapped Imogen's head off the moment she mentioned geranium petals, and in order to keep the peace both Imogen and Debby had steered clear of the subject. They were both beginning to be a little more interested in their appearance than before, but this took the form of trying their hair in different styles and making sure that their best frocks were always ironed before they put them on. It was only Rita who truly cared about her looks. Imogen accepted that when one has coal black hair one also has pale skin which does not take kindly to being exposed to the sun, whilst Debby occasionally wished aloud that her nose and mouth were smaller and her skin less sallow. 'Shove your head in the flour bin,' Rita had said nastily when Debby had moaned that she was so brown she was beginning to look like a foreigner. 'Don't you remember that story in the French book which we read at school? The girl with the big mouth who was told to make it smaller by repeating *petite pomme, petite pomme, petite pomme* before she went to bed each night, only she forgot which fruit the teacher had told her and so she said *petite poire, petite poire, petite poire* until her mouth was so huge it met round the back of her neck? Yours is like that, so if I were you I wouldn't worry about being tanned. No boy is going to look twice at you with a gob that size.'

Remembering, Imogen sighed to herself. What on earth was the matter with Rita? She had always been sharp, quick to criticise, but just lately she had seemed to take pleasure in being really horrible, particularly to Debby. Why? Everyone liked Debby; even Rita had done so, though she still picked on her. But there was just no understanding Rita, and Imogen made up her mind that she would take the other girl on one side the next day and ask her bluntly to stop creating friction. Things had been so pleasant when the five of them were together . . . come to think of it, Imogen realised, things were still okay when they were with the boys; it was just when there were only the three of them that Rita started to be nasty. Oh, not always to Debby, sometimes to Imogen herself, but Imogen always hit back, whereas Debby just went very quiet.

But this time was different, Imogen reminded herself, just before she slid into sleep. This time Debby had answered back, defended herself, maybe even attacked. Well, it served Rita jolly well right, and Imogen hoped, though without much conviction, that it might prevent Rita from criticising the younger girl in future.

Imogen usually slept deeply and dreamlessly, but perhaps because her mind was still active she went straight from sleep into a most peculiar dream. She was walking along beside a high chain-link fence; she trod on summer grass, like a hay meadow, starred with bright flowers, poppies, corn cockles and ox-eye daisies. But on the other side of the fence the earth was packed hard, and presently she saw men coming out from ramshackle buildings, men whose lagging bare feet scuffed up clouds of dust as they walked, and as they drew close she saw that they were skeletally thin, and though several of them looked towards her they made no sign that they were aware of her presence. More and more men poured out of the buildings, and with a sensation of sick horror Imogen saw that at intervals around the perimeter of the high fence there were towers upon which men in uniform sat, each one with a rifle laid across his knees. Staring, she suddenly saw, amidst all the skeletal strangers, someone she knew. She stared, her eyes watering, and it was Debby, but not the plump and smiling Debby she knew. This was a skinny waif, dressed in rags, her dark eyes fixed imploringly upon Imogen's face. She crept nearer the fence and spoke in a tiny whisper. 'Help me!' she said, and, as though the plea had been some sort of mantra, the men around her spoke the same words in low guttural tones. Imogen put her hand through the fence, even as the scene began to whirl in the topsy-turvy way dreams do, to whirl and to shrink until it was no larger than a postage stamp and she could only just make out the two tiny figures, Debby in the compound and herself on the outside. Then she was waking, sweat running down her neck, hauling herself upright in bed whilst her heart hammered unevenly and looking across to where Debby slumbered, fearing that the bed might be empty, that Debby might have been carried off to the terrible place of her dream.

But Debby was there, snoring a little, and presently Imogen lay down once more. It was only a dream, she told herself fiercely, only a dream. Gosh, I hope I never have a dream like that again! And I wonder why I had it now? Of course, people are saying that the Germans and Japanese are doing terrible things, but . . . oh, dear, will I ever be able to sleep again?

She lay for some time, gradually growing calmer, but as soon as she closed her eyes she began to toss and turn and she must have woken Debby, for suddenly the younger girl was standing by her bed and shaking her shoulder. 'You're having a nightmare, Immy,' Debby said softly. 'You poor thing. I used to have terrible nightmares when we first came to the Linnet but Auntie said I'd grow out of them, and I have, pretty well. Do you want to come into my bed or will you be all right now I've woken you up?'

'I'll be all right, but thanks, Debby,' Imogen said. 'I had a really horrible dream. I thought I'd never be able to sleep again, but I'll be all right now. Thanks ever so much; you're a real pal.' She slithered down her bed and, to her own surprise, presently slept.

Chapter Ten

Despite her broken night, Imogen woke, as she usually did, just before the alarm went off. She had a theory that the clock must make some little noise prior to starting to ring its bell and it was that which woke her. She leapt out of bed and began to wash, adjuring Debby to get a move on because the warm summer air coming through the window meant that they could work at the harvest, as they had the previous day, from daybreak until dusk.

'Ooh, aren't you horribly hearty,' Debby grumbled, climbing rather stiffly out of her own bed. 'Did you have a good night? After your nightmare, I mean?'

Imogen sloshed water into the round blue basin, soaped her face and neck, then ducked her head under the water to rinse off the suds before she rubbed herself dry and began to dress. 'Nightmare?' she said vaguely. 'Did I have a nightmare? I can't remember what it was about; in fact all I can remember is you waking me up. Here, I've finished. We needn't save any water for Rita because she'll have brought her own up last night. I keep meaning to ask Auntie if we can all have a go at sleeping in Jill's room, turn and turn about. I don't see why Rita should have it all to herself, do you?'

Debby, happily splashing water about, reached for the towel. 'I don't know,' she said doubtfully. 'I think the reason I stopped having nightmares was because I knew you or

Rita would wake me. It's the fear of nightmares that's the worst thing about them, I think. So if you want to take a turn at sleeping alone, I suppose I'll have to put up with sleeping with Rita. I just hope she's forgotten we fell out yesterday, but one thing I will say for her, she doesn't usually bear a grudge.'

'True, but that's just about the only thing you can say in her favour,' Imogen said ruefully. She slipped on the old dungarees she always wore for farm work, shoved her feet into a pair of plimsolls and went over to the door. 'Come on, lazy bones. Mrs P gave Auntie four eggs and four rashers of bacon so we could have a cooked breakfast like the one she gives the boys on harvest days.'

'I'm ready,' Debby said and the two girls abandoned the bedroom and clattered down the stairs to where Auntie was already at the range.

'Morning, girls,' she said cheerfully as they entered the kitchen. 'I heard you stirring so I knew it wouldn't be long before you were down, wooed by the smell of frying bacon. Where's Rita?'

Imogen was beginning to say that she was probably still sulking when she clapped a hand to her mouth, then spoke through her fingers. 'Oh Lor', I forgot! Jill took her alarm clock away with her when she joined the WAAF. I'll just nip up and give Rita a shake, though I can't imagine she'll still be in bed with that smell wafting up the stairs towards her.'

She left the room as she spoke, ran up the stairs, tapped perfunctorily on Jill's bedroom door and burst into the room. Rita was neither in bed nor at the washstand, and the room was in considerable disarray. Imogen sighed. She must have got up early and gone straight to the harvest field – or more likely she's gone to the farm to have breakfast with the Pilgrims and the boys – without saying a word to us. But it is rather odd, because as Debby said earlier, Rita doesn't usually bear a grudge. Perhaps she really is sorry for being nasty to Debby yesterday so she's started the chores early and will have finished them by the time she comes in for breakfast.

As all the girls did, Rita had pulled back the curtains, rolled up the blackout blind and thrown open the window, and now a slight breeze scented with summer wafted into the room. Imogen had been about to return to the kitchen but she paused, frowning. Something was different, something was here which should not have been, or possibly something was missing. She looked carefully at the muddle of clothing and possessions on the floor. Rita had been in this room for three nights; how on earth had she managed to get it in such a mess? They all knew Debby was the tidy one, but even so . . .

Imogen scanned the room again, and this time she saw what had caught her attention. Pinned to the pillow was a note, and even from across the room Imogen could see that it was in Rita's round, rather sprawly writing. Feeling almost like a spy in a novel, she tiptoed across the room and unpinned it. It was addressed to Auntie, but Imogen felt no scruple in unfolding the piece of paper and reading the brief contents. *I'm not staying here,* Rita had written. *Nobody likes me. Imogen and Debby are jealous cats and they want to keep Woody and Josh to themselves. Well, they're welcome. I'm off. Sorry, Auntie. From Rita.* Imogen was still standing by the bed, staring down at the note with complete stupefaction, when Debby joined her.

She looked round the littered floor, then at the note

in Imogen's hand, then up into her friend's face. 'What on earth . . .' she began. 'Where's Rita?'

Imogen shrugged helplessly. 'Run away,' she said briefly. 'Oh, dear, trust Rita to go off in the middle of the wheat harvest! We'd best tell Auntie, though I don't imagine she's gone far. She's probably hiding in one of the outhouses, or maybe she's gone down to the Pilgrims' place. I mean, I bet she spent all her pocket money ages ago and you can't stow away on a bus or a train these days. I'm sure she can't have gone far.'

They thundered down the stairs once more, waving the note, and Auntie, dishing up bacon and eggs and thick rounds of home-made bread, listened in bemusement whilst Imogen and Debby, in chorus, told her not only about the note but also about the litter of clothing on the bedroom floor.

Auntie sighed, fished up her spectacles which she wore on a cord round her neck, took the note with fingers already greasy from handling bacon and read it aloud. She was about to put it down on the table when Debby spoke urgently. 'Hang on, Auntie; there's a PS on the other side of the paper.'

Auntie turned it over and read in silence, and Imogen saw her mouth begin to work, and her eyes to fill with tears, before she spoke. 'You'd better read it for yourselves,' she said, laying the note down on the table and fishing out her handkerchief. It simply read: *I'm sorry, Auntie. I do love you. Your Rita. xxx*

Auntie sat down with a thump on the nearest chair. 'What happened yesterday?' she said in a resigned tone. 'You needn't tell me Rita started it, because she nearly always does. But one of you must have said something to send her flying off. I suppose it was you, Immy my love. I can't imagine our little peacemaker losing her temper, not even with Rita.'

Debby took a deep breath and then exhaled it in a long sigh. 'It was me,' she admitted. 'Rita said that when she went back home she would be pointed out as the girl who lived in the house with no windows, and I said better a hotel with no windows than a yellow star on your clothing – and your house too – which shows you are an "undesirable" and could be sent to a concentration camp.' She looked appealingly at Auntie. 'I know I shouldn't have said it; I know my grandparents told me not to speak or think of such things . . .'

Auntie crossed the kitchen and enveloped Debby in a warm and loving hug. 'You did the right thing. It's time Rita realised that there are others, many, many others, not just worse off than herself but suffering unimaginable horrors. In fact, I think even kind little Imogen here should know that the world can be a wicked place. You've learned it the hard way, Debby, but it hasn't made you believe all men are evil. It's time Rita learned that Mrs Jeffries's windows can scarcely be put in the category of war crimes. And now come and eat your breakfast, because part of our war effort is to provide food for the country and the harvest won't wait, so sit down, the pair of you, so I can dish up.'

All three of them sat down at the table and began to eat, but naturally enough the main topic of conversation was Rita, and where she had gone. 'We won't despair too soon,' Auntie said briskly, wiping a slice of bread around her plate. 'You two must go up to the farm, ask if anybody has seen her and explain she's lit out. If I hadn't known the reason I'd have thought it would be kindest to keep quiet and wait until she comes back with her tail between her legs, but I'd take a bet that she said something cutting even after you'd mentioned the yellow stars.'

Debby blushed and looked anxiously at Imogen. 'She didn't mean it; I'm pretty sure she didn't,' she said uneasily. 'She was cross, you know, and – and asked why I didn't wear a yellow star here. Because I was just as undesirable to her as I was to the Germans.'

Auntie clasped her forehead. 'That girl!' she said. 'Of course she didn't mean it – she was just hitting out the way she always does. Dear Debby, try to forget it. And now I'll go up to Jill's bedroom and see if I can find any clues, and I'm afraid you two had better come back here if she's not with the harvesters.' She clapped her hands briskly. 'Off with you! If I don't see you within about an hour I'll assume that all is well.'

Before leaving the kitchen, Auntie remembered that Rita had had no breakfast, or not what you might call an official breakfast at any rate. Bearing this in mind, she went into the pantry and found that half a loaf and a pat of butter as well as a bottle of cold tea and a bag of apples was missing. Oddly enough, this cheered Auntie considerably, because it was the sort of food the children took whenever they went off on an impromptu picnic. So having checked carefully that nothing else had gone, Auntie climbed the stairs and entered Jill's room, where Rita had been sleeping, and looked with dismay at the untidy mass of garments on the floor. She opened the wardrobe and saw at once that Jill's haversack was missing; no doubt it was now hanging on Rita's shoulder with the food and bottle of cold tea inside, as well as such garments as Rita had seen fit to take with her. Jill's best blue dance dress, a pre-war relic, had gone as well as some of Rita's own stuff. Two pairs of knickers, a white blouse and her grey pleated school skirt, Auntie calculated. Grimly, she began to tidy, to put away, to make the bed and to return anything of Rita's to the attic room the three girls shared. Up there she examined Rita's bed closely, then lifted the mattress and withdrew from beneath it a small pile of letters, all addressed to Rita in Mrs Jeffries's large and careless hand. Auntie nodded grimly to herself, but she finished tidying the room and made the beds before going downstairs to sit at the kitchen table and beginning to read the letters, telling herself that this was her duty though normally she would never have read a letter addressed to anyone but herself. The letters did not say much but it was very clear where Rita got her prejudices from: every single letter contained grumbles about the small private hotel run by a Jewish family a few doors away from Mrs Jeffries's establishment. She even blamed them for the fact that she had still not managed to get glass put in all her windows, though in the last letter she grudgingly admitted that a neighbour had managed to acquire some sort of Perspex – or was it celluloid? – so that at least light could now enter the building.

Auntie put down the last letter and sighed. When they found Rita, she, Auntie, would have to speak seriously to her. She would have to tell her what happened to Jewish people under Nazi rule; she just hoped that when she did so Rita would apologise to Debby and take back every word. Imogen would have to know as well, having been present when Debby had told her what Rita had said. And she supposed that Woody and Josh should be told too.

Auntie sighed; never before had she regretted Jill's absence quite so passionately. Jill would know how to treat the subject without upsetting what had once been a harmonious relationship between the three girls. Automatically Auntie got up from her place at the table, scooped the letters into her overall pocket and then thought she saw one way out of her difficulty. She would show the letters to Imogen and Debby when they came in, and hope that this would make them regard Rita's cruel words as being merely an echo of Mrs Jeffries's feelings. Perhaps that would be the best way to deal with the dilemma.

When the girls returned from the harvest field to say that no one had seen Rita, Auntie's immediate thought was that perhaps the girl had gone home to Liverpool. After all, she was an intelligent youngster and must know that Debby would repeat her words to Auntie, if no one else. But there were the rail and bus fares to be considered. Auntie kept a drawstring purse behind the clock on the mantelpiece in the kitchen, and there was always a float in the money drawer behind the bar. It was possible that Rita might have raided one or both, might have left a note in either saying how much she'd taken, but when Auntie checked she could see at a glance when she opened purse and drawer that neither had been touched. Not wishing to admit that there was a possibility money might be missing, she nevertheless felt impelled to ask Imogen and Debby to check their cash. Imogen had given a little snort of amusement. 'I'm no saver,' she had admitted readily. 'Neither is Debby, for that matter. Last time we were in the village we bought liquorice sticks and a quarter of mint humbugs, which was all we had coupons for. Rita isn't keen on liquorice, but as far as I can remember she spent the same as we did and got Little Gems, because she said they lasted longest.'

'Then if she's not gone home, where could she be?' Auntie asked. 'Have you looked in your hut down by the river? She took half a loaf, some butter and a bottle of cold tea. Maybe she'll just stay out all day and come home this evening after you're both in bed, with her tail between her legs.'

'I should think that's very unlikely; Rita's far too proud to come back and admit she was wrong to say what she did,' Imogen observed. 'Look at the note she left for you, Auntie. She more or less said she was running away because we had been nasty to her. But no, we've not looked in the hut yet, or the Lookout. I suppose she might easily be at one or the other, planning to come home, as you say, late at night with some story she's concocted. Only I do think you ought to tell the police, just in case we don't find her.'

'Right you are,' Auntie said briskly. 'I know where your hut is down by the river, so I'll go and check that whilst you two go to this Lookout of yours. And I remember her saying once that she had a heap of cousins all living in various parts of Liverpool. They were evacuated as she was, but I believe she said that most of them had gone home. Even if she hesitated to go back to her mother – and there's nothing in any of these letters to suggest that she might be wanted at home – she could always seek refuge with the aunts and uncles.' She turned to appealing to the two girls. 'Wouldn't you say that was a possibility?'

Debby looked doubtful, but Imogen nodded slowly. 'Yes, it's possible. But the same difficulties apply, Auntie. She had no money and her relatives are a long way away. Honestly, I do think you should just let the police know she's gone missing. I remember reading somewhere that there had been several cases of unhappy evacuees running away from cruel foster parents, and managing to get home by one means or another.'

Auntie reached out and gave her a playful slap. 'Thank you very much!' she said. 'So now I'm a cruel foster mother, am I? But knowing Rita, she is likelier to say that she's been badly treated than to admit the truth. All right, once we've checked the hut and the Lookout we'll all go into the village and telephone the police station.' She brightened. 'For all we know, she might already have given herself up.'

As so often happened when her unruly tongue had said things she would afterwards regret, a part of Rita wanted to rush over to Debby and apologise. She knew it was scarcely Debby's fault that her mother had been unable to obtain glass to replace all her shattered windows, but Mrs Jeffries's constant refrain that the Jewish owners of the small hotel further up the street had taken her trade had made an impression on her daughter. Added to this was her jealousy of the warm friendship which had sprung up, first between Imogen and Debby and later between the two girls and Woody and Josh. It never occurred to her that it was her sharp tongue and constant criticism which had made the others wary. And now, of course, she had done the unforgivable. No one had ever referred to the fact that Debby was Jewish and now she had not only mentioned it, she had taunted the younger girl, virtually saying that she approved of the things the Nazis were doing in Dachau and Auschwitz. Rita shuddered; sometimes she doubted her own sanity. What a wicked and untruthful thing to say! She had looked across the harvest field, to where Debby and Imogen were collecting the sheaves; if only Imogen would leave Debby alone for a moment she would go across and say she was sorry, apologise properly for once, admit she had been horribly wrong.

But even as the thought occurred, she knew she would not do it. It would mean apologising, eating humble pie, and treating Debby in future with kid gloves. But it would mean not just admitting to a fault, which was foreign to her nature, but banishing the jealousy she felt whenever she saw Debby and Imogen with their heads together over some joke or other. So she said nothing but continued to work, telling herself that the time to apologise was not yet, not acknowledging that the right time to apologise would simply never come, because she would keep putting it off, as she always did when her tongue betrayed her into saying something she did not mean.

When the harvesters stopped for the generous meal which Mrs Pilgrim provided at around five o'clock, Rita was sure that Debby would have told not only Imogen but everyone else within earshot. They would all be thinking her despicable and some of them, girls at the village school who had suffered from Rita's tongue themselves, might be planning some sort of revenge. The fact that her spiteful remarks were usually laughed off or ignored would be forgotten. She remembered once calling Debby and Imogen Nazi-lovers, and though she had afterwards pretended it had been a joke, she was sure it would be held against her now. So instead of joining them she went over to the generous display of food, took a large slice of harvest cake and made off. She went slowly, half hoping that someone would call out, ask her where she was going, and had they done so, she told herself, she would have returned and done all the things she knew she should do. But nobody noticed, and when she knew that teatime had passed and the labourers would have started work again she was full of righteous indignation. If they had cared tuppence about her they would have noticed her absence. Debby became, in her eyes, no longer the injured party but the wrongdoer. She should have approached Rita again; she must have known she hadn't meant a word she'd said; it was Debby's duty, positively her duty, to be available for the apology which, Rita told herself, hovered on her lips.

Having eaten half her slice of harvest cake, however, she realised she was thirsty. She did not go back to the harvest field but made her way through the trees and down the steep slope to the grassy plateau where they had built their hut. Inside the hut she knew she would find tin mugs; she would dip one in the river and have a drink, finish off the rest of her cake and return to the Linnet in time for supper. Presently, hunger satisfied and thirst slaked, she settled down on the soft grass to watch the river and mull over her grievances, but it was a warm day and she had been working hard. Presently, she slept.

It was late when she was woken by an owl drifting across her resting place, a white barn owl, intent upon its hunting, uttering a soft too-woo as it went. Dreamily, Rita sat up and looked round her with some surprise. What on earth was she doing here? They had all been helping with the harvest, but that had been in the golden afternoon; now it was night and she was alone. Getting to her feet, she felt a prickle of fear, and with it annoyance. Typical! Imogen and Debby had just gone off, leaving her asleep, a prey to any wild animal which passed. But then she remembered that it had not been they who had left her, but she who had left them. She had better get back to the Canary and Linnet or she would be in trouble. Auntie was easy-going, but she did have rules and one of them was that the girls must be indoors well before dusk fell and in bed by eight thirty at the latest. Rita knew that this was because by nine o'clock at night the pub was usually busy and occasionally, when closing time arrived, it was all Jacky and Auntie could do to eject some drinkers who would have preferred to remain in the bar until the early hours. By and large, it was not the men from the air force station, but others who sometimes exceeded their welcome. The boys from the ack-ack batteries in the surrounding area came galloping up on old bicycles, on foot and very occasionally in an ancient car they all shared, and though Auntie was as fond of them as she was of the air crews she still liked to have the girls upstairs and in bed before her customers grew rowdy.

Rita combed her hair with her fingers, brushed bits of earth and twigs from her dungarees and set off. She was surprised when she reached the pub to find it in darkness, but she knew that she could gain admittance through the kitchen window closest to the back door, and presently she was standing in the kitchen and gazing with some horror at the clock. It lacked ten minutes to midnight. For a moment she wondered why no one was waiting up for her, but then she realised that if the other girls had suspected her of sneaking home before them it was unlikely that they would risk her wrath by disturbing her in Jill's room. As for Auntie, she would simply assume that Rita had come quietly in and gone straight to bed whilst she herself was still pulling pints in the bar.

Satisfied that she was not going to get into trouble for being late, Rita entered the bedroom, undressed and slid into Jill's bed. How she wished the older girl was here! She told herself that Jill would understand, would take her side, would make it unnecessary for her to do more than mumble a quick apology. And presently, despite the fact that she had slept deeply all evening, she slept again.

The next time she woke, in the small hours, all the optimism which she had felt earlier had evaporated. She tossed and turned and even wept a little. She would be in trouble on every count: saying unforgivable things to Debby – nasty, spoilt little Debby – as well as coming in late. Auntie would tick her off for not letting anyone know she was home when she reached the Canary and Linnet, and worst of all, Imogen and Debby would make sure that everyone knew that she had uttered remarks that made it look as if it was she who was the Nazi-lover. She actually remembered that Debby had accused her of approving of what was going on in Dachau and Auschwitz . . . lies, all lies, but not lies that it was easy to disprove. So what should she do? The answer seemed simple: she would run away. She contemplated returning to Liverpool and her mother's boarding house, but the more she thought about it, the less the idea appealed. She needed to show everyone that she was an adult person who could make her own decisions and live her own life. She did not need Imogen or Debby, far less Woody or Josh. She did not need Auntie either, though if Jill had been at home it might have been a different story.

She lay still, considering her options. If she did not return to the boarding house she supposed she could go to the cousins, but speedily dismissed the thought. The cousins were all older than her, and already gainfully employed. She thought they worked in the many factories which had sprung up around Liverpool, factories which made a variety of different things – munitions, parts for aeroplanes, uniforms and parachutes – and paid good wages to competent young women. She could do that! But then there was the problem of where she would live. If she returned to her mother she would be sucked into helping in the boarding house, and that would scarcely prove her to be a person of worth. And she knew the cousins were crammed into poor accommodation, sleeping on sofas or Box and Coxing it, which meant for instance that when Jane, working a day shift, climbed out of her bed to go to work, Elsie, working a night shift, would climb between the same sheets.

Rita wrinkled her nose; going to the cousins was out. She wanted to prove herself independent and capable, did not intend to find herself regarded as a nuisance; returning to Liverpool was a bad idea then.

It was tempting to decide to go to the only other town she knew much about, which was Lincoln, since Norwich was too near, too obvious. The three girls had visited Jill, who was stationed at one of the big airfields outside that city, and had liked it very much. But on thinking it over, Rita heaved a deep sigh. If she went to Lincoln she knew what would undoubtedly happen: it was sod's law, as she had heard the men in the bar saying, that she would walk straight into Jill or Laurie or one of the other airmen who had frequented the Canary and Linnet. They would undoubtedly see to it that she was dispatched straight home again. The fact that this thought gave her comfort was something of a shock and she had to tell herself firmly that she had no wish for her adventure to end in ignominy. There must be another city where she might find both a job and accommodation, and as soon as she was firmly established she would write to Auntie and this time she really would apologise, both for the carelessly cruel words she had said to Debby and for running away. She supposed, miserably, that everyone would assume she had gone because she was unhappy at the Linnet, but even as the thought entered her mind she noticed that the sky beyond her window was no longer black and star-studded, but was beginning to pale. She realised that if she did not get out of bed and get moving she was likely to fall asleep and not wake again until the girls and Auntie were beginning to stir and think about getting up.

Rita got stiffly out of bed, and dressed hastily. Then she pulled Jill's haversack out of the wardrobe and began to stuff clothes into it. She had filled it with everything she thought essential and actually had her hand on the door knob when she remembered, guiltily, that she had not packed toothbrush, flannel and soap. She added these to the bag, feeling rather bad over taking Jill's best dress and her own school skirt and blouse, but telling herself that she must have respectable clothing if her flight was to succeed. Then she opened the door with the upmost caution and set off down the stairs. She avoided the one that creaked the worst, but guessed that, after a long day harvesting, the other girls would still be sleeping soundly, whilst Auntie often remarked that it would take a brigade of guards marching through her room to wake her. This was obviously true, since Rita gained the kitchen without rousing anyone. To be sure, Rufus, curled up on his blanket under the kitchen table, thumped a sleepy tail, but he made no effort to get to his feet, though he watched with considerable interest as Rita went into the pantry, helped herself to bread, butter, apples and the bottle of cold tea left over from the harvest supper. Packing the food and tea into Jill's haversack, she slipped into her coat, knotted a spotted headscarf under her chin and let herself out into a newborn morning which felt full of promise.

She considered her penniless state, but decided that even if she 'borrowed' some cash and left a note promising to pay Auntie back, it would scarcely be a good start to her new venture. So she walked at a comfortable pace into the village, for hurrying would be noticed, and she was well known so near the Linnet. Here, too, no one stirred, though a dog barked as she passed his kennel, and when she gained the winding country road which led to the next small village she saw smoke beginning to rise from chimneys and knew that very soon now the inhabitants would be going about their business.

Rita walked on. She knew that people thumbed lifts, had been with Mrs Pilgrim when that kind lady had stopped to pick up hopeful members of the forces or someone she knew from one of the surrounding villages, so as soon as she reached the main road she prepared to show drivers that she was hitch-hiking, as they called it. She felt very self-conscious waving down a vehicle which turned out to be an army lorry, but the driver grinned and told her to hop aboard and asked where she was bound.

'For the city,' Rita said briefly. She told herself that she knew better than to reveal more than the most innocuous of details for fear that the man might remember giving her a lift and tell someone searching for her where she had gone.

The driver, a man in his forties with sandy hair and a thin, knobbly face, grinned. 'Well, you ain't a Waaf or a Wren or an army lass,' he said cheerfully, 'because if you was, you'd be in uniform. So let me guess: you're goin' to sign on . . . or have you got a factory job in your eye? The pay's mortal good . . . how old are you, sweet' art?'

Warning bells sounded in Rita's head. 'Old enough to know it's rude to ask a woman her age,' she said coldly. 'How old are *you*?'

The driver laughed; he had, Rita decided, a most unpleasant laugh, more like a neigh. He slowed his vehicle as they approached a crossroads, however, and turned towards her. 'My age ain't no secret,' he said loftily. He stared at her as he drew his vehicle to a halt, then reached out a hand and pushed her headscarf back so that he could see her curly fair hair. 'Let's have a little guessing game,' he suggested. 'I'd guess you at, say, eighteen or nineteen; what would you put me at?'

Rita opened her mouth to say something placating but her tongue as usual let her down. 'Oh, I'd put you at fifty or sixty,' she said airily.

The driver had been looking quite pleasant, but now a flush stained his thin, acne-marked face, and he reached out and slapped her, not all that lightly, across the cheek nearest him. 'You saucy mare,' he said between gritted teeth. 'Get out of me cab! If an insult is all I get for helping you on your way . . .'

Rita was horrified. She reached out a hand and patted his arm. 'I'm very, very sorry, and you're quite right, I was rude and horrid,' she said in a small voice. 'And you're right about my age too; I'm eighteen and a half. And now please take me the rest of the way into the city and I'll tell you anything you want to know.'

The driver pulled away from the crossing and smiled at her, clearly mollified. 'Right you are, sweet' art,' he said jovially. 'Let's hear the tale, then!'

That first lift had taught her a thing or two, Rita concluded later as she waved goodbye to the driver and his lorry. She had boarded the lorry in full daylight and she made up her mind that she would not take any lifts offered once it began to get dark. Though the driver had behaved perfectly properly, she had seen an odd sort of gleam in his eyes a couple of times and got the definite feeling that a slapped face as reprimand for her rudeness might, in other circumstances, have been something far worse. She did not quite know what revenge the man might have taken, but she had a horrid feeling that it was the sort of revenge Auntie and Jill had warned them about in hushed tones.

So having waved the lorry driver off she began to

ponder what she should do next, and his suggestion that she might join one of the forces was tempting. She would get paid, fed and clothed, and once she was in uniform she was highly unlikely to be spotted as a runaway.

As she had asked, she had been dropped off at the railway station, so her next move must be to ask the way to the recruiting office. But having discovered that it was only a short walk away she found herself hesitating. She had no objection to lying about her age but knew she would have to get rid of her plait because grown-up people rarely plaited their hair, and when she approached the recruiting office she began to waver. She had heard that recruiting was going down as the war progressed and conscription reached its peak. Suppose they turned her down, yet made a note of her details, just in case? She had no address she could give them, a sign of guilt in itself. She hung around for perhaps half an hour, then turned and headed for the marketplace. Whenever they visited the city they always made a beeline for it because you could buy all sorts of things there. Rita had removed the haversack whilst sitting in the lorry, but now she slipped both arms through the straps so that it rested quite comfortably in the small of her back, then dug her hands into the pocket of her coat and was both surprised and delighted to find a sixpence and three pennies which she had not known she possessed. She remembered going into Mrs Bailey's shop a couple of days before and buying the only sweets the old lady had in stock: Fox's Glacier Mints. She did not recall being given change, but she must have been.

Made bold by the feeling that she was affluent she reached the market and went straight to the first stall, which happened to be selling fish, and fish of course was not rationed, so the stall was quite busy. Rita pushed her way through the people waiting to be served and went behind the counter. Back there, the smell of the innards and entrails of fish which had been gutted and filleted for sale was almost overpowering, and she was tempted to cut and run, but the enormously fat woman in the blue and white striped apron turned and saw her and raised a thick grey eyebrow. 'You're the wrong side of the perishin' stall, my woman,' she said reprovingly. 'You've got to take your turn, like all them others, and Friday's fish day if you're a Catholic so we're rare busy.'

Rita looked up into a round, red-cheeked face and saw a pair of very shrewd boot-button eyes looking down at her. All the way to the market she had been concocting a variety of dramatic stories to account for her desire to work – a sick mother, an ailing sister, a teacher who had asked her to do her shopping and given her money which had been stolen from her as she made her way towards the market – but under those sharp and knowing little eyes, truth won the day.

'I want a job,' she said bluntly. 'Any chance of you needing some help? I'm a hard worker, honest to God I am.' All the while she had been talking the fat woman had been gutting a large fish which she proceeded to fillet and then to throw on the scales.

'Four fillets come to five and eleven; we'll call it five and six,' she told her customer. 'That's one each for you, your hubby and them fellers what's boardin' with you. Awright?'

The customer groaned, but comically. 'Fust time I heared cod fillets was wuth more'n gold,' she said resignedly, fishing two half-crowns and a sixpence out of her shabby little purse, whilst the fat woman, taking the money and throwing it into a drawer under the counter, raised those bushy eyebrows at Rita.

'Well, gal? Can you skin a skate? It's hard on the fingers but I can show you the best way to do it.' She looked at the increasing crowd awaiting her attention. 'Come to that I could do with someone else to wrap the goods and take the money. I'd pay you three bob an hour . . .' she chuckled hoarsely, 'and all the fish heads you can eat. Are you on?'

Rita longed to say that desperate though she was, she was not that desperate, but common sense for once prevailed. 'I'm on,' she said briefly, and took the enormous skate which was held out to her. She looked hopefully into the woman's sharp little eyes. 'Show me how to skin it,' she suggested. She moved her fingers on the surface of the fish and dropped it back on the counter with a squeak. 'It's – it's like sandpaper!' she exclaimed. 'Where do I start?'

The woman laughed, picked up an oddly shaped knife and skinned the fish in seconds, shaking her head at Rita. 'Don't you a-worrit yourself, my woman; I were teasin' when I suggested you might learn to skin,' she said. 'Just you put 'em on the scales when the customers say what they want, tell me the weight and I'll price 'em. You can take the money, but don't pick the fish up without you put a piece of newspaper around 'em first, 'cos folk don't like their money smellin' of fish . . .' she winked at Rita, 'even though my fish is fresh as a daisy and only smell of the sea. Now no more chattin', 'cos I want to sell every fish on this stall before the day's out.'

And by the time the day was out every fish had been sold and Rita had learned the art of filleting and had grown almost used to the smell of fish. She was glad the fat woman had had no crabs and lobsters, but decided that her labour had been worth it when she trotted back from the standpipe with a bucket full of water, and was paid generously for her work.

She beamed at Mrs Boston, who said she had done well but added that the money included a task which she had not yet done: that of washing down the stall and its surroundings, for the market authorities insisted that there should be no whiff of fish left to prove that the stall had not been properly cleaned. Rita sighed but tipped strong-smelling bleach from a big commercial bottle into the bucket, and then, at Mrs Boston's command, picked up the stiffly bristled broom, tipped the bleach and water over the concrete and began to brush.

It wasn't until she was thanking Mrs Boston and saying yes, if she was able, she would try to return the following Friday that she realised how very tired she was; obviously she would have to find somewhere to sleep. There was a pub quite close to the church which had a board outside offering bed and breakfast for a sum which would pretty well do away with her earnings; she could not see herself surviving on whatever was left until the following Friday. Yet she was clutching the very first money she had ever earned, and this made her reluctant to go far from the marketplace. There were other stalls selling other goods; if only she had not gone first to the fish stall she might have got herself a job selling vegetables or second-hand clothing; anything, in fact, which would be available on the market for six days of the week and not just one. As she brushed she put the point to Mrs Boston and was disappointed though not particularly surprised when that knowing woman shook her head. 'What with rationing and that, the stalls are mainly run by the farmers themselves; they don't employ no outside labour.' She looked shrewdly at Rita. 'I don't meself, as a rule, but today my son Freddy what normally help on the stall have gone off with his old dad in the trawler, so you fell lucky. Tomorrer, Saturday, we stand King's Lynn market and don't come here again until next Friday, and then only if the men have a good catch.'

Rita finished scrubbing down and emptied the now filthy fishy water down a nearby drain, then returned to the stall. 'Thank you very much, Mrs Boston,' she said politely. 'I'd best be getting back to the bus station; I told you I lived in the country, didn't I?'

'You did,' Mrs Boston admitted. 'But I'd still like to know why a neat young woman like yourself want to work on a fish stall. Care to tell me?'

'To earn some money,' Rita said promptly. 'I thought I would like to join the WAAF, but . . .'

Mrs Boston nodded sagely. 'But they ain't recruitin' right now. I heared it from several gals, but mostly they goes in for the factories. We've plenty of them around them here. Pay's good, and provided you don't do munitions working conditions is good, too.'

Rita was beginning to reply when she glanced up at the clock tower which loomed over the marketplace. 'Oh, dear, it's past six o'clock. I don't imagine anyone will be employing staff now until tomorrow,' she said. 'But thanks for your advice, Mrs Boston; I'll catch the early bus into the city in the morning and see what factory jobs are available. And if I can't find one, I'll maybe see you again in a week's time.'

The day was still warm, but clearly Mrs Boston was a creature of habit. She took off her striped overall, which by now was extremely fishy, and tucked it into an American oilcloth bag which had been hanging up behind the stall. Then she donned an old black serge coat which had seen better days and plonked on her head a felt hat with violets round the brim. 'I'm headin' for the bus station meself,' she announced, and they set off together, Rita thinking whilst Mrs Boston talked. She was not going to be able to join one of the services if they were no longer recruiting, but when Mrs Boston returned to the subject of the factories, and the way they employed young people who wanted to earn good money, Rita realised this must mean that smaller establishments whose proprietors could not pay high wages would be in need of staff. If this was indeed so, then provided she could find somewhere cheap to spend the night she could start job-hunting again first thing in the morning, and the best place she knew for a vagrant needing a free bed was a farmer's barn. She tried to forget that she had promised herself she would not remain in the city a moment longer than she needed because this was where Auntie and the others would look for her first. They all knew that she had no money with her – or almost none – and would guess she must find paid employment or give up her daring escape and crawl back to the Canary and Linnet with her tail between her legs.

August evenings are short, however, and Rita also remembered her vow not to take lifts from anyone at dusk, but a bus was not like thumbing a lift and she could pay her way as far as the bus fare was concerned. By now they had reached Surrey Street, and even as they did so the nearest double-decker began to draw out. Rita shouted a goodbye over her shoulder to Mrs Boston; then, without checking the destination board, she leapt for the platform, climbed the stairs and settled herself in the front seat, slipping the haversack off her shoulders. She had no idea how long it would be before the bus left the suburbs and gained open countryside, but paid the conductress a shilling, deciding she would just abandon the bus when she saw agricultural buildings near the road. Satisfied with her plan, she sat watching the passing scene. The bus stopped several times and began to fill up, and presently Rita had to move over a little when a tall man in a flat cap, an open-necked shirt and corduroys came and sat beside her. 'You'll ha' to move that bloody great bag, pretty miss, else my feet'll stick out into the aisle,' he said. 'Where are you a-goin'? If you're gettin' off first we could mebbe swap seats, save a lot of fiddlin' around when we reach my stop.'

Rita looked at him with disfavour. He had a boil on the back of his neck, badly cut hair poking from beneath the ancient cap and a great many spots and blackheads; and his small, light-coloured eyes were sly. An unsavoury character, she thought, trying to move nearer the window, for at present their thighs were positively rubbing against one another. But he was looking at her enquiringly, and she realised he was still waiting to hear at which stop she would alight.

Putting on her coldest voice, Rita told him that she would be getting off quite soon but refused to change places. 'I can get past you easily,' she informed him, and turned her shoulder, pressing her nose against the glass and hoping that suitable country for her purpose would soon arrive.

She was just beginning to relax, to think that her unwanted companion was no longer interested in her or her destination, when a sharp elbow dug her in the ribs. 'Didn't you hear me, pretty lady?' the man said. He had a whining, unpleasant voice, with overtones of aggression. 'Iffen you's gettin' off at my stop we could walk into the village together.' He wrinkled his nose when she did not reply. 'God awmighty, don't you jest stink o' fish!'

A thousand replies, all of them rude, sprang to Rita's lips and were quickly suppressed. She longed to tell him that even if she did smell of fish she wasn't covered in boils and blackheads, or that he himself stank of cow manure, but after her experience with the lorry driver she knew better than to give her tongue full rein. He was clearly the village idiot, but there was no point in antagonising him, so instead she pointed out coldly, without turning away from the window, that she had been working on Mrs Boston's fish stall, so had a perfectly legitimate reason for smelling of that good lady's wares.

The man gave a suggestive snigger. 'That's what you say,' he taunted. 'I say you're a dirty little tart what's been plyin' her trade along Gentleman's Walk, and now you bring your horrible pong on to our nice clean bus.' Abruptly his voice softened. 'But I don't mind the smell, I like it. And I like you, pretty lady. If you come along o' Dicky, he'll give you a present . . .'

But Rita had heard enough. The bus was slowing,

drawing in to the verge, and the man had one filthy hand on her thigh. She thrust the hand away and jumped up, pushed past his knobbly knees and crashed down the stairs, her heart beating so loudly that it almost deafened her.

She would have jumped off the bus while it was still moving, but the conductress seized her arm, tutting disproval. 'That in't allowed to leave the bus until that's stationary,' she said reprovingly. 'And as I recall, you paid me for the next two stages. Changed your mind?'

Rita glanced quickly behind her and saw the man's big ill-fitting boots and corduroy trousers; he was beginning to descend. The moment the bus stopped and the conductress's grip on her arm relaxed, Rita jumped from the platform on to the verge. 'I – I made a mistake,' she said breathlessly. 'What time does the first bus leave tomorrow?'

The conductress had her finger poised on the bell but she did not press it. 'Workers' bus?' she said, eyeing Rita up and down. 'That go at ten to seven; you pick it up from here.' She laughed. 'Only t'other side of the road, of course.'

Rita thanked her, then suddenly realised that she had left her haversack on the bus. She turned to go back but her erstwhile travelling companion jumped off the platform and cannoned into her – she was sure deliberately – and by the time she picked herself up the bus was well away, charging towards its next stop.

No one else had got off the bus here, and looking round her Rita realised that there were only three dwellings within sight. Two were cottages, both in a poor state of repair with drooping thatched roofs and unkempt gardens. The third was a farm set well back from the road up a long and twisting track.

Rita felt a stab of real dismay. This was not a real bus stop, but it would have been ideal had the wretched Dicky not been staring gloatingly at her. This was just what he had wanted, she thought miserably, to catch her by herself and either attack her or insult her in some way. But if she behaved as though she knew the people in the cottages or at the farm, she might well come off the victor; she must brazen it out. She turned on Dicky. 'I left my haversack on the bus because of you, and it contained important material,' she said angrily. 'When I get to the farm and he asks for the things I was bringing I shall tell him who is to blame.'

He stared at her, his mouth dropping open and a tide of red creeping up his scrawny neck. 'I din't mean no harm,' he muttered. 'Don't you say no word to Mr Thompson, else Ma and meself won't have no roof over our heads. Please, pretty lady, Dicky never meant no harm.'

Rita thought he looked both frightened and abashed, but she still hesitated to turn her back on him. However, there was no help for it. Dusk was creeping over the land and she was miserably tired. The red brick farm was surrounded by outbuildings but she suspected they were all too near the house to be a safe refuge. However, there was a large barn a mere quarter of a mile or so away; if she could just shake off her unwanted companion she could spend the night in the barn and catch the workers' bus next morning.

Scowling, she stood and watched Dicky as he shambled up to the nearest cottage. He hesitated in the doorway and, realising that for the moment at least she had the advantage of him, she wagged a reproving finger. 'Remember what I said,' she warned. 'If I hear one more squeak out of you, I'll tell Mr – Mr . . .' For the life of her she could not remember the man's name, but hopefully she had said enough, for Dicky hunched his shoulders, ducked his head under the lintel and disappeared into the cottage.

Rita felt relief wash over her in a warm tide. The conductress had been helpful and friendly; no doubt she would find the haversack, realise it must be Rita's and put it aboard the workers' bus next morning, so things had not turned out so badly after all. She still had most of the money she had earned from selling fish and tomorrow she would return to the city and search for a proper job. She would make certain, however, that first she found a stream or a pond; somewhere she could wash and rid herself of the smell of fish.

Now that Dicky was gone she wondered whether to go up to the farm just in case he was watching from behind the small lead-paned windows of the cottage, but decided she was too tired and instead made for the narrow track which bordered a field of what looked like barley and led, if not straight, at least in the general direction of the barn she could see on the horizon.

As she walked she realised it was very quiet; she could hear birds calling to one another and saw that the sun had sunk out of sight, leaving the sky a clear, singing green, whilst the moon lay on its back awaiting its turn to take over the sky. A blackbird shrilled a warning and to her right some small animal scuttled between the tightly packed stalks, and she heard from the pasture on her left a rabbit thump a warning on the turf and saw others sit up, ears erect, as they wondered whether to flee or remain.

Rita began to walk more quickly. She could not rid herself of the suspicion she was being followed. It had been some while since they had had rain and her feet moved quietly through the thick white dust, but behind her she was almost sure she could hear soft footsteps. She began to be very afraid, and to wonder what she should do for the best. If she continued along the track until it reached the barn she would be very vulnerable, but if she cut across the pasture to the farm she could explain how Dicky had insulted her, had knocked her over and was now following her. Surely that would be sufficient to make the farmer, or his wife, whichever opened the door, take her in?

She had turned off the lane now and was fast approaching the farm. From a distance it had seemed a building of some importance, with well grown trees at its back and well maintained outbuildings on three sides, but close to it looked rather run down, the thatch needing attention and the yard patched with cow dung where the beasts had been led to and from the milking parlour. Rita was just through the wide, lopsided gate when somebody seized her by the shoulders, and a voice close to her ear said: 'Where the devil do you think you're going? I could bloody kill you!'

She was opening her mouth to scream when she saw the back door of the farm fly open, and she collapsed on the cobbles as blackness overwhelmed her.

Chapter Eleven

Rita came round to find herself staring into a face she knew well, a face whose concern faded into a broad grin as its owner saw that she had regained consciousness. 'Well, what a welcome!' Woody said. 'Mind you, I blame Josh here for grabbing you, but we've chased you all the way from the market, you young horror. Josh was afraid you'd disappear into the farmhouse and we wouldn't be able to take you home in triumph.' He was helping Rita to her feet as he spoke, and when she was upright she looked round and saw she had quite an audience. A plump little woman, presumably the farmer's wife, was trying to usher her into the house whilst an elderly man, a large slab of bread and cheese in one hand, was chewing ruminatively and staring at her with unabashed curiosity. He was flanked by a couple of farm workers, also chewing. And there was Josh, his light brown hair standing on end, and Woody, smiling down at her, both obviously pleased and relieved to have found her.

Woody turned to the farmer's wife. 'You must be wondering what's going on . . .' he began, but the woman put a plump arm around Rita's waist and led her into the kitchen, where the table was laid and the kettle hopped merrily over the flame.

'Never mind explaining until we've all had a cup of tea, and this young woman has recovered from her fainting fit,' she said placidly. 'I dare say you could all do with a bite to eat as well.' She jerked her thumb at the three elderly men. 'Sit down, Abel Thompson, and you as well, fellers. I'll make a plate of sandwiches,' she nodded to Woody, 'while you get down the mugs from the sideboard and make us all a nice cup of tea. Then you can tell the tale, which should be a good one, by the looks of you.'

Rita, sinking into the offered chair, cast Woody a desperate look; it was a look which said *Don't tell*, but Woody shook his head very slightly and bent over her. 'Lies won't help,' he hissed. 'Fortunately we've found you before the local papers have got hold of the story, but a great many people know you ran off and must be told that you're back, so we'll start as we mean to go on, and tell the truth.'

Rita would have argued, had in fact opened her mouth to do so, when, unbidden, a picture of Dicky with his dirty hand on her thigh popped into her mind. If the boys had not come along – and she still could not imagine how they had appeared with such magical suddenness – she might have got herself into all sorts of trouble, even if not through Dicky. So instead of following her usual course, she nodded. 'But you tell it,' she urged him as their hostess bustled up to the table.

First, however, Woody put the most important question of all. 'Are you on the telephone, Mrs Thompson?' he asked anxiously. 'We've got half the county hunting for this young lady, and we must telephone the local constabulary so that they can let everyone know Rita's been found.'

His hostess shook her head regretfully. 'No, that we

in't,' she admitted. 'But there's a public box at the end of the lane. It won't take one of you lads more'n ten minutes to run down there and make the call.'

'I'll go,' Josh said eagerly. He beamed at the farmer's wife. 'If I could borrow a bicycle . . .'

Mr Thompson gave permission at once and Josh shot off, arriving back well within the allotted time. He burst into the kitchen with only the lightest of knocks to say that he had rung the police station first and then the village shop. 'You know what a gossip Mrs Bailey is, and how the bush telegraph system works,' he said, pink-cheeked from his ride. 'They're sending a police car out to pick us up. I told them we were with the Thompsons at Stonyridge Farm, and the sergeant said he knew it well.' He grinned at Rita. 'How much of the story have you told?'

'We haven't told anyone anything; we saved it for when you came back,' Woody assured him. 'But now we're all here, I'll fire ahead.'

Rita guessed that Woody had been rehearsing in his mind how best to relate the story, and certainly he launched into it without any hesitation. He gave few details of the reason for Rita's departure, merely saying that she had fallen out with one of the other evacuees and decided to make her way into the city where she might find congenial work.

Rita giggled. 'I don't think filleting fish and cleaning herring is particularly congenial,' she observed. 'But it was good of Mrs Boston to give me work, when you consider how inexperienced I am. *And* she let me take money and give change. And she paid me pretty well, considering. So go on, Woody: how did you find me, and why didn't you approach me on the fish stall? It would have saved us all a lot of bother if you had.'

'By the time we got to the fish stall everyone had left, but on the stall next door the feller was still cleaning down. We'd already gone through the rest of the market with a fine-tooth comb but no one had seen hide nor hair of a girl with a long blonde plait. This chap, though, said he'd seen a bit of a girl with a spotted headscarf tied under her chin working for Mrs Boston. We asked him where the fish lady lived and whether she and the girl had gone off together, and he told us that Mrs B usually went to the bus station. It seemed likely that young Rita here had gone with her, so that was where we headed, and we'd barely arrived when we saw Rita leaping on a bus. It would have been great if we could have grabbed someone and shouted "Follow that bus", but of course we hadn't even a bicycle on which to give chase. However, just as we were going to give up and telephone Auntie to say that Rita was alive and well and heading for the coast, another driver called us over. "Don't worry, lads," he said. "I saw you'd missed the 15, but I'm drivin' the relief bus, leavin' almost at once, so you won't lose much if you jump aboard now." We dithered for a second, but then the chap roared his engine and we bundled aboard.'

Rita stared from Woody to Josh, wide-eyed. 'I saw the bus that was following us pull out and pass us when I was asking the conductress what time the workers' bus left in the morning. So that was you! Oh, if only I'd known!'

'Yes, it was us, but the driver chose that very moment to overtake and if it hadn't been for Josh we'd probably have thought you were still aboard. But Josh spotted you and shouted to the conductor to ring the bell since he'd just seen his little sister getting off the bus behind.'

Josh chuckled. 'Poor feller, he must have thought either I was mad or he was,' he said. 'The minute the bus stopped we baled out and followed you – and that tall, loopy-looking chap – as fast as we could go. You and whatsisname seemed to be chatting to each other, and we didn't like to interfere, but then he sloped off into one of the cottages and we began to walk more quickly to catch you up. I might add we were pretty cross with you. Auntie has been in tears and everyone was dreadfully upset and imagining the worst, of course.'

'I'm sorry,' Rita said in a very small voice. 'And I'm very grateful that you did catch me, because I was running away from that man – the one who went into the cottage – and goodness knows what might have happened if he'd caught me before I'd reached the farmhouse. I knew he was following me, because I could hear his feet in the dust . . . oh!'

Josh and Woody exchanged grins. 'That was *us*, you stupid girl,' Woody said. 'And you were in far more danger from us than from anyone else. Honestly, Rita, do you never think what will happen as a result of your actions? Oh-ho, my fine lady, you're going to have a great deal of explaining to do when we get you home.'

Although Woody might have seemed light-hearted, almost joky, in fact he was beginning to realise that Rita was indeed about to face the telling-off of her life, and for the first time he felt sorry for her. She had acted foolishly and not given a thought to the consequences, but he was pretty sure that on this occasion at least she was well and truly in for it. As they drank the cups of tea Mrs Thompson had poured Woody looked at Rita's chalk-white face and wondered if there was anything else he could do to prepare her for what was to come. In some respects, he knew she deserved to suffer some of the anguish which she had doled out to others, but although she thought herself so grown up – and certainly she looked far older than her years – he did not think she had any idea of the storm which would burst around her head as soon as they got back to the Linnet, or the ability to accept that she had done wrong and apologise from the heart. This time, it would not be just Auntie handing out a dressing down, it was the authorities who oversaw the welfare of evacuated children. Auntie would be very cross and upset, but Rita would think that a fluent apology and a warm hug would be sufficient to melt Auntie's wrath. She would remember how cross Auntie had been when Imogen had nearly died in the snow, and think that her own behaviour, though reprehensible, was no worse than Imogen's.

Woody looked again at Rita and saw her give an enormous yawn, saw how the heavy lids drooped over her blue eyes; saw, too, the dark hollows beneath those eyes, and felt a rush of pity. When all was said and done she was only a kid, a kid proud of her ability to shin up the mighty beech to the lookout platform, or any other tree for that matter. He knew she had not been deliberately wicked and began to plan what he would say if his opinion was asked.

When the police car drew up in the farmyard he was not tremendously surprised to see a large, commanding-looking woman in the front seat. Doubtless the authorities had not wanted to put the police driver in the uncomfortable position of having all the responsibility for getting a young girl back to where she belonged.

And his guess was probably right, he thought, as the large woman got out of the car, straightened her hat, and marched towards the back door. Woody was watching through the small window to the right of the door, and realised that he was the only one who knew that retribution, if you could call it that, had arrived. He cleared his throat, but before he could speak the visitor rapped smartly on the door and, not waiting for her knock to be answered, walked into the room.

'Mrs Thompson?' Her keen gaze swept the assembled company sitting round the kitchen table with their mugs of tea, and settled unerringly upon the farmer's wife. 'I gather you've got our runaway. I'm Mrs Caldecott, Women's Voluntary Service. Come to collect . . .' she opened a dark green handbag hanging from her shoulder and produced a small notebook, which she flicked open, 'to collect Miss Rita Jeffries.'

Rita, who had been sitting facing away from the door, pushed her chair back and got to her feet. 'I'm Rita Jeffries,' she said in a small voice. 'Have you – have you come to take me home? I'm so sorry . . . Mrs Thompson has been awfully kind . . . and of course Woody and Josh found me, and explained . . .'

Mrs Caldecott swept on as though Rita had not spoken. 'Are we all ready?' She turned to Woody and Josh. 'I gather you are the young men who found her. You've done very well; I'm sure all concerned are grateful.' She looked back at the farmer's wife. 'Thank you very much for helping this foolish young person,' she said perfunctorily, and

Woody thought she sounded as though she did not mean a word of it. As soon as Rita had put on her coat, she grabbed the girl's arm and began to pull her towards the back door, whilst Rita was still trying to thank the Thompsons for their kindness.

Once outside Mr Thompson carried the lamp which illumined the many cow pats they had to avoid. Woody and Josh followed, and Woody could not help giving a private grin when Rita wrenched her arm out of the older woman's grip and dived into the long back seat of the police car. 'There's no need to behave as if I were your prisoner,' she said irritably over her shoulder. 'Or as if you thought I might cut and run. Well, you'd be wrong, because I know I've behaved badly, but all I want right now is my bed, and I assume that's where you're taking me. Back to the Canary and Linnet, I mean.'

Mrs Caldecott, a large woman with small brown eyes and grey-streaked dark hair worn in an uncompromising bob, flushed angrily, but before she could answer Woody had grabbed her arm and shaken his head slightly. 'Rita's dog-tired. She's had a dreadful day,' he murmured. 'She'll say things she doesn't mean, because she's worn out. She's very grateful that you've come to take her home.' He reached over and swung the passenger door wide. 'And, you know, you did rather behave as though she were your prisoner.'

'I don't need you to tell me my business, young man,' Mrs Caldecott said stiffly. 'The idea!' But when she caught Woody's eye she gave a small but reluctant smile. 'I dare say I did overreact,' she admitted. 'And now you lads get in beside Miss Hoity-toity and we'll be on our way.'

The driver did a neat three-point turn, muttering, as

the tyres slid on the cowpats, that he'd cleaned the car earlier that day and now he would have to clean it again. Then he swung into the lane and Woody and Josh settled back in their seats and prepared to enjoy the well sprung, comfortable ride back to the Canary and Linnet. Mrs Caldecott and the driver talked in low tones, and Woody thought Rita was asleep, but as they were driving through the village she rubbed her eyes vigorously and turned to him.

'Gosh, I'm tired,' she said in a small voice. 'I've got no idea of the time; is it very late? Do you think Auntie and the others will still be up?'

Josh interrupted before Woody could speak. 'I should think they jolly well will be,' he said reprovingly. 'And not only awake, Rita, but dying to give you what for. Even Debby, who Auntie calls the peacemaker, is cross with you, not for running away, though that was bad enough, but for upsetting Auntie. And Auntie's upset because she imagines folk will think she ill-treated you . . .'

Woody dug his companion in the ribs. It was so unusual for Josh to be angry that he had kept quiet at first, but now, remembering Rita's white, exhausted face, he thought it was time to intervene.

'All right, all right, Josh old fellow; I think you've said enough,' he murmured. 'Let Auntie speak for herself. I reckon Rita realises there's trouble just round the corner.'

A few minutes later the big car swung into the car park, and in its hooded beams Woody saw that there was another vehicle parked close to the front door. He had begun to say that they had clearly got a visitor when the dim blue headlights lit up the boxy shape and he gasped even as Rita, who had been leaning back, suddenly sat upright. But it was left to Josh to identify what they were seeing. 'It's an ambulance!' he said, speaking so loudly that both passenger and driver turned in their seats. 'Oh, what can have happened?'

The moment the police car stopped both back doors flew open and the youngsters tumbled out, ignoring Mrs Caldecott's instructions that they should wait for her, and made for the door. Rita was ahead of the boys, but Woody pushed her aside and had his hand on the door knob when it was opened from within and they saw Imogen standing there.

She was tear-streaked and clutching a coat which Woody knew was not her own. She stared at him for a moment as though she couldn't believe her eyes, and then she flung her arms around his neck and he felt her tears wet on his cheek. 'Oh, Woody, Woody, it's Auntie,' she wailed. 'We called the doctor, me and Debby. She started to talk funny – Auntie, I mean, not Debby – and she couldn't use her left hand. She was frightened; her eyes went huge. Then she said, "Fetch Dr Vaughan," and oh, Woody, before we could even move she fell off her chair and crashed on to the floor. Dr Vaughan told us she'd had a stroke and says she'll be all right, but she has to go to hospital. She's in the ambulance now, and I was just going to take her coat out to her, but the ambulance men had wrapped her in blankets and said not to bother with coats or shoes or hats, but to bring them to the hospital when the staff asked us to do so. Oh, Woody, I'm so glad to see you! Did you find Rita?'

'She's here,' Woody said briefly, jerking his chin at Rita. 'I think we'd better have a conference.' He lowered his voice. 'Can we talk privately? Only Mrs Caldecott, the woman who was sent to bring Rita back, mustn't realise you're here alone.'

'Well, we aren't, not exactly,' Imogen said. She had let go of Woody and now they stood together in the doorway watching as the ambulance turned neatly in the confines of the car park, the driver hooting at the police car to get out of the way. 'Jacky was here, the same as always, to open the pub. Me and Debby thought Auntie had just fainted – from all the stress, you know – and would come round and take over. Only I reckon Jacky knew better, because he came into the kitchen, took one look at Auntie – me and Debby were trying to pick her up off the floor – and dispatched people in every direction. He sent one of the customers to fetch Mrs Jacky, and sent me for the doctor. Jacky's old, but he's sensible.'

By this time they had moved through into the kitchen, followed by Rita and Mrs Caldecott, but at Woody's instigation Imogen had kept her voice low, and Woody hoped that the WVS woman had not heard. Nevertheless, she reacted to the situation with the sort of prompt efficiency which Woody guessed she had learned from experience. She looked round the kitchen, then through the open door which led to the bar. 'What on earth were the evacuation authorities doing, to allow you to be homed on licensed premises?' she said. 'I never heard of such a thing, but I suppose the landlord must be a person of good repute.'

'There isn't a landlord, only a landlady, and she's a person of very good repute,' Rita said angrily, and Woody had to bunch his fingers into fists to stop himself from hitting her. Trust Rita to put the cat among the pigeons, given half a chance.

He could see that Mrs Caldecott was puzzled, and feared the worst. Sure enough, she turned to the driver, who had followed her into the kitchen, saying briskly: 'Well, there's nothing else for it. If there's no responsible adult here these three children – I take it there are only the three of you? – will have to go to a children's home in Norwich until we can send them back to their parents. I don't imagine that this Miss Marcy will be able to cope. Dear me, a spinster, in charge both of a public house and of three lively young girls; whatever were the authorities thinking of?'

The police driver raised an eyebrow, looking longingly into the brightly lit bar and then back at Mrs Caldecott. 'Someone's in charge all right,' he pointed out. 'There's a man and a woman working behind the bar. Can't we leave these kids in their charge, at least until tomorrow? Then, as soon as the office is open, you'll be able to sort things out satisfactorily.'

Debby, who had not said a word until now, broke in at this point. 'By tomorrow Auntie will be better and the hospital will send her home,' she said firmly. 'And we won't go to a children's home; we're needed here. Who's going to feed Pandora and the hens, to say nothing of the pig-which-mustn't-be-named? Who's going to go down to the end of the lane for the four-pint milk jug which they leave out for us? Who's going to clean down the bar and wash and dry all the empty glasses? And what about Rufus?'

Mrs Caldecott began to say, grimly, that none of this was her concern; she was only responsible for the child who had run away and would thank everyone present to let her think. Seeing that she was having second thoughts, Woody pressed home the advantage.

He addressed himself to the police driver. 'Would you run us all up to Pilgrim Farm? It's where Josh and I are billeted and Mrs Pilgrim is a good sort. She'll make up beds for the girls and take care of them rather than see them sent miles away. And Debby's right about the work they do, you know. If they sleep at Pilgrim's we can all come down first thing tomorrow and do the chores. The farmers are harvesting the wheat, so we can help with that, but of course the girls will want to get to the hospital as soon as possible. I'm sure Mrs P will see they can do so.'

By now Jacky had announced closing time and come through from the bar and there was a good deal of discussion between Mrs Caldecott, the police driver and the cellar man. Mrs Jacky had followed her husband through with a tray of empty glasses and offered to sleep in Auntie's bed and give an eye to the children, but this Mrs Caldecott would not allow. 'I should be obliged if you would stay here and supervise the children when they come back from the farm the young man mentioned,' she said stiffly. 'But you haven't been authorised to take evacuees, I gather.'

Mrs Jacky was old, but she was game, and her thin wrinkled cheeks flushed angrily at the implied criticism. 'No we in't, do we take 'em like a shot,' she said stiffly. 'But we live in a tied cottage, two up two down, what means no room to swing a cat. Still 'n' all, no harm in my man and myself stayin' here overnight and seein' the work gets done.' She looked consideringly at the other woman. 'I dare say you won't want the girls in the bar cleanin' down and collectin' the dirties and that.'

Mrs Caldecott began to swell with disapproval, so

Woody broke in, biting back a chuckle. 'It's all right. Auntie has never allowed the girls to so much as enter the bar,' he said, crossing his fingers behind his back. He turned to the policeman. 'And now that everything's settled, perhaps you wouldn't mind taking us to Pilgrim Farm. We'll have to explain to Mrs Pilgrim, of course, but I'm sure this good lady . . .' he indicated Mrs Caldecott with a jerk of the thumb, 'can explain far better than we could.' He gave her an ingratiating smile. 'Isn't that so, Mrs C?'

Mrs Caldecott hesitated, saying undecidedly that she thought Rita should probably return to her mother, but the police driver, clearly anxious to get the whole matter settled, nodded approvingly at Woody. 'You've got a head on your shoulders, young man,' he said. 'The kids can go to this Mrs Pilgrim for tonight at least – we can't possibly take the runaway all the way to Liverpool now; not enough petrol for one thing – and we'll let tomorrow take care of itself.'

As Woody had clearly expected, Mrs Pilgrim agreed at once to take Auntie's evacuees for one night. However, she scorned Woody's suggestion that she might make the boys shakedowns on the parlour carpet in order that the girls might have their beds, though this would have meant Imogen and Debby top-to-toeing it.

'The girls can have my boys' room; there's a couple of single beds all made up for when they come home on leave, and a camp bed for when they bring a friend along. As for Rufus, he can sleep with our dogs in the barn,' Mrs Pilgrim said. She smiled kindly at the five of them. 'Now, I know you lads haven't had a bite since breakfast, so I made up a plate of sandwiches, and there's a big jug of hot milk on the back of the stove.' She looked shrewdly at Rita's strained white face, and patted her cheek. 'That's all right, my woman, they can't kill you for it,' she said bracingly. 'You'll feel better with some grub inside o' you. And tomorrow, once I've done my chores, I'll get the car out and run you girls down to the hospital. You lads can give a hand with the harvest, 'cos there's no room in my little ol' car for the lot of us.'

Having eaten the sandwiches and drunk the hot milk the girls were led up to their temporary accommodation and prepared for bed, saying very little. Without any discussion, it was Rita who climbed into the little camp bed. Imogen and Debby mumbled good night, and were soon sleeping soundly, but tired though she was Rita found it impossible to fall asleep. She lay in the dark listening to the ticking of the alarm clock which their hostess had set for nine o'clock since she wanted them, she said, to get a good night's sleep. And it was not until shortly after two a.m. that Rita was able to relax sufficiently to drift off.

But then, of course, the nightmares started. She and Auntie were together in a tiny boat, afloat on a choppy sea. She had seized the oars, telling Auntie to sit still and say nothing, because she, Rita Jeffries, could row far better than the older woman. Despite Auntie's objections, the dream Rita took the oars and began to pull towards the shore, but even as she did so a huge octopus rose out of the depths and wound itself round the right hand oar, dragging it out of Rita's grasp and crunching it to matchwood with its strong and slippery tentacles.

Rita was annoyed, but not despondent. She stood up

in the stern of the boat, pushed the remaining oar into the water and began to waggle it as though it was a rudder. The boat began to move forward once more, though the sea grew wilder. They were going well, and Rita was thinking they would easily make the shore, when a gigantic fish, a shark no less, seized the dangling oar and crunched it as though it were made of paper.

The dream Rita gave an angry sob. 'It's your fault!' she exclaimed, even whilst tears poured down her cheeks. 'You must have called up the octopus and the shark just to show me that I couldn't row our little boat to the shore. It's all your fault, Auntie!'

Auntie got up from her seat in the bows and leaned over the side. 'It was *my* fault, it's always my fault,' she wailed. And then, quite simply, she flopped into the water and was pulled down into the cold grey depths by a long purplish tentacle.

Rita screamed and awoke. Daylight was filtering into the room round the edges of the blackout blind, but though the time on the alarm clock was only six a.m. she was far too frightened to let herself fall asleep again. Instead, she tried to decide on her best course of action, for the previous night Mrs Caldecott had made it plain that she thought Rita should return to her mother. Stupid woman, Rita said to herself. If I'd wanted to go home I could at least have set off in that direction, and how dare she think I ran away because Auntie was unkind! Why, she's the kindest person I've ever known, much kinder than my mother. I won't go home, I simply won't. If they make me, I'll run back to Auntie. And I've already proved that I can earn my own living, and lots of girls not much older than me work in factories. If only I can live with

Auntie at the Canary and Linnet, if only the girls will forgive me, then as soon as I'm fourteen I shouldn't mind leaving school in the least, and getting a job of some sort. If the forces won't have me perhaps I can be a Land Girl; I'd really like to be a Land Girl. The Pilgrims have two and could do with two more. If Imogen leaves school too we might both join the Land Army. Then she and I could be best friends . . . oh, whatever am I thinking! I've been mean enough to Debby already without taking her pal away. And I do like Debby, only I don't think she'd care for the land, much. I remember her saying when we were talking about our futures that she would like to go to university and I'm sure she could. She's really clever, though she hates showing it. Much cleverer than Imogen or me, so if she went off to university that would just leave Immy and myself . . . there I go again! But oh, how I just wish I wasn't the odd one out.

Whilst half her mind grappled with her own problems, the other half was taking in every detail of the strange room. Posters on the walls, photographs everywhere, an old wardrobe with the door swinging back to reveal stained working clothes in one half and a couple of smart shirts and two dark suits in the other, all, presumably, the property of the Pilgrim boys. There was a dressing table with a big mirror, and a chest of drawers, each drawer labelled with an initial . . .

'You awake, Immy?' Rita, who had sat up on one elbow the better to look about the room, hastily withdrew into her bedclothes like a snail into its shell. She had no desire, as yet, to face even Immy, far less Debby. She lay very still, therefore, and strained her ears to hear every word.

'Debby?' That was Imogen's voice, pitched so low that

Rita could scarcely hear it. 'Have you been awake for long? And is *she* awake?'

There was a slight rustle of bedclothes; Debby, presumably, turning to glance across at the camp bed, then more rustling as she turned back. 'No, she's asleep. Why?'

'Well, I thought we ought to talk about what we'll say to Auntie when we go to the hospital. I know she's had a stroke, and strokes can be dangerous, but she's ever so strong is Auntie. Dr Vaughan thinks she'll pull through, only . . . well, will they let us go back to the Linnet? Or will they say Auntie's not a suitable person, because of the stroke?'

'I don't know.' Debby must have turned cautiously, for once again the bedclothes rustled. 'But I do know one thing, Immy. Nothing, but nothing, will ever be the same again.'

Imogen frowned, Rita thought, though she could barely see her face in the dim light. 'I don't see why not,' she said slowly. 'After all, it's not as though Rita was unhappy, or tried to run home, so what makes you think we can't just go back to how we were before?'

Debby shrugged. 'It's as though, by running away, Rita broke the pattern,' she said slowly. 'It's – it's a bit like when you throw a pebble into a really still pond which is reflecting the sky and the reeds and everything. Your pebble makes ripples and the ripples go wider and wider . . .' She broke off. 'I'm not very good at explaining; you'll just have to wait and see. I don't want to be right, I don't want things to change, but I'm pretty sure they will.'

When the alarm went off Imogen was first out of bed, closely followed by Rita. Imogen dived for the washstand, sloshing water from the ewer into the basin, whilst Rita tore off her borrowed nightgown – one of Mrs Pilgrim's, so large that the previous evening Debby had remarked with a giggle that it could have contained all three of them – and began to scramble into her clothes.

'We've got to talk,' Rita said as Imogen finished her washing and gestured to Rita to take her place. 'Did you hear what Mrs Caldecott said last night, about my being sent home? Well, I won't go; if they try to make me I'll run away again. I'll – I'll . . .' Her voice faded into silence and she turned hopefully to Imogen. 'You'd back me up, wouldn't you, Immy? You won't let them send me home. I've been silly, but not wicked, and I can't wait to tell Auntie how sorry I am.'

Imogen sighed deeply. Every time she had woken in the night – and she had woken often – she had wondered how best to make the authorities and Auntie see that Rita was truly sorry, had acted without thought, and would never be so foolish again. But Debby's words still reverberated in her head. What her friend was saying, in effect, was that the future cannot wipe out the past. Rita would have to abide by whatever decision was made, though Imogen could not believe that Auntie would ever reject any of her foster children. The authorities, however, were a different matter.

So she grinned at Rita and gave her a playful punch on the shoulder. 'Let's wait and see what happens,' she said diplomatically, and left the room.

Mrs Caldecott called for the three girls at ten o'clock and drove them straight to the hospital, but only Rita was allowed on the ward.

'I know you're anxious to see Miss Marcy,' she told Imogen and Debby. 'But the ward sister said only Rita might visit on this occasion. She understands Rita wants to apologise for the way she's behaved, so they'll allow her ten minutes. If you two sit on the bench by the little round lawn, Rita will join you quite soon.'

Imogen and Debby sat on the bench, suddenly so nervous that they found it impossible to talk but sat hand in hand, staring at the revolving doors with frightened eyes. Imogen was the first to spot Rita and Mrs Caldecott's large, commanding figure, and knew at once that something was wrong by Rita's drooping head, and when she got near, by the tear tracks on her pale cheeks. She and Debby both jumped off the bench and went towards the couple. 'How is Auntie?' Imogen asked.

'Miss Marcy is still very weak,' Mrs Caldecott answered. 'I'll leave Rita to tell you what she said. I'll go and sit in the car, but you mustn't be more than five minutes.' She gave them a thin smile, but Imogen suddenly saw that she was not a bad person, and was doing her best to help them to cope with what was to come. 'Is that clear?' she continued. 'Five minutes, no more.'

As soon as she was out of hearing, Debby and Imogen turned to Rita. Neither said anything, for there was no need: one look at Rita's swollen eyes and trembling mouth told their own story.

But it had to be put into words, of course. 'I said I was sorry, I said it over and over, I begged her not to send me away,' Rita said in a tear-thickened voice. 'But she just said "No" and shook her head. They wouldn't let me see her alone, but the nurse was quite nice. I'm to leave today; Mrs Caldecott's already arranged for my mother to come for me. I asked her if Auntie was going to keep you and Debby, because if so it really isn't fair, but she said she had no idea.'

Imogen was just thinking how typical it was of Rita to be interested only in her own future when Mrs Caldecott beckoned from the distant car park. They ran towards her and piled into the car, Imogen and Debby in the back seat and Rita in the front passenger one. As soon as the car had left the hospital and was heading for the village, Imogen leaned forward. 'Is Auntie better? When will we be able to visit?' she asked. 'Did you tell her we were waiting outside, Mrs Caldecott? Only I'd hate her to think that we didn't care. She's terribly kind; we've been so happy . . .'

Mrs Caldecott hooted at a man in a small van drawing out ahead of her. 'Yes, I told her. She wants to see you, and the staff assure me she's making a good recovery, but they say it's a bit soon yet for anyone but relatives. Her niece is coming down from Lincoln, so she'll be Miss Marcy's first proper visitor.' She shot a quick look at Imogen over her shoulder. 'She knows you'll be anxious, but I told her we'd arranged for the cellar man and his wife to move into the Canary and Linnet to run the pub until she's better, and in the meantime Mrs Pilgrim has agreed to take you, Debby and the dog. You will have to go down to the Canary and Linnet every day to care for the livestock and give the Wellbeloveds a hand . . .'

'Who are the Wellbeloveds?' Debby chipped in. 'What a wizard name . . . but who are they?'

For the first time since picking them up that morning, Mrs Caldecott chuckled. 'You know them better as Jacky and Mrs Jacky,' she explained. 'But really they are Mr

Jack and Mrs Doris Wellbeloved. I'm taking you back to the Canary and Linnet now and you must all pack up your belongings and prepare to move out.'

'But we're only going as far as Pilgrim's, aren't we?' Debby said anxiously. 'Imogen and I haven't done anything. Surely, if Auntie's really getting better, we shall only be at the farm for a week or so?'

Mrs Caldecott slowed to let a bus pull out from its stop, and when she spoke again her voice was vague. 'My dear child, I don't know everything. Now, I gather that Farmer Pilgrim is harvesting at present, so if you and Imogen go up to the farm as soon as you've packed your stuff I'm sure they'll be glad of your help, and I dare say it might keep you out of mischief for a few hours.'

'Can I go too?' Rita asked eagerly. 'Just till my mother arrives, I mean.'

Mrs Caldecott glanced sideways at her passenger and Imogen thought she saw sympathy in her small brown eyes. 'No, my dear, I'm taking you straight to the station when you've packed your belongings, because your mother wants to get home again as soon as possible. She's had to arrange for a neighbour to look after the boarding house . . .'

Imogen cut in, seeing the look of sheer misery on Rita's face. 'Debby and I don't want to go up to the farm if Rita can't come too,' she said quickly. 'Can we come to the station with you, Mrs Caldecott, and see her on her way? It's horrid to leave somewhere where you've been happy without folk to wave you off.'

Mrs Caldecott looked doubtful and seemed about to refuse Imogen's request, but then she relented. 'You can come to the station with us by all means,' she said. 'But I'm afraid you'll have to go back to the village by bus and walk to the farm from there. Petrol is a precious commodity and I have other people to visit who live on the far side of the city. I can give you money for your bus fares.'

The three girls were profuse in their thanks and as soon as they reached the Linnet they rushed inside and cantered up the stairs to their room. Imogen, ahead of the other two, thought how strange it was that already the place seemed different, almost as though it, too, missed Auntie and knew that things had changed.

In their attic bedroom, they worked with feverish haste, eager not to give Mrs Caldecott any excuse to say she could not take all three of them into the city. Mrs Jacky toiled slowly up the stairs to say that they need not clean the room until they returned from their trip, and even her footfall was so different from Auntie's quicker, lighter tread that Imogen had to fight back tears.

'She's using too much bleach; everywhere smells horrid,' Rita murmured, as the old woman began to descend the stairs once more. 'And what on earth is she cooking? I'm not sorry we shan't be here for dinner!'

Imogen stifled a laugh. 'It's pigswill. Why, Rita, Auntie boils up all the potato peelings and the onion skins and stuff like that every day; you can't have forgotten the smell of it.'

Debby chuckled, but Rita shot her a scornful look. 'It smells different. Auntie's pigswill smells delicious, almost as though it was a nice dinner cooking,' she said. 'Debby, if you don't want that poster, I wouldn't mind it.'

'Feel free,' Debby said obligingly. She rammed her parents' wedding photograph into her already bulging suitcase, snapped the lock shut and cast a lingering look around the attic where they had slept for nearly three years. 'When I think of all the fun we've had . . .' she was beginning when a shout came echoing up the stairs.

It was Mrs Caldecott. 'Come *along*, girls,' she called. 'Don't forget we have to go up to the farm first, to dump your suitcases. And Mrs Jeffries has made it plain that she'll be very annoyed indeed if she misses her train back to Liverpool. If you aren't ready in five minutes . . .'

'We're ready now,' Rita said, casting an impatient glance at her two companions. 'Come on, you two. My mother hates to be kept waiting.'

Debby promptly grabbed her case and followed Rita's example, but Imogen lingered for a moment. She hardly knew why she did so, but she found herself eager to take one last look at the room which had been their retreat for so long. We must come back when we've seen Rita off and make the room respectable again, she told herself. The blackout blind needed repairing and they had all abandoned small things such as night lights, an electric torch whose battery had failed, comics, magazines and even clothing which no longer fitted any of them, so the room was in desperate need of tidying.

But then she heard the back door opening, so she grabbed her case and followed Debby, chiding herself for believing even for a moment that they would never come back here, that Auntie would refuse to take responsibility even for Debby and herself. She thundered down the stairs and into the familiar kitchen, blinking back sudden tears when she saw that it was Mrs Jacky rolling out pastry on the big wooden table, and Jacky seizing the cauldron of pigswill, clearly intent upon feeding the pigs before setting off for the harvest field. Because she was last out, it was she who sat in the front passenger seat this time whilst Rita and Debby sat in the back. No chance for whispered conversations, then, between herself and Debby, but perhaps that was a good thing. Although Rita had shown little sign of distress since they had left the hospital behind them, Imogen knew very well that the other girl was deeply unhappy, and perhaps it would be some consolation to be able to chat to Debby as the car took her ever nearer to the meeting with Mrs Jeffries.

'Goodness, Rita, wharron earth have you got in this perishin' suitcase? I'm sure it weren't as heavy as this when you left three years ago!' Mrs Jeffries chuckled. 'Don't say you've been and gone and stole the family silver from that old woman what took you in! So what made you decide to run home to your old mam? I suppose you got the blame for something what weren't your fault. Well, there's been so much bomb damage in the city that folk is clamouring for beds, so I'm full to the roof tiles, even though we've still got no glass in half the winders. You'll have to share a bed with me until you can leave school and get yourself a billet somewhere out Love Lane way, because that's where the big factories are, and that's where you'd best look for work. It were all very well you bein' evacuated when the bombs was raining down, but now you might as well earn your keep.'

Debby and Imogen stared at Mrs Jeffries, almost

unwilling to believe their ears. On the only other occasion when they had met Mrs Jeffries, she'd clearly been on her best behaviour in order to come across as a caring mother, concerned with her child's welfare. How different was the reality! No wonder Rita had not wanted to go home; no wonder she had not been as keen as Imogen for her mother to visit the Canary and Linnet. But now she had to put a good face on it, and to Imogen's relief she skated neatly round the question of running away and instead introduced Mrs Caldecott. That lady, clearly as surprised as Imogen and Debby, greeted Mrs Jeffries rather stiffly. 'I think you may have been misinformed,' she began. 'There has been no suggestion that Miss Marcy was not a caring foster parent; indeed, all the young people in her charge are desperate to stay with her.'

Mrs Jeffries gave a scornful sniff. 'You can't tar my girl with the same brush as you tar them others,' she said belligerently. 'In my view there's always a reason for everything. Why should my Rita run away if she were so happy, answer me that!'

Rita began to mutter that it wasn't exactly Auntie who had driven her to run away, but then she caught the accusing eyes of Imogen and Debby and changed her mind. 'It weren't Auntie: me and Debby had a row. I said awful things, things I didn't mean, and then I was ashamed, so I ran off. Oh, Mam, make them let me stay! Tell 'em I'll look after Auntie like a proper nurse and never give no trouble. Tell 'em I mean to go to university, like what Debby says she will. Tell 'em anything, so long as you make them let me stay!'

Mrs Caldecott's cheeks went red with embarrassment and she began to stutter, but it was clear that Mrs Jeffries had made up her mind. When she told the story of her daughter's sudden arrival home she would tell it her way. Rita would be the innocent victim of an old woman's spite, and though this was manifestly untrue it would go down in history as 'what happened to Rita Jeffries', until either Mrs Jeffries thought up a better tale or Rita moved away from home and was forgotten.

Perhaps it was a good thing that at that moment the train for which they waited came hissing and clattering alongside the platform. Mrs Jeffries held out her hand to shake Mrs Caldecott's, and Imogen was struck by the difference between those two hands. Mrs Caldecott's was clean, with well-trimmed nails; Mrs Jeffries's was somewhat grimy and the nails were painted scarlet, looking so long and pointed that Imogen was reminded of the wicked queen in Snow White.

'Thank you for looking after my girl,' Mrs Jeffries said rather grudgingly as the hands met. She turned to Imogen and Debby. 'Best say goodbye now, you two, 'cos railway trains don't wait for no man . . .' she chuckled, 'nor women neither.' She hefted Rita's suitcase on to the train and gave Rita a not unkind push in the same direction. 'Get me a winder seat,' she ordered, and began to climb ponderously aboard. Imogen had one last glimpse of her friend's set white face, and then the porter was coming along the platform, blowing his whistle and waving his flag. The train began to move and Imogen started forward.

'We never said goodbye properly,' she wailed. 'Oh, Debby, we let her go without telling her how sorry we were, and how much we shall miss her. Oh, stop the train, someone stop the train!' She began to run along the platform, but stopped when she felt Debby's small hands grip her wrist.

'It's all right, it's all right, Immy,' Debby said soothingly, and Imogen realised that the tears which had filled her eyes had splashed down her cheeks. 'It was hearing all the lies her mother was making up about Auntie which made us forget to say a proper goodbye. When we get back to the farm we'll write her a nice long letter, telling her we love her and shall miss her. And after supper we'll get the boys to add a PS to the letter so she'll know everyone's forgiven her, not just us.'

'Oh, Debby, I do love you,' Imogen said. 'We'll be friends for all our lives long, won't we? And when it's our turn to go home, we'll go together.'

Chapter Twelve

1959

The young woman sitting on the bench was brought back to the present by a ray of sunshine falling on her face, and when she opened her eyes she realised that the rain had stopped. She had dressed with care that morning in the peach-coloured jersey wool suit which Will had always loved, and now she jumped up, a hand flying to her mouth. If the seat had marked it . . . but then she remembered that the suit was protected by an old brown mackintosh and relaxed for a moment, though she brushed the seat carefully before sitting down again. Brown? Brown was not her colour, never had been; what was it that was tugging at her memory? Odd, the things one remembers . . .

Abruptly, she sat upright. She had not thought about her dream of the Canary and Linnet in ruins for years, but now that it had come back to her she remembered everything. The woman in brown who had called Imogen's name . . . but dreams were only dreams, she chided herself.

She glanced at the house behind her and got to her feet once more, and even as she shook the rain from the shoulders of her mackintosh she heard a small sound at her feet and looked down to find a tortoiseshell cat stropping itself against her legs. She bent and stroked it, noting that it was well fed and quite young. Clearly it belonged to somebody and would doubtless make off as soon as it realised it was unlikely to get any sort of welcome here. But as she went up the side path – sadly overgrown – to take a look at the front of the pub the cat followed, and when she reached the courtyard which Auntie had called her parking area it darted ahead of her, rearing up on its hind legs to grab a whirling leaf.

But the moment she rounded the corner, the young woman forgot the cat when she saw something else which brought her to an abrupt halt. A house agent's board, announcing that the premises were for sale, proclaimed its message to anyone passing by on the main road. The woman went closer, to read the small print, thinking that the agent could not be a local man or he would have put his board up at the back rather than the front, for locals popping in for a drink or the men from the RAF station had always come via the lane. But then, the agent would scarcely expect a local to put in an offer for the ramshackle place that the Canary and Linnet had become, so it stood to reason that the board had been put in the most obvious spot for anyone who might be looking for somewhere to buy.

Having read that the property was freehold and contained, in addition to the house, three acres of good land, the woman turned away from the board, and looked long and hard at the place where she had spent the happiest years of her childhood. The back of the house had been a shock and in a way the front was a shock too, only this time a pleasant one. Someone had cleared the path to the front door and tidied the beds beneath the bow windows. Here there was no missing glass, no crumbling wood, no scarred paintwork. And even as she took a couple of steps towards it the front door opened and a figure shambled out carrying a bucket and, when he saw her, blinking in mild surprise. She guessed he was in his fifties, and when he tilted his cap to the back of his head and scratched his brow an elusive likeness caught at her throat.

'Jacky?' she said uncertainly.

'That's me,' the man said. 'But I don't know as I reckernise you, missie. Unless you was meaning t'other Jacky – my brother Ralph – 'cos the older we gets the more like one another we grows.'

With a tremendous effort of memory the woman remembered that Jacky and his wife had had two sons, Ralph and Tommy. She had only met them once, at the very end of her sojourn at the pub, when the girls had left the Pilgrims and moved back to the Canary and Linnet to help Auntie with her chores. The two brothers had come home to celebrate VE day. She remembered noticing even then the strong family resemblance between all the Jacky family – or perhaps she should say the Wellbeloveds. But the man had set down his bucket, and now jerked his thumb at the house agent's board. 'Are you lookin' to buy? The poor old Linnet is in a bad state, 'cos it's been empty for years. But the owner is payin' us to clean it up, make good the winders and so on. Hev you bin round the back?'

'I hev – I mean I have,' the young woman said quickly. 'But I'm not interested in buying – well, not unless it's very cheap indeed, that is.' She cleared her throat and looked speculatively at the man. 'Forgive me, but I believe you must be Jacky Wellbeloved's son Tommy. I knew your father very well during the war.'

'You did?' A broad beam spread across the man's sunburned face. 'My dad's been dead this dunnamany years, but Mam's still livin' in the cottage next door to ours.' He grinned, showing a set of teeth far too white to be his own. 'I don't say nothin' agin young Mr Pilgrim – his ma and pa were rare good to us Wellbeloveds – but when my ma drops off her perch they'll do away with them two cottages and build somethin' a bit more modern. A' course the rent'll go up, but my Millie, she hanker after a proper oven and that. And Ralph don't live at home no longer. Him and his Sandra hev got a flat over the general shop in the village, which suit them quite well since they've got no kids.' He beamed at the young woman. 'Two boys and a girl, that's us.' He looked at her narrowly. 'But don't go tellin' me you was in the forces, 'cos you're too young, so how come you knew my dad?'

The young woman explained that she had been an evacuee, billeted at the Canary and Linnet, and Tommy Wellbeloved nodded sagely. 'I heared tell of them,' he said thoughtfully. He picked up his bucket. 'But I'd better get on,' he observed. 'The owner want every weed took out and the beds planted with suffin' colourful, though God know what it will be, 'cos this ain't the time of year for beddin' plants.' As he spoke he started heaving out the knee-high weeds and dumping them in his bucket. The young woman watched until the bucket was full, and was about to turn round and go back the way she had come – for she knew that if anyone else did turn up it would be by the lane from the village, and not the main road – when Tommy cleared his throat. 'If you've got five minutes to spare I dare say you might pop up to the cottage and hev a chat with my old ma,' he said. 'She'd be right grateful. She don't see many folk these days – don't get out much, in fact. Well, she's past eighty, deaf as a post, and her sight's failing. But as she tells it she were right fond of the little gals what stayed at the old Linnet.'

'I will, if I have time,' the woman promised. She looked up at the sky and the racing clouds. 'I've – I've arranged to meet someone here, but I forgot about bus times, so I've got a couple of hours to kill. Will it be all right, if it starts to rain again, for me to take shelter in the pub? I looked through the window and though the kitchen's a bit of a mess I couldn't see any sign that the rain was getting in.'

Tommy chuckled. 'Feel free,' he said generously. 'Or you could go up to our cottage, have a mardle with my ma. Come to that, you might go up to the farm. Mr and Mrs Pilgrim would likely offer you dinner.'

'If I have time,' the woman temporised. She told herself that she had given up all hope that any of her old friends would come, yet she could not bear to think that she might be away from the Linnet at the crucial moment if they did. She glanced at her wristwatch. If she stayed here until three o'clock . . . but she realised it would be an act of kindness to visit the old lady who had been good to her in the past, so she asked Jacky's son – she could not think of him as Mr Wellbeloved – to keep an eye out for any strangers and to direct them to his mother's cottage. 'I wrote to the others reminding them that our twentieth anniversary was today and asking them to meet me here,' she explained. So if you see anyone . . .'

Tommy Wellbeloved agreed to do as she asked, and she set off, calling over her shoulder as she did so: 'This will be a trip down memory lane indeed!'

An hour later she kissed Mrs Jacky's soft, wrinkled cheek and set off to return to the Canary and Linnet, reaching it just as Tommy dumped his last bucket of weeds on the huge pile of rubbish to which he meant to set fire as soon as it had dried sufficiently and announced that he was off for his dinner. 'No one hin't gone by,' he told her. 'That don't look like rain, them clouds is too high, but I've cleaned up the kitchen so's you can have somewhere dry to sit if your pals turn up.' He eyed her consideringly. 'Mr Pilgrim, he let me off mornings to clear up here, but afternoons I work on the farm, so I shan't be seein' you again, but that's nice to have met you and I reckon you've give my old ma somethin' to think about for many a long day. If you do take shelter in the kitchen of the Linnet make sure you lock the back door when you leave. You know where the key is kept?'

The young woman nodded, not sorry to wave him off; when they came – *if* they came – they would want no one else at their reunion. She glanced at her wristwatch again, already resigned to disappointment. They would not come, but she would keep faith regardless. As she pushed open the creaking back door and entered the kitchen she was suddenly reminded of the poem which every schoolchild learns:

'Is there anybody there?' said the Traveller,
Knocking on the moonlit door;
And his horse in the silence champed the grasses
Of the forest's ferny floor.

But only a host of phantom listeners dwelt in the lone house then, and I'm a listener, the young woman told herself, aware that she was straining her ears to catch the longed-for sound of an approaching footstep, perhaps a voice, a whistle, anything in fact which would indicate that the letters she had penned with such care, such high hopes, would bring at least one of the recipients. Sighing, she picked out the chair which had once been Auntie's and sank into it, and thought gratefully that Auntie had always known a thing or two; even lacking its cushioned seat, this was easily the most comfortable chair in the room.

She closed her eyes and went over in her mind, for the hundredth time, how she had tried to reach the people she wanted. She had always sent Christmas cards to them all, had received cards in return, yet until now it had simply never occurred to her to suggest a meeting. Having thought of it, however, she had been all eagerness, assembling her addresses and sending off what began as a suggestion and ended as an invitation, dispatching the letters carefully: Debby's first, because she and her husband now lived in France; the others a couple of weeks later. She had included Jill in Auntie's letter, still too ashamed of what she had done to write directly. In fact, if Jill simply did not come to the pub she knew it would serve her right, though it was Jill she most longed to see. She glanced around the kitchen, so different yet so familiar, and reminded herself of Jill's sweet nature, of her generosity; surely she would come, if only to say that despite the long silence they might still be friends?

She moved Auntie's chair until she got a clear view through the window. What a fool she had been to provide herself with nothing to read! Old Mrs Jacky had offered her some elderly magazines, but she had refused, though with heartfelt thanks. She had told Mrs Jacky that when the others arrived they meant to go to the pub in the village for chicken and chips, but now, alone in what had once been the bustling heart of the Canary and Linnet, she regretted her refusal. To be sure, she had glanced at the magazines whilst they chatted and seen they were dog-eared and at least three years old, but they would have helped to pass the time.

Closing her eyes, she let memories wash over her once more. She thought about the letters, winging their way to the recipients, dropping through letterboxes, being opened, being read, aloud or in guilty silence . . .

Chapter Thirteen

Debby awoke, as she so often did, when the sun rose high enough to send a beam through the uncurtained window of their bedroom. Very carefully, so as not to wake Stan, she turned so that she could look into his sleeping face. Once it had been a very beautiful face, and when he lay as he was lying now, so that she could only see his right, uninjured side, he was beautiful still. His blue eyes were fringed with almost girlishly long dark lashes and he had a firm mouth and a cleft chin. His fair hair curled crisply and he wore it long to disguise at least some of the scars, though Debby knew that after so long he hardly ever thought about his looks.

However, there had been a time when his scars had very nearly ruined her life, because when they met again in the late 'forties he had been convinced that no one could possibly love him, far less want to marry him. And Debby, telling him over and over that she had fallen in love with him when she was just a child, and would continue to love him whatever anyone might think, had had to behave in a thoroughly unladylike manner to persuade him that she meant every word she uttered.

'There will never be anyone else but you for me, Stan Mielcza . . . I mean Stanislaw Micza . . .' she had said. 'Oh, God, how can I make you believe that I want to marry you more than anything else on earth when I can't even get your bloody name right? Look, if you won't marry me then I'll just move in and live with you . . . it isn't what a nice girl would do, but I'm desperate!'

Debby had taken Stan to meet her grandfather, and the conversation had taken place in the garden of the little house on the Wirral, Stan in his best blues – at that time he was still in the air force – and suddenly he was grinning, grabbing her, lifting her up, kissing her chin, her cheek, her mouth . . . and then he had stood her down and, with his hands on her shoulders, tilted his head as though considering.

'Your grandfather thinks we should marry, you think we should marry . . . who am I to argue?' he said in his almost unaccented English. 'But I refuse to saddle you with a name you can't even begin to pronounce. If your grandfather has no objection I shall become . . . oh, Mr Smith, or Mr Jones . . . even Mr Nobody, if you like. And then as soon as it's legal we'll marry and you can start bossing me about and helping me to find the sort of work I'd most like.'

'Oh, Stan, I don't deserve you,' Debby had said, standing on tiptoe to kiss that strong cleft chin. 'Any name you like, you said; what about us both becoming Viner? I'm sure nothing could please my grandfather more, because when we have children they'll carry on the name . . . but only if you don't dislike it, of course,' she finished hurriedly.

So Stanislaw Mielczarek became Stanley Viner, and though at first he could only find jobs he disliked, and honestly believed when he failed at an interview that it was the fault of his terrible scars, Debby knew he was wrong. 'What you would really like is a place of your own, something similar to your father's farm in Poland. Well, my darling, that isn't possible yet, not in Poland at any rate. The Russians have changed boundaries, given away land . . . but one of these days, if you can just find something you like and we can afford . . .'

He had grinned down at her, but behind his smile, she knew, was a deal of buried frustration. He hated having to rely on her salary as a medical secretary – they had met again after the war when he had come into her hospital for physiotherapy on a badly broken ankle – though he never said so. After they were married they moved in with old Mr Viner and Stan tried hard to find work which suited him, without success.

Then Grandfather Viner had died, leaving everything he possessed to Stan and Debby: his nice little house on the Wirral and a number of shares which, his solicitor told them, they could sell for a good sum. At the same time a friend had pointed out to Debby that a gîte in France had come on the market at a ridiculously low price. 'No one's even made an offer,' the other girl had said disgustedly, for she worked for an estate agent specialising in French properties. 'I remember you telling me once that your feller had been brought up on a farm in the country. Why don't you take a couple of days off and go and have a shufti? Even if it's out of the question, you could make your trip into a little holiday; at least you'd get away from this damned awful climate for a bit.'

That had been ten years ago, and they had taken Debby's friend's advice and set off for the Continent the very next week. Stan had taken one look at the crumbling house and weed-ridden pastures of La Petite Chaumière and put in an offer which was immediately accepted, though they had agonised over it once it was too late to retract. Then they had moved in, labouring from dawn till dusk, and had never regretted it. It was the most propitious decision of our lives, Debby mused now, staring out through the open window as the leaves of the olives in the groves behind their vineyard showed green-grey one moment and silver the next as the breeze caught them, and maybe no couple ever has perfect happiness, but we've got the next best thing: a beautiful home in glorious country, the help and friendship of the neighbours and a steadily increasing bank balance.

Now, she could look back and laugh at the fears which had almost made her decide they could not possibly make a living in a strange country. In fact, even after they had moved in, she had suffered from qualms. But very soon she had begun to see the change in Stan. His delight in the land, and the expertise which he had picked up not only from books but also from their neighbours, had helped to convince her that the move had been the right one. And now, ten years on, their wild gamble had paid off. By sitting up and staring out of the window she could see the vineyard, the leaves beginning to turn scarlet and gold. Beyond the vines were the olive groves, where the sheep liked to foregather in the cool of the early morning, and though she could not pick out much detail from here she could see, in her mind's eye, the woolly bodies, spangled with dew, already beginning to steam gently as the sun reached them. And beyond the olive groves reared the foothills, climbing to the distant mountains, misty blue with distance like a stage set, their snow caps in winter promising cool streams and green grass when the plain below them sweltered in the heat.

Sighing, Debby slipped out of bed and went over to the washstand; she would leave the room quietly so as not to wake Stan, because today was the day when she was to start her journey into the past. It sounded romantic, put like that, and she remembered how she had felt when she had picked up the cream-coloured envelope from the polished wooden boards of the tiny hall and recognised the neat, slightly slanting handwriting.

Immediately, her heart had begun an uneven thump. She, Imogen, Rita and the others exchanged Christmas cards but had long stopped writing letters as such. Looking back over the years which had elapsed since they had been everything to one another she tried to remember why they had drifted apart. In her case, of course, it had been the move to another country. La Petite Chaumière had been in a terrible state, the gîte a wreck, the land untended, but they had thrown themselves into the work with such enthusiasm that, Debby thought now, they had scarcely noticed the years passing. In five years the farmhouse was habitable, and Debby had felt she could stop working on the land for long enough to have a baby. Rachel, now three, was the apple of both their eyes, and Debby knew that now things were easier they would have more children. They had crops in the fields in addition to the vines and olives, and were the proud owners of two great percherons which pulled the plough, carted hay and lent their enormous strength to every other task required of them.

When she first stopped working on the land Debby

had ridden her bicycle daily into town. She had taken a job in a café, where her command of languages proved useful as visitors began to arrive, and when Rachel was born she accompanied her mother everywhere. She was a happy child, popular with both the café owners and their clients. But that was all in the past; now she and Stan could manage without her wage, because they were producing all they needed. They had pigs, poultry and half a dozen sheep, and were not only keeping their heads above water but beginning to thrive, as was the vineyard, the olive grove and the small but productive orchard beyond.

Yet Debby felt she could tell none of this to Imogen, Rita, or even Jill. Partly, this was due to the fact that to explain why they had fled from England would mean revealing Stan's inability to find satisfactory work and his sensitivity about his appearance, and this Debby had vowed she would never do. Everyone assumed that Stan was just an ex-member of the Royal Air Force, and that Debby, attracted by the coincidence of their having the same surname, had begun to go around with him, fallen in love, and wed.

So the arrival of the letter suggesting a reunion, since very soon it would be twenty years since their first meeting, meant that a decision must be reached. She had a perfect excuse for not going, of course. France was a long way from Norfolk, and if she wrote offering her good wishes and explaining that she and her husband could not simply abandon the farm it would be accepted as reason enough for non-attendance.

Having made up her mind, she had shown Stan the letter, and to her surprise and slight dismay he had said that she really must go. 'Maybe I can't leave the farm,' he reminded her, 'but you can. And anyway, those friends of yours, those little evacuees, were once a part of your life. Why, I don't suppose they even know that our place is doing okay, and they should.' And with the words he had slid his arm round her waist, pulling her against him, and given her a loving kiss.

'Of course they know we're okay,' Debby said indignantly. 'I send them all Christmas cards.' Another thought occurred to her. '*If* I go – and take note I'm not saying I will – then who will do the housework whilst you're looking after the farm? And what about Rachel? Who would take care of the most important member of our household?'

Stan pinched her nose. 'I'll cope, you little unbeliever. You won't be gone for more than three or four days, I don't suppose; surely you trust me to look after things for such a short time?'

But as the day when she must depart – if she was to depart at all – came nearer, Debby's reluctance to go increased. What did she know of Imogen, Rita and Jill? They would be strangers to one another, ships that pass in the night. Yet she longed to see Auntie again, and from that point of view knew she should accept the invitation. Once her home had been made respectable she had scrawled an invitation every Christmas: *Come to France and see how beautiful La Petite Chaumière is. You know we would love to have you.*

Auntie always thanked her politely, said she would indeed cross the Channel one of these fine days, but had not yet done so. It occurred to Debby for the first time that Auntie had never suggested that Debby should come to her, but that was only natural. She was no longer landlady of the Canary and Linnet but lived in a cottage on the outskirts of the next village, and managed to give the impression that she was too busy to undertake a long journey.

She had still been dithering, not sure whether to go or stay, when Stan had taken matters into his own hands. Without consulting her he had arranged everything. Madame Bouvier who came in twice a week to help out would come every day until Debby returned. Henri and Philippe, who were employed in the vineyard and the orchard for part of the year, would come to La Petite Chaumière whenever they were needed whilst she was away, and Stan had caught the bus to the nearest big town and arranged tickets and a passage across the Channel with a travel agent. He had got Madame to wash and press Debby's only smart outfit, a light green coat and skirt, and had arranged for a taxi to take her on the first stage of her journey. It would arrive at seven o'clock this very day.

Debby tiptoed down the stairs into the kitchen and picked up the bellows to get the fire going. Though they had taken many French habits to their hearts, she and Stan still liked to start each day with a homely brew, so presently she poured tea into Stan's big breakfast cup, added milk and sugar and headed for the stairs.

'So far, everything's gone smoothly,' she said later as she and Stan climbed into the rackety old taxi owned – and driven – by Monsieur Guillaume. 'I'm going to be at the station in plenty of time. Oh, Stan, it is good of you and Rachel to come and see me off. I promise I'll be back as soon as I possibly can.' She kissed her daughter's cheek. 'You'll be a good girl for your daddy whilst I'm away, won't you?'

As the car surged noisily on to the main road, Stan flung an arm round her shoulders and kissed the side of her neck, grinning as he caught the driver's eye in the rear-view mirror. 'I'm not seeing you off,' he said in French. 'I'm coming with you, and so is our petit chou. It's about time we all had a holiday and I can't wait to meet this Auntie of yours. I know you say she came to visit me in hospital, but the only face I remember from those dark days is yours, my darling.'

'But – but . . .'

'Don't argue,' he said, grinning. 'I've made all the arrangements – it's a good time of year to be away. The grapes have been picked and those crops which are still not ready will have a fortnight in which to ripen. Henri and Philippe will have a cushy time of it. So stop worrying, mon petit chou, and look forward to our little holiday.'

Debby beamed at him. She felt as though a heavy weight had rolled off her shoulders; she could rely on Stan to take care of them. 'But are you sure you don't mind? After all, these are my friends; you've never even met them.'

'Mind?' Stan said incredulously. 'And as for my never meeting your pals, you're the one who's always telling me I have, even though I have no memory of it. Do you think they'll recognise me? It's been a lot of years since I was helped down from that tree by my little angel, my very own Debby, so it's about time I met them officially.' He glanced down at her, his expression rueful. 'Remember it was I who refused to let you have a proper wedding; now I'm making up for it.'

Rita was sitting in her small office, crunching toast, with a cup of tea to hand, when there was a perfunctory knock on the door and Phyllis Brown poked her head into the room.

'You awright, Miss Jeffries?' she asked. She sighed dramatically and wagged a reproving finger at Rita. 'If your mam could see you now, she'd have a perishin' blue fit. She always said no one could work proper unless they had a full breakfast inside of 'em and here's you, snatchin' a snack when you're the owner of three of the best guest-houses in Liverpool, with a table reserved in all the dining rooms so's you can eat whenever you're so inclined.'

Rita sighed. 'Hotels, not guesthouses,' she corrected automatically. 'Really, Phyllis, you cluck round me like an old hen with one chick, and you don't have the excuse of having known me since I was a scruffy teenager, like most of the staff.' Rita thought that having staff who had known her mother and probably her grandmother as well was one of the disadvantages of a family run business, but on the other hand she knew that not one of her elderly employees would cheat her, or see her cheated by anyone else. 'Tea and toast is my idea of a good break-fast; I couldn't face a plateful of greasy bacon and eggs at this hour of the morning. So I do beg of you, Phyllis, not to try to change the habits of a lifetime.' She held out a hand. 'Is that the post you've got there? Pass me the register, would you? I know most of these will be bills or invoices, but there's one at least which looks as though it might be a booking.'

Phyllis fanned the letters out on the desk before her employer and fetched the heavy, leather-bound register, opening it at that day's date. 'It's pretty full, and it'll get fuller as Christmas approaches,' she remarked. 'We's doin' a special Yuletide offer, ain't we? But it's a bit early for holiday bookings.' She peered inquisitively at the cream-coloured envelope which Rita had abstracted from the rest of the correspondence. 'That one looks interestin'.'

Rita had glanced quickly at the envelope and immediately recognised the writing. Instinctively, she shuffled it back into the pile of post and reached to take the register the girl was holding out. 'Thank you, Phyllis. I take it this is just the post for this hotel, though it looks an awful lot. If you'd be good enough to collect the correspondence from the Elms and the Oaks, I'll deal with the whole lot at once.'

'Righty-ho,' Phyllis said breezily. She was younger than the majority of Rita's staff, but Rita had long ago recognised that she had potential. She was already Rita's deputy and most trusted employee and would, one day soon, take over the running of the newest and most modern hotel, the Sycamores.

Once she was alone, Rita opened the cream-coloured envelope and swiftly scanned the contents. She read it through twice, a scowl gradually descending on her brow. So they had decided on a reunion, had they? She had exchanged Christmas cards with the other girls from the Canary and Linnet, but had never even thought of meeting up; why should she? She had been the first to leave, to break free, and though it had taken years she had at last forgiven Auntie's refusal to allow her to return. She supposed, reluctantly, that they had all known good behaviour was essential if they were to remain at the pub under Jill and Auntie's gentle rule. Thinking back, she felt once more the desperate misery, the sharp stab of pain, which had overcome her as Mrs Caldecott had explained as gently as she could that Auntie and Jill were adamant, but in her heart she understood that her expulsion had come about because of her own wickedness, and was deserved.

But even now she could not bear to remember her banishment from Eden; instead she let her mind go back to that very first meeting with the other two girls. She could see it all: Imogen's shiny black bob of hair, her white face and blue, dark-shadowed eyes. And Debby, equally exhausted, small and plump, her fawn-coloured curls a tangle, her lower lip trembling with the fear that the three of them, chance met yet linked for ever, might be parted. And she, equally pale, chewing the end of her long blonde plait and insisting that they must find a lavatory before they burst.

And Auntie, coming out of Mrs Bailey's shop and seeing them gathered around the billeting officer's car, offering rescue without a second thought. Auntie was tall and very slim; an unkind person might call her gaunt. Her skin was white, but it was a healthy white and in no way connected with exhaustion. Her beautiful hair was sandy – later on in their acquaintance she would tell them that it was called Plantagenet gold – and her eyes were green, beautifully clear and set beneath surprised-looking brows. Rita remembered how they had twinkled as she had offered to take the three little waifs, and promised – how untruthfully! – that they would never see the inside of the public bar.

They met Jill later that same evening and in Rita's recollection at least it had been love at first sight. Yet so far as Rita could recall Jill was not beautiful or unusual; she was a brown girl, brown-haired, brown-eyed and tanned. When Rita had been told she must leave, the only tears she had shed had been at Auntie's bedside, and in the first months back in Liverpool she had written long, impassioned letters to Jill, addressing them to various airfields, for by then Jill had been in the WAAF and seldom stationed in one place for long. But the letters had slowed and eventually ceased as life claimed Rita, and she began her upward climb.

A tap on the door brought her back to the present, but it was only Phyllis, bringing the desired correspondence. Rita took it with a word of thanks and began to work her way through the tottering pile of bills, invoices, advertising material and staff applications, but all the time she was thinking about the planned reunion.

Why had she herself never thought to visit the Canary and Linnet, she wondered now. Why had she simply concentrated on becoming a very successful business-woman? She had friends on the staff, good friends. Her mother had died eight years previously, but she could name half a dozen employees who had, at various times, taken over from her in order that she might have a holiday. The very first time she had gone to Italy she had met and married Luigi. He was a fellow hotelier and she had learned a good deal from him before their mutual hot temper and sheer, undiluted selfishness had made living together impossible. Besides, he had thought his one Italian hotel more important than her three Liverpool ones. Then she had discovered him in bed with one of his waitresses, and though she had very soon realised she did not love Luigi she had no intention of sharing him with a sharp-tongued little Venetian, so since Luigi was equally unwilling to change his ways a divorce had been the best answer.

Her second mistake had been to believe the words of a confidence trickster, who had shammed devotion and then left one night with the takings. She had never looked seriously at a man since, and had told Phyllis that men and marriage were simply traps for the unwary, proceeding to make her hotels the most important things in her life.

She made the last entry in the hotel register and rang the bell on her desk so that she might begin to dictate letters, pay bills and do the rest of her paperwork with her secretary. But when the hour for staff lunches arrived she sat on behind her desk, chin in hand, and let her mind wander back to the Canary and Linnet. Reflecting now on that past life, she admitted to herself that she had always had a soft spot for Woody. He had admired her agility as she swarmed up the great beech they called the Lookout, and when there had been altercations he had sometimes taken her side.

But Woody was Imogen's – if he belonged to anyone, that was – and though she, Rita, had written to him on and off for a couple of years their tentative friendship, if you could call it that, had never become anything more. Even exchanging Christmas cards had not survived their diverging lives, though she sometimes wondered whether he had married, what he was doing now, whether he had left the air force.

But the thought of Woody married was so absurd

that she felt a smile twitch at her lips. In her mind, Woody was a boy still, with a quiff of hair which would never lie flat, a rueful grin which revealed a chipped tooth and a voice which broke into falsetto when he least expected it.

The opening of the door cut across her thoughts, and Phyllis scarcely had a chance to open her mouth before Rita was replying to what she knew would be implied criticism. 'All right, all right, I'm coming,' she said, then hesitated, glancing at the letter – the invitation – which lay on the desk before her. Abruptly she made up her mind and held the sheet out to the younger woman. 'Read that!' she commanded, and when Phyllis had perused it she took it back and raised her eyebrows. 'What do you think? Though I warn you, I've not got the slightest intention of going all that way just to meet girls I've not even thought about for years.'

She rose as she spoke and together the two made their way to the hotel dining room, where their table was already laid for them in the corner and they could exchange conversation without being overheard. As they sat down, Rita repeated her question. 'What do you think?' she said insistently. 'If you were me . . .'

Phyllis smiled, but the glance she gave Rita was shrewd. 'I'd go like a shot. You say you've not thought about those girls and that old pub for ages, but you talk about them quite often, you know. Auntie sounds a wonderful person, taking in three kids who might have been real little rogues, and that Jill must have been grand too. And don't pretend you never think of them, because the Christmas cards which come from the people you knew during the war are the ones you always put in a little cluster on the counter top in the Elms. And that's your favourite hotel, the one you spend the most time in, as well as having your little flat on the fourth floor. So you do think of your pals from the Canary and Linnet days, and with affection, what's more.'

As she spoke, she slid a large slice of steak pie on to her plate and reached for the dish of mashed potatoes whilst Rita helped herself to salad; lucky Phyllis ate like a horse and remained as slim as a wand, whilst Rita herself had to watch every mouthful.

'And you could do with some time off,' Phyllis said through mashed potato. 'You know I'll hold the fort, and so will Madge and Val and Suzie . . .'

'Oh, I know you're all very capable . . .' Rita began, but was interrupted.

'You want to go, you know you do,' Phyllis said placidly. 'It's writ' all over your perishin' face! Why not admit it and start makin' plans?' She grinned cheekily at her employer. 'You want them to know what a success you've made of the business, don't you? Aw, c'mon, admit you're only human!'

'Why should I care whether they know or not?' Rita said loftily, then spoiled it with a giggle. 'I can't go to a reunion carrying a banner saying I'm a big success, and they probably wouldn't care anyway.' She sniffed. 'But I bet fat little Debby won't have stopped the world in its tracks! I know she lives in France now, so probably she and her feller couldn't make a go of whatever they were doing in Britain and thought life would be easier over there. I think Auntie said in her last letter that they had some sort of farm, but I can't say I'm very keen to see her again. She was a real little cry-baby, always running away from something . . .'

Phyllis cut a large piece of her pie and pushed it into her mouth. Rita made a mental note to tell her that when she ate in the dining room she really must make an effort to improve her table manners. Some people would take the huff at such criticism but Phyllis, Rita knew, would be grateful for the advice and might even, in future, take a smaller mouthful of pie. 'I gather you didn't like Debby, but since she lives in France I should think we can safely assume that she won't attend this 'ere reunion,' Phyllis said thickly. 'But Auntie still lives in the next village, don't she? Am I right in thinking Jill lives next door?'

Rita stared at Phyllis, her eyes rounding with astonishment. 'How do you know so much about my old pals?' she asked suspiciously. 'Do I talk in my sleep? Have you been hovering outside my bedroom door, hoping to hear what I really think of you?'

Phyllis giggled. 'I always read the Christmas cards, 'cos there's nothing private about them, and when one of them contains a letter I might give it the once over, just to see whether you want it filed or not. After all, the cards and the letters inside 'em are stuck on the counter for anyone to see. If I'd thought they were private I wouldn't of read 'em, o' course. It's apple cake an' custard for afters. D'you want some?'

'To answer your questions in order, yes, Jill moved in next door to Auntie after Auntie had another slight stroke,' Rita said rather coldly. 'And I'll have some pud, as a treat.'

Millie, who was waiting on, delivered their desserts, promised a tray of coffee in the staff room, and whisked out of sight. For a moment the two young women ate in silence, which was broken by Rita. 'Thank you, dear Phyllis, for your much prized advice,' she said sarcastically. 'You have quite made up my mind for me. As the Yanks say, I'll take a rain check on this one. So you needn't start planning your takeover just yet; I won't be going to Norfolk.'

But a couple of days later Rita sent the boot boy, one of the few males in her kingdom, down to the station to purchase a first-class ticket. Then Rita went off by herself on a shopping expedition and bought the most expensive clothes she had ever possessed: a slim skirt with a back pleat and a wide-lapelled jacket in deep blue, the jacket cinched in at the waist with a wide blue belt. Underneath the jacket she wore a roll-necked pink jumper, and on her short, curly blonde hair a perky little candy pink beret, tilted at just the right angle. The sales lady persuaded her to add a pair of incredibly high, pin-heeled court shoes, a clutch bag and matching gloves, which completed the ensemble, and when she looked at herself in the long mirror she beheld a beautiful stranger. Left to herself, she would have chosen something less arresting, but admitted when she walked into the foyer of the Elms Hotel and saw the glances which followed her that she had done the right thing.

'Don't walk, stalk,' Phyllis advised, as Rita approached the reception desk. 'Imagine you're a model on a catwalk – it's bound to impress them because, dear Rita, you look a million dollars! And don't try to pretend you aren't off to your reunion in a couple of days, because I wouldn't believe you. Only don't, for goodness' sake, wear those lovely clothes until the day itself arrives. Your old mac and your comfortable flatties will do for the journey, since I'm sure you'll drive the MG with the roof down, letting all the dust in. You can borrow my weekend case, the one I bought to attend that course on hotel management.'

'Thanks,' Rita said briefly, and afterwards realised, as she got into her bright red MG, that that one word had been her only acknowledgement that she really did intend to undertake the tedious journey and join in the reunion.

Imogen did not know she was asleep until something woke her – a small noise perhaps – and then she looked round her wildly, wondering where on earth she was and what had roused her. She had slumped back in the chair as she slept and now she sat upright, heart hammering, then slowing to a more normal pace as she remembered. This was the kitchen of the Canary and Linnet, not as it had been but as it now was, and what had woken her, she realised with an inward smile, was the tortoiseshell cat. It had squeezed through an incredibly tiny gap between the window and the wall and jumped lightly to the ground, where it stood, tail erect, ears pricked, gazing up into her face. 'Who are you? What are you doing in my kitchen?' it seemed to enquire, fixing her with its big yellow eyes, innocent yet knowing, like the eyes of all the cats Imogen had ever known.

Imogen patted her knee and the cat jumped up at once, emitting a purr so deep and loud that it seemed as though it could not possibly be coming from such a small creature. She tickled it under its pointed little chin and wondered, aloud, whether it was related to the farm cat which used to come into the pub for whatever it could get when the girls were living here. That one had been a proper little thief, though Auntie had treated it as she treated all children and animals, and refused to let it be punished for its thefts. 'It's nature, and the Pilgrims don't feed their cats,' she told the children. 'It doesn't hurt me to put down a saucer of milk and a few scraps from time to time.'

Now, Imogen glanced at her wristwatch, convinced that she must have slept for hours and missed the arrival – and departure – of those she had come here to meet, and might as well go home. But her watch, amazingly, seemed to show that she had only slept for about ten minutes and that there was still some time before the next train – assuming the others came by train – arrived.

Yet the dream had seemed to last a lot longer than a mere ten minutes. She had dreamed herself back into the past, not the past she had shared with Rita and Debby, but the one she had lived with the man she had married, her dear Will Carpenter; married and then fought with, repudiated, and finally run from. She had blamed him, castigated him, tried to make him take all the responsibility for something which, she had known even at the time, he could not have prevented . . . ah, but she had been a fool, breaking into a thousand pieces something which had been good, reducing their loving relationship to rubble.

The cat settled itself more comfortably on her knee, and Imogen leaned back, gently caressing the smooth, velvety back. Now she remembered another cat, a cat which had unwittingly caused so much trouble. So far as she could remember, that had been a black cat.

Imogen moved to stand up, but the cat gave a squeak of protest and began to make bread on her lap; an old trick. Imogen laughed but bent her head to look through the kitchen window and saw, without surprise, that it was raining again; raining heavily, what was more.

Sighing, she settled back in her chair and began to stroke the cat again, reflecting that for a long time she had been unable to look at a cat, particularly a black one, without a shudder of revulsion. She had known it was foolish, known that her aversion would pass because not even she, in the depths of the depression which had assailed her, could continue to dislike a whole species.

The cat stopped kneading her lap and Imogen began to drowse once more. The patter of rain on the window-panes was soporific and she felt herself sliding into sleep. At first she fought it, but another glance at her watch convinced her that no one was likely to arrive quite yet. And sleep did not only help to pass the time but also conserved energy. Imogen slept . . .

Imogen came out of the surgery, crossed the road and headed for the seat upon which Will sat. It was a burning hot summer's day and she was wearing her loosest, coolest summer dress and sandals. The little park where they had agreed to meet was suffering from the drought, the grass turning brown and the roses drooping heavy heads. Beads of sweat formed on Imogen's brow, but it would have needed a positive inferno to spoil her pleasure in the news she was about to impart.

Will had been too nervous, he said, to go to the surgery with her for the result of the test, but now he jumped to his feet, apparently knowing by osmosis that his wife was near, for Imogen had stolen along, soft-footed, wanting to surprise him.

There were children everywhere. A tiny tot in a pink dress, with a matching bow in her curls, staggered from the grass to the path, then sat down abruptly on a well-padded behind. Imogen smiled at the child but saw that Will had eyes only for her. 'Well, what did they tell you?' he said. 'Not that I need to ask, because it's written all over your face.' He took her hands and squeezed them, then drew her towards him and, despite the fact that they were surrounded by people, kissed her lingeringly. 'We're going to be Mummy and Daddy Carpenter, isn't that right? Oh, my darling, who's a clever girl then?'

He gave her an exuberant squeeze and Imogen wagged a reproving finger. 'Everyone's looking!' she hissed. 'Behave yourself, Mr C. You can't go round kissing strange women in city parks.'

'And what a strange woman you are,' Will said affectionately. 'I hope you told the doctor that he had hit the nail on the head when he said that we were too anxious. We thought one only had to stop using birth control to get pregnant and of course the more we longed to start a family, the more anxious we became . . .'

'Five years of wondering whether we'd ever have a baby,' Imogen said reminiscently. 'Five years of looking at other women with babies in pink, or blue, or lemon or white . . . oh, Will, the doctor even got out a sort of calendar and told me our little one should arrive in January. Gosh, however shall we wait so long?'

Will linked his arm with hers and they strolled towards the park gates. 'Let's go back to the flat and open that bottle of champagne which has been lurking on the bottom shelf of the fridge for longer than I care to admit. I think we ought to celebrate, don't you?'

They reached the flat and Imogen bent to retrieve the envelopes which were scattered over the doormat. 'Post! Only by the look of it it's all estate agents' prospectuses. I say, darling, wouldn't it be just wonderful if one of these . . .' she flourished a handful of house details, 'was the very thing we're looking for: a cheap cottage in a nice little village, so we could bring our child up in the country.'

Will laughed. 'Fairy tales might come true,' he said. 'Go and sit on the sofa whilst I pour us both a drink. Then we'll look through them and see what's what.'

He left the room and presently returned with two slim glasses full of golden liquid. He settled himself beside his wife and was about to hand her her champagne when she gave a squeak. 'Oh, Will, do you remember that empty cottage we saw in Cornerstowe? You said wouldn't it be nice if it was on the market and within our means.' She handed him a sheet of paper. 'And there it is, the very same, Farthing Cottage! I'll pack up a picnic and you can put some petrol in the Rover's greedy old tank and we'll go down tomorrow and take a closer look.'

She felt that their luck had changed at last, what with her pregnancy being confirmed and the details of the cottage dropping on to their mat, all in one day. Even the village was absolutely ideal: a small place, almost a hamlet, but just within commuting distance for Will's London job.

Everything went according to plan. To their great delight, Farthing Cottage did not only have a large garden, it also had an acre of what was described as 'useful pasture', though Will intended to plough the land and plant it just as soon as they could move in. The cottage itself was dilapidated but Will was a practical man he had done all the work on their tiny flat – and he was certain that, given time, they could turn it into a delightful and desirable residence.

That first visit to the cottage was one of many and the more they saw it, the more they loved it. A friend of Imogen's surveyed the place for free and said that the roof was sound, though in the two little bedrooms cramped up under the thatch rain had come in through broken windows and a good many floorboards would need replacing. And the chimney was full of birds' nests and quite unusable, though a sweep would see to that, whilst the pump – the only water supply – had to be primed before every use. It had been many years since anyone had painted or whitewashed, a great deal of the woodwork was wormy and would have to be replaced, and several of the stones in the paved kitchen floor were cracked and uneven.

But Will brushed all this aside. 'Oh, I know it's a lot of work, but it'll be quite safe to put our furniture, such as it is, on the ground floor, and until we've done the bedrooms we can sleep on camp beds in the kitchen.' He grinned at Imogen, who was cleaning the flat they would soon abandon. 'Remember, this is an adventure, sweetheart! It's necessary to have an adventure once in a while!'

But though they might suffer from moments of doubt, both Imogen and Will knew they would be able to cope and longed to start on the repairs, so they put in an offer which was so speedily accepted that they exchanged terrified looks. 'Oh, Will, have we paid more than we should?' Imogen asked anxiously as they left the estate agent's office. 'Only I do love it; not just Farthing Cottage, but the village and the green and the little pub . . . oh, everything about it. It's just the sort of place we've dreamed of owning, just the sort of place to bring up babies. Only suppose we have twins, a boy and a girl? We'll need more bedrooms . . .'

Will wiped imaginary perspiration off his forehead, then nuzzled a kiss into the side of her neck. 'We've done it now: too late to retract, and anyway, I don't want to,' he said. 'You're daft, you are! We shouldn't count our babies before they're hatched! And we've got vacant possession, which means we can start moving stuff from our flat to Farthing Cottage just as soon as we like.'

The baby was due in the New Year, the exact date being 10 January, though when Imogen attended the clinic she was told that first babies seldom come when they're expected. However, they moved into the cottage as soon as they could, to take advantage of the glorious summer weather. Imogen had always loved gardens and gardening, so if she wasn't painting or plastering within the house she could be found in the garden, digging, wrenching up the waist-high weeds, planting and watering. It had been Will's dream to own and run a market garden, though it might be several years before this particular dream came to fruition; market gardens were not built in a day. Imogen shared his urge to become proper country people and not just commuters, and was determined to do everything in her power to see that this dream, too, became a reality.

She had left her job in order to cope with the work on Farthing Cottage, but had decided that if anything came up in the village which was within her capabilities she would apply for it, though not until the baby was born. Mrs Grindley, who ran the little general store and post office, had said she could do with someone who understood book-keeping. ''Twould only be a couple of days a week,' she had explained, 'but I don't understand this double-entry stuff. Ever since Mr Grindley went off with that flighty flibbertigibbet, leavin' me to make what I could of the business, I've fair longed for someone what understood figures to give me a hand. If you'd be willin', Mrs Carpenter, I reckon atwixt the two of us we'd manage just fine.'

Imogen formed the habit of walking down to the station to meet Will on his way home from work. Because of the expense, they had decided to use the car only when it was absolutely necessary; his season ticket was a good deal cheaper than petrol and the wear and tear on their beloved vehicle.

One day she must have been a little later than usual for she and Will met in the middle of the village green. Will gave her an exuberant kiss, and Imogen was about to remonstrate when she suddenly gasped and clapped a hand to her waist. 'Will? I've just had the oddest feeling. You know when you were a kid and you caught a tiddler and held it for a few minutes in your cupped hands? And its little tail sort of fluttered? It was a feeling like that, inside me, where the baby is. Oh, Will, it's the first sign he's given me that he's real, and alive, and longing to come out.' She smoothed a protective hand over her still flat stomach. 'How nice that he chose to wriggle for the first time just as we approached our new home! I feel sure that I won't get that horrid sickness again.'

'I'm sure you're right, but can I try to feel it?' Will said eagerly, but though she agreed that he might, he could feel nothing.

'I knew you wouldn't – feel anything, I mean – because it was such a tiny, tiddley wriggle,' Imogen said. 'Perhaps, in the circumstances, we ought to call it Tom Tiddler's Cottage instead of Farthing.'

But Will just laughed. 'Farthing Cottage is good enough for me, and I expect Tom Tiddler will be satisfied with whatever we choose to call it,' he said. And from that moment on, the baby became Tom Tiddler, though Imogen pointed out that if she had a girl they would have to call her Thomasina.

Imogen continued to work hard in both the house and the garden until she was almost seven months gone, and what finally stopped her was the onset of winter. Farthing Cottage had never known insulation against the cold, but Imogen and Will did their best with thick curtains at the windows, home-made 'sausages' against the bottom of every door and a roaring fire in the living room, as well as another in the range. It had been a glorious summer, the best on record, but it soon became obvious that they were going to pay for it with a truly terrible winter.

They began to measure waiting time for the new addition in weeks rather than months, and Imogen had never felt healthier, but Will was anxious, saying that competent though he felt himself to be, he had no desire to end up delivering Tom Tiddler himself. At one point he actually suggested they should move into town when the birth was imminent, but Imogen pooh-poohed his worries. 'I expect they'll send an ambulance for me from the hospital, and I'm sure this dreadful weather isn't going to last,' she said airily. 'And even if the ambulance can't get through I know the Rover is in tip-top condition, so you can drive me.'

'Suppose the baby comes when I'm not here?' Will asked anxiously. 'I can't take time off before Tom Tiddler has even arrived because I'll need to do so when the pair of you come out of hospital. Still, Ida Roscoe's a sensible woman and she's promised to pop in every day once Christmas is over. She'll ring for the ambulance – or for me, if necessary.'

Ida Roscoe was a tiny, energetic woman in her mid-sixties, with a wrinkled face, grey hair pulled back into a bun on the back of her head, and shrewd brown eyes. She described herself cheerfully as a "char" and had been happy to add the Carpenters to her list of employers. She promised Will that she would see Imogen was never alone for long, and not only did she pop in for a few minutes every weekday, but she also scrubbed floors, thundered up the stairs to tidy the bedrooms, changed sheets and pillow cases when necessary, and generally confirmed Imogen in her belief that Ida was a treasure.

By early January the work on the cottage was almost completed and Will decreed that enough was enough. One of the two bedrooms had been converted into a nursery and when they could afford it the little scullery would become a bathroom, though for now they carted cans of hot water up the short steep flight of stairs and washed in their room.

At first time had seemed to fly. Imogen, with a great deal of help and advice from Ida, made baby clothes and knitted warm little cardigans, bootees, and a rather odd-looking shawl. She told Will indignantly that what he had rudely called holes were in fact the lacy design she had copied from a woman's magazine, but she did not think he believed her.

As luck would have it, the weather, which had been terrible, eased just about the time the baby was due to be born. The thaw did not last, but though it was still cold and frosty most of the snow had melted. They awoke in the mornings to a fairy tale-like scene of trees outlined in white icing sugar and puddles reflecting an ice-blue sky, so that Imogen was happy to stay indoors and keep the fire in the living room supplied with the logs which Will cut and stacked in the old chicken house.

By the middle of the month she began to suffer for the first time from some of the consequences of her condition, and the district nurse told her that this was not uncommon and added, rather depressingly, that first babies were often two to three weeks late. Backache plagued her if she spent too long on her feet, and she had to watch her diet since she had started to suffer from dreadful heartburn. And when the frost seemed determined to remain she only walked down to meet Will's train when she saw someone else setting out too, for a fall, in her condition, was the last thing she wanted.

'I'm bigger than that haystack,' she moaned as they walked, arms entwined, back from the station one dark afternoon. 'If Tom Tiddler decides to be one of those babies who won't put in an appearance until they're three weeks late I bags be the one who smacks his little bottom and hears his first cry.'

But a week or so after the baby was due, Imogen fairly danced to the station, her eyes like stars. 'First sign of imminent arrival,' she told Will, cuddling his arm, for it was horribly cold still. 'He's stopped kicking and wriggling, bless him! The district nurse says babies do that when one is near one's time; it's almost as though they're preparing for the big dive down.'

'Gosh, the things I'm learning,' Will said. 'Tomorrow's Saturday; how would you like a trip into Wickenham? A ride in the car might hurry things up and I know you wanted to buy a little present for Ida to say thank you for all her help. There'll be far more choice in one of the big stores than you'd ever find in the village shop.'

'Well, I had meant to buy her cigarettes because she smokes like a chimney,' Imogen confessed. 'But I'd far rather buy her a really pretty headscarf, because the one she's got is dyed orange from the cigarette fumes, and she does like to look smart. Oh, Will, you are kind to me! A trip out would be wonderful and it would take my mind off Tom Tiddler. I know I want him to start getting born, but there are moments when every old wives' tale I've ever heard pops into my head and I start expecting the worst.'

They reached Farthing Cottage and went in to find a welcoming blaze from the living room fire and a delicious scent coming from the oven. Will rolled his eyes. 'You marvellous woman. Of all the food I love, beef casserole comes out on top. So it's decided then? We'll get up early tomorrow and attack the shops!'

* * *

They set out early next day, for although Imogen tried to put together a packed lunch, Will was firm. 'We'll go to that posh restaurant on the top floor of that big store on the main street,' he said.

Imogen pulled a face. 'What's wrong with my sandwiches? Don't forget, any day now we're going to be a real family, so we mustn't splash money around. And I've made a batch of scones, so we could have had them for our elevenses.'

Will chuckled. 'Did you say stones?' he enquired innocently. 'The last lot you made, if you remember, I broke a tooth on.'

Imogen leaned over and gave him a playful punch between the shoulder blades. Will was driving carefully because of the icy conditions, and had turned to upbraid her when she gave a sudden squawk as a movement ahead of them caught her eye. 'Will! Look out – it's a cat . . . !'

She heard Will swear, felt the car jerk and swerve, and after that everything happened at once. Will slammed on the brakes and she catapulted into the windscreen. She felt the impact, felt something wet trickling down her face, and the last thing she heard before she plunged into darkness was Will's voice. 'Immy? Oh my God, Immy . . .'

She awoke what could have been hours or days later to find a man in a white coat bending over her with what looked like a long pair of tweezers. He must have noticed her eyelids fluttering apart and stopped his work for a moment to explain. 'You went through the windscreen, my dear, when your husband had to stop rather abruptly.

You've got some nasty cuts, with the glass still in them; I'm picking out every piece, and when that's done we'll give you something to make you sleep. When you wake up, you'll be stitched and bandaged and fine.'

Imogen made a tremendous effort and tried to smile. 'Will? My husband?' she whispered.

'He's fine,' a woman's voice said soothingly. 'He's waiting outside Theatre, very anxious to see you. He told us you're going to have a baby quite soon, so we are to take especial care of you. Now just you relax, my dear, and let Dr Samuels get on with his work. He's given you a little shot of something to numb the pain.'

Imogen moved her head a trifle and saw a woman in nurse's uniform holding a kidney basin, heard the tinkle as a piece of glass was dropped into it, and plunged once more into unconsciousness.

After that, the nightmare began in earnest. Will was there, white and shaking, gripping her hand and murmuring loving words into her ear. He told her the baby had started, that she was now on the labour ward and that she had no need to worry. Everyone said she and Tom Tiddler would be fine; she must just do exactly as the staff told her and all would be well. She begged him not to leave her, but a large woman – not the one who had assisted the doctor to remove the glass – told her briskly that this was women's work, and men on a labour ward were just a nuisance.

She was on the labour ward for thirty hours, attended by various nurses, several of whom showed signs of worry at the baby's slow arrival, and there were occasional visits from a very young and very frightened doctor. She was given gas and air, but when this merely made her even sleepier and less capable of obeying the command to 'bear down' they took it away and tried bullying. 'The baby's in the birth canal and can't breathe until it comes out,' a particularly sharp-tongued nurse told her. 'Your baby's doing its best to get born; now it's up to you to help it. Push, Mrs Carpenter, push with all your strength; give the baby a chance of life.'

'I am pushing. I'm pushing as hard as I possibly can,' Imogen panted. She tried to struggle into a squatting position, but every time she attained it someone pushed her back, saying that the correct way to give birth was when supine.

For the first time in the nightmare scenario, Imogen fought back. She reared up on the birthing couch and pushed feebly at the hands trying to hold her down. 'Get – my – husband,' she screamed, or rather she thought she screamed; all that emerged was a husky whisper.

It had its effect, however. The young doctor suddenly took command. 'Fetch Mr Ramsden,' he shouted, and when the nurse said coldly that it was not necessary, that Mrs Carpenter must just try a little harder, he ordered her out of the room and presently a tall, balding man with kind eyes was at her side, patting her shoulder, telling her that he would have to perform a Caesarean section, that he was very sorry . . .

She felt the mask over her face, the sweetish smell of the anaesthetic, a hand gripping her arm, subdued voices . . . then silence, darkness, and a desolation greater than she had ever imagined.

She came round dizzily, to find herself in a high hospital bed, with Will holding her hand whilst tears chased themselves down his cheeks. She ached all over, and a questing hand at her stomach found a dressing of some description. What did it mean? She had a vague memory of having had an accident but she was pretty sure her injuries had been to the head, so why should the dressing be on her stomach? It took a long while to turn her head so that she might look into Will's eyes. 'What happened?' she whispered. 'I banged my head – I remember that – but I don't remember . . . oh my God, my God, my God! Was it Tom Tiddler? Oh, Will, I can't *remember*.'

'Better not think about it,' Will said huskily. 'It's all over; all you've got to do now is to get yourself fit and strong again. As soon as you're well enough, we'll go back to the cottage. Once you're there, you'll remember everything. I've rung them at work and explained what's happened, so I'll be staying at home to look after you . . .'

By now, Imogen had summoned up enough strength to look about her. She was in a smallish room, with five other beds in which reposed five other women, and at the end of each bed was a cot. She peered at the end of her own bed. No cot.

She was about to panic, then remembered that her ordeal had only just happened; these other women had probably given birth to their babies days, possibly even weeks, before. But when she looked into Will's eyes, she read a terrible message there.

Very, very slowly, she withdrew one hand from under the covers. It was white and feeble; not at all like her own hand. Will, seeing her holding it out towards him, took it in his and bent his head to catch her whisper. 'Tom Tiddler? Is he . . . was he . . . there was a nice man who said everything would be all right. Was he telling me the truth?'

There was a long, long pause and then Will put his arms round her. 'Just as soon as you're well enough we'll make ourselves another Tom Tiddler,' he said. 'But oh, my darling, our first little fellow didn't make it. He's – he's gone to Jesus, sweetheart.'

Imogen stared at him for an unbelieving moment and then she gave a great gulping, tearing sob and buried her head in her pillow. 'Go away,' she cried. 'If it hadn't been for . . . if you'd thought before . . . oh God, if only, if only . . .'

Chapter Fourteen

Imogen remained in hospital until almost the end of February. The hospital was a small one, and though at first she had begged to be moved to a ward where she did not have to see other women nursing their babies the sister had told her, not unkindly, that she must not be so over-sensitive. 'This is a maternity hospital, so we have no other wards, and Mr Ramsden, who did the Caesarean section, wants to keep you under his eye,' she explained. 'At least two of the women in Room 3 lost their first baby and will tell you that their second child soon followed, though we do advise a six-month wait before trying again. Try to be patient, Mrs Carpenter, and remember how fortunate you have been. You were involved in a very nasty car accident and your head hit the windscreen with enough force to cause you to lose consciousness, yet because of the prompt action taken by the doctor in charge you will scarcely be scarred at all, and if you wear your hair in a fringe for a few months . . .'

Imogen sighed. 'I'm not ungrateful, I just want to get home,' she said. 'I'm sure I'd get well quicker if I were at home. Most of the other women are discharged after a week or so . . .'

'They're the ones who have a friend or relative who can move into the house until the patient is well enough to be left on her own,' Sister explained. 'Your husband told us your mother died soon after the war, and anyway you've had a Caesarean section, so your wound needs time to heal. But Mr Ramsden will be doing his rounds today and perhaps he will agree that you should go into a convalescent home until you have fully recovered.'

'Thank you,' Imogen said. 'When my husband visits this evening I'll ask him to bring me some clothes.'

'We'll see,' Sister said, and patted Imogen's shoulder as the younger woman smiled tentatively up at her. 'It's nice to see you smile, Mrs Carpenter. The convalescent home is by the sea, so you should begin to recover your spirits as well as your strength.'

That evening when Will visited the hospital, he asked Sister why Imogen could not come straight home. 'She's had major surgery, Mr Carpenter,' Sister explained, 'and must not lift or carry heavy objects for a considerable while. Furthermore, you've told us your work takes you daily to London, so a few weeks in our convalescent home, being brought gradually back to normal health, can do your wife nothing but good.'

Will had expected Imogen to object, but she did not do so. The home was a long way from Farthing Cottage, but he told her that he would visit at least twice a week. 'The Rover's been mended and is as good as it ever was,' he told her bracingly. 'So no fear that I won't arrive on the dot when you get your discharge.

A few weeks later, Will took time off work and arrived at the home with a suitcase containing the clothes for which Imogen had longed. He had taken the greatest care in the selection: a blue cardigan, a pretty white blouse and a smart navy skirt which had seen better days but he knew Imogen loved, though the staff at the home had reminded him tactfully that Mrs Carpenter's wound, albeit healing beautifully, would be best without the pressure of tight garments.

When he entered the dormitory which Imogen had shared with three other women he was telling himself that now everything would be all right. Imogen had blamed him bitterly for the accident, blamed him for the death of the baby, though she had never said a word about the scars across her forehead where she had hit the windscreen. But surely, now that she was becoming her old self again – or he hoped she was – she would accept that he was no more guilty than she was herself. She had punched his shoulder, though only in fun, seconds before that damned cat had run out in front of him. He had borne the responsibility, explained that he'd have slammed his foot on the brake the moment he saw the movement of anything heading across the road. He had told her that it might have been a child, and then regretted the words as he saw her big, dark blue eyes fill with tears.

He put the case down on Imogen's bed and kissed her, feeling her immediately go stiff with rejection. He tried not to mind, but it was hard when all he wanted to do was hold her in his arms and regain the loving trust they had always shared, even if it meant accepting responsibility for something which, he knew, was in no way his fault.

'Will! You've brought my clothes? What a silly thing to say – you're scarcely likely to bring anyone else's.' Imogen clicked the case open, pouncing on the contents and snuggling clothing against her cheek. 'My favourite things; aren't you clever?' She stood up to draw the curtains around the bed. 'Go and wait for me in the day room. I can dress in a trice,' she lowered her voice to a confidential whisper, 'if it means getting away from here.'

Will was halfway out of the curtains when he stopped to look over his shoulder. 'Why can't I stay and help you with buttons and things?' he said, almost shyly. 'I am your husband, after all.'

He had not meant to sound hurt, but somehow that was how it came out, and when he looked at Imogen's face he knew he had said the wrong thing. She gave him a cool and antagonistic look whose meaning he could not fail to interpret and he slunk out of the day room, glad that there were no other patients to see his humiliation. He told himself that it had been his tactlessness which had annoyed her. Once she was out of here, all would be well.

'Well, darling, as you can see, I haven't wasted my time during your absence. What do you think?' Will had driven the car between the brand new wooden gates and parked it on a patch of ground which had once been home to an ancient chicken-house and was now converted into a small gravelled sweep, just wide enough to turn the car.

Imogen had been very quiet on the drive home but now she began to look about her. 'New paint,' she said. 'I like the green front door, only I thought we'd agreed that it should be yellow.'

'Yes, I know, but green paint was all I could get, and do you know I believe I prefer it to yellow anyway? It's such an old building . . .'

'You've dug the garden.' It was a statement, not a question. 'I suppose you'll plant spuds; isn't that what you said was best for the land?'

'That's right,' Will said eagerly. So she had been listening after all when, during visiting, he had tried to tell her how he was employing his time. 'I know you can't see it from here, but old Geoff Barnett, the thatcher who lives in the village, has done some patching and he's made a reed bird to stand on the ridge of the roof. I should have pointed it out as we came round the bend, but I forgot you'd not seen it before. What do you think?'

There was a long pause and Will, anxious that everything should go well, got hastily out of the car and went round to the passenger side. He tried to help Imogen out of the car, but she stepped past him and moved back to admire the reed pheasant on the ridge. He waited for her comment, but she did not speak, so he inserted the key in the lock and pushed open the front door, then stood aside. 'Come into the lovely warmth of your newly decorated parlour,' he said. 'Did you like the pheasant? I think it's a work of art.'

'It's very nice,' Imogen said in a small, flat voice. She looked around the living room, into which the front door opened directly. 'I like the pictures; where did you get them?'

Will smiled. 'Oh, from the local auction. They're only prints; I got them quite cheap. But come into the kitchen. It's my *pièce de résistance*.'

They walked across the room and through the door into the kitchen, and Imogen saw that the old cooking range had been replaced by a more modern version. For the first time since they had left the hospital, she gave him a tiny smile. 'Oh, it's a Rayburn. I've always wanted one of these. Did it cost a great deal of money? Only I never could get the temperature right on the old range.'

'It actually cost more to install than to buy, even though I did most of the work myself,' Will admitted. He pulled a chair out and would have helped Imogen to sit down, but she shook her head.

'I'm not an invalid, and as the locals at the Linnet used to say I in't made of icing sugar, neither, so let me get on with things at my own speed.'

'Sorry. But after all, pet, you were in the convalescent home only a couple of hours ago,' Will said. 'I've a meal in the oven. It's nothing special; just a couple of baking potatoes – can't you smell them? – and a bought pie, because as you know I'm no hand at cooking. I don't want to leave it too long, but if you want to see the rest of the cottage first . . .'

'I don't; want to see the rest of the cottage I mean,' Imogen said quickly. 'Did you bring my case in? . . . Then while you fetch it I'll lay the table.'

Presently they settled down to eat the meal Will had prepared, though he noticed that Imogen ate little more than a few mouthfuls. They had told him at the home to 'feed her up', but he thought that nagging her wouldn't help. She had been very active before the accident, and he imagined that was what had given her such a good appetite; perhaps now that she was home again it would gradually return. So when he cleared the plates away he made no comment, merely saying that he could tell she must be tired. 'You go upstairs and get ready for bed,' he suggested. 'I'll deal with the pots, and follow you when I've closed down for the night.'

Imogen was still sitting at the table, though she had pushed her chair back, but now she stood up and faced him, pale but determined. 'I'm not going upstairs; please don't try to make me. It's – it's too soon. I'm going to sleep on the sofa in the living room tonight.'

Will stared at her, knowing his astonished pain must show on his face. 'But you won't need to look at . . . I mean, you can go straight to our room,' he said. 'I've cleared the second one. Look, I had a plumber round to give me a quote for turning it into a bathroom . . . I thought you might prefer it . . .'

He stopped speaking; Imogen was shaking her head and there was a mulishness about her mouth with which he had become painfully familiar since the accident. 'It's too soon. Don't you realise, every room in this house, every inch of the garden, makes me remember our plans for Tom Tiddler. I thought it was the same for you, but I can tell I was wrong. You've put him out of your mind and you expect me to do the same. Well, maybe I'll be able to forget him eventually – after all, I only saw him for a second before they took him away – but for the time being his little spirit . . .'

Tears welled up and Will tried to take her in his arms, but she repulsed him. 'Don't touch me!' she said sharply. And then, as he stepped back, it seemed that for one moment she softened. 'Will, I'm sorry, but that's how I feel at the moment. I hope it will pass, but until it does . . . oh, can't you see? He – he was like you to look at, not in the least like me. Every time I look at you, I see his little face . . .'

Her voice became choked with tears and Will took her unresisting hand and kissed the palm. 'I'm sorry, sweetheart. Now I understand how you feel I'll do my best to respect your wishes. But Immy, as soon as you feel able . . .'

'Of course,' Imogen said, and a tiny, wintry smile flickered across her face for an instant. 'When you fetch a blanket and a pillow, perhaps you could bring my suitcase down. I'll need my nightie, my slippers and my wash bag, so if you wouldn't mind . . .'

'I'll do whatever you want, whatever will help you to get well again,' Will said, but this, apparently, was the wrong thing to say.

The gentler look left his wife's face and a frown etched itself between her soft, winged brows. 'I'm not an invalid,' she reminded him crossly. 'Don't treat me like a child . . .'

It was too much for both of them. Imogen flung herself on the sofa and buried her head in the cushions, racked with sobs, whilst Will stood helpless, not daring to touch her, as tears trickled down his cheeks.

But when the May blossom starred the hawthorn hedges, Will began to lose heart, for it seemed to him that Imogen spent her days mooning around the house doing almost nothing, and when he came home it was to find her listless and apparently indifferent to his hopeful chatter. He went off to work as he had always done, walking to the station and catching the train to town, but Imogen stayed at home, made no attempt to find a job as she had promised, and no longer came to meet him at the station. She still slept on the sofa and – Will could tell – spent a great deal of the day in tears. She missed Ida, who had had to take other work during Imogen's long absence, but refused to try to find another charlady, telling Will that they could not afford it until she was earning again, but adding that in any case she did not want another woman interfering in her house.

When she said this, Will saw her look round and pull a face. For the first time perhaps, Will thought, she must have realised how she had neglected their little home. Dust was thick on every available surface, and clothes lay in untidy heaps, for Imogen insisted that her possessions must not go up the stairs any more than she would herself. Unwashed dishes and pans encrusted with partly eaten food were piled up on the draining board, waiting for Will to deal with them, and wet clothes dripped from the airer which Will festooned with washing and hauled up to the ceiling in bad weather, drying in the warmth from the Rayburn and the living room fire.

Will cleared his throat awkwardly. It was so difficult to gauge her mood, to be understanding, never critical. 'I can see you don't want anyone to come into the house just now . . . but it's only surface dirt. If we work together we can get it respectable . . .' he began, but was swiftly and ruthlessly interrupted.

'It's quite all right; you needn't try to spare my feelings. But I don't need any help. It's about time I flicked a duster round. When I've done that, if I decide *I* need a charlady – *if*, Will – then *I* shall employ one. I've not touched the money in our post office savings book so I could pay her with some of that . . .'

'Oh, darling, I'm sure if you had some help . . .' He stopped speaking as his wife brushed past him, going through the back door and slamming it behind her.

Will sighed and went over to the sink. He pumped

cold water into the kettle and stood it on top of the Rayburn. You fool, you said the wrong thing again, he accused himself. He glanced through the window and saw that the rain, which had held off while he walked up from the station, was beginning to fall once more. She won't come in again until she's cooled down, he thought. I ought to do a caveman act and go out and fetch her, but it would only make her furious. Oh, how I wish I could talk to Ida, persuade her to come back, explain . . . but I'd be accused of interfering and that would be another black mark against me.

The kettle began to whistle. Will carried it over to the sink and poured its contents into the bowl, then began to wash the pots. When Imogen came back indoors she said nothing for a moment and then picked up a tea towel and began to dry up. After a minute she said awkwardly: 'Sorry I was cross. By the way, when I was in the post office the other afternoon Mrs Grindley mentioned her books again. I said I would give her a hand with them.'

The remark gave Will hope that things would improve, so a few days later when the plumber appeared in his office with three sketches of nice, modern bathrooms which, he said, would fit easily into their spare room, Will was delighted. Things had seemed easier at home ever since Imogen had begun to do a little housework and he decided he must stop being such a ninny: he would show her the sketches and see if they might lure her into climbing the stairs.

He glanced out of the window of his office and saw bright buds bursting into leaf and pale sunshine falling on the frail petals of a big pot of primroses. This was central London, he told himself; how much lovelier were the primroses and violets on the mossy banks of the lane which led to Farthing Cottage. Spring was supposed to have a softening effect on the heart; how much he hoped it would work its magic on poor, unhappy little Imogen.

Will glanced from the scene outside to the sketches in his hand and decided to leave work early. He would buy Imogen some chocolates and some of the wine she liked and then he would produce the sketches. He knew she missed the luxury – and convenience – of a bath and decided to add a bottle of bath salts to his other purchases, then called his secretary through to advise him on where best to buy these delightful presents.

He took Miss Gibson's advice and soon found what he sought. The bath salts were pink and fragrant, the chocolates soft-centred, the wine sparkling; he added a chiffon scarf in palest blue, her favourite colour, and as he waited on the platform that afternoon his hopes were high. Surely she would see his only desire was to please her, to make her understand – and reciprocate – his love for her!

He caught an earlier train and as it approached the station he thought how lovely it would be if Imogen were to be waiting for him. He could imagine her pleasure in his gifts and thought how they would walk home, sharing the chocolates, holding the wine up to the spring sunshine, even opening the bath salts to sniff them as they walked. And then, when she was laughing, he would bring the sketches out of his pocket . . .

She was not at the station, of course; why would she be? She had probably forgotten all about the promised bathroom. Buoyed up by hope, however, he burst into the kitchen. Imogen was sitting at the kitchen table, idly scanning the pages of the church magazine, a monthly affair which was no doubt filled with exciting information about village life. She looked up as he entered and gave him a tentative smile.

'Hello! Shall I put the kettle on? You're early, aren't you?'

'I managed to catch the earlier train. I've got you . . . here . . . it's your favourite colour; I saw it in a shop window . . . and some wine, and chocolates too!' He produced the wisp of chiffon and handed it to her, saw her eyes soften, and put the chocolates down on the table between them. 'I thought . . . look, the plumber's sketches have arrived. Do you remember me telling you . . .'

Without warning, Imogen jumped to her feet. She snatched the sketches from him and crumpled them in her hand, not even looking at them. When he protested, said she was not giving the man a chance, she said coldly, 'We talked about converting the scullery into a bathroom, if you cast your mind back. If you make the second bedroom into a bathroom, where will our visitors sleep? Or do you intend to keep me a prisoner here, never seeing anyone but you?'

The unfairness of the remark was like a kick in the stomach, and for a moment Will was so astonished that he simply gaped. Then he responded, his voice rising as he did so. 'How dare you say such a thing? I've begged you to let me bring friends home, people from my office, even villagers like dear old Ida or that fat woman who never stops talking, and you've never once agreed.'

'They aren't my friends,' Imogen began, but Will was thinking of all the lonely nights when he had lain in his bed, longing to hear a step on the stair, the creak of the bedroom door as Imogen crept into the room, and ignored the remark. He thought of the clutter in their living room, a clutter of clothing and possessions which Imogen wanted to keep to hand instead of putting upstairs, where they belonged. He thought of the back-breaking spring work of digging, manuring and planting the garden, all done by himself and without one word of praise – of acknowledgement even – from his wife. He thought of the expensive food he had bought to try to tempt her appetite which she had pushed round her plate and then emptied into the bin. Then he thought of the meals which awaited him each evening: beans on toast, cheese on toast, poached egg on toast. He had never complained, not even when he finished eating and then had to tackle the washing up alone. In fact, Will was suffering as much from the strain of examining every word before he let it escape from his lips as from the fact that he was doing the work of two people at home on top of his job in the insurance office, and now the dam was about to burst.

He began to detail the tasks he had done, unhelped by so much as a word or a look, but then he realised she was not listening. She was justifying her behaviour, blaming him for doing everything, so that she was idle not from choice but because he had greedily taken the work for himself, and suddenly Will's patience snapped. He crossed the kitchen in a couple of strides, grabbed her by the shoulders and shook her as hard as he could, and as he shook, he shouted. All the worries and frustrations of the past weeks were voiced aloud for the first time. He reminded her that she was his wife, that she had made promises – promises in church furthermore – that she clearly had no intention of keeping . . .

And as though his anger had lit a flame within her, Imogen began shouting too. She said that all he wanted was a housekeeper, or did he expect her to do the heavy digging which would be needed to turn the pasture land into a market garden?

'Oh, very funny, when you can't even be bothered to wash up the pots at the weekend when I – I, Imogen Carpenter – have cooked a proper meal,' he yelled. 'I've done my best to please you, I've worked as hard as any man could, doing your jobs as well as my own, but that's all over, you lazy little madam! You said you didn't want to be treated as an invalid; then stop behaving like one. And we'll start by *both* of us going upstairs and comparing the sketches with the little bedroom.'

He moved to grab her wrist but she hit his approaching hand as hard as she could, snatched up the crumpled sketches and threw them into the heart of the fire. Then she dusted her hands together, as though ridding them of a noxious touch, and threw herself down on the sofa. He saw the tears begin but from the look on her face he realised they were tears of anger. 'Get out and stay out,' she shrieked. 'I hate you, Will Carpenter!'

He crossed to the sofa and grabbed her, hustling her towards the stairs, but she fought back, kicking and biting, her fingers curled into claws, and suddenly he knew he had to get out, get away, or they might both do things they would bitterly regret. He let go of her and she hurtled back to the sofa, burying her head in the cushions whilst he stood looking down at her. He saw the white nape of her neck, somehow defenceless and childlike, and knew that trying to talk things out when they were both so angry would not be a good idea.

The anger which had flared when she threw the sketches into the fire suddenly seemed excessive, unnecessary. He was ashamed, wished it had never happened, yet he knew that, like a volcano, he had simply had to erupt, to voice the feelings of frustration and unhappiness with which he had lived for so many weeks.

He bent down and touched her shoulder and felt the immediate rigidity of rejection, but nevertheless he spoke. 'Imogen? I'm going away now, since that seems to be what you want. I'll leave it a couple of days, a week perhaps – I'm sure you can manage that long without me – and then I'll come back and maybe we can discuss the situation like two sensible people and not like a couple of wildcats. Imogen? Did you hear me?'

A tiny sigh came from the crumpled little figure face down amongst the sofa cushions and for a moment Will had to fight an urge to take her in his arms. He thought of all their other fights – and there had been many in the early days of their marriage – but such fights had been partly in play, always resolved. 'Kiss and make up' and 'never let the sun go down upon your wrath' had been the happy principles by which they had run their married life. How had it all come to this?

'Imogen, did you hear what I said?' Will repeated. 'I'm going away for a while. Did you hear me?'

When she did not reply or acknowledge in any way that he had spoken he felt a renewal of his anger beginning to build up and knew he really must get out, could not afford to let the quarrel flare once more.

He was halfway to the back door when it occurred to

him that he would need a clean shirt, his washing kit and his pyjamas. He addressed the slim figure still face down on the sofa. 'Imogen? I'm going upstairs to pack a few things, all right?'

No answer. Will sighed and headed for the stairs. It didn't take him long to pack an overnight bag, though he ended up filling their big suitcase with almost every garment he possessed. Why not? He was suddenly filled with the horrid suspicion that after he left she might go upstairs and either hurl his possessions out of the window, to lie on the half-dug ground until he reclaimed them, or stick them in the Rayburn.

As he came quietly down the stairs again, he was aware that he was half hoping to find a tearful but repentant wife awaiting him. If he had, he would be the first one to kiss and make up. But when he reached the foot of the stairs he saw that she had drawn a chair up to the fire and was leafing through a women's magazine, and paid him not the slightest attention. When he told her that she could contact him at the office if she needed anything, she gave him a look so cold and disdainful that he shot out of the kitchen, slammed the door behind him and slung his suitcase on to the back seat of the Rover.

He reflected that Imogen had the post office savings book, so would not lack money. He decided he would return to Farthing Cottage in two or three days and not a moment before. He would bring with him something easy, like fish and chips, and hope that they might discuss their situation over a meal. He thought – or rather, hoped – that two or three whole days and nights alone in the cottage, with no one to wash the dishes and put them away, no one, in fact, to come should she call, would be enough to bring her to her senses.

Having settled in his mind that Imogen would not lack for money he realised, abruptly, that he had very little cash on him. He had a season ticket for the train, of course, but he did not much fancy a night spent in the waiting room or curled up on the back seat of the car. If he went to a friend they would naturally want to know why he was suddenly homeless and would inevitably conclude that there had been a quarrel and his wife had thrown him out. However, he had a cheque book and he knew his bank balance was healthy, so he could afford a couple of nights in a bed and breakfast.

He drove back to London, left the Rover in the office car park, and took his overnight bag in search of a pub that would offer him a room. He approached the Boot and Bottle, a hostelry where he had frequently gone with his fellow workers for a pie and a pint, which he knew charged ten shillings a night for bed and breakfast. He signed in, paid for two nights in advance, asked the landlord to put together a plate of sandwiches and a pint of bitter and headed for the stairs. He knew from experience that the clientele of the bed and breakfast side of the business consisted mainly of travellers dealing in various commodities, knew also that they were not generally curious about their fellow clients, and once he had ensured that the room was clean and the bed comfortable he made his way his way down to the lounge bar and soon fell into conversation with a couple of the other residents, one of whom specialised in fancy biscuits and the other representing a large firm of chocolate manufacturers. By the time he sought his bed he realised that he had enjoyed the evening, even enjoyed the food and the beer, because he had not had to prepare it and it was eaten in undemanding company, with much laughter and a general of air of bonhomie, for the talk had turned on the peculiarities of women in general and wives in particular. He felt normal, a man amongst men.

'My missus makes me ring her up at least twice a week, telling her where I am and the name and telephone number of each B and B,' the chocolate rep said. He was a small, fat man with a crop of untidy brown hair and a tendency to wheeze after talking for long. He raised his eyebrows in a comical gesture. 'Do I look as though I inveigle barmaids up to me room for a spot of the old 'ow's your father?' he asked plaintively. 'But there you are; my good lady thinks that because she fancied me twenty years back, others may do the same.'

Will laughed with the rest. 'Are you ever suspicious?' he asked, only half jokingly. 'Do you imagine that your missus carries on when you aren't there?'

The fat little man blew out his cheeks and gave a long whistle. 'Nah,' he said dismissively. 'We've got six kids, four boys and two girls. She's got no time, let alone no inclination, to play arahnd.'

Again Will laughed with the rest, but when he was alone he thought rather guiltily that it had never occurred to him to wonder what Imogen did when he was working at his desk in the city, and knew that it would never occur to her that he might be unfaithful. And though he tried to deny it, the moment he thought of Imogen, alone in the cottage, he was attacked by guilt. She was such a sweetie, or rather she had been such a sweetie; how could he have simply walked out on her, knowing she had no relatives to whom to turn, suspecting that she had lost touch with most of her friends?

But it was no good repining, and anyway he would make it up to her when he returned to the cottage, somehow get past the guard she had kept between them. And, remembering the fat little man with the jealous wife, he comforted himself with the thought that at least neither he nor Imogen, no matter how furious, had accused the other of infidelity. That's a point in our favour, he told himself as he snuggled down in the single bed. His last thought as sleep overcame him was to wonder with a good deal of pleasant anticipation what the landlady would give them for breakfast. Even if it was just coffee and toast it would be prepared by someone else! But poor Imogen would be making do with tea and bread and margarine. He decided he would make her a proper cooked breakfast when the day following his return dawned.

Satisfied, he slept.

Will allowed three days to pass before once again he drove the Rover along the winding country roads, and as he approached Cornerstowe, and the cottage, apprehension began to build. How would she greet him? With anger, or reproaches? Or perhaps with shy friendliness? You could never tell. He arrived at the village green, which was deserted save for two old men sitting on a bench, savouring the last warm rays of the sun, and then turned into their lane. As he parked the car he saw that there were no lights visible in the cottage, nor smoke ascending from the chimney. He tapped lightly on the back door, then tried to open it and found it locked.

Frowning, he fished the key out from under the flower pot, turned it and entered the kitchen. He immediately knew that the place was empty, that the Rayburn had not been lit, nor the fire in the living room kindled. He crossed the room and put a match to the paraffin lamp which hung above the scrubbed wooden table, and as the lamp hissed into life he saw the note.

His heart gave an uneasy lurch but he forced himself to pick up the sheet of paper and sit down, taking a few uneven breaths as he started to read. He knew of course that it was from Imogen and read it carefully, taking his time. It began abruptly.

Will, you said you were going away for a couple of days and that we would talk when you came back. I'm going away too. I feel cabined, cribbed and confined, as Shakespeare put it. Before we married I earned my own living and can do it again, given time and opportunity and somewhere to lay my head. Please don't be cross. I shouldn't have blamed you over losing Tom Tiddler; it was no one's fault, but it's changed me. The Imogen who screamed at you and told you to get out wasn't the one you married. That one's dead and buried, so forget me as I mean to forget you. Imogen.

Will read the letter three times, aware of a coldness in the pit of his stomach. The last thing he wanted, he realised, was to lose her altogether. His own eyes blurred as he saw that her tear stains had almost obliterated her signature. He looked wildly round the unaccustomedly tidy kitchen and realised he did not have the slightest idea where to begin to look for her.

Suddenly he could not breathe. He had to get out of the cottage, away from the village; he must go back to London, go to work tomorrow as usual, and wait for her to contact him when – if – she wanted to come home. Numbly, he locked the door, got back into the car, and drove away.

When Will went into the office next day he was immediately accosted by his boss, who entered his room breezily, already talking as he came. 'Morning, young Carpenter. Have you talked to your secretary yet? What do you think?'

Will, who had just started to open his correspondence, looked up cautiously. Mr Carruthers had told him several times that he would progress faster in the firm if he took advantage of offers to stand in for branch managers when locums were needed. Before Imogen fell pregnant he had occasionally done this and had rather enjoyed the change of scene and extra responsibility, but since moving to Farthing Cottage he had felt unable to consider leaving his wife even for a couple of weeks. Now, however, he decided he would at least listen to any proposal Mr Carruthers might put forward. Accordingly, he pushed his mail to one side and eyed his boss. 'No, I haven't seen Miss Gibson yet, so you'd better explain. Fire ahead,' he said.

Mr Carruthers did so and it was immediately obvious to Will that his suggestion might, in the long run, be just what he needed. The manager of the Jersey branch meant to retire – indeed he had to do so – when he reached his sixty-fifth birthday in a few weeks. All had been arranged; his deputy was to have taken over, but then had accepted a job with a French insurance firm paying a salary well in excess of what he was currently earning.

'So if you decide to take the plunge, St Helier will want you at once,' Mr Carruthers finished. 'At first it would be as relief manager for just a couple of weeks.' He looked at Will under his lids. 'But you've been to St Helier before, and liked the people, the set-up, the island . . . what would you say to something more permanent? That little wife of yours . . . she might welcome a change of scene . . .'

Will, though tempted by the thought of making such a move, had started to say that Imogen was not yet able to cope without him, but Mr Carruthers's last sentence gave him pause. After his stint in the St Helier branch a few years before, he and Imogen had spent a wonderful holiday on Jersey, staying for a fortnight in a beautiful little cottage a stone's throw from the beach, yet near enough to walk into town, for the island was small; nothing, he thought rather confusedly, was very far from anywhere else. It had been one of the happiest times they had had, and the thought of Imogen's possible pleasure when he told her that they might live on the island was sufficient to make him say at once that he would accept the position.

He had been looking down at his hands, clasping each other on the desk top, but now he raised his eyes to his boss's face. 'Do you know, it might be the answer?' he said slowly. 'I don't know if you've guessed, but ever since we – we lost our baby, my wife's been uneasy in Farthing Cottage. She says it reminds her . . .'

'Quite,' Mr Carruthers interrupted. 'My sister-in-law lost a child, and for a few months my brother thought

. . . but let's just say I quite understand, and think that a move away from . . . away from the area might be the very thing for you both. You would need to make arrangements; the firm will put you up in a boarding house, of course, until you find somewhere you would like to rent. Property in Jersey's expensive but rents are reasonable, and I imagine you would let your cottage to begin with, just in case it didn't work out?'

And so it was arranged. Will put the cottage in the hands of a letting agent recommended by Mr Carruthers, packed his favourite books, his photographs of Imogen and the clothes she had made for Tom Tiddler in tea chests still smelling faintly of their fragrant cargo, and tried not to think what would happen if he had made the wrong decision. As he slipped the keys to Farthing Cottage through the agent's letterbox and listened to them fall, he wondered when – and if – he would ever return.

Chapter Fifteen

Imogen awoke. She sat up on one elbow and stared around the room, actually wondering where she was, though this only lasted for a moment. She was in the living room where she had slept ever since her return from the convalescent home; nothing unusual there. She frowned, trying to think back. Something had happened the previous evening, something cataclysmic, something that had caused the strange feeling she had that things had changed.

Imogen swung her legs off the sofa and stood up. She was just thinking resentfully that Will might have lit the Rayburn before he left for work when events jolted into place. There had been an awful row and Will had said he was leaving her and Farthing Cottage for a while. Well, that was all right by her. He could go any time and the further the better, but he might have lit the Rayburn first; didn't he know how she loved her first cup of tea? He must have come quietly down the stairs whilst she slept, walked straight across the living room and out through the front door. Indignation filled her.

But as she stumped crossly over to the sink and began to work the pump, banishing the last shreds of sleep, recollection came, clear and unwanted. He had left last night, which meant that he could not possibly have started the Rayburn or made her a cup of tea this morning. Well, she had wanted her independence and now she had it; strange how little satisfaction the thought gave her.

Now, with the filled kettle in one hand, she remembered that Will had always tried to keep the Rayburn glowing because he said it was a beast to relight. Ten minutes later Imogen pulled a face, knowing that he had spoken no more than the truth, for she must have used the best part of a box of matches with no result. She lit the paraffin stove instead, stood the kettle on it and then glanced stairwards. She remembered how she had shouted, how she had told him to get out, and felt a tiny twinge of guilt. Had she meant him to leave? She was just wondering whether she had gone too far when the kettle began to hiss and she reached for the teapot. Damn Will Carpenter! Let him go as far and as fast as possible; she had her own life to lead.

But had he really gone? A part of her hoped he had, and yet . . . Perhaps this was just a bad dream, and he would come downstairs presently. On the thought she ran lightly up the stairs, making as little noise as possible, to the tiny landing. Once there she did not even have to open their bedroom door, which already stood wide. One glance was sufficient: it was not a dream but horrid reality. The wardrobe gaped, empty of clothing, and the big suitcase which lived on top of it had gone. Imogen crossed the room and pulled open the top drawer of the chest – it was empty. She turned to look at the bed, neatly made with Will's hospital corners, and did not need to check for his dressing gown and slippers. They were gone along with all the rest.

Well, she had told him to go and he had obeyed, and

if he thought she was going to hang around waiting for him to apologise he had another think coming. As for loneliness, hadn't she been lonely ever since they moved into Farthing Cottage? Of course she had. She refused to remember the happy busyness of the months of her pregnancy, how she had thrown herself into country life, proud as a peacock when Will commended a cake she had baked, eager to help when a room needed redecorating or seedlings planting out. She made herself a cup of tea and then decided she had better get dressed. After that, she would do some shopping in the village. She checked that their post office savings book was still in the dresser drawer, then examined the contents of the pantry. She needed coffee and sugar, and bread of course. She made a note.

All through the day her mind was in a whirl. One moment she decided she would ring Will at work and demand his return, the next that she would leave Farthing Cottage and forget he even existed. The problem was, where would she go? By the end of the second day, her mind was made up. She would go to London, for where better to hide – until one chose to be found, of course – than in a populous capital city? And she would write a note for Will which would leave him in no doubt that she could look after herself.

She was sipping her tea as she made these plans and was aware at once of considerable relief. She told herself that she had not missed Will; she had just missed having someone else in the house. She would pack her bag – though she would not take everything she possessed as Will had done, just a few necessities – go down to the post office in the village and draw on the account she and Will had kept for the market garden they had hoped to start. Then she would shake the dust of Farthing Cottage, and Cornerstowe, from her neat little brogues, and start on her new life.

She slept well that night for the first time since she had returned from the convalescent home, though she would never have admitted it, even to herself. She had packed the evening before and it was not until she reached the village that she realised she had used the little case she had filled ready to take with her to the hospital when Tom Tiddler began his entry into this cold, cruel world.

Oddly, this set her back on her heels in a way nothing else had done, not the packing itself nor the tidying of Farthing Cottage, nor the writing of the note. But she had made up her mind that emotion was something she could no longer afford, so she forced back the tears and hummed a happy tune as she stowed away the contents of their post office savings account in her old leather handbag and headed for the station.

Within a week Imogen had found work and a flat share near Euston Station and her confidence had begun to return. Within a month she was promoted from office junior to the secretarial pool, and life began to follow a set routine. The first flat was shared by four girls and by the weekend it was usually squalid, for though they took turns to cook, clean and take their washing to the local launderette they rarely stuck to the rota and Imogen grew tired of sour milk, a filthy refrigerator and finding her chocolate biscuits had been nicked. Also, two of the girls brought men in, so when a friend at work suggested that

Imogen might like to share her own accommodation, nine stops from the office on the Circle line, she jumped at the chance. The journey on the Tube was not a long one and she came to recognise other girls heading in the same direction, though they never spoke but merely exchanged smiles.

One of the girls was a loud-mouthed Brummy with a laugh like the bray of a donkey and a bottom of such noble proportions that she took up almost two seats. By listening to their conversations Imogen learned her name was Hattie, and she usually avoided her for her loud remarks drowned out any other conversation.

Yet it was the noisy Hattie who was responsible for Imogen's bright idea. After three months Imogen missed Will so badly that it was a constant physical ache, and one evening, when she got aboard the Tube, the only seat available was directly behind that upon which Hattie was perched. Sighing, she resigned herself to being battered by the other girl's loud voice, taking little notice of the actual words until Hattie heaved herself out of her seat and clapped her companion on the shoulder. 'So that's that – she's organising a reunion of the girls what flew the barrage balloons on Number 48,' she said. 'The war's been over fifteen years and she don't know how to get in touch with anyone bar meself, but they say there's one born every minute . . .'

She was still jabbering as she climbed down on to the platform but Imogen sat where she was, staring into space. A reunion! Hattie's remark had made her realise that it was actually September and in a few weeks it would be twenty years since the evacuees had first arrived at the Canary and Linnet. A reunion!

She had longed to get in touch with Will, to apologise and explain, yet her pride would not let her make a direct approach. If she did so and he turned her away, it would break her heart. She wanted to meet him casually, accidentally on purpose, with other people around to – to cushion the shock, she thought wildly. She could invite everyone, and then if Will didn't come . . . but he would if he could, she was suddenly sure.

After a couple of weeks, everyone had answered her invitation except Will. Did it mean he had never received it? Or had simply pushed it aside? Perhaps he had a new life – and girlfriend – and had no interest in meeting up with a part of his past. But she did not really believe the latter idea; his good manners would not allow him to ignore an invitation, even if he felt he could not accept. She remembered how kind and thoughtful he had always been . . . oh, God, why had she ever let it come to this?

She comforted herself with the recollection that he no longer lived in England but had taken a managerial position in the Channel Islands, so his reply would naturally arrive later than the others. She had rung his London office when she had discovered that he was no longer living in Farthing Cottage and been told by a snooty young woman with a suppressed Cockney accent that Mr Carpenter had left. She had been close to despair then, but she had rung again later and asked to speak to Mr Carruthers.

She had done the right thing. Mr Carruthers told her that Will had moved to the Jersey branch and was doing very well. Could he pass a message on? Shyly, feeling like a spy in an enemy camp, Imogen had asked for the telephone number of Will's new office, and had then lacked the courage to ring.

But she had sent off his invitation, and told herself that she would telephone if the reunion failed to bring him back to the Canary and Linnet.

When Imogen had sat down in Auntie's creaking old rocking chair, she had told herself severely she really must not fall asleep again. Remembering times past was all very well, but there would be quite enough of that when the others arrived. She, who had engineered this meeting, would have to explain that she had not known the Canary and Linnet was no longer a hostelry where friends could meet but merely a shell of its former self.

She imagined that peaceable Debby would simply accept the explanation and that quick-tempered Rita would be full of reproaches, but would come round; she usually did. Jill, of course, must have known all about the Canary and Linnet, because she lived next door to Auntie and Auntie lived only four or five miles from the pub which she had once run so successfully.

A sound from outside made Imogen get up from the chair and peer out through the window, but it was only a blackbird, examining the ivy-clad wall for insects, so she returned to her seat, glancing at her wristwatch as she did so. Heavens, how time crawled when you were waiting for something to happen! But it was passing, albeit slowly; the others should be within moments of getting off the train and catching a taxi or a bus. Provided the train was on time, they could be here in minutes. She got to her feet; perhaps it would be best if she set out at once and walked to the village to meet them. Then she remembered that

Rita had said in her last Christmas card that she had just bought a little red MG, having passed her driving test at last, so the chances were that Rita at least would be arriving by car, and now that she considered she realised that Debby and her husband might have found it easier to hire a vehicle than depend on the reliability of public transport. And hadn't Mrs Jacky said that the village bus now only ran three days a week? All in all, it seemed safer to stay where she was.

The blackbird rustled in the ivy again, then chattered for a moment and gave its warning whistle. Imogen, who had sat upright at the first sound, wagged an admonitory finger. 'You don't fool me . . .' she was beginning when the back door creaked open and someone pushed it wide, entered the kitchen and after one swift glance around rushed at Imogen, almost knocking her over as she struggled to her feet.

'Immy, darling!' Warm arms were round her and a warm mouth was kissing her cheek, then Jill was holding her back, looking her up and down. 'Oh, Immy, how long have you been here? I'm so sorry Laurie couldn't make the reunion, but I wouldn't miss it for the world, and nor would Mum, of course. I gather you know we now live next door to one another? Laurie talks about leaving the RAF because he gets moved around so much, but I don't think it will happen for years. Still, I go out to see him quite often, and of course he comes home between postings, so it's not too bad. In fact, I sometimes think our marriage is even stronger because we're apart so much – it's so wonderful when we *can* be together! Oh, my love, it's so good to see you, but I have to tell you you're not looking your best.' Another warm hug.

'You've had a horrid time, I know – I saw the note you sent with the invitation – but believe me, love, although grief doesn't go away it does become more bearable as time passes.'

Imogen remembered the letter from Auntie telling her that Jill too had lost a baby not long after the end of the war. She felt the tears begin and scrubbed impatiently at her eyes. 'I know you're right,' she said, scooping her handbag up from where she had cast it down and giving Jill her most cheerful smile. 'And I'm so glad you came early, because one of the main reasons for the reunion was so I could apologise for something I did . . . oh, years ago.'

Jill stared at her. 'Something you did?' she echoed. 'Immy, darling, I'm sure I don't know what you could possibly mean.' She laughed. 'As I'm sure you must be well aware, you were always my favourite evacuee! Oh, I was fond of Rita in a way, and Debby the peacemaker was very loveable, but you and I were two of a kind . . .'

She would have gone on but Imogen, desperate to admit her fault, spoke across her. 'Do shut up a minute, Jill, and let me get it off my conscience before anyone else arrives. I've lost count of the number of times I've tried to write to say I was sorry and beg you to forgive me, but I never sent any of the letters, so this might be my last chance to put things right between us. Do you remember that time when Auntie got cross when her Home Chat magazine went missing?'

The older girl was staring at her. 'I wondered why you never wrote to me,' she said slowly. 'I must admit I was rather hurt – I thought we'd been such friends. But then the invitation arrived, and I hoped . . . but what has that wretched magazine got to do with anything? Auntie was so upset when we came down to breakfast and it had disappeared. Had you thrown it away by mistake? I couldn't find it anywhere, and heaven knows I tried hard enough. Was it you?'

'Yes, in a way,' Imogen said slowly. 'One night I came downstairs when everyone else was in bed – I wanted a drink of water – and you were putting *Home Chat* in the middle of the kitchen table, and – and sort of smiling. I was just going to ask what you were doing when I thought I'd guessed – I'd been watching you and Laurie for some time – but I couldn't be sure. So I scuttled back to the attic and waited until I heard your bedroom door open and close. Then I came back downstairs, picked up the *Home Chat* and thrust it into the Aga. I was pretty sure that the magazine meant that Laurie could go up to your room in safety. And – and I decided to put a stop to it. What a little prude I was! But I was jealous on two counts, you see, because I'd had a hopeless crush on Laurie ever since he came into our lives, but I loved you, too, Jillywinks, and couldn't bear to share you. And when I realised the significance of that beastly little magazine . . . well, I hid in the pantry until I heard the key grate in the lock and looked through the crack and saw Laurie come tiptoeing into the kitchen. He stared at the table and then heaved an enormous sigh and I think that was when I realised what a dreadful thing I'd done. He looked so haggard, Jill, so grey-faced and weary! At that moment I knew I'd done a wicked thing and I was afraid I'd ruined your lives, yours and Laurie's. I was so scared, crouching in the pantry, and I suddenly thought that Laurie might decide to get himself a snack and find me there. I truly wished I could have undone the last half hour, but it was no use wishing, so I waited until I heard him heading for the box room and then I went back to my own bed.

'And next day, when Auntie made such a fuss about *Home Chat* because she was using one of its knitting patterns, I was so unhappy I very nearly confessed, but I couldn't, because to admit what I'd done was the equivalent of telling tales on you and Laurie, and that was something we'd all been taught never to do; sneaking's horrid. I felt even more guilty because I thought that Laurie might stop coming to the Canary and Linnet, when he was free to do so.'

'Oh, Immy, fancy you guessing that the magazine meant it was – well, okay for Laurie to come to my room. It was wrong of us, of course, but in wartime . . .' Jill said remorsefully.

'I was a selfish little beast,' Imogen said slowly. 'But I had to tell you – it's been on my conscience ever since.'

'And soon after that Laurie was posted,' Jill said. 'He knew that there were times when we let one of the bedrooms, usually to a wife of one of the RAF station personnel, and Auntie and I doubled up. It was going to be Laurie's last forty-eight for ages and naturally enough he wanted to . . . well, shall we say he needed to know that if he came upstairs and into my room, he wouldn't find a stranger or, worse, Auntie in the bed.' She chuckled, though eyeing her companion somewhat warily. 'I was almost always last to go up; I'd bank the fire down, lay the table for breakfast and so on first. But our days were pretty full what with one thing and another, and I told Laurie that if – if the coast was clear

I'd leave *Home Chat* on the kitchen table when I went upstairs. I didn't fancy leaving a note for him, you see, but it was a simple matter to arrange that if he saw *Home Chat* lying on the table when he arrived he would be safe to come to my room, but if it wasn't there he'd either use the camp bed in the box room or bed down on one of the old pews in the bar. Simple, wasn't it?'

Vastly relieved, Imogen nodded. 'I suppose I was a proper little prude, but that's how you are when you're thirteen or fourteen. I guess I wanted Laurie for myself, though I didn't realise it then. And I wanted you as my bezzie, as we say in Liverpool . . .'

Jill linked her arm with Imogen's and gave it a tug. 'Fancy you remembering that one little incident after all these years,' she marvelled. 'Well, if it's any satisfaction to you, both Laurie and I would have forgiven you years ago had we known what you'd done. And now, since you've got your confession off your chest, you can jolly well listen to mine . . . my confession, I mean.'

Imogen stared. 'I can't believe you ever did anything like I did,' she said slowly. 'You are the most honest, straightforward person I know. But go ahead, tell me . . . I bet it's nothing much, nothing like what I did.'

'Grammar, girl,' Jill said, laughing. 'For years I've thought you three girls knew, anyway, but something you said just now – or rather something you *didn't* say – leads me to believe you don't. Did you notice I said Mum wouldn't miss it for the world?'

Imogen frowned. 'Ye-es,' she said slowly. 'But honest to God, Jilly, I've never met your mother . . . in fact we never gave anyone but Auntie a thought. But why are you laughing? I thought your father was Auntie's brother, and that was why you had the same surname.'

'Well, if you aren't the most innocent creature I know,' Jill said. 'Didn't you ever talk about us when you were tucked away in your attic? Did it never occur to you that Auntie was my mother? In those days it wasn't acceptable to have a baby before you were married. Auntie fell in love with a young man and would have married him, but he was killed in a road accident. She had been meaning to tell him she was expecting a baby the day the crash happened. Gosh, Immy, I was certain you all knew . . . oh, not when you first arrived, but by the time you left.'

'Well I never!' Imogen said blankly. 'But until today you never slipped up and called Auntie "Mum", and she never let on that you were anything but her niece.'

Jill grinned. 'I didn't know she *was* my mother until I was seven, and then I was old enough to agree that it was a big secret and must never be told to anyone outside the family. Secrets are the breath of life to kids, anyway, but mostly I forgot all about it and simply thought of Auntie as just that. But I don't need to tell you that Auntie or Mum is the best person I know.' Jill stood up. 'Now, I'm sorry I never told you that the Linnet wasn't a suitable place for a meeting, but I knew the others would want to go all over the pub and tell their partners all about their time there and I wanted to talk to you alone. You said in your note to Mum that you and William had parted, and I knew from our own experience that the awful thing that happened to you can cause even good relations to founder . . . but Imogen, you mustn't let it ruin your lives. Casting blame is a pointless exercise, which hurts both parties and does no good to anyone. Do you promise to see Will and make it up?'

'That's the real reason why I planned the reunion, to meet Will again on neutral ground,' Imogen said gloomily. 'However, first catch your hare. But if we find each other . . . oh, Jill, if only!'

They had left the kitchen and gone through into the bar. Jill turned to Imogen. 'You invited him to the reunion, of course.'

She would have said more, but Imogen gave a wail. 'Yes, but I've had no reply to my letter. Remember, we've been apart for five months!'

'And you haven't even been in touch, let alone met, for five whole months?' Jill asked incredulously. 'Oh, Immy!'

Imogen hung her head. 'That's right. You see, we more or less agreed that we would give each other space because we'd had some terrible fights after we lost Tom Tiddler. I went for an interview with the manager of a building society and got a secretarial job . . .'

Jill's mobile eyebrows went up. 'Where is this job? Are you still living at Farthing Cottage?'

'The job's in London and I've got a flat share with an awfully nice girl, quite near the Limerick Building Society, which is where I'm working. But I – I'm afraid Will must have got truly fed up with me because I went back to the cottage a few weeks ago and there's a young couple living there, with a toddler. So then I did try to contact him at work, and was told that he'd been promoted to manager of the St Helier branch, in Jersey. Since I hadn't sent him my London address or told him I was earning a good salary – at first I was still too angry – I suppose he felt that he couldn't afford to leave the cottage empty. Oh, Jill, I was so unhappy! I don't think I was in my right mind when we parted, yet perhaps it was the best thing to do. I've got it out of my system, you see, and now all I want is to tell Will how sorry I am and to beg him to let us try again.' She hesitated, looking shyly up at the older girl. 'Do you think he'll come?'

Jill gave her a fierce hug. 'Oh, darling Immy, I hope so,' she said. 'Remember, Laurie and I lost a child ten years ago, but in the end it strengthened our marriage. Happiness comes from within, so just you admit to Will that you made a terrible mistake and want to put it right. And listen – I can hear voices, so prepare yourself for a nostalgic tour of the old place before we all migrate to the Golden Lion.'

It was over and it had been pretty successful, Auntie told herself, sitting on the platform, waiting for the train which would take her home. She leaned back and let the memories wash over her. It had been a tiring day, yet strangely satisfying, though whenever she thought of Imogen's little white face getting paler and paler as the time passed she was shaken with pity. It was easy to see that the child had expected great things from the reunion; what a shame it was that the person who had masterminded the whole idea had been the most disappointed, the most let down. But useless to think about that; time heals all wounds, she told herself.

Auntie turned her thoughts to the others, first to Rita, the oldest of the three evacuees who had lived at the Canary and Linnet. Auntie tried to forget that it had been

Rita who had spoiled everything and concentrated on the Rita of now and not the Rita of then. As soon as the sports car had roared to a halt outside the Linnet's kitchen she had known what Rita wanted from the reunion, Auntie told herself now. She wanted everyone to know that she is a successful businesswoman, a hotelier par excellence who despite her comparative youth will go on to greater things. She had been the first one to mention her unsuccessful marriages, but instead of failures she presented them as happy escapes from unworthy partners. She had talked of engaging first-class chefs and experienced waiters and waitresses. Being Rita, she had boasted about her expensive cars and luxurious lifestyle. Like the others, she had gone over every inch of the Canary and Linnet, peering into all the rooms, looking impatient when Imogen and Debby had to turn away to hide tears when they went up to their attic bedroom and saw the three little rusty camp beds, side by side, almost exactly as they had been so many years before, when they had contained the hopes and aspirations of three little girls. Auntie could not say how much Rita remembered, but when she had glanced quickly at the other woman and seen her turn away she had thought that maybe Rita did care.

Debby had clutched her husband and kissed her little girl's soft neck. 'Mummy slept in the middle bed,' Auntie had heard her whisper. 'I was so happy here, darling.' She had turned to her husband. 'I know there was a war on, Stan, and you were in the thick of it, but we were . . .' her voice had broken, 'we were the lucky ones. We heard the news and worried when Liverpool was bombed, but it was almost as though we occupied a different world, a world where war could never touch us. I ought to feel guilty, but all I feel is – is glad.' And at those words, Auntie had seen Stan's large, tanned hand take Debby's and then they had all begun to descend the stairs once more.

When they had entered the bar the smell of the place had taken Auntie's mind back to those far off happy times; she remembered the young Imogen sliding into the bar of an evening to collect dirty glasses, then her and Rita hefting a full bucket of pig meal and potato peelings, cabbage leaves and sprout stalks, carrying it between them right to the end of the garden where the pig-which-must-not-be-named lived in pampered splendour in the old pigsty. There was another pig, of course, a young sow called, for some reason, Pandora. Were they at the stage when they knew that the pig-which-must-not-be-named had an ugly fate in store, or did they still believe my protestations that no one ever named boy pigs? We did not mean to deceive them, Jill and I, but the truth would have hurt them, and neither Jill nor myself could have borne to see them hurt.

What little sillies they were, and how we loved them, Auntie thought. They believed whatever they were told, and why not? We knew that if they were told the truth they would probably have planned a rescue attempt, and carted the pig off to some secret destination in the middle of the night. The fact that we might then be prosecuted, because during the war it was illegal to "hide" a pig, would simply never have occurred to them. No, we were right, and they had the consolation of Pandora and her constant production of piglets, as well as those birthday hens.

The hens had been a present from all three girls, and since Auntie did not believe in caging birds they had ranged far and wide and given the children something else to do: finding the eggs was soon a daily task which Rita, Imogen and Debby much enjoyed.

'Aren't you glad we thought to buy the hens for your birthday, Auntie?' Imogen had said one day, handing over four large brown eggs. 'For your next birthday we might give you a cockerel, then we could have baby chicks. Auntie, why do you have to have a cockerel before you can have baby chicks? I asked Mrs Pilgrim but she just said to get along wi' me, so now I'm asking you!'

Questions, questions, Auntie thought happily. I bought the cockerel myself, before they could spend their pocket money on me, bless their kind little hearts. And though I always managed to get around the question they asked most often – "How old are you really, Auntie?" – I wouldn't mind now admitting to seventy, only of course they're too polite to ask. Because if I did nothing else of worth in my life, I reckon that bringing up three little girls in wartime should stand to my credit. It wasn't always easy, but it was always fun.

Everyone said the reunion had been a great success, though Imogen had had to fight back tears of disappointment over Will's absence. She had explained that her husband could not make the rendezvous, and was nobly backed up by Jill and Auntie. Auntie had put a comforting arm round her as they left the Canary and Linnet and headed for the Golden Lion. 'It's all right, my little chickadee,' she had whispered. 'If you want my opinion, your husband won't fancy meeting you for the first time for ages in front of a great many people, all of whom he actually knows.' She had grinned her elfish, childlike grin and given Imogen's thin shoulders a comforting squeeze. 'You just ring him on Monday and arrange a rendezvous on Jersey, or in London, whichever suits him.'

They had dropped behind the others and Imogen's voice became a whisper. 'Fancy Josh becoming a GP! And his wife is a doctor as well. It just goes to show that folk can do anything they set their mind to.'

Auntie had chuckled. 'And our shy little Debby is a mum and a farmer's wife, with the most delightful husband and a dear little girl – Rachel, isn't it? And Rita's got what she wanted as well – to be a successful businesswoman. As for you, Immy, you're a whole person, or you will be when you and that husband of yours start acting like grown-ups again, and not like spoilt children.'

Imogen blushed and mumbled what might have been agreement or apology. She had agreed to go home with Auntie and Jill and share a meal before setting off on the last train for London, but as she saw Auntie settled on the tiny platform and was about to take a seat beside her she clapped a hand to her mouth. The old box Brownie! It had been Will's very first present to her and she had meant to take photographs not only of the Canary and Linnet but also of everyone attending the reunion, yet she had completely forgotten about it until this moment. She touched Auntie's arm. 'I know the train's due in about five minutes, but I've just remembered I didn't take a single photograph of the old Linnet,' she said apologetically. 'When Will and I meet again – and I'm sure we shall one day – I'll have nothing to show him. So I'm going back now to take a picture, and then I'll catch the next train and come straight to your cottage, I promise.'

Auntie had been leaning back with her eyes closed, but she smiled and nodded approval, and Jill, sitting next to her and staring up the track in the direction from which their train would come, got to her feet and grinned at Imogen. 'Good hunting,' she said cheerfully. 'And don't forget that I took at least six photographs with my old camera; I'll let you have prints as soon as I can get them developed.' She kissed Imogen lightly on the forehead and then gave her shoulders a little shake. 'You'll be all right,' she said bracingly. 'We'll still have plenty of time for a meal before you have to return to London. And don't think I didn't notice you pushing your nice lunch round and round the plate and eating nothing, because I did.'

'Sorry,' Imogen said apologetically. 'I – I wasn't really hungry. I'm off now. See you later, then.'

Dusk was falling, and in the distance the approaching train whistled, a romantic sound on an October evening when a light breeze was whirling the leaves into crisp, colourful piles, making the dusty platform momentarily into a thing of beauty. As the train drew in, Auntie got stiffly to her feet and Jill took her arm and helped her into an empty compartment.

'It's all over, and though I'm worn to a bone I enjoyed every minute,' Auntie said, smiling at the younger woman. 'It's been the best day of my life, seeing my children once more; after all this time I never expected to be so fortunate as to share their thoughts again even for a little while. Things have gone right for Debby and Rita, and even for

Josh, though I never knew him as well as the girls, of course. It's only Immy . . . I wanted to tell her never to put all her eggs in one basket, because that's the way to Weeping Cross. But despite the fact that he didn't come, we don't know that he won't. Oh, Jill, my dear, if only I could be sure . . .'

Jill leaned over and took the older woman's hand. 'It will all come right for Immy; I promise you it will, Mum,' she said. 'Ah, here comes the porter slamming doors and waving his flag . . . we'll be home before you know it!'

Imogen turned away from the station, slipped her mackintosh on and began to walk towards the Canary and Linnet, swinging the box Brownie on its rather worn strap and telling herself that she must stop believing Will could have come had he truly wanted to. Instead, she sang a happy little song under her breath and strode out, for dusk was deepening and her excuse of taking a photograph of the old pub was becoming less credible by the minute.

She bypassed the new estate in the gathering gloom, seeing that lights were coming on in the big, impersonal houses, and plunged into the trees, scuffing through the drifts of autumn leaves, hearing all the little night noises which had once frightened her and the other evacuees, until Auntie and Jill had explained that, with the darkness, a whole new community came to life. The night-people were badgers, foxes, stoats and weasels – shades of *The Wind in the Willows* – to say nothing of hedgehogs, birds, and the mice and voles, frogs and toads who were the prey of the larger creatures.

Imogen jumped as a barn owl passed her, floating on

silent white wings, its great golden eyes too intent on its hunt to pay attention to a mere human. She began to smile at its single-mindedness, then, abruptly, was conscious of another sound: a footfall? She remembered the man who had accosted her earlier in the day, the one who looked like a retired colonel. Suppose he – or someone else – was lurking in the trees, full of righteous indignation that anyone should be abroad after dark. He might think she was up to no good . . .

But of course it was only her imagination; when she stood still for a moment and listened, there was no sound other than the night noises which she had already recognised. Yet even so, she quickened her pace, and presently found herself gazing through the trees at the reassuring bulk of the Canary and Linnet. She had arrived. And what exactly did she expect to find? A repentant Will, anxious to apologise for his non-appearance at the reunion? She scoffed at the mere thought; why should he do any such thing? She really must try to control her stupid imagination.

She came out from the sheltering trees and lifted the camera, then lowered it again. If she took a photograph all she would see would be a black building against what was left of the sky, which was mostly a pale green line on the far horizon. She might as well admit defeat and go back to the station.

Yet suddenly she remembered the Lookout, and her sudden conviction, earlier in the day, that if Will did come it would be to the old beech, where they could be alone to discuss . . . what? Their future? Their past? The dreadful way she had behaved? She had reached the back door of the Canary and Linnet, the door which led straight into the kitchen and could be opened by the key which was always kept under the sixth flowerpot along in the collapsing porch. For a moment she toyed with the idea of going in, lighting the lamp which hung from the ceiling, and trying to take a photo to show Will when they eventually met. Then she dismissed the idea as sheer fantasy. Besides, she found she did not want to go back into the deserted house; it was downright creepy even to imagine herself fumbling amongst the flower pots, finding the key . . .

A sound from the trees she had just left made her prick up her ears for a moment and then, suddenly, she lost patience with herself. She moved away from the back door, opened her mouth and positively bawled. 'Will Carpenter, what the devil are you playing at? I know you're there, so you might as well come out.'

Nothing. No answering call, no reassuring footsteps as someone scuffed through the autumn leaves which lay so thick under the trees and hedges. And suddenly, Imogen knew why. Of course he would not answer to that name here . . .

She filled her lungs and fairly shrieked. 'Woody! Oh, Woody, my darling, don't play games with your Immy! I've been so unhappy, so wicked! Tell me you forgive me, tell me we can start again!'

And this time the footsteps were coming so fast that she barely had time to turn towards them before she was in his arms, both of them hugging with all their strength, Imogen at least letting tears of joy bubble down her cheeks.

After a few minutes he held her away from him, the better to examine her pale, exhausted face. 'Little idiot,' he said tenderly. 'For a moment I didn't recognise you in that old brown coat, but then you called my name. It was the first time anyone had called me Woody since I was a kid.'

He put his arm round her waist and began to lead her away from the pub and into the trees, but Imogen hung back. There was an important question which needed answering.

'And what if I'd not remembered that here you were always known as Woody? Would you have stayed hidden? Because all day I've kept getting the feeling you were behind the next tree, or crouching in a bush, or up at the Lookout, looking down on us. Oh, Woody, you really were here all along, weren't you?'

'I was,' Woody agreed. 'But I couldn't bear the thought of all the watching eyes so I stayed out of sight. I was absolutely sure, you see, that once all the others had gone you'd remember that your old pal was Woody, not Will, and it was poor Will who was connected with the worst hurt you've ever encountered, whereas Woody . . .'

They were making their way through the wood now, and above their heads a great moon was shedding light on the countryside they both loved, lighting their path between the trees. Imogen leaned her head into the hollow of her companion's shoulder.

'Woody?'

'Yes, love?'

'Is – is this going to be the happy-ever-after bit?'

In the dark she could not see his face, but she felt his amusement.

'If that's what you want,' he said softly. 'If that's what you truly want, my love.'

'It is,' Imogen said. 'And – and if there's never another Tom Tiddler it won't matter, will it?'

'Not a jot,' Woody said firmly. 'But there will be another Tom Tiddler, I'm sure of it. And I think this is the time for a chorus of that song we used to sing when we were particularly happy.' He laughed. 'Back in the good old days, when I was Woody Carpenter and you were little Immy Clarke.'

She did not need to ask him which song but began to sing softly, not moving her head from its comfortable resting place.

Don't sit under the apple tree with anyone else but me,
Anyone else but me, anyone else but me, no, no, no,
Don't sit under the apple tree with anyone else but me,
Till I come marching home.

ALSO AVAILABLE BY KATIE FLYNN

The Forget-Me-Not Summer

Katie Flynn

Liverpool 1936

Miranda and her mother, Arabella, live comfortably in a nice area. But when her mother tells her she can no longer afford their present lifestyle, they have a blazing row, and Miranda goes to bed angry and upset. When she wakes the next morning, however, her mother has disappeared.

She raises the alarm but everyone is baffled, and when searches fail to discover Arabella's whereabouts, Miranda is forced to live with her Aunt Vi and cousin Beth, who resent her presence and treat her badly.

Miranda is miserable, but when she meets a neighbour, Steve, things begin to look up and Steve promises to help his new friend in her search, and does so until war intervenes...

arrow books

ALSO AVAILABLE IN ARROW

A Christmas to Remember

Katie Flynn

A few days before Christmas Tess Williams rushes into Albert Payne's tobacconist shop, with two boys in hot pursuit, saying she's a thief. Albert chases the boys away, and though Tess does not realise it, this incident changes her life.

Tess lives with her grandmother, Edie, in a small flat on Heyworth Street. She has recently returned from Bell Farm, where she was evacuated during the war, and is being bullied by her schoolmates, but when the handsome Snowy White comes to her rescue she thinks her troubles are over, and returns for a working holiday to Bell Farm and her old friend Jonty.

This leaves Edie to her own devices, however, and Tess is jealous of the friendship which blossoms between her grandmother and the tobacconist. Yet though Tess resents Albert, it is to him she turns when things start to go wrong...

arrow books